D1204969

BY THE SAME AUTHOR

MARGINAL MAN

Charu Nivedita

translated from the Tamil by the author along with
Dr. Vasantha K. Krishnaraj, Gayathri R., T.R. Vivek, V. Sivakumar
edited by Susanna Marian Correya

Based on *New Exile (Tamil):* ©2014 Charu Nivedita

English Translation, Marginal Man

English translation and all editorial material copyright © 2018
Zero Degree Publishing

First Edition: January 2018
By Zero Degree Publishing

ISBN 978-81-935283-3-4

ZDP Title: 5

Logo design: Aditya R.

Zero Degree Publishing
12/7,Bay Line Apartments, 2nd Cross Street,
R.K. Nagar, Thiruvanmiyur, Chennai 600 041"
Mob : 9840065000 | www.zerodegreepublishing.com"
Email : zerodegreepublishing@gmail.com

Typeset by : Compuprint, Chennai 86.

Publishers' Note

Writers are the cultural identity, the memory of the aeon, the conscience and the voice of the society. By the sheer magic of their art, they surpass the barriers of language, land and culture. Any country should pride itself on possessing writers – national assets – whose works in translation have the potential to catapult them into international renown.

The Latin American Boom during the 1960s and '70s was a launchpad era that thrust names such as Julio Cortázar, Gabriel García Márquez, Carlos Fuentes, Jorge Luis Borges and Mario Vargas Llosa into the Anglophone literary world where they enjoyed a plausive reception.

Publication of translated nineteenth-century Russian literature fetched Tolstoy and Chekhov iconic status. Due to the availability of and the demand for their works in translation, Haruki Murakami of Japan and Orhan Pamuk of Turkey have become bestselling writers to watch in the present day and age.

What we understand from all of this is that translation and publication are fruitful endeavors that engage national writers and their oeuvres with the world at large and vice versa.

Zero Degree Publishing aims to introduce to the world some of the finest specimens of modern Indian literature, to begin with, we take great pride in introducing Tamil literature in English translation because, as Henry Gratton Doyle said, "It is better to have read a great work of another culture in translation than never to have read it at all."

– Gayathri Ramasubramanian & Ramjee Narasiman
Publishers

to

gayathri, sriram and ramjee

who made this

happen

Freshness in fiction is like freshness in fish. Go down to the market, prod a carp or two, check the gills, watch for eyebright. Give the great white NATO shark a miss (bland), pass on Bengal river fish (duff), steer clear of the latest electric eel from Norway. They've been poked to death. But what's this *piranha* doing here? Don't let the name scare you. *Charu Nivedita's* reputation runs ahead of him. Stick your toe in the water. He could make short work of it but watch him size you up: he's alive and watching you back, unlike your average punter who puts out a book and turns away. He's said to eat human flesh, but don't we all. Don't be deceived by the devil-may-care attitude: he cares deeply, insanely, oceanically for life and love and the things that matter. I could list them but it's best if you find out for yourself, and have a feast in the bargain. Piranha's delicious, daring, and doesn't cost the earth. Take *Charu Nivedita* home, scale him, gut him, grill him; take him with a pinch of salt, a twist of lemon. You'll never eat better, and you'll never touch stale fiction again.

IRWIN ALLAN SEALY

Autobiography? No, that is a right reserved for the important people of this world at the end of their lives, a refined style. Fiction, of events and facts strictly real; autofiction, if you will, to have entrusted the language of an adventure to the adventure of a language, outside of the wisdom and the syntax of the novel, traditional or new. Interactions, threads of words, alliterations, assonances, dissonances, writing before or after literature, concrete, as we say, music.

Serge Doubrovsky, "Fils"

Prologue

In 1914, the king of Nilambur prayed to Lord Guruvayurappan to solve every problem that dogged his kingdom. To return the favor, he donated one of his elephants to the temple. The ten-year-old elephant was named Kesavan. This elephant, like the smartest boy in the class, was the smartest in the herd. It kept fast with the humans twice a month on *Ekadashi* days. This smart-as-a-whip elephant was special in more ways than one. It would deign to carry only Guruvayurappan, no one else and nothing else. No matter how much you cajoled it, bribed it or threatened it, it would not participate in any other temple feasts and fests. Any number of jabs with the mahout's goad would elicit nothing more than a few silent tears. Such was the steadfast stubbornness of the elephant.

The festival idol is called *thiruveli* in Malayalam. In Kerala, the *thiruveli* is placed at the center of a flat wooden plank. Kesavan would stoop only to the bearer of the *thiruveli,* in order that he might climb onto his back. Even if a person brandished the biggest bunch of bananas in front of him, he would have to climb the elephant from the back just because he was not holding the *thiruveli*.

Starvation and isolation were the consequences of his stubbornness, but even the lack of food and company did not alter his nature. He endured all with silent dignity and tears. One day, it was decided that Kesavan would not carry the *thiruveli* any longer. In its stead, he would carry loads. The elephant, though obstinate, did not have a rebellious streak. The mahouts feared he would go into musth and run amok, leaving powder and pulp in his wake. No grinding spree ensued. The elephant carried on like a martyr.

In 1970, on the *Ekadashi* day of the month of *Margazhi*, another elephant was supplied to bear the *thiruveli*. Kesavan lay all alone, weeping during the merrymaking.

In the beginning there was the sky. From the sky came the air, and from the air came fire; from fire came water, and from the water came land. So says the *Pancha Bhoota* theory. That day, however, water turned into fire when Kesavan's tears turned into drops of flame. Soon there was a fire raging round the temple, threatening to make ash of all and sundry. Kesavan trumpeted like never before and the whole of Guruvayur heard it. He started to dump sacks of sand onto the flames that were soon snuffed. If not for the elephant's intellect, Guruvayur would have turned into a crematorium.

Due to his heroic deed, Kesavan was allowed to carry the *thiruveli* like he did before. Like the tiger that never changes its stripes, Kesavan never changed his ways. Only the bearer of the *thiruveli* was allowed to climb him from the front.

On the day of *Vaikunta Ekadashi*, as Kesavan was carrying the *thiruveli*, he collapsed. The idol was simply transferred to another elephant's back. The last sight Kesavan's dying eyes saw was the idol being carried by another elephant. He had made good his resolution to carry only Guruvayurappan all his life and to bend his knee before him and no other. This was the elephant's dying thought as he breathed his last.

* * *

Dear Reader,

Perhaps you will like this novel, perhaps you will not.

Regardless, to those of you who have bothered to pick up this book, I would like to return the favor.

Here's a print of a *yantra* for you. Keep it in your house. It should face north or east. Karuvurar, a renowned *siddhar*, recommends it, not this marginal man.

It doesn't matter whether you are a believer; you have nothing to lose by giving the *yantra* a try. Karuvarar holds the copyright to it. I'm not sure what the man's real name was. No *siddhar* worried about such things back then. He is called Karuvurar because he lived in Karur. Many of the books he wrote are still in existence. In them, he compiled the many secrets of *mantras, tantras, yantras* and yoga.

These days, if a bloke donates so much as a light bulb worth a couple of hundreds to a temple, he gets his entire family tree painted on it – "Donated by Mylapore

Muthukumarappa Mudali and Brothers" – in the hope of being remembered for all eternity. But the *siddhars* of the past, who knew the art of transmuting copper into gold, preferred anonymity.

Karuvurar was a disciple of Bhogar, but I am not going to explain why Bhogar's name is Bhogar, where he comes from, who he was and what he did, because if I do, this might become a work of spirituality which the literary world will frown upon because it is in vogue to frown upon all things spiritual nowadays.

வ லம் றியும் எ ▽	ய ஔௌம் ஸ்ரீம் ஒ □	ந ஐம் ஐயும் அ ○	ம ஈம் கிலிம் இ ☆	சி நம சவ்வும் உ ✡
ந ஐம் ஐயும் அ ○	ம ஈம் கிலிம் இ ☆	சி நம சவ்வும் உ ✡	வ லம் றியும் எ ▽	ய ஔௌம் ஸ்ரீம் ஒ □
சி நம சவ்வும் உ ✡	வ லம் றியும் எ ▽	ய ஔௌம் ஸ்ரீம் ஒ □	ந ஐம் ஐயும் அ ○	ம ஈம் கிலிம் இ ☆
ய ஔௌம் ஸ்ரீம் ஒ □	ந ஐம் ஐயும் அ ○	ம ஈம் கிலிம் இ ☆	சி நம சவ்வும் உ ✡	வ லம் றியும் எ ▽
ம ஈம் கிலிம் இ ☆	சி நம சவ்வும் உ ✡	வ லம் றியும் எ ▽	ய ஔௌம் ஸ்ரீம் ஒ □	ந ஐம் ஐயும் அ ○

PART – I

CHAPTER ONE

1 – Of Mongrels and Scoundrels

Early one morning, I was walking along the Marina. It was bustling with roller-skating youngsters. The more seasoned and skilful youth on wheels were whizzing across the road at a breakneck speed. Traffic was barred on Beach Road from five to seven in the morning. Four policemen were posted – two at Gandhi's statue and two at Netaji's statue – to ensure that nothing on rubber wheels passed. There were, of course, days when the policemen left Gandhi and Netaji to watch the motorcyclists having a field day.

Wrestlers, members of laughter clubs, yoga and karate enthusiasts – there was no lack of action on the beach that morning. Large crowds were pooling around the roadside stalls that sold papaya and raw vegetable salads. Pushcarts selling vegetable soups and fresh juices jostled for space. Gooseberry, curry leaf, amaranth, carrot, ginger, *thoothuvalai* and bitter gourd – the vast array of botanical specimens being pulped and squeezed for the health-conscious crowd boggled my mind.

I walked from the lighthouse to the public swimming pool and all the way back. It was at some point during my walk back that I noticed a stray dog on the pavement, blood oozing from his ear. A speeding car must have hit him. Strangely, he wasn't howling in pain. That left me wondering: was the animal shocked, or was it I who was blind to his pain? The dog licked the blood that had dripped onto the ground and limped away.

The plight of strays in this country is pitiful and pathetic. They have to scrounge and scavenge for food. Their spaces and their lives are under constant threat from the *Homo* sadistic *sapiens* and their equally sadistic smoke-breathing monsters on wheels. Young hooligans pelt stones at these dogs like they're the whores of Babylon. When they fall ill, they just keel over and die, often in great pain and agony.

The only thing their dismal lives allow them is sex. This privilege they enjoy freely and to their hearts' content – whenever, wherever. No indignant protesters accuse them of running the morality of Indian culture. Cops don't harass them by asking to see their marriage license and then thwacking them with *lathis*. They don't have to marry or sweat over in-laws. They are not hit with scandals of illicit sex and do not face the ignominy of men who suffer from erectile dysfunction. (It is said that blood pressure tablets are responsible for erectile dysfunction. Medical research suggests Indians are more susceptible than others to hypertension and as a result, to pill-induced penile problems. As this is a sensitive issue that concerns the male ego and honor, nobody speaks openly of it.)

Traditional Siddha medication offers a number of remedies for this condition. One of the most useful methods is the use of the *ashwaganda* root. Theraiyar cites yet another affliction and another remedy. Let me introduce you to Theraiyar on paper. Like Tolkappiyar, he was also a disciple of the sage Agasthya, one of the seven most important sages of the Indic tradition. Both men lived in Kabadapuram during the second Sangam era – 4000 B.C. or thereabouts."

The story I am about to tell you can be found in the *Bogar Nigandu.*

Tholkappiyar suffered from persistent headaches that seemed to have no cure. It was Agasthya who discovered their cause. *Hatha* yogis practice a cleansing ritual in which water is passed through one nostril up into the skull and then pushed out through the other. When Tolkappiyar was engaged in this ritual, toad larva entered his skull along with the water and remained there. In time, the larva developed into a fully formed froglet.

Agasthya cut open Tolkappiyar's head with a knife. He planned to surgically remove the frog using a scissor-like blade. One of his students expressed concern that the instrument might cause brain damage. This student took a vessel filled with water and held it near Tolkappiyar's head, and out jumped the toad! This student was none other than Theraiyar. He became one of the founding fathers of Indian medicine and discovered the secret of eternal youth – fresh ginger in the morning, dried ginger at noon, *haritaki* in the evening. Being on this diet for forty-eight days will have even a nonagenarian gamboling about like a lamb in spring time. I owe my sex drive to this diet. It helps me have sex with Anjali for hours on end.

As I was saying, dogs don't have the same problems with sex that humans do, but post-ejaculation, the canine's organ turns stiff as a post and the bitch is unable to extricate herself for a good thirty minutes. This results in considerable pain and embarrassment for mating dogs. Disgusted women often spit at them and young boys stone them.

There was a stray dog that lived in a dump near my house. Blood and pus oozed from its sores which it scratched at continuously. Like some religions preach, this dog or its parents or some forefather must have committed some grave sin in this birth or one of their previous births to have been born a dog and to suffer this predicament. Pelting stones at this dog was a sport – like darts – for the little scoundrels from the slum who would harass the creature on their way to school. The animal wasn't clever enough to seek a safe haven. Perundevi would shoo the little human aggressors away if she had to see them. I ignored them. After all, breathing slum-air does a number on your brain.

As was custom, on one particular day, the boys stoned the dog. Suddenly, a guerilla war broke out. The little midgets were ambushed by a pack of dogs that had been hiding behind the garbage dump. I made no effort to intervene.

The next incident I am going to describe involves these same boys. One of my neighbors, a sixty-five-year-old man has a Great Dane called Bruno. He lives with his wife in their own little house with a garden. The wretched brats didn't spare Bruno either and they lobbed stones over the gate at him every day. Bruno's angry barks roused the entire neighborhood, but this only seemed to stoke the boys into playing the stoning game with greater delight.

I have two dogs – Baba and Blackie. Baba is a Labrador, an affectionate creature and a stranger to anger. He licks everyone he meets and likes cuddles, no matter who they come from. Perundevi says that even if a thief were to enter the house, Baba would run off with him. Blackie, on the other hand, was cut from an entirely different cloth. Like most Great Danes, he has an intimidating presence and will not let even a fly enter the house. Fearing for both the boys and the Great Dane, we kept the dog from the garden. Hence, they focused on Bruno.

My neighbor actually did try talking to the slum boys. He scolded them and even chased them away. One day, during this *tamasha*, one of the boys unzipped his fly and flashed his willie at the old man. They returned the next day too, armed with stones. Suddenly, the gate opened and Bruno leapt out. The old man finally allowed the dog its much deserved canine revenge. One of the boys, who was running for his life, was knocked down by a car and died on the spot.

2 – Pussy's in the Well!

It upsets me that Perundevi appears in my dreams to spy on me. It makes me feel vulnerable. When I was a student in Thanjavur, I sometimes had sex with my neighbor, a thirteen-year-old girl called Mekhala – or as much sex that is possible with a girl her age. I didn't know much about sex then, but those breasts of hers seemed to be beckoning me so desperately to squeeze them. Whenever we found ourselves alone, we would grope each other. There was no love involved though, and, truth be told, when I left Thanjavur for Delhi, I hadn't really mastered the art of entering a female body.

One night, Mekhala appeared in my dreams. When Perundevi woke up the next morning, I noticed that she looked a little upset. When I enquired after the reason, she said that she had dreamt of me cavorting with a girl. When I realized that this woman had managed to slither into my dreams like a thief on the sly, I was consumed with fear. I tried not to dream from that night on, but that endeavor led to a different problem altogether. Without dreams, sleep abandoned me like a fickle lover.

One night, I was startled by the wailing of an animal while desperately trying to fall asleep. There was a slight drizzle outside. We were then based in Chinmaya Nagar, a snakepit. Perundevi could instinctively sense the presence of a snake. It had to do with the smell of screwpine when the snake was about. The Chinmaya Nagar snakes never did transgress their boundaries. They just spread the screwpine scent wherever they went, sticking to their non-interference policy.

The mating ritual of snakes is a wonder. In Indian mythology, they represent lust and sexual union and a tantric *mudra.*

In a village near Nong Khai in Thailand, I once drank the warm blood of a snake obtained by making a slit right below its head. The drink was sold on the streets and it had quite a novel taste. These days, I don't think I can find it in me to even swat a fly. Perundevi is chiefly responsible for this transformation. One day, I watched from the balcony as she was drawing the *kolam* on our street. Several crows, perched on the compound wall, watched her in action. As soon as she had finished and left the spot, they flocked down and began to eat of the rice flour, filling their mouths with as much of it as they could. I noticed that they inclined their beaks at an angle to ingest more of the flour than would be possible if they ate it with their beaks in a straight position. They looked beautiful with the beaks coated with rice flour. When I recounted this to Perundevi, she told me that she never used the cheap version of *kolam* flour that people generally use.

People usually add lime to the rice flour to brighten the *kolam*, but lime is a crow-deterrent. *Kolams*, Perundevi explained, were not merely aesthetic eye-catchers. The flour used to draw them acted as a supplementary source of nutrition for crows, squirrels, sparrows and ants. A squirrel feeding on the *kolam* flour is a charming sight indeed. After feasting on what was on offer in the front yard, the crows would perch themselves on the stone slab intended for the washing of clothes in the backyard and raise a fresh racket. Perundevi would immediately rush to fetch them water. Perundevi taught me so much about compassion to living creatures. What I learned from her, I could never have learned from a million books. Don't you dare mess with me, beware!

Let's talk about this night I was desperately trying to sleep. I wasn't sure whether the distress call was coming from a cat or a dog. I followed the direction of the sound and found myself looking down the neighbor's well where I found a cat, its front claws on the wall and its hind-legs in the water. There was no one in the neighbor's house, so I called Perundevi. She came running, took one look at the wailing cat, and ran inside to fetch a rope and a bucket. When she returned, she cooed lovingly to the creature.

The cat's sounds grew louder. Fearing something terrible was happening, I placed a call to Blue Cross. They said they would be with us in an hour (our house was not exactly a stone's throw from their hospital). In the meanwhile, Perundevi had started singing to the cat like it was a toddler being put to bed. She slowly lowered the bucket into the water, but the cat panicked and lost its grip on the wall, falling into the water.

I could see something gleaming in the cat's eyes – the desperation to live. Perundevi continued her litany of tender words. "Mama will rescue you. She won't let you die," she said, lowering her bucket again. As if under her spell, the cat stopped wailing and jumped into the bucket. Perundevi slowly raised the bucket, but the stupid cat lost its balance and fell back into the water.

I don't think I would have been able to rescue the animal even if I climbed down into the well. I didn't share Perundevi's instincts when it came to understanding animals by sound and smell. I was also afraid of being attacked by the cat. I have observed that when you try to rescue someone, you end up perishing along with them.

One rainy night, a friend and I stopped for *idlis* at a wayside stall near Udayam Theater in K. K. Nagar. When the *idlis* did not appear after a good wait, my friend called out impatiently, "Hey, are the *idlis* ready?" He placed his hand on a metal rod in front of the shop and started screaming like he was possessed. I realized that he was being electrocuted and without thinking – because such situations demand acting – I tried to pull him away and I too began to convulse violently. Luckily, fate chose to intervene in the form of one of the workers in the shop who sensibly went and switched off the mains. If not for him, both my friend and I would have featured in the obituary section of the newspapers. Our deaths would have been just two of the many fatalities that occur in the city with depressing regularity.

More rescue attempts ensued. It was quite some time before the cat finally managed to climb into the bucket and crouch into safety. As soon as the bucket was on terra firma, the cat leapt out and off it ran, without so much as a meow in acknowledgement. Perundevi lamented the fact that the creature had vanished before she could dry its fur with a towel and offer it some milk. I was just relieved that it survived the ordeal.

3 – Baba's Death and the Arrival of Baba II

Death, or even its imminent arrival, has never filled me with fear. I didn't grieve when my parents died for they had both lived long and full lives, but their lives were mechanical. They had worked hard and eaten well. Had I consumed half the amount of salt and sugar that my father had had, you'd find me dead in bed a week from now. My father was ninety when he passed and my mother, eighty-five. Neither of them had ever once seen a doctor. Work, food and TV series – that was their whole life. They saved to build a house and once that house got built, their life's mission was complete.

Neither life nor death came easy for my younger brother Selvam. He was not a bright student, and in this country, crime and politics are the only careers available to those who are not cut out for school, though, admittedly, one does need some talent to become a successful criminal. In fact, a criminal needs to be cleverer than people who actually work for a living. Education – or the lack of it, rather – was not the only problem Selvam faced. There was his body – the boy needed to defecate at least ten or fifteen times a day though he was hale and healthy in every other respect. Nothing came of doctors and treatment, and he eventually accepted his condition.

When he was very young, Selvam swallowed a nail and had to be operated upon. The surgery affected his vocal cords and his voice never broke. He started a poultry farm with my father's money, but every last one of the birds died, leaving him with debts up to his nose. He went on to open a small grocery store. That tanked too. Selvam had no vices – did not smoke cigarettes, drink, whore or read books. He never even raised his voice.

When his dashing looks brought him a marriage proposal from a rich family, everyone thought he'd hit the jackpot. All the bride's family wanted was a man with a clean slate and no bad habits. Selvam fit the bill. To cap it all, our families knew each other. But with Selvam, fate had a way of throwing a spanner in the works. To everyone's utter astonishment, he declared that the girl – a real ravisher – was not to his taste. Apparently, he was in love with someone else.

Of course there had to be a hitch – the girl belonged to a different religion. Still, this wasn't an impediment as ours was a family of multiple faiths. I asked to meet the woman, but he kept evading a definite response. One day, when I came down to Chennai from Delhi, he announced he was already married and invited me home. When I saw his Juliet, I was aghast. Five feet off the ground with protruding teeth like half an umbrella and shrunken like a mummified Egyptian. As if that wasn't enough, she was ten years his senior and a divorcee to boot. And oh, she was also infertile. I wasn't surprised my brother wanted to keep her away from our critical eyes. He rather hesitantly invited me to dinner once. Since my sister-in-law had been informed of my non-preference of rice, she had made *chapattis*. They were hard as cowpats. I left without finishing dinner.

After marriage, Selvam tried his hand at carpentry which wasn't a paying vocation even though he slogged all day under the brick-baking sun. A few years later, he took up with an electrician. At the age of forty, he was diagnosed with terminal cancer. In three months, he was dead. I never expected him to die as early as he did. A good number of cancer patients manage to cheat death. It's probably got to do with the will to live, but in Selvam's case, the lack of that will. As soon as he got the diagnosis, he called me. "*Anney*, there's a function at a friend's house. You must come." I agreed because it was the first such request he'd made. A few days later, he called again. "*Anney*, my friend wants to give you the invitation in person. When should he drop by?" When I saw the invitation, I realized the folly of having contact with one's relatives. Selvam's friend's daughter had attained puberty and he wanted me to grace the occasion. My name featured prominently in the card with clear mention that I was a writer. Despite the assurances, I failed to show up. Selvam rang me incessantly. I ignored him. Then, I heard of his death. My sister-in-law said, "He kept reiterating his last wish which was to see you."

Peering into the coffin, I was shocked to find not my brother Selvam, but a body with hardly any flesh or even frame, deep-sunken eyes and hollow cheeks. It not even fit to be called a body, let alone my brother's body. I burst into tears. That was the first time I cried at anyone's death. I learned that Selvam had been on a liquid diet for three months.

The next time I cried copiously was when my Baba died. I remember vividly how she died – her head falling back to the ground as I stroked her. We gave the vet some money to bury Baba in the pet cemetery and went home as Perundevi said that the sight of our dog being put in the ground would be unbearable. She wept for two whole days. Unable to come to terms with her grief, I bought a puppy which became Baba II. We had promised ourselves that we would never have another dog again, but Baba's death made us change our minds.

Though Selvam's death soon became a distant memory, I was unable to forget Baba who had been like a child to me, who had shared a decade of her life with me, a faithful shadow. It's been six years, but the grief is still as strong as it was on the day she died. I wondered where Baba's soul was romping. Would she be thinking of me? Why did she cling on to life until I returned home from my journey? The moment I stroked her head, she breathed her last, why?

When Baba was in heat, there used to be blood all over the house. She would bleed for a month and we would have to keep scrubbing the floors clean until her cycle was done. Baba died, without having had sex.

Perundevi declared that Baba II was none other than our late Baba reborn as a male. A few days after Baba II arrived, another dog, a Great Dane, entered our lives. We named him Blackie. Perundevi bought him for our son, Madan. I warned her that our lives would be ruined. It was hard caring for one dog, and now there were two! Two demanding dogs in the household! Having a Great Dane was an expensive affair. His food supplies alone would burn a hole in our pockets. But Perundevi turned a deaf ear to all my appeals. Instead of cooking for the dogs, we decided to feed them Pedigree.

All seemed well until Blackie refused to touch Pedigree. Like our dear departed Baba, he turned out to be a fussy chap when it came to food. He would retch and pass bloody stools. Luckily, it wasn't hard to find a vet in Mylapore. His name was Varun. He told me to keep Blackie on a diet of curd and rice for a few days, but the vomiting resumed after six months. He then suggested Pedigree mixed with crushed biscuits. Blackie ate, but developed a skin disease. Rice and eggs didn't work; rice and chicken worked for a while, but Blackie hated the local chicken. We had to buy canned chicken imported from Germany that was available in Varun's hospital.

If – on the days I was unable to make it to the hospital – I served Blackie some locally available chicken, he would take one sniff and walk away. Will a tiger eat grass even when it's starving? No matter how hungry he was, Blackie had to eat like a king. Soon enough, even the German chicken stopped agreeing with Blackie, and both dogs developed skin infections.

Varun suggested we quit Pedigree and try balls of rice, fish, potatoes and carrots. The making of said dog meal is not as easy as it sounds. The dogs had to be fed the mixture twice a day. The rice, the vegetables and the fish had to be boiled and cooled before the dogs could eat them. The fish had to be boneless. We had to ensure that the larder was stocked with fish, meat and vegetables at all times. And our dogs knew how to demand their chow, so we'd better have it ready when it's supposed to be!

We finally settled on a diet of Pedigree and boneless shark. Bony fish made the pets bleed. I had to buy the shark from Nadukuppam where I once spotted a small variety of turbot, which is also a boneless fish, and much cheaper than shark. If one shark cost me a thousand bucks, four turbots cost me a hundred. Baba was content, but Blackie took one disdainful sniff and moved away, highly offended.

My dogs kept me on my toes. I had to take them for their morning and evening strolls, administer their medicines, and like a pimp or a dog broker, find sexual partners for them.

Now that's another story altogether. When I saw Baba trying to mount Blackie, I realized that the former had come of age. I chased him away. You, dear reader, may wonder how and why, I, an author specialized in the absurd, the erotic, and the absurd erotic, could do this. I don't worry myself silly over incest and homosexuality. It's just that I saw fear in Blackie's eyes when Baba tried to mount him. Rape *is* a crime after all, isn't it? But there was another vexing problem. Chasing Baba away when he had a boner might cause him to fear sex. Varun also had similar apprehensions, so I kept both pets under constant surveillance as a precautionary and a preventive measure.

It soon became obvious that a healthy Labrador bitch would have to be found for Baba. I wanted a pedigreed dog, a pure-breed, with no history of ailments, *especially* skin diseases. Finally Jagan, Varun's twenty-year-old assistant, managed to find a dog that ticked all my boxes. He agreed to oversee the mating. Pulling back Baba's foreskin, Jagan stroked his organ till it was hard enough. Then, he made Baba mount the bitch. With gloved hands, he kept inserting Baba's organ into the bitch's opening. There was an assistant filming both dogs making whoopee. Taken aback, I asked, "Are you making animal porn in my presence?" They informed me that the bitch's owner demanded proof of the mating. Who could be so horny as to want *that*? I had no idea.

A lot of money rides on the dog-breeding business. A Labrador pup is priced at ten grand, so if a Labrador bitch has a litter of ten, the owner can make a handsome profit. This, I suppose, was the rationale of the video. The only downside is that Labrador pups are gullible and can hence be easily lured away by strangers.

Jagan's efforts were futile as Baba seemed to be stronger than the other labradors and even his dick was enormous. At one point, I thought that Jagan himself would turn into a male dog. The bloke was so keen on thrusting Baba's organ into the bitch. An hour later, exhausted and disillusioned, Jagan told me that such was typical of first attempts, and he left.

4 – The Arrival of Baba I

I had no room for dogs in my life until I met Perundevi.
One rainy night, she changed everything. I woke up to
the shrill cries of a pup. Perundevi rescued it from its
misery and brought it home. The pup took to us at once.
We named her Baba. During the ten years of her life, she
played guardian angel on four legs to Perundevi. If I raised
a hand to Perundevi, that hand was in danger of being
caught between sharp jaws, but if Perundevi raised a hand
to me, or even whacked me over the head, you wouldn't see
even a muscle twitch. We never put Baba on a leash. We
thought it cruel.

In coastal towns, the sea-facing front would be overrun
with garbage. In Nagore, the western part of the sea-
facing town is the low-caste colony where corpses were
cremated. Destiny usually conspired to ensure that I lived
in a shithole that was decidedly downmarket. In Chennai,
I lived in Chinmaya Nagar for a really long time before
moving to Mylapore, the southern part of the city.

Come the monsoon, and Chinmaya Nagar would turn
into a swamp. During the torrential rains of 2005, sewage

from the neighboring Cooum River invaded homes. The sewage was tolerable when you consider the fact that even the contents of the two backed-up toilets spilled over. Worse still, a blockage in the underground sewage conduit caused human excreta from the toilets in the homes above ours to enter our place via the bathroom pipes.

Our flat was on the ground level of a multi-storied living space. Chunks of dirty yellow turd swirled around our ankles. Groaning and howling in despair, Perundevi clambered onto the bed and remained huddled there with Baba. She climbed down only after two days when the gray water had receded. Using the toilet was out of the question, so she ate sparingly – a couple of biscuits and a few spoonsful of water. My stomach was yet to be tamed. It was hungry as a starving wild beast, so I made some garlic curry and steaming hot rice which I ate with relish, seated at the dining table, surrounded by shit.

I ate heartily because there was a toilet on the terrace that could be used. Perundevi refused, arguing that whatever went down that toilet too would find its way into our apartment.

The power remained despite the rains. This was miraculous, but also dangerous. One day, there was front-page news of an electrocution in Kilpauk. The man had been trying to turn off the mains because his house was flooded. I wonder how and why politicians are spared from such miserable fates.

Even as the level of the shit-ridden water was rising to my knee, I busied myself with the writing of a novel that was being serialized in a Malayalam weekly. I took the handwritten chapters to a barely functioning cyber café, got them typed, proofread and e-mailed to the translator.

On the streets, the sludge was waist-high. There were naked electric cables lying in the storm water that posed a serious threat of their own. *Jala samadhi* was guaranteed should anyone get sucked down an open manhole. The water was teeming with snakes of all sizes and appetites. If I rant anymore about my pathetic circumstances, my critics will accuse me of wallowing in self-pity or call this my attempt at obtaining belated commiserations.

Several families flew the locality, seeking refuge in the homes of unaffected kith and kin. That was not an available option in my case. As the water rose, I kept shifting my stack of books to a higher place. They ended up on the loft. There was also the minor concern of having to transport a hydrophobic Baba on a dinghy. If the water rose any further, we would all have to head for the terrace unless we wished to drown.

The realization that a number of people had abandoned their pets and scooted from the scene in these circumstances filled me with nothing but revulsion and disgust for the human race. My friend in Thanjavur, a writer and a human rights activist, had a Doberman called Chief. The dog had to be tied as it compulsively tailed its owner. Once, he left the dog untied in his haste to drop me off, and the creature opened the gate and did a three-kilometer run all the way to the bus stop. When this very friend was transferred to Chennai, he rejected Chief to the streets like the day's garbage, a plantain peel, chewed betel, a bubblegum wrapper, and left town. Chief was four years old then.

I never met my "human rights activist" friend again post this incident though we lived in the same town.

I happened to come across an even more distressing occurrence in the newspaper. The goods van of a train coming from the north was opened, and what was found was a terrified Dalmatian dog. The dog had been trapped in pitch darkness for three days, all alone and barking in fear. The two-day journey time must be included too in this ordeal. The frightened animal tried to bite those who approached it. Finally, it was rescued by Blue cross. When I saw the picture in the papers, I could clearly glimpse, in his eyes, the fear the dog had experienced. Maybe the people who had looked after him had been transferred elsewhere. To avoid the expense of taking him with them they had surreptitiously abandoned him in the goods van.

After experimenting with several diets for Baba, we eventually found out only beef suited her. It was around that time we had moved to Mylapore.

Every two days, I made a trip to the beef butcher. The availability of beef is dependent on the time of day and the day of the week. Even beef did not help Baba very long. Cleaning dog puke ranks among the most unsavory activities a man could engage in. The stench was unbearable, but we were left with no choice. To us, the dog was like an ailing child.

As a pup, Baba had a peculiar habit. Hard times relegated us to a barely furnished house with neither washbasin nor wall-mirror. When I needed to shave, I would prop a small mirror against the wall and squat on the floor, like my father used to. This was when Baba would come running and clamber onto my lap. This continued till she was four.

In her tenth year, Baba was no longer able to retain any food. She died a very poignant and poetic death, the sort of death you see in movies. I was out of town, but news of Baba's condition saw me throwing my plans and appointments out the window and rushing home.

When the frail little creature saw me, she tried to lift her head, but couldn't. I ran to her side as her head fell back to the floor. I was crying.

I stroked the head of my dying dog gently. Gazing into my eyes, she breathed her last.

5 – A Bite-Sized Story

When Puja was in college, her neighbors had a dog. One day, it had clamped its jaws shut around a human shank. The woman of the house was so angry that she wanted to finish off the mongrel. Her twelve-year-old daughter and eight-year-old son chased the dog with a rod and a rock. Intuition told the frenzied dog that its life was under threat, but despite that knowledge, it did not try and harm its masters. The lady screamed with rage, 'Kill him! Kill him!' and the boy plunked down the rock on the head of the dog. After watching this gruesome act by the neighbours, Puja's family moved to another place in few days.

"Udhaya, do we kill one of our children for doing something wrong?" Puja asked tearfully.

6 – The Great Killer who Walked like a Duck

Anjali once told me the story of a 40-year-old Shri Vaishnavite lady who, aided by her two younger brothers, killed an elderly, wealthy Brahmin couple residing in Madippakkam – one of the Brahmin ghettos of Chennai. The couple lived on the first floor and had rented out the ground floor to the Shri Vaishnavites who snuck into the upstairs house one day and bludgeoned the unsuspecting couple to death.

It was a simple open-and-shut case for the Tamil Nadu police and the trio was arrested in two days. But what was to be done with them? If they had murdered the prime minister or some big shot politician, they would have been slapped with the death penalty or life imprisonment. But if you kill someone unimportant like your neighbor, the same rule doesn't apply. All you'll have to do is hang around in prison for a couple of years and walk out to a normal life.

This is how justice works in India.

The Brahmin couple that got murdered had two children who had settled off in the U. S. Most middle-class

Indians aspire to send their children to the U. S. and I hear such talk during my walks in Nageshwara Rao Park. If it's not about sending their children there, the talk is about children who are living it up there after settling.

I had a friend called Mohan whose daughter lived in New Jersey. He went to the U. S. for a while to look after his grandchild and he returned to India within a month when he said he'd be there for six. When we asked him about his quick return, he said, "U. S. is such a boring place! It has no life. You have to stay cooped up in the house all day. Even if you go outside, there is nothing to do. I used to visit a park near my daughter's house; it was beautiful, but how long was I supposed to sit there? I met some elderly people in the park, all of them like me – unpaid babysitters who had come all the way from Mylapore to New Jersey. We would sit in the park and gossip about life back in Mylapore until we returned to our respective children's places. After a month, I decided I'd had enough."

"Didn't you make any American friends?"

"Even if I had any, what would I do with them? What would we talk about?"

He was right. Once you've lived in Mylapore, you'll find it hard to live anywhere else. With a temple on almost every street, Mylapore is Chennai's temple town. There's the Sai Baba Temple, Kolavizhi Amman Temple which is the temple of Mylapore's guardian deity, Adi Kesava Perumal Temple, Madhava Perumal Temple, Kapaleeswarar Temple, Mundakkani Amman Temple and three Hanuman temples. The place is heavily punctuated with cafés and there's also Nageshwara Rao Park if you feel like you could use a walk.

The people Mohan met in the U. S. spoke dearly of all these places and the murdered Brahmin couple was no different.

A sixty-year-old priest from Tirupati went to Nanganallur, another Brahmin ghetto in Chennai, to call on his daughter and granddaughter. A bunch of goons accosted them during their morning walk and one of the fellows shouted smut at his daughter. When the priest raised his voice in her defense, the goon brandished an *arivaal* and with it, spilled the old man's brains.

The locals notified the authorities with bulging pockets about the terrorizing goons. When the chief minister caught wind of the goon situation, he jotted on the police file, "Brahmin area. Do the needful." The chief minister had been raised in a socio-political tradition that believed that the Brahmin had to be dealt with first if a Brahmin and a snake were encountered at the same time. The authorities, competent in reading between the lines, knew what was wanted of them. The file was left to gather dust. Nanganallur remains an absolute dump.

Call it the randomness of life or destiny where anything can happen to anyone at any time in any place. That murder was not envisaged, blueprinted and committed for reasons of enmity or hatred. It could just as easily have been you or me in that priest's unfortunate place. And I can't help wondering what might have been the reaction of the priest's daughter and three-year-old granddaughter when the rowdies' *arivaal* split his skull and his brain spilled out right there on the ground. Would they ever be able to forget that moment for the rest of their lives? How would it have affected their minds? But what I really wanted to say is that those who killed the priest would soon be out of prison and committing other murders. In fact, they would already have been accused of at least three other murder cases at the time of commission of the latest murder.

In my opinion, your lifespan depends on your hood and its inhabitants. Mylapore, my current address, is home to several big names – ministers, judges, actors and the like. During the inundation, when the rest of Chennai looks like a human aquarium in need of cleaning, the residents of Mylapore and the Boat Club area – the fanciest address in town – continue to strut the walkways like runways round the clock in imported rainproof sneakers. There is a slim chance of skull-splitting and gut-spilling here.

Just before I set out for the Himalayas, I met a thirty-year old man called Kumar who had murdered at least six people. Kumar was an acquaintance of my friend Manickam who gave me the rundown of the former's criminal history. Intrigued by his account, I insisted to meet Kumar, who, despite his notoriety, skillfully evaded the grasp of the long hands of the law. In under two hours, Kumar was with us, nattily dressed. He even wore shoes. Over drinks, I asked him about the *arivaal*, the instrument of death in most murders that happen in Tamil Nadu.

Every town boasts its own distinctive *arivaal*. The town of Thiruppachethi in Sivagangai is perhaps the most storied where the weapon is concerned. Thirupachethi's *arivaals*, however, according to Kumar, were welterweight. Real heavyweight *arivaals* are forged only in Namakkal. The Namakkal blades weighed anywhere between three and six kilos. A Namakkal *arivaal*, with one well-aimed swing, could accomplish what the guillotine did. Kumar added that the *mandai porul arivaal* that came without the beaked-edge was the blade for a clean beheading, while the serrated *maan porul arivaal* was ideal for a gutting – it took just one stick to spill blood, bone and entrails.

Despite education being government-funded, Kumar quit school after the eighth grade. Corporal punishment, heavily practiced in schools, had embittered him. He was bereft of his mother at a young age. His father found himself another woman and neglected his son. He ended up being raised by his maternal grandmother and his habitat was the street. He was a Dalit. And this meant he got kicked around like a stray dog for sport.

Kumar and his grandmother lived in a tiny asbestos shack. There was a *pucca* house next to theirs. When Kumar stood near this house to talk to a friend, its owner directed a barrage of abuses at him. "You motherfucker! I don't want filthy scum standing outside my property! There are young girls in this house! Buzz off before I call the police to beat you to a pulp!"

Incidents such as these filled Kumar with the desire to exact revenge from just about everyone he thought had wronged him. Once, before he had reached adulthood, Kumar and his friends were drinking at a construction site. The watchman who detected their clandestine activity ordered them out of the premises. Every mouth spat filth – son of a bitch, son of this, son of that and son of whatnot.

Kumar took out his *mandai porul arivaal* and aimed for the watchman's head. His alcohol-induced stupor caused him to miss his mark and the blade cut through the watchman's shoulder and all the way down to his chest. His friends cut and ran like scattered sheep. It was hard, even with the finessed arm and wrist movements of a butcher, to extricate an *arivaal* lodged in human flesh. When it was out, he used it to hack the head off. The arms and legs followed. In one hand he held the head and in the other one of the legs, with the pride of a cricketer holding his man-of-the-match trophy and replica check and walked to the nearest police station. Placing the anatomical remnants of his victim outside the "tesan" (Kumar's best attempt at pronouncing "station"), he respectfully woke up the drooling constable and recounted the sequence of events that had led up to the murder. "Away with you, you halfwit!" said the groggy-eyed constable. Kumar left and returned in a flash, brandishing the watchman's scalp.

Since no witnesses came forward and since the murderer had not attained the legal age, he was tossed into a juvenile correctional home where he spent a few years and emerged a free man.

On his return to his neck of the woods, Kumar discovered that he now commanded respect from the same folks who had dared to spit at him earlier. The shopkeeper of the *pucca* house fervently addressed him as "sir," for fear that Kumar's perception of the slightest disrespect might cost him his head.

Kumar's next murder was planned and executed with an express profit-motive. The plan was to attack a motorist at the traffic signal and bolt with the bike. The first part of the plan went swimmingly. He had mounted the bike, but had cut his thigh while trying to put the *arivaal* back in his cummerbund. To make bad matters worse, the bike wouldn't start and a heavily bleeding thigh didn't help his cause. A traffic cop tried to nab him, but the sight of the *arivaal* gobbled his gumption. "Dey, dey, I have three children. Please spare me," he pleaded fearfully. Leaving the bike on the road, Kumar limped to a nearby shop. "*Akka*, would you mind giving a wounded man a little place to sit?" he said to the woman at the cash-counter. He took a huge swig from the bottle of soda on the table. In the meantime, the traffic cop had arrived with reinforcements of men.

"Did you attack the motorist with intention of stealing his bike?" the officer asked. When Kumar replied in the affirmative, he received a cuffing. Kumar was sentenced to only a few months in prison for this crime. The traffic cop lied under oath in the witness box, claiming he was so busy directing heavy traffic that he hadn't seen a thing.

As for Kumar's third murder, I thought it was worthy of being adapted into a stage-play.

An engineer's wife was having an affair with his assistant. When the husband learned of it, he felt scandalized, and instead of confronting the paramours, contacted Kumar.

The engineer introduced Kumar to his assistant as a friend. Kumar's mandate was to befriend the assistant, lure him to the lakeside on the pretext of a little revelry and finish the job there. Finish he did, with the flourish of a homicide-fetishist. He decapitated the corpse and displayed the limbs. He captured the carnage on his cellphone and sent it to his client. He then packed each limb into a gunny bag filled with rocks and sank each bag at a different place in the lake.

Nearly a month later, the decomposed fragments of the assistant's limbs were discovered. Yet again, no witnesses and no viable forensic evidence. Kumar the Killer simply couldn't be nabbed but for human vanity. The cuckolded engineer, keen to acquaint his wife with the cost of her infidelity, showed her the video of the hacking. "You thought you could play me dirty? Look what I did to your Romeo."

The police were promptly informed. The engineer and Kumar spent some time in prison before being let out into the world again.

As Kumar was readying to leave, I asked him one last question about his modus operandi. "When pistols are so ubiquitous in Uttar Pradesh and Bihar and so accessible elsewhere, why do you make do with cumbersome *arivaals?*"

"If I'd used a pistol, I wouldn't be sitting here," he said. "It's harder to get bailed out of prison for a firearms offence." The more I gave his speech thought, the more convinced I became that Kumar was safer inside the prison.

When the time came to depart on a happy high, Manickam offered to see Kumar off at the bus stand. When Manickam returned, he was all complaints. "Did you hear the condescending way the rascal talked? All that talk and no money to even buy a bus ticket or even a cigarette! Wangled a hundred from me!" It turned out that Kumar's shoes were "borrowed" as well. No wonder the great killer walked like a duck.

7 – Victim: Feline, Perpetrator: Canine

Ismail was the keeper of a large bungalow whose owners were living overseas for an indefinite period of time. Having plenty of time to spare and a quest for some extra income, he offered to run errands for us. He sought a little bit extra not just by way of coin but also by way of sex. A very much married Ismail, unhappy with his wife, was bonking a maidservant of similar marital status in the bungalow he was supposed to be guarding. She was responsible for general upkeep.

Perundevi wasn't pleased to hear about their affair. She decreed that Ismail would not put one toe on our threshold until after he divorced his current wife and legally married the maidservant. Now that she had barred Ismail, the household chores fell to my lot.

Determined to not let Ismail rot in his sinful state, Perundevi took it upon herself to reform him by telling him moral stories that actually brought about realization and an apparent transformation. "You're my mother," he said, prostrating himself before her.

If things had ended there, this story would not have been written. Perundevi gave him an abandoned kitten and exhorted him to take good care of it. She also gave him a daily stipend of fifteen rupees to buy "Chintoo" some milk.

After a few days, Ismail's promise of fidelity began to fray. "You'll never change your stripes. Don't ever come near my house again," an incensed Perundevi told Ismail.

The very next day, I was horror-stricken when I saw Blackie come running to me with Chintoo gripped between his canine jaws. The kitten had somehow escaped from Ismail's place and found its way to our house. Before my very eyes, I saw one pet murder another. Blackie, like all Great Danes, was as big as a pony. He would obey every command I issued, but on the day of the murder, he simply refused to obey. It deposited the kitten on the floor and there it lay dying before me. Something about that kitten's death rattled my bones.

"Why did you let the kitten out?" I asked Ismail.

"Well, Madam scolded me rather harshly, so I didn't have the nerve to ask her for the milk allowance. The cat was starving. It must have sneaked out to search for a bite," he replied indifferently.

8 – *Jalebi* Chicken

I know a millionaire in Mylapore. He is a chicken seller. His top-quality produce has made him something of a local celebrity. The industrially processed broiler chicken you usually get in Tamil Nadu is stringy and hard to chew, like a week-old chapatti. Country chicken is not a tad better. While it is not as stringy, it gives the jaws a workout. I had lost faith in chicken and hence stopped eating it. Then, I heard of the millionaire's Mylapore chicken stall. His chicken slid down my throat with the ease of a syrupy *jalebi*. No wonder the owner of that shop had become as rich as he had.

After a while, I stopped eating chicken altogether. If you ever hear the desperate clucking of a chicken facing the knife, you would quit chicken too. I sometimes hear chickens clucking in my sleep.

9 – Dog Personalities

An actress' pet dog sank its teeth into Jagan's hand once. It wasn't the dog's fault, though. It was Jagan's, because he'd assumed it was a pedigreed dog. Pet dogs don't tend to bite people, but this dog was a hardened stray that the actress had adopted recently.

Fear is encoded in the DNA of stray dogs. Biting is their only defense mechanism which is why I do not blame the stray for having bitten Jagan.

Let me educate you a little bit about the standard operating procedure to be adhered to when dealing with the species *Canis familiaris*. The canine has to be spoken to first if you intend to win its trust. Leave it up to the dog to decide if you're friendly or hostile. Speak to the animal kindly and welcomingly and extend your wrist. If the dog sniffs at it, it is a signal that it's willing to be touched. Your hand just might become a tasty chew-toy if you don't adhere to the protocol.

10 – Whitey, a Street Dog, My Friend

I seem to get along very well with street dogs. I had a four-legged friend who lived in my lane. When I first saw him, every last square inch of his body was infested with sores. A few months later, as if by some miracle, he was healed. I could see shoots of white fur reappearing. I named him Whitey. Whenever I ventured out, he'd come sprinting to me like we'd been best friends for ages. When sore-stricken, he shied away from physical contact. Feeling the urge to reciprocate this dog's affection, I began feeding him biscuits. I even offered him branded dog food, but he was partial to cashew cookies.

I used to walk the length of Beach Road every morning. When I set out for my walk at five in the morning, I would find Whitey sleeping under a car. He would usually accompany me to the mouth of the lane. Today he followed me further. The two of us, man and dog, prayed before the Santhome cathedral for five minutes before pacing up to the lighthouse.

Even at that early hour, traffic wasn't sparse. Cars and bikes were zipping by like their riders were being pursued through one of hell's circles by the devil himself. I feared that some rash rider might hit Whitey or run him over. I looked at him. He was standing right beside me, returning my gaze, wagging his tail. I decided against crossing the road and abandoned my morning walk altogether. Whitey serenely escorted me back home and curled up on my doorstep.

Whitey was ever on the alert and kept his vigilant eye trained on scavengers and North-Indian blanket sellers.

The influx of North Indians into Tamil Nadu would have been unimaginable forty years ago when the Dravidian parties first seized power, piggybacking on emotive slogans such as "The North waxes while the South wanes." Today it is the North that seems to be waning. It is nearly impossible to find South Indians in labor-intensive jobs. There is a heavy demand and a voluntary supply of migrant labor from up north. The Dravidian parties overexerted themselves to uproot Hindi, but the northern language was already entrenched too deep. Most of the workers in the restaurants here are from Uttar Pradesh and Bihar – even in mofussil towns whose inhabitants would never have heard a word of Hindi. Today, a working knowledge of Hindi is essential if you wish to be attended to even in a place as hoary as Mylapore's Rayar Café.

Perundevi was convinced that the blanket-sellers were doubling as the local thieves' informants. Using trade as their cover, they made careful note of which houses were locked, how many members lived in a household, and their everyday schedules. If the thieves had a field day, the informants would have a wad shoved into the back pockets of their pants. Perundevi's theory couldn't be pooh-poohed entirely. Chennai did get rocked by a spate of robberies around that time and the culprits turned out to be slave-laborers from the stone quarries of Rajasthan.

It is not uncommon even for poor and lower middle-class families of Tamil Nadu to be in ownership of gold worth a hundred grand. Middle-class households could, at a conservative estimate, be in possession of 250 grams, five-hundred grand there. Most of it is found on a woman's nose, dangling from her ears, round her neck and on both her arms (mostly from wrist to elbow). The rest of it is stashed in steel almirahs.

In one particularly gruesome, widely covered incident, a gang of Rajasthani blanket-sellers broke into a house they'd been sussing out for quite some time at around two in the morning. They attacked the family with crowbars, killing them all. A twelve-year-old was among the killed. She had been pinned to the wall and held in a chokehold until she died. Under the pressure of a public outcry, the police bucked up for once and swung into action. The gang was intercepted during their flight to Rajasthan. The jewelry was recovered but all its owners were dead.

Whitey's eternal vigilance and ferocity deterred the blanket-sellers from entering our street, but not the scavengers. Local men knew the art of handling local dogs; they chased the dog away with sticks and stones. The scavengers presented a peculiar sight as they went about their business. Their filthy torsos were indistinguishable from the garbage dump. They usually came bare-bodied, with a high-density sack slung over one shoulder.

They had their eyes peeled primarily for milk sachets and plastic tumblers (that fetched them seventeen bucks per kg), beer and soda cans (a kilo of these sold for twenty-five), cardboard boxes (twenty-eight a kilo) and beer bottles (full, half-full, half-empty, or empty – it made no matter). And some of them were specialists in ferreting out ferrous scrap alone.

Perundevi was one among the few who practiced the segregation of wet and dry waste. The scavengers were attracted only to the dry half. They would tear open the wet bag to find nothing of even marginal commercial value. The contents of the bag they deemed useless would be scattered far and wide, creating an almighty mess. Appalled, Perundevi would curse them. The scavengers did not ruffle my feathers. I was no stranger to the circumstances of their lot because I was born in them. If I were a practitioner of my caste-ordained profession, I would have been no different than them. Perundevi would give a deaf ear to my take on the issue, and her vocal battles with the scavengers raged on.

"You will never understand how a woman feels about certain things, so, the best thing for you to do is to mind your own business," she would admonish me.

She feared that the street, if abandoned in its garbage-ridden state, would attract undesirable nuisance-cases, and since my travels kept me away most of the time, she had to look out for herself. Like a hawk with an eye on its prey, she would keep an eye on the dustbins and holler at the scavengers and drive them away. They responded to her with obscenities.

The scavengers broke Whitey's hind leg. It was their "how do you like that" to us. We took Whitey to the vet who had to surgically amputate his leg, but the dog did not lose its spirit. It continued to run like it had three legs more instead of one leg less.

Perundevi the zealot had an idea. Why not have the garbage bin removed from the vicinity? Using her influence, she made a few phone calls and – what do you know – the bin was removed. Once the bin was gone, the sanitation workers showed up at six every morning and at noon with their pushcarts to collect the garbage. When there was the bin, all the residents of our street had to do was hand the garbage to their maids who simply tossed it into the giant roadside bin. They exerted their collective influence and had the bin brought back. They were livid with Perundevi for causing them all this trouble, and the fact that she was a woman only angered them further. "How can a woman be so arrogant? Wait, we'll teach her a lesson," they said.

Not one to back away from a fight like a spineless coward, she opened another front. First, she brought the problem to the attention of the city's mayor; second, she adopted a Gandhian strategy – she went from house to house like an evangelizer and explained the merits of not having a garbage bin in the neighborhood. When she told them how the garbage dump was responsible for their children's illnesses, she managed to win them over. The bin was once again removed. We spent four thousand rupees a month for the maintenance of the premises. We had hired two people to rake the leaves. They also swept the ground and watered it twice a day. Only after this was done, Perundevi would draw the *kolam*. We paid the sanitation workers 1500 rupees. Considering their measly monthly payment, this couldn't be called a bribe. The remaining five hundred bucks was paid to incentivize the dude who supervised the workers.

While the entire country was turning into one giant garbage heap, one woman was fighting a dogged battle to keep one street clean. Three sanitation workers – Chandra, Devanai and Gajendran – collected the garbage from our street. They took it in turns to come. If one of them failed to turn up in the morning, Perundevi would phone the other two. On most days Gajendran wouldn't answer her calls as he'd be nursing a hangover, and if Chandra too didn't answer, she would call Durai, the supervisor, immediately. If none of them turned up, the place would stink to high heaven. Sometimes, it felt like Perundevi was running a mini-municipality by herself.

At around ten one morning, Devanai was knocking at our gate. The garbage in the kitchen was spilling out of the trash bag. I asked her to wait while I took care of first things first. Just then, I heard Perundevi whisper something to Parvathy, our maid. Fearing that Devanai might leave without taking the garbage, I kept yelling for her to hold on. I saw Parvathy run to the gate and tell Devanai to come later in the afternoon as there was no garbage to be dumped now.

"The garbage bag is overflowing, Parvathy!" I shouted.

Perundevi came to me and whispered, "Gajendran is on leave today, Udhaya. If Devanai collects the garbage now, no one will come in the afternoon."

"But it's overflowing! Can't you see? Why couldn't we have just handed it to her now?"

"You don't get it, Udhaya. If nobody comes in the afternoon, then all the garbage will pile up before our house and I will have to sweep it away."

Something else happened that day. I don't usually pay attention to Perundevi's many telephone conversations as they mostly veer around all things spiritual. But this time, she spoke of something else altogether.

"Durai, I need some help. The house in front of ours is being renovated. I think the rubbish they dumped outside has found its way into the sewage pipe and blocked it. Could you come and take a look at it? If you can't, just let me know so that I can call the mayor and ask *him* to do something about it. Oh, so you're coming, are you? Are you *sure*? Well, that's settled then."

In a few minutes, a huge lorry arrived with the words "Chennai Corporation Solid Waste" emblazoned on it. The lorry was much larger than the garbage truck. While I was wondering how it managed to wend its way through all the narrow streets, a water lorry too arrived. Perundevi assumed the role of a traffic cop, standing in the middle of the road and issuing instructions to clear the way for the water lorry. After the workers who had come in the solid waste lorry had cleared the blockage in the underground sewage system (taking forty-five minutes), they came to Perundevi for their "incentives." I was in my room when I heard Durai say, "What is the meaning of this, Madam? You have given us only four hundred rupees when there are five of us."

She said, "Of course, you'll probably hope for a biscuit of gold each when you next see me."

One day, I noticed that Whitey was troubled by a flea-infestation. When I tried to medicate him, he scooted. Blackie would not allow Whitey into the house, so we did not encourage Whitey in either. Whitey would visit thrice a day, eat his cashew cookies and leave. He would stand guard at the gate and wait for me. Soon enough, Blackie and Baba were also flea-stricken. Madan said he would deposit Whitey with the Blue Cross, insisting that his own pets were more important than a street dog. Even though he did not put his threat into action, it surprised me all the same that he could differentiate between a dog with and a dog without a home.

Around that time, some new neighbors moved in. They had a Labrador called Buddy. The son, Raja, a college student, was an ardent devotee of Sai Baba. All day, I would hear *bhajans* being chanted or played in their house. Upon learning that I too was a Sai Baba devotee, Raja started coming over on Thursdays to give me the *prasad*. Perundevi remarked, mightily impressed, "I've never seen such a nice boy!"

I did have my doubts, but I never voiced them openly. How could a boy so young be so spiritually inclined?

When Buddy the Labrador caught the flea infestation, Raja realized that Whitey was responsible for it. He came to me and said that he was going to hand over the stray to the municipality. Stunned and saddened, I asked Perundevi, "Did you hear what the 'nice boy' said?"

"A person is made up of both good and bad traits," she philosophized.

Do you know how street dogs are culled? Have you seen them being rounded up and caught by the municipality workers? Did you hear their pathetic howls when they are caught? As per the government's orders, these dogs are to be killed with a lethal shot, but that doesn't happen. The men, fearing that the dogs might bite them while they are being injected, kill them by bashing them on the head with an iron rod. This I have witnessed with my own eyes and this is just one of the reasons I detest man, the most vicious of all living creatures.

11 – A Close Shave with Death

Devika asked me whether I'd be interested in watching *Chanakya* at the Music Academy. She was a dear friend to Perundevi and a top cop, the head of the anti-corruption wing.

We lived on the ground floor of an apartment complex in Chinmaya Nagar. On the floor above was a family that had moved in recently. Quite often, their refuse would rain down onto our laundry on the line and soil it completely.

After a drink, they would simply toss the bottles off the balcony. Even their dog took after them, taking a dump at everybody else's door. Following a series of complaints from Perundevi and the other residents, our shoes started vanishing from outside our houses.

I never butt into these affairs. If you want to throw dishwater down my shirt or even piss on my head, go right ahead. I was young when I realized the futility of getting into a tangle with numpties and knaves.

My father used to grow tomatoes on a small patch of land. While he was waiting for them to ripen, the neighbor's goat made an unwelcome visit and polished them all off.

"It's okay, don't worry about it," I'd often have to tell him.

The grueling work involved explained the film of tears that would come over his reddening eyes. The heated exchange between him and the neighbor degenerated into a fisting match once. Had I not come to his rescue equipped with an *arivaal*, they would have strangled him to death. This vicious cycle of revenge continued. I once banded together a group of friends and gave my neighbors a sound thrashing. They returned the favor with a near fatal attack on me. I miraculously managed to escape.

After my near meet-and-greet with death, I stepped out of that notorious world. I immersed myself in books and music. But the literary world too is peopled with its strongmen, its henchmen, its thugs and its hired snipers. Not a day went by that I didn't receive abusive mail. Most of what I received was very articulate and colorful, and very generous in the outpouring of filth. The correspondents were mostly from the US of A, Europe and India. They all seemed to have a personal problem with me. Perundevi was the subject of several of these letters. One moralizing correspondent had the audacity to ask me if I wasn't ashamed of living with a second-hand wife.

Soon after we married, I asked Perundevi why she preferred to keep her hair short after the fashion of Lady Diana. She told me that after her husband from her previous marriage had died, ultra-orthodox Brahmin custom dictated that she keep her head shorn. Once it grew back, she decided to sport a bob cut. It would have been a surprise to not receive those obscene e-mails considering the society I live in.

Our plan to watch *Chanakya* unfortunately coincided with the Residents' Association meeting of our apartment. I was usually a no-show, but this time, we had all reason to attend. While several residents had had their footwear pinched, my son Madan was robbed of his bicycle. In addition to all of that, there were plenty of other niggles wanting resolution. As is usually the case with such meetings, this one ended in pandemonium without us getting even remotely close to solving our problems. Perundevi returned exhausted and exasperated.

After that mayhem, Perundevi had a duplicate key made for the main gate. This she gave to the folks who lived above us who invariably came home at midnight. Despite this, they continued to knock on our window to be let in. They would say that the key had been misplaced and cheekily ask Perundevi to have another made for them. Although this was not Perundevi's responsibility in the slightest, she acceded to their demand. After all, she was a social worker. Like a woman losing her bobby-pins, these bothers kept losing their key and continued to disturb us by knocking on the window at ungodly hours.

This is an essential strategy for problem-free living and survival in India which I discovered when I was working in the postal department. Whenever the Postmaster General – the PMG – and I were happened to be in the same lift, I would ignore him, but the other employees would bow and scrape before him. I did not wish to make an exhibition of my boldness or my indifference to authority, but if I greeted him, he would realize that I was a postal employee. His next question would invariably be: "Which section?" and if I were to reply, "Stenos' Pool," I would return to a table with a mountain of documents to be typed before I even reached it. A rider saying that I had to finish them all within the hour would accompany them. I had been in one of these situations before and it was then that I'd stumbled on this practical philosophy of remaining hidden from or invisible to others. If I lay low, the PMG would assume I was a member of the public and leave me alone. Okay, that was quite a digression. Let's return to the point.

Perundevi and I set out to watch *Chanakya*, in the hopes that it would be a pleasurable pursuit. Devika had sent an official jeep to pick us up. She said she would join our party midway. En route, Perundevi exclaimed, "Look, there's Madan's cycle!" When he saw the police vehicle, the chap on the cycle froze. The peabrain hadn't bothered to sandpaper Madan's name that was painted on the cycle. After all, who would expect a bicycle stolen in Chinmaya Nagar to be spotted a good five kilometers away in Ramavaram? We parceled the custodian of the cycle and offered him a joyride with us.

"This I bought from stranger man standing Ashok Pillar – six hundred only," said the boy who looked to be about twenty, but he yielded even before the police had begun to grill him. Perundevi was thrilled to have got the cycle back.

The play was a disaster from start to finish. It was past ten when that eyesore of a spectacle ended. We took our supper at a 'military' hotel that served curried blood and head of goat. Perundevi and Devika did not object despite the fact that they were vegetarians. Perundevi had actually learned to cook animal meat just for me, but offal is out of her culinary orbit, which is why I am at the mercy of restaurants like this one to sate my occasional craving for that good stuff.

It was past midnight when we reached home. No sooner did we enter our house than we heard the screams of the young man from upstairs at our window. "Aunty! Aunty!"

"Don't open the door," I said nonchalantly.

"Why not? It sounds like the poor chap is in distress," she said, and off she went.

I dropped onto the bed as she went to open the gate. The boy was not a stranger, so I didn't care to accompany her. The next thing I heard was Perundevi's terrified scream. "Oh God! Udhaya!"

Three burly men and women were brutally beating her up. One of them was even trying to strangle her. Madan too got roughed up in the pell-mell. If not for man's instinctive fear of dogs, if not for Baba zapping to her rescue and lunging at the attackers and sending them running helter-skelter, Perundevi would have been dead.

"I'll kill you, bastard!" yelled one of the scooting thugs who was bleeding from the eye. He was the head of the family that lived on the floor above. He had come with his son and his son-in-law.

We dialed the cops who arrived after five minutes. Devika turned up a quarter of an hour later. The assailants were long gone.

Perundevi had to be carried to the police station to register her complaint. She was a woman with the strength of a spring chicken. She would come close to fainting when I played Black Sabbath and Cradle of Filth. Her body began to convulse, foam dribbled from her mouth. She soon lost consciousness and we rushed her to the hospital on a stretcher.

Not a single head from our apartment popped out to check what the fracas was all about. After ringing the police, I rang Gangadharan, the owner of the complex, as he was responsible for this whole sorry affair. He had rented out the flat to these roughnecks because his tongue was hanging for money. He was also present during the Residents' Association meeting earlier that day during which Perundevi had spoken in his favor, much to the fury of the tenants upstairs. Gangadharan's wife answered the phone. Trembling with rage, I demanded to speak to her husband that very moment.

"He is sleeping," came her calm reply.

Agitatedly, I described to her what had transpired.

"Why did you have to fight with the other tenants? Can't you live amicably with them?"

"Just give the phone to your husband," I said.

But the woman hung up.

The x-ray revealed that Perundevi had suffered a hairline cervical fracture. She had to spend a week in a government hospital. Since hers was a police case, we couldn't treat her in a private hospital. The general ward was like a refugee camp; due to the shortage of beds, a number of patients lay on rags spread on the floor. We paid some extra money and had her shifted to a private room on the fourth floor. It turned out that there was no water supply up there. In order to use the toilet, water had to be fetched from the third floor for which an attendant had to be bribed. With no water to bathe, Perundevi decided to make a trip home. Her attackers, whose plea for bail was being heard, received this intelligence.

"She's checked herself into a hospital despite the fact that she's in a sound physical condition," said the defense attorney. "She even goes home occasionally." He thus managed to successfully argue them out of jail. I gathered that the hooligans had hired a mole to keep an eye on us at all times.

How much more abuse would Perundevi's sinewy body endure? It started with her father. How many more fists? How many more blows? Her desperate scream from the other night was still ringing in my ears.

Attending to Perundevi in the hospital made me realize why people in India hesitate to approach the law. What passed for medical care in the hospital was only marginally removed from being manhandled.

There were several temples, mosques and churches around the hospital. Beginning at four in the morning, all these religious places battled it out to dominate the airwaves. The Mariamman devotees were the loudest. Even at eleven in the night, L.R. Easwari's devotional medleys would be on full blast.

So much happened in the hospital that I do not know what is or isn't worthy of being written. To use the lift to get from the third floor to the fourth, five rupees had to be slipped to the operator. On her third day of her stay in hospital, the head nurse came to Perundevi and unashamedly said, "Keep us in mind, madam. We slog day and night." She was a heavyset woman of fifty. Bewildered, Perundevi took out a hundred from her purse and handed it to her, but the head nurse was not happy. "What is this, madam? There are four of us, and we *all* work from morning to night. Please don't insult us like this." When Perundevi handed her a five-hundred rupee note, the woman was all smiles. It left me dumbfounded that she could be so brazen as to demand such a hefty bribe despite seeing the woman with the cop-badge making frequent appearances.

It was around six one evening when I was about to make a trip home from the hospital when an auto screeched to a halt at the entrance. A man in a *lungi*, one hand chopped off at the wrist, stumbled out. He was with a woman who was carrying his severed hand in a bloodstained plastic bag. Had he been operated immediately, there was a fat chance that his hand could have been saved, but the nurses on duty dismissed him, saying, "The doctor is not here."

The nurse saw me looking at her, baffled. She explained, "If we admit such cases, we will be in a stew with the law. These chaps chop off hands, legs and heads in a drunken rage. We can save ourselves the trouble of shuttling between the hospital and the court this way."

"I see," I said, removing myself swiftly from the scene.

As I was going back and forth from the hospital, Perundevi's parents asked me, "Where does Madan eat?"

"Motherfuckers," I muttered to myself. Then I replied. "I have no time to think of where he eats, drinks, bathes or shits. My brains are addled."

I heard later that Madan had been taking his meals in their house.

Their enquiry was probably their jab at me for being an irresponsible father. And would you look at who it came from? But I refrained from getting into words with them for the sake of Madan's stomach.

None of Perundevi's relatives – not even her parents – paid her a visit or made a courtesy-call to enquire after her. Her parents took on Madan to excuse themselves.

Once we returned home, we were given police protection for eight days. Two constables took it in turns to guard our house. The men in the apartment above us had already had another run-in with them the previous week. Janakaraj, one of the constables, recounted the incident to me.

"The fellow who misbehaved with me is as rotten as rotten can be. I did not catch him in a headlock or punch his teeth down his throat because I'm a softie. I avoid trouble as much as I possibly can. But I assure you that I have them on my radar."

I felt bad for the constables who had to stay up and out in the cold of night. I invited them in, but they refused, saying that they would be unable to nab any troublemakers if they were not on the alert. With the swarms of mosquitoes with vampire's cravings that were active during the night, it was a wonder they still had blood in their bodies. Even mosquito-repellent coils proved ineffective. Janakaraj subjected me to a daily hour-long sermon on mosquitoes. Even after the eight-day police protection ceased, he would pay us a visit during his morning rounds to talk at length about his favorite subject. "I don't understand the world. We have sent one of our women into space but we still haven't got rid of mosquitoes."

"Pathetic," I gravely nodded in agreement.

"Have you noticed something, sir? The mosquitoes used to be tiny little chaps before. Now, they're bigger than flies and their stings itch like the pox."

Sometimes, I wondered if the man had been born and raised with pesky mosquitoes.

To avoid the trap of such pointless conversations, I desist from making conversation. Another reason for my lack of sociability is my hatred for these harassing know-it-alls who talk like they've swallowed the ocean of knowledge and churned it for days to extract the nectar of everlasting wisdom they are determined to dispense to anyone and everyone within arm's length.

Before my second visit to Paris in 2001, Kannappan, a senior officer in the postal department came to me with his queries.

"Why are you going to Paris?"

"I was invited to lecture at a literary conference."

"A lecture on what?"

"Literature."

"That's a little too obvious. What's your concentration?"

"Postmodernism and contemporary Tamil literature."

"Take my advice and read Ramanichandran before you leave," Kannappan said gratuitously. Ramanichandran is *the* most famous purveyor of pulp in Tamil. Her connection to postmodernism is as strong as mine to the sport of lacrosse.

Thereafter, whenever I ran into him, he would ask if I'd managed to read the masterpieces of his recommendation. I always replied in the negative, fearing that a "yes" would effectuate a long-drawn conversation on the writer's œuvre. He happened to be my superior and I couldn't risk a haggle with him over a subject we were bound to vary on, a subject he considered himself an expert in.

While Perundevi was still in hospital, I had a meeting with Harish, a friend who lived in California. He brought me a tin of tuna. I put it in the fridge and forgot all about it. A couple of days later, I noticed it sitting there, untouched, and began looking all over the place for a knife to open the can. We had two knives, of which one was sharp enough to cleanly cut a goat. Neither could be found.

When Perundevi returned home, I asked her about the knives and she confessed that she had hidden them. I had gone out with friends for drinks a couple of days after our incident. Perundevi explained that she had hidden the knives because she didn't want them lying around when I came home drunk. I was alarmed. "I wouldn't even kill an ant! Do you think I would kill *you*? I love you more than my life. Don't you know that? Do you really fear *me*?" I protested.

"I know you love me, Udhaya, but sometimes, all I feel is terror."

It filled me with anxiety to think about how long she would subject herself to living in fear. She also told me that her coworkers were afraid to accompany her anywhere, so, wherever she had to go, she went alone.

"What bullshit! Why are they afraid of you? It should be the other way round."

"They see me as a trouble magnet. They fear that if the thugs come, they might get roughed up too."

In spite of the police protection and the close friendship of Devika, we were convinced that no one and nothing could keep harm from befalling us.

It was crazy. Whenever I saw – or even imagined – the person who had sworn to kill me, I trembled in fear. Who *was* this fellow, and what did I ever do to him for him to want so desperately to kill me? Whenever these thoughts harassed me, I felt anger against Perundevi. The owner of the apartment was going about his life without a hitch as were the other tenants. Why did she, of all people, have to get so deeply involved in things? Because of her, both of us had to live in constant fear, all because she had meddled in something that had naught to do with her. For how long would we continue to look over our shoulders?

As I masticated on these thoughts, a police officer told me that the guy upstairs has close ties with the leader of some political party. Coincidentally, the leader was also a friend of my friend Basheer. I explained our predicament to Basheer and asked him to talk to the leader. He was to convince him that no loyalties tied us to Gangadharan, and that there was no reason for the goons upstairs to target us.

Basheer arranged a meeting with the leader during Pongal. We had to wait for hours to see the man, and I was again moved to anger for being put in this spot all on Perundevi's account. When the leader finally arrived, I had to reiterate that miserable account and he listened to me with rapt attention. When I finished, a thickset fellow who had been standing near the leader said, "*Anney*, we'd planned to finish off this fellow if our people hadn't been released on Monday." The leader raised his hand, signaling him to shut up. He turned back to me and said, "You can leave now. Leave everything to me. You won't have any problems." Once we were outside, Basheer told me, "The leader will lay off those thugs. No one dares to flout his word. Don't sweat it anymore."

Begging that leader to save our lives was the most mortifying things I had to do.

Sometime later, misfortune after misfortune befell our attackers. As it was a case of attempted murder, they had to cough up a lot of cash and consequently, their business crashed and burned. Their daughter had a stillborn baby, and even in that fragile physical and emotional condition, she had to answer summons from the court and the police station. The respect these folks enjoyed among the locals diminished sharply, and within a few days, they were reduced to such a miserable state that they folded their hands in greeting whenever they encountered me.

Perundevi began to pray for their welfare. The police had done everything they could to ensure that they would be moved to court on charges of assault with intent to murder. When they had gone into hiding, the police nabbed them in Andhra Pradesh. But finally, when we were asked to testify against our assailants, we refused.

"There is no point punishing them any further," I told the baffled policemen. "Fate has punished them enough."

The people who had subjected us to one of the worst ordeals of our lives eventually packed their backs and left the neighborhood and settled elsewhere.

12 – The Art of Buying Fish

I love the fish market. It is a microcosm in itself. I'd recommend a visit even if you're a vegetarian, just for the sake of the experience. Nadukuppam on Lloyds Road is my favorite. There, a person can buy anything from a lobster worth a thousand bucks to a mackerel worth twenty. Its democracy only serves to boost its appeal. I visit once in five days and buy shark and Asian sea bass from a very dignified fifty-year-old woman. If the fish is kept in the freezer after being marinated in salt and turmeric, it will not rot. During the DMK regime between 2006 and 2011, blackouts in the state could last for as many as twenty hours a day, but Chennai, being the state capital, had to endure the heat and the darkness for only a couple of hours.

Perundevi grumbled that I was being gypped by the fishmongers. This is something married men have to live with because women all over the world think their husbands are gullible fools. Before I left for Thailand, I'd told her to go to Nadukuppam if she needed fish. On my return, she told me she'd found a woman who sold for less.

"What you buy for eight-hundred, I bought for six," she announced smugly. The next time Perundevi went to the market, I went with her, wanting to see the seller she was talking about. When we got there, I realized that we'd both been buying from the same woman. There was something about her that lured buyers. Perundevi told me, "From now on, *I'm* buying the fish. You stay away."

Like barring a man from buying fish was not enough, Perundevi would bug me, saying that Ismail, the neighbor, brought home a bag full of fish for a mere hundred rupees. So, she sent me with him one day to learn the art of negotiation.

I suggested we take an auto because, left to Ismail, he would have preferred to go the distance on foot. Ismail, on reaching the Lighthouse, asked the driver to turn right towards Nochikuppam. If we drove straight till Queen Mary's College and turned left we would have reached Nadukuppam, but Ismail said, "They ask for astronomical sums there." I smiled noncommittally. Ismail was already several paces ahead of me by the time I'd alighted from the auto. "Let's take a look first," he said. There must have been at least a hundred shops and he stopped at each one of them, enquiring about prices. The women selling the fish were adorned with chunky gold neckpieces. Unlike the middle-class folks, these people seemed to prefer squandering their money on tasteless jewelry rather than investing it for their children's education.

Most of Mylapore's children receive a twelve-year education at P. S. Senior Secondary, Rosary Matriculation,

S. S. K., Vidya Mandir or St. Raphael's and move on to college, get a degree and get settled. But Nochikuppam's children rarely get that chance. These women could very well use their money and their gold to provide for their children's immediate and future needs, but why on earth don't they? I followed Ismail who evinced no interest in such social and cultural issues and instead kept raving about the art of buying fish.

"Listen to me carefully. If a fishmonger asks you for six hundred, you must quote two hundred."

"What? Two hundred?"

"Watch this," he said, pointing to a couple of large barracuda fish. He asked the vendor the price.

"Six hundred," was her reply.

"Two hundred," he said, and the bargaining began in right earnest.

"Did you come here with money to buy fish or two empty pockets and a mouth full of crap?"

"Ah! Damn you! You can keep your bloody fish!" Ismail retorted, moving to the next vendor.

"Fine! Three hundred. I'm settling for that pittance only because you're a regular."

"Two fifty?"

"Well, how about you try your luck at the other stalls? If you get two barracudas for *that* price, come back to me and I'll throw in these two for zilch."

Ismail moved on, saying that one should not tarry long at a particular stall, and that all of them should be visited.

At one, he bought some Bengal carp for thirty and at another, he bargained outrageously and bought two sharks priced at eight hundred rupees for three hundred.

On the way back, he stopped at the stall where he had bargained for the barracuda and asked the woman, "Now what do you say?"

"*Five* hundred."

"Whoa, whoa, whoa! Just a little while ago, you said *three* hundred," he reminded her.

"That was a while ago. Now it's five hundred."

Finally, the deal was concluded. The fish were sold for three hundred rupees.

We took the fish we had bought to another group of women whose task it was to scale and slice the fish. Ismail handed them over to the woman who usually did the job for him, but her knife was rusty and she was struggling to get the job done. I felt sorry for her. In Nadukuppam, scaling and slicing was a man's job. They had big and sharp knives that accomplished the task in a jiffy.

"Why don't you use better knives?" I asked one of them.

"There are too many tosspots here," she said. "If we get sharper tools, there'd be four deaths a day."

My legs and hips began to ache. There was a slight drizzle and we could hear the roar of the waves. Fishermen were on their boats, unfazed by the giant rollers. In the distance, I could see the faint outline of several ships. It began to rain. Ismail opened his umbrella and held it over the woman. Folding up his *lungi*, he squatted beside her as she worked, talking about fish and life in general. I couldn't stand in one place for long. It took the woman more than an hour to cut the fish. Besides, the auto driver was still waiting.

"I thought you sent him away," Ismail said.

"If I had, it would have been difficult to catch another to get back home."

Buying fish from Nadukuppam was preferable to buying it for three hundred after a two-hour long wait. I made a mental note to tell Perundevi that all the money in the world could not compensate for those two lost hours.

As I was late, Perundevi had made a radish gravy for lunch. I felt miserable: all this fish at our disposal and I had to eat vegetables! Suddenly I spied Ismail at the gate. I told him we were out of onions, so he'd brought some. "It's okay. Lunch has already been prepared. Thanks." He was about to leave when I added, "Once your gravy is cooked, would you mind sending some across? Just a little…" When I went back inside, I saw that the maid had begun cleaning the fish. Normally, I am not satisfied unless I do this myself. If I am too occupied, Perundevi does it, but as a rule, we never let the maid clean fish.

Ismail's fish gravy was simple yet tasty and I wondered what had gone into its preparation. The next day, Perundevi took out some fish from the freezer and made a curry – it was heavenly! Her cooking was guided purely by olfaction, for, being a Shri Vaishnavite, she was a vegetarian. Though she didn't eat meat, she prepared it fantastically. She never did allow me to bring mutton and beef home. I didn't want to anymore either because I no longer had the heart to eat it. After Madan had eaten, he announced, "I will never eat fish again for the rest of my life!" He did not care for meats and apparently, the fish hadn't been scaled properly. The woman in Nochikuppam hadn't been thorough and neither had our maidservant. I never visited Nochikuppam again.

13 – Brownie

Not long after I had made Whitey's acquaintance, he came home with another dog in tow, a brown one, and I promptly named it Brownie. The two had starkly different canine personalities.

Whitey understood that patience is a virtue and would wait for hours to get his biscuits. Brownie couldn't wait. He probably had bitches to chase and important conferences with other local dogs to attend.

Whitey would accept biscuits from my hand. Brownie would rather I put them on the floor.

When I touched Brownie for the first time, he seemed to tell me that I was the first man to ever do so.

"Probably the last one too, dear," I thought.

14 – The Wife-Mother

Perundevi did what no other woman in this world or any other could have done – she lived with me and endured me. Perhaps I might have been a desirable man, a good husband, if I wasn't a writer.

It was ten in the night when my friends knocked at the door. They were all in high spirits and wanted to drink with me in my house. I agreed. Perundevi made chapattis and chicken curry for us. Our drunken revelry ended at four in the morning with glasses, bottles and bodies scattered on the floor.

This was not a one-time occurrence.

There was a poet-friend of mine who spent a whole day in my house – drinking. He spent the next day sleeping on the verandah. He woke up to retch, and who would clean the reeking puddle of puke but Perundevi? He woke up every thirty minutes with a request for a cup of buttermilk. Perundevi uncomplainingly obliged him. She stayed home that day to nurse him.

There were two things I did that many wouldn't dare to do.

Seventeen years ago, I married Perundevi without having got my divorce papers. My illegitimate marriage could have cost me my government job, but I did not mind losing it. Besides, there was a fat chance of ending up in a dingy prison cell if someone decided to slap bigamy charges on me. I had braced myself for that turn of events as well.

Even when I was fastening the *mangal sutra* around Perundevi's neck, I felt apprehensive, anticipating the cinematic arrival of the cops who would haul me off in handcuffs as my bride stood and watched helplessly.

We were married in Mylapore's Kapaleeswarar Temple. The priests would not agree to marry us without the production of proper documents. It was Krishna who saved the situation by exerting his influence. Many of my friends did not attend the wedding as they thought I was pulling an April Fools' prank on them. Besides Krishna, there was only one other happy guest at the wedding, our son Madan.

We arrived at the temple at 6:30 in the morning for the marriage that was to be solemnized at 8. The place was empty, save for the officiating priest. Perundevi swept the *mandapam* clean. Later, when she appeared as a bride, the priest was taken aback. Not a soul from Perundevi's family had come for the wedding.

My parents were delayed and they happened to be in possession of the *mangal sutra*. Just as Krishna was about to send someone to buy one from one of the jewelry boutiques near the temple, my parents arrived.

I married Perundevi within fifteen days of meeting her. She was a unique breed of woman. She bought, preserved and cooked meat for me despite being a *brahmin*. She dried fish herself as she knew that fish loaded with salt from the fish stalls would send my blood pressure skyrocketing. She took to cooking snail curry for me when she was told it was helped to cure piles. Any other woman who was a vegetarian would have drawn the line at chicken, but Perundevi was not just any other woman.

15 – The Bait

The murrel is available in Nochikuppam only on Sundays and only one person sells it. By the time I reach the place at 10 a.m., all the big fish would have been sold, so I would call the fellow beforehand and tell him to keep one for me. During my trips to the market, I got acquainted with a person called Murugesan. He would buy the kind of fish I liked and also cut it into neat slices. One day as he was cutting the fish, I heard the knife strike metal. The tip of the knife had become blunt and a close scrutiny revealed that a bait was lodged in the fish head. I love fish head curry and if I had eaten the head without chewing it I would have swallowed the bait. Nervously, I wondered what might have happened to me if that had occurred. As it was a Sunday, the market was very crowded and four or five of us were standing before Murugesan. He sent some of them to other vendors but even with so many people crowding around him he was able to discover the bait only because he was good at his job. If he had been careless, the bait wouldn't have been visible, so pleased with his efficiency, I gave him an extra hundred rupees.

On reaching home, I excitedly told Perundevi what had transpired but she became annoyed. 'It's because of people like you that workers are getting spoilt. He was only doing his job so why give him the extra money?'

'Isn't my life more precious than the hundred rupees?' I asked. 'What are you trying to say?' I relapsed into silence.

16 – Whitey Again

Did you wonder about what happened to Whitey after I left for the Himalayas? I had given a lot of thought to it, in fact. People who are into spirituality are a bit dense so I decided to target Raja's Achilles heel. One day I told him that I was going to the Himalayas to retreat and at once he fell at my feet. I pulled him up and said piously that Baba had appeared to me in a dream and asked me to give him a message. Eyes brimming over with tears, he asked me what it was. 'Baba said, 'Your neighbour Raja will take care of Whitey',' I said.

Astonished, he asked me why Baba had not appeared in his dream. 'For that, you need to evolve further. If you want further proof, Baba also said, 'Ask him to read page number 333 of my sacred autobiography.' It's the same page that describes the incident about Baba's visit to a devotee's house in the form of a beggar and a street dog. Need I say more? By this time, I expect Whitey must have shed his proletarian identity and become a bourgeois.

17 – *Les deux belles noires*

I am seated on the lawn of the India International Center in Delhi. A Chinese poet is reading a poem. Suddenly a cat, which resembled a Pomeranian more closely than it did its own kind, materializes from somewhere and snuggles into my lap like we go back a decade. It promptly falls asleep. This little tableau plays out for four days.

There were debating sessions in the conference room from morning to noon. Later, at six o'clock, there were reading sessions on the lawn. I usually sat myself down there at five-thirty. The first time the cat approached me, I was both surprised and amused. Over the next few days, it seemed to have a preference for me over everyone assembled in the lawn.

As for me, I've never seen such a beautiful cat before. I would run my fingers through its soft, velvety fur and when I stopped, it would look at me questioningly.

Soon, it was the last day of the conference. The springtime evening was pleasant and mild. That evening, Asma, a poet from Algeria, was observing me and the cat from a short distance. On the first day, she'd tried to lure the cat out of my lap, but the creature clung to me like a babe to its mother. She'd tried to pick it up, but the cat showed her that it was clearly not wanting to be picked up. Disappointed, she seated herself at a distance and contented herself with watching us.

On the fifth day, she walked up to me and, eyeing my pastel green t-shirt, remarked, "The colors complement each other rather well, no?" She was referring to the contrast between the cat's glossy black fur and my shirt. In a mellow voice, she said something in Arabic to the cat that looked up at her, ears twitching. With an air of condescension, the cat left my lap for hers. Not long after, it tired of her and sauntered back to me.

That evening, Asma and I drank ourselves silly. When it was time to part, she embraced and kissed me.

"Je ne t'oublie pas, le chat noir aussi,… vous deux," she whispered tenderly into my ear.

18 – Men and Women

"One of my friends was staying in a ladies' hostel in Chennai. One day, a man entered the bathroom, but managed to escape before he was caught. A little while after the incident, my friend was sitting around with a couple of roommates, eating apples, when the intruder barged in, bolted the door and grabbed the apple-knife. He threatened the other two girls at knifepoint and asked my friend to strip naked. She didn't. Enraged, he held her in a chokehold, the knife pressed to her throat. My friend didn't try to save herself. For her, death was more welcome than humiliation. He asked the other two if there were people outside. They lied that the coast was clear. He walked outside, leaving the knife behind. Big mistake. The girls who were standing outside caught hold of him and beat him up. When they took him to the hostel warden, she let him go scot free. When the shocked girls demanded to know why, she replied, 'I've taken his picture. What good is it going to the police?' She then showed them the picture she'd clicked on her phone.

"But the real horror was not the intrusion. It was the discovery of a tiny installed camera in the bathroom. It soon came to light that in every bathroom was found a camera. Goodness only knew for how long they'd been there. What were the odds their pictures were not being flashed on some porn site that very hour? Robbed of their peace and their dignity, they cannot sleep, they cannot think straight. This is the life of Indian women," said Puja.

I said, "Men suffer too, Puja. I'll tell you a story Kannan told me. As you know, he works in the software industry. One fine day, when he turned up for work, he found a woman sitting in his chair. Before he could get one word out of his mouth, she authoritatively told him to find himself another seat. When Kannan yelled at this bossy bitch whose ass-cheeks were barely covered, she had the nerve to complain to the boss that he was harassing her. The story was soon picked up by his colleagues who actually suspected him of doing so, but his boss – who was thankfully not a fool – debunked the complaint and saved his ass. But he lost face in the office and there was nothing he could do to clear his reputation."

CHAPTER TWO

1 – Caverta from the Side-Street Sexologist

One of the "regulars" I meet in the park during my morning walks is Ranganathan, a friend of Santhanam's. He prefers listening to our conversations to taking part in them. Frequent work travel means he is able to make it to the park in the mornings only once or twice a week. A great Perumal devotee, he is quite handsome – tall with an enviable physique, glowing complexion and a charming smile. His lack of a moustache seems only to enhance his looks. We would sometimes see him walking with a woman in tow, and on such occasions, he studiously ignored us.

"Do you know why this chap frequents Madhava Perumal and Kesava Perumal temples?" Santhanam once asked me. "He does so to befriend ladies who come there."

I remembered these words of Santhanam whenever I saw Ranganathan in the park thereafter.

When Santhanam failed to turn up one day, Ranga and I were walking in an eight-formation between two trees as it is said that it was better than walking in a straight line.

Ranga, a man of few words, surprisingly began the conversation.

"Were you out of town?"

"No."

"Oh, I thought you were."

"Wait, sorry, I was. I went to Goa."

"Did you get *it* in Goa?"

"No, the BJP has Goa in a chokehold. Not much they can do in that position. Liquor is freely available though."

"Who'd go all the way to Goa for liquor when Pondicherry's just three hours away?"

"True that."

After few minutes of silence, he asked, "Do you drink daily?"

"I can't afford such luxuries daily, so I drink weekly."

"Scotch?"

"I prefer Rémy Martin."

"Ah, Rémy Martin! My favorite. Do spare me a bottle if you happen to find two."

"Of course."

"Does a full bottle cost three thousand rupees?"

"No, six thousand now."

"The last time I bought a bottle, it was three. If it's double, I don't want it. How many pegs do you usually have? Two?"

"Six."

"Oh, you can down *six* pegs?'

"I can, once a week."

"I'd like to join you sometime."

"Be my guest, Ranga."

After an hour, we parted ways. I cursed myself, "You hopeless fucker! You son of a bitch!"

I was cornered by Ranga again on another day when Santhanam was a no-show. As usual, it was he who began the talking.

"I need to tell you something, but you need to promise to keep it to yourself and not tell Santhanam."

"Alright."

"Last month, my boss and I went on a 'business trip' to Bangkok. He arranged a real dish for the pair of us. Twelve thousand a night. He asked me to go first, but the moment she touched me, everything was over, the way a gun goes off when you touch it. And like that wasn't mortifying enough, she went out and told my boss about what happened and he ticked me off for wasting his money. I was so ashamed that I could have put a bullet through my brain. Do you know of a remedy? I've sired two kids, but sex… the mere thought of it sets my mind and body on fire. I have a feeling you can help me out here, but again, don't tell Santhanam."

"I know of an effective pill."

"Is it Viagra? They say Viagra's risky."

"Viagra *is* risky and not easy to come by, but there is Caverta. Twenty-five milligrams will solve your penile problems."

"And it's not risky?"

"If it was, you think a drug store would shelve it?"

"Have *you* tried it?"

"No, I eat *haritaki* daily. I don't need Caverta."

"I tried *haritaki* too. It was useless."

"You must have taken it for a week and stopped. You're supposed to take it daily for three months, except on the days you drink. It's not like Viagra – pop it into your mouth and your dick springs to life like a jack-in-the-box."

"Is Caverta widely available? Will it be given to me if I ask for it?"

"Yes and yes."

Cursing him for reducing me to a sleazy side-street sexologist, I exited the park.

I didn't see Ranga for a few days. When he did turn up in the park, he buttonholed me the moment Santhanam was out of earshot.

"I tried in a lot of places, but I couldn't find it anywhere. I got strange looks from some of the pharmacists that made me feel embarrassed. Would you mind getting it for me?"

I agreed.

That evening, I went to the drugstore near my place and asked for Caverta.

"How many milligrams?" the pharmacist asked me.

I immediately grew suspicious. If such a small drugstore had it, then how could the other bigger ones not? It seemed impossible. I went around enquiring in several drugstores and it was available in every single one of them. I realized that I'd been foxed. Ranga was a daisy who couldn't go to a chemist's and ask for Caverta like a man, so he conned me into doing it for him.

For the thousandth time, I promised to never associate with such "common men."

When Ranga asked me whether I'd bought the drug the next day, I gave him a piece of my mind.

"You made a bloody ass of me! I deserve to be flogged for listening to you, let alone trying to help you."

From then on, I stopped helloing Ranga.

I had a similar experience with yet another "common man."

Santhanam is a voracious reader, but not anywhere in the neighborhood of Professor Subramanian of IIT. An admirer of Abraham Lincoln, Subramanian once lent Santhanam a book on the American president when the latter visited his house with a friend who never sniffed a single book. This pathetic friend was called Padmanabhan. Now Padmanabhan worked for a firm and his demanding job never allowed him such indulgences, but he also wanted a book from the professor and was therefore given one. The professor was restless when he lent his books and kept dropping broad hints about people who failed to return books they'd borrowed from him.

One day, Santhanam and Padmanabhan were walking in the park, each carrying a book the size of a pillow to return it to the professor.

Amused, I suggested they deposit the books on the park bench and retrieve them once they'd finished their walk, but they refused, saying that the professor would have their heads on a platter.

Curious to see Padmanabhan's book, I took it from him. It was Gurcharan Das' retelling of the Mahabharata.

My interest did not go unnoticed, and Padmanabhan said, "I've not opened the book yet. I'll lend it to you once I buy my own copy."

"Asshole, you are beyond redemption!" I said to myself.

Nowadays I don't hit the beach for my daily walks because the heat of the sun might burn me like a fifteenth-century heretic. I go to the park instead, which is shady as a forest till nine.

But, there are also some inconveniences to be endured during a walk in the park, such as dealing with the "common man" which is simply beyond me. One of the common man's lunatic ilk once asked me, "Is Da Vinci dead, sir?"

"Yes, he died several centuries ago."

"No, I meant Krishna da Vinci, a Tamil writer."

"Oh, he died a couple of years ago."

"What happened to him? He was quite young, wasn't he?"

"I have no idea."

"I thought you'd know because you were all comrades."

It was obvious that the bloke had never used the word "comrade" in speech before. He sounded as awkward as a drunk trying to sound sober in front of a cop. Speaking of cops, I have never seen anyone talk to them with the unaffected ease of Kokkarakko. Kokkarakko treats a cop like his homie. Once, while driving he put his hand out the window and tapped his cigarette ash. A cop on a motorbike pulled him over. Kokkarakko was cucumber-cool when he answered the cop who was soon on his way, shouting and ranting like he'd just emerged from a drunken brawl.

I was quite alarmed by the whole incident, but Kokkarakko merely shrugged his shoulders and said nonchalantly, "I think a cigarette must've blistered his fat ass once which is why he has a problem with cigarettes."

Unlike Kokkarakko, the "common man" becomes very flustered in the presence of a writer and starts blurting out insensible guff.

One of my brothers-in-law – and it is my opinion that there can be no one as dumb as or dumber than a brother-in-law – started speaking to me in high Tamil one day.

"May I enquire after your health and your welfare and your missus?'

It is well known that a Tamil writer lives like a stray dog or a social outcast. While even mediocre Indian writers who write in English land lucrative book contracts and become rich overnight with money to wipe their backsides and blow their noses in, the Tamil writer languishes in the wilderness, unknown and unread.

I was looking for a French translator for one of my novels and found one in Paris. His translated titles were published by Gallimard, but his fee was rather steep. Twenty-five rupees a word. In that case, a thousand-word essay would fetch him a jaw-dropping twenty-five thousand rupees! But in Tamil a word is worth only half a rupee and some magazines just send you a free copy. With all this in mind, should you snicker or laugh out loud at a Tamil writer?

I asked my brother-in-law, "What's wrong? Why are you talking like someone who got half his brain eaten by a crow?"

"I spoke to you that way because you are a writer – a Tamil writer!"

"You imbecile! I am not a Tamil writer. Here, take a look at this *ArtReview Asia* article I've written in English. So there! I'm an English writer and you shall talk to me in English."

Now do you see how the "common man" loses his marbles in the presence of a writer?

I would usually leave for the park by six in the morning, but one day, after I was delayed, I spent some time meditating and having a chat with Santhanam. It was nine when I decided to return home.

Suddenly, a "common man" speared before me and said, "I hardly see you here these days."

"I come every day."

"But I never see you."

"What time do you come?"

"Around this time."

"I come at six. I was delayed today."

"I see. What are you writing about now?"

"Nothing."

"Oh," he looked at me like I'd just told him I have terminal cancer of the balls. "Why?"

"I don't know."

"Must be writer's block."

He began guffawing at his own statement like it was the joke of the century.

I felt like asking him: "On the days you don't fuck your wife, do you consider yourself to be suffering from fucker's block?" But not everyone has the liberty of speaking his mind. Such privileges belong exclusively to the "common man."

Another "common man" I know is the brother of a female friend. Brothers of female friends are fools too, like brothers-in-law.

One day, he asked me, "How do you write?"

At that moment, I deeply regretted being a writer. *You jelly-brained dunce! In all my life I've never been asked such a ludicrous question,* I thought.

"I type on a computer," said I, following the biblical prescription of giving a stupid answer to a stupid question.

"That's not what I meant," he said, twiddling his fingers and moving his mouth like a fish. "I want to know *how* you write."

Formerly, I was able to answer questions of this base variety with a straight face, but my temperament has changed now as my face has.

Cocking an eyebrow, I asked him, "Do you read books?"

"I used to back in college, but I don't have the time now."

"What kind of books did you use to read?"

"*Cine Blitz, Time Pass...*"

"Who's your favorite writer?"

"No one in particular. I'm content to just flip through the pages."

Such encounters have forced me to withdraw from my fellow human beings and this I do not regret for a split-second. There is more pleasure to be found in engaging with trees, squirrels, crows, monkeys, cats and dogs. I do not expect anyone who has not experienced this pleasure to sympathize with me.

One of Perundevi's friends paid us a visit with her husband. I knew the friend, but I'd never met the husband before. He never helloed me or shook my hand. When the two women whisked upstairs to sit and gaze at the aquarium, the friend's husband spoke his first words to me.

"How much rent do you pay for this house?"

Unprepared for such a question, I sheepishly said I had no idea. I honestly didn't know what the rent was, so I had to explain stuff to him: "Five years ago, when we moved into this house, the rent was twenty grand. It's been hiked a couple of times over the past two years. I don't know what it is now. You should probably ask Perundevi."

There was something else that rankled me. How on earth did he figure out that the house was rented?

This incident left a marked impression on me. How can a person who is unacquainted with another person be so audacious as to ask the person what the person pays for his house?

Hang on. The interrogation, I mean the "conversation," didn't end there.

"What was your advance payment?"

What the fuck, man? What're you gonna ask me next? How many times a week I have sex with my wife?

"Again, I don't know. Perundevi's the one you should ask."

The inquisitive man mercifully fell silent when he realized he wouldn't get a straight or proper answer out of me.

But the worst was yet to come.

When I grumbled to Perundevi about our visitor's insolent curiosity, she, in his defense, accused me of thinking "perversely."

"He's a very nice man. Not everyone can be as intellectual as you are, Udhaya."

I once found myself in a bizarre situation involving a saree-seller who set himself up as the "Judge" to the "Accused" – me.

I'm talking about the time we were in Chinmaya Nagar. The man had been selling *sarees* to Perundevi's family for years as his father and his father's father had before him. His coming was a ritual in itself. He would spread a mat on the floor, sit like the Buddha on one end of it, and with a magician's flourish, pull out more sarees than I imagined his bundle had. I'm not sure if we were paying for the quality of the saree or for what rolled of his silver tongue. Women from all the houses in the vicinity would flock to our place at his arrival, but I don't think it was to stare open-mouthed at him.

His coming to our house was a monthly affair. I asked Perundevi, "Why do you keep buying so many sarees?"

"Look, Udhaya," she said, "I'm not a social butterfly. I don't like to go out and I don't nag you to take me to the beach, to the movies or to fancy restaurants. I don't even like to go to the temple because the crowds make me uncomfortable. A saree or two a month is my only indulgence."

"Alright, but tell that fellow to change his timings. He always barges in when I'm lunching."

And like his unwelcome intrusion during my lunch hour wasn't bad enough, he wouldn't let me enjoy my food in peace either. He kept talking to me and I was expected to answer him the whole time he was there. That got under my skin.

One day, there was fish curry for lunch. The following conversation ensued:

"You're eating fish, *saar*?"

"Yes."

"But today is Saturday, *saar*."

"Yes."

"You shouldn't eat fish on Saturdays, *saar*."

"I see."

"Moreover, today is *Karthikai*. You must not eat meat on this auspicious day, *saar*."

"I see."

"Hereafter, take care to avoid meat on Saturdays and *Karthikai* days, *saar*."

"Oh, please! Don't come here talking to me like I've seduced another man's wife. Keep your nose where it belongs."

That very day, the saree-seller went to Perundevi's parental home and complained that I had harshly scolded him.

If this is the common man's understanding of me, then what about my readers and those who are familiar with my body of work?

The first thing I do on returning from my morning walk at nine is remove the shark from the freezer as Baba and Blackie have to be fed at ten and a half-minute delay would not sit well with them. At the gate sits Whitey, my next customer, patiently waiting. I give him four biscuits after which I walk Baba and then Blackie. Blackie is a dog who looks like a horse and he absolutely terrifies the weak of heart who lay eyes on him. The dog senses their fear and, like a four-legged demon, creates mayhem. Then, he stands back and watches the panorama unfold before striding back into the house. (And just so you know, he gets more looks from college girls than skinny dudes on muscled bikes.)

Once the walk is over, I cook the fish and put it under the fan to cool. I add some Pedigree to it and feed the dogs – first Blackie and then Baba. The feeding takes half an hour. Blackie is fed first because he's a fussy eater. If he refuses to eat, I offer his food to Baba. Baba and I are alike in that we can never refuse food. He and I can eat like we've been starving since the day of our births.

My stomach groans in hunger when the task of feeding my four-legged children is complete.

I like to think of my kitchen as a factory in which I am a manual laborer. For breakfast, I finely chop or slice, capsicums, carrots, zucchini, olives, onions and tomatoes. I halve the salad and season my half with a squeeze of lemon, pepper it and have it either for breakfast or for dinner. But I can't live on salads my whole life, can I? For the sake of variety, I have couscous or pasta for lunch. On Saturdays, I have *idlis* with my friends at the Sai Mess. Post breakfast, I dice five carrots, three beetroots and an apple for my ABC juice. I toss in some pomegranates and gooseberries. The fruits go into the juicer one by one. The preparation takes three-quarters of an hour. Perundevi and I drink it in installments, emptying our glasses at four in the evening.

It was *after* all this that the actual "labor" began.

I would skin and chop ginger, garlic and onions, and assemble the rest of the ingredients required for the gravy. The greens came next, and there was a new variety on the menu every day. They had to be washed till the water ran clear, and then chopped. If the greens in question were drumstick leaves, even with Perundevi's assistance, the work would stretch itself out till one in the afternoon.

Our menu would feature *paruppu usili* at least twice a week. Show me a man who has peeled the banana flower in its entirety and I will prostrate before him. It takes at least forty-five minutes to peel a single banana flower. One has to remove the matchstick-like stem and the gauzy petal that resembles a dragonfly's wing. I do all this without complaint. If you are not a connoisseur of food like I am, you can save yourself all this trouble and survive on *rasam* and rice. I cannot subsist on said dish, being an aficionado of world cuisine – European, Asian, Islamic, Brahmin.

I'm dogged once the cooking is done. And if it's Sunday, it's mandatory-trip-to-the-fish-market-day. Fish is available in abundance on Sundays – especially shark and murrel. The less fastidious clean these fish in ten minutes. I clean then for an hour.

But wait, there's a problem.

I've heard several Brahmins living in apartments complaining that they couldn't bear the odour that emanates from their neighbour's place when they cook meat. But those comments irked me and I always retorted back. But it was a wake-up call for me when I couldn't tolerate the gut-wrenching smell of meat that was cooked by one of my neighbours of the Mandaveli flat where I was residing five years back and that was when I realised the problem of the Brahmin households. Nevertheless I can vouch that the meat was prepared by Perundevi or me, invariably sends out an aroma and not a stink.

A decade ago, I was overcome with a desire to eat duck. Although I was told that it would stink, I was bent on trying it. I asked Krishna for a recipe. Though he is a Brahmin, he knows his meats. He gave me the contact number of a female friend who was a cordon bleu in a five-star restaurant. When she shared her recipe with me, she too mentioned that duck meat has a strong smell. I shared this bit of information with Perundevi, whose duck yielded a delicate aroma instead of a stench. She told me it was the turmeric that did the trick.

It is not only "common men" who torment me. If I were to make a list of all my tormentors, my own friends' names would figure at the top. I had a student-friend called Arasu, twenty-one. He called me *appa* as I was something of a father-figure to him. I happened to be cooking when he called. I texted him, saying that I would call back when my hands were free. I never did get around to calling him back. From that day on, he messaged me compulsively, asking why I didn't return his call.

"I take calls only till nine a.m.," I explained. "I'll call you tomorrow."

But the next day, I was laden with work and hence couldn't call him.

He began sending me e-mail after e-mail.

Bizarrely, by that time, *I* was starting to obsess over *him*.

Arasu Arasu

His name kept popping up in my mind the whole time. I couldn't read or write. I realized that madness is not limited to the "common man" and the reader. Even the writer is susceptible to it.

A group of writers was having a discussion, and I felt like an alien among them. They were all talking with deep sentimentality and with sighs of nostalgia about their respective hometowns, going on and on like a song in a Bharathi Raja movie, not inclined to stop. The places they were waxing on about so eloquently were – in simple, unexaggerated, "common man" terms – total shitholes. If, by some stroke of misfortune, you find yourself waiting at a bus stop in any one of the towns these mouthy men were so reverentially praising, the stench of urine would make you wish you'd been born without a nose.

A writer described Mayiladuthurai as a glorious place, and another spoke glowingly of Tirunelveli, romanticizing the stink of piss and the sight of shit, the potholed, rubbish-flanked roads and the open gutters. All this seemed wonderful to the writers just because they had been born in those places.

Dear God!

Anjali was standing at the window. She was on the phone, talking to her husband, Suresh. No, wait, scratch that. She wasn't exactly *talking* to him. All she did was respond with a "hmm" from time to time or she would respond with one of the following:

"Yes, go on. I'm listening…"

"No, no. It's nothing like that…"

"You were saying?"

"When are you returning?"

"Sorry, come again?"

I was standing behind her as she was talking to him in this fashion. I brushed her hair back with my fingers and nibbled her earlobe. Foreplay with this woman when she was talking to her husband aroused me, so you can imagine what making love with her did to me. I lifted her up and lay her on the bed. I stripped her and kissed her naked body.

Her "hmm" sounded different now, alive. She bit her

lips, closed her eyes and arched her back, stifling her moans of pleasure so as to not arouse her husband's suspicion.

I could hear him clearly.

I licked her opening and she became wet. That was when I heard Suresh ask, "Didn't you say that the walls have become damp and are leaking? Did you complain to the municipality?"

"Hmm…"

As I slid my "pipe" into her crevice, Suresh asked, "Did the plumber come?"

It amused me to hear his questions, the poor man. It was almost like he half-knew that someone was fucking his wife in their marital bed.

I began to move inside her. She tried as hard as she could to control the moaning, not wanting to make any noises that would give her away, but when she climaxed, she gasped.

"You sound strange," Suresh said.

"Oh, it's nothing," she lied, "just a stomachache."

The phone conversation finished when I did.

Frenziedly, she jumped on me, growling, "You *rascal*!"

And the feral cat began to wildly bite my neck.

2 – Some Spiritual Business

Nathan told me, "The guru's *satsang* is going to be held in Chennai. You must make it a point to attend. It's a rare opportunity."

The "guru" my old friend Nathan was talking about was a fellow called Kushaldas. I disliked the man not only because of his half-baked discourses but also because of his habit of making renunciates out of young women. How could a girl in her twenties renounce her sexual nature? Even if she found it possible, was it healthy? I had my doubts.

It so happened that a twenty-five-year-old woman – a friend of a friend – got obsessed with Kushaldas and entered his ashram to become a monk. There, they chopped off her long hair and made her wear saffron robes. But what irked me most of all was the manner in which Kushaldas paraded about in clothes that made him look more like a pop musician than like a spiritual teacher. I wondered why such an extravagant person who owned more clothes than the entire population of Mylapore forced young girls to wear plain saffron robes.

The twenty-five-year-old girl I told you about was the only child of her parents. Before she entered the ashram, she was working in a software company and earning a fantastic salary. Her parents lamented that they were like orphans after their child left, but Kushaldas' company – yes, company – will insist that they do not let people join without first obtaining permission from their families. This girl threatened to commit suicide and her parents were forced to give their consent.

Whenever I looked at Nathan, my curiosity about Kushaldas was stirred. Everyone considered Nathan to be a lost soul. Before he met Kushaldas he was forever in the drunk tank, but ever since he met him, he didn't drink even a single drop. Now, he is well settled with a good job, a good wife and a child. He often goes to the mountains, practices meditation, and leads a peaceful life in general.

"According to our *guru*, you must be a little mad to fully experience life," Nathan told me. "Kazantzakis' Zorba told Basil the same thing. He told him he had everything but he lacked one thing. When Basil asked him what that one thing was, Zorba told him that he lacked madness. Guru says, 'Don't think about life, just live it,' just as Zorba tells Basil that he should try living life instead of writing about it."

Nathan admitted that Kushaldas and Kazantzakis had like minds, but in his opinion, Kushaldas was better than Kazantzakis.

"Guru is an expert," Nathan continued. "He knows what he's doing. He teaches meditation, but he first teaches us why and how it is used as a tool to discover the truths of the universe. You casually told me once, Udhaya, that when you close your outer eyes, your inner eye opens. If you wish to have a truly spiritual experience, you need to meet my guru."

It is my opinion that all these "gurus," are just Osho's dummies – and Kushal is by far the worst of the lot. I couldn't bear to think of how he was poisoning the minds of youngsters.

Kushaldas spoke like a religious fundamentalist.

"You people are in love with America," he once said during a speech. "Do you know that 45% of the American population is on drugs for mental illness?"

In all my life, I've never heard such bullshit.

India in its present state can be compared to Europe in the Dark Ages. The kind of economic disparity and injustice seen in India cannot be seen anywhere else. Politicians siphon millions and claim that they are below the poverty line while in Chhattisgarh, people are dying like flies. Smut masquerades as film. At voting booths, actors and actresses throw tantrums because they have to stand in queue. The kith and kin of politicians enter the film industry and get paid astronomical sums. The poor and the non-influential have to lick the feet and kiss the asses of the rich and the influential if they want their children to be admitted in schools that discriminate on the basis of looks, caste and wealth. Not a day goes by that a rape does not happen in every Indian state. And we poke fun at America!

What the so-called expertise Kushaldas claims to have is something I've had ever since I was twenty. There is a yoga exercise called *nauli* which I mastered at the age of twenty. It is one of the reasons why I'm able to live like a happy-go-lucky youth at the age of sixty. There is yet another exercise called *uttiyana* that will help make *nauli* easier.

Here's what you have to do: keep your legs wide apart and bend forward keeping your hands pressed to your thighs. Exhale slowly and pull your stomach inside and tighten your gastric muscles which have relaxed.

When you tighten the stomach muscles, the two lateral portions of the stomach will become concave and the middle portion will stand firm like a log. Stand in this position for a few seconds, then relax the muscles and inhale. You can do this twice or thrice. Press your hands firmly on both thighs and move your bowels to the left and right.

Uttiyana and *nauli* help regulate bowel movements and the flow of semen. It deworms the stomach, increases your appetite and reduces acid formation. It also relieves one of ulcers and stomachaches.

If I decide to become a *yogi* this very moment – an English-speaking *yogi*, not a Tamil-speaking one – I will become as famous as Osho in three years. Growing a beard like his might be a problem, but oh well, I don't think J. Krishnamurthy had a beard either.

I haven't read Osho's books or heard his speeches, but those who follow him are often surprised by the parallels between my writings and Osho's teachings. I don't read Osho because I don't want people saying I'm influenced by him and that I'm his shadow. Osho and I are shadows of the Buddha who was himself a shadow of those who came before him.

Kokkarakko likes Osho. Once, when I was browsing through his collection of books, I came across a book by Osho called *Books I Have Loved*. In that book, Osho had listed all of his personal favorites, and one of them happened to be *Zorba the Greek*.

In Tamil Nadu, only characters like Kushaldas can become spiritual leaders. Now you might come and ask me why I didn't go ahead and become one myself. I'll tell you why. The answer is simple: I am not interested in spirituality. Also, I don t like human beings. How can a hater of human beings conduct discourses surrounded by millions of people?

If I decide to live like Osho, my name will become a brand after I die, won't it? How can I allow myself to become a brand and a company when all of my writings are against business and authority? Besides, spirituality has become a third-rate business – another reason why I want to have nothing to do with it.

When I saw Kushaldas' disciples, I felt that even politicians' aides were better off. Kushal's followers are more like slaves. What kind of spirituality is it that creates slaves out of human beings? I think it's better to be a crazed fan of an actor than to be a slave of Kushaldas.

Kushaldas has a slave-making strategy which actors don't have. And he tells people to "be happy." How the hell can a slave be happy? Kushaldas can be happy because he is a dictator who enjoys his position.

In India, a woman cannot venture out after dark because there is a 99 per cent chance of her getting raped – gang-raped. Here, the people are content to live like gutter rats while their rulers live like kings. Can you call such a pigsty a spiritual land? Travel in one of those trains that transport people to the suburbs of Mumbai and you will see what this country actually is. At least a body could be found on the Mumbai railway tracks every day. Women cannot travel alone in trains as they get raped and thrown onto the tracks. Our corporate gurus compare such a country to America and declaim against the latter, calling it corrupt, evil and rotten. A huge number of people in India are living like animals, but are told by the corporate gurus that they have better lives and lifestyles than Americans.

I paid five thousand rupees to take part in a program conducted by Kushaldas on the premises of a Chennai college. As I was a writer, I was given a front row seat that cost eight thousand. On the first day, the crowd assembled at six-thirty in the evening to listen to Kushaldas who would be speaking in an hour. He prattled on till nine-thirty and all I learned from him was nothing. He kept harping on middle school ethics class clichés like "Be good human beings," "Plant trees" and "Be happy."

Sixteen thousand people attended the program. The price of registration ranged from 1.5K to 8K. If we assume that the average cost of registration is 3K, then Kushaldas and Co. would have made fifty million. Fifty million in three days! Now you see what a huge business spirituality is. Is there any other business in India that rakes in such huge profits?

But this is not what I meant to tell you. His sermon, which began at 7:30 the next morning, was also an inane affair. There was no yoga – only shallow talk – and when we were given a twenty-minute restroom break after two hours, I thought of slipping away. Screw the five thousand rupees. I couldn't endure another minute of Kushaldas' torture. When I tried to escape, the guru's people who were standing guard at the gates refused to let me leave the place. What right did they have to confine me against my will? I tried reasoning – even pleading – with them to let me go but to no avail.

"If you leave, others will follow suit," one of the fellows said.

"So let them!" I said. "Why do you want to stop people who want to leave from leaving?"

Very gently and politely, they refused to let me go.

I lost my patience. In all my life, no one had ever dared to confine me or restrict my movements. I pushed them aside and moved towards the gate but they pulled me back. After a good struggle, I managed to get out of there. After all that pushing and pulling, my shirt was drenched with sweat. Wrestling with those six fellows built like bouncers made my chest hurt as I'd undergone bypass surgery a few years ago. My pulse rate skyrocketed and it took an hour to return to normal.

How can such cruelty be allowed by those who preach love and spirituality? What happened to me also happened to another woman I knew. Kushaldas failed to impress her too, so she tried to leave at eight in the evening but was forbidden. She told those bouncer dudes she wasn't feeling well but they didn't care a hang. She told me that she'd argued with them for an hour and a half.

On the first day of the program, you should have seen the pushing, shoving and jostling to get out of the place through one small gate. There were sixteen thousand people, it was nine-thirty at night, and the place was poorly lit. A woman caught in that madding crowd started screaming in agony. If one person had to stumble, there would have been a disaster. I'll never understand how the government allowed such a huge crowd to congregate in such a small place.

Above all, isn't it illegal to hold a person against his will and forbid him from leaving a place? My departure wouldn't have affected whatever Kushaldas had going on in any manner. For holding me back against my will, Kushaldas' bouncers should have been booked under Section 342 of the Indian Penal Code and made to spend a year in prison. They also caused me physical hurt when they were wrestling with me. What if I succumbed to the pain in my chest?

The manner in which the bouncers were marshaling

that horde of sixteen thousand was just obscene. What Chennai witnessed upon the release of *Enthiran* was nothing compared to the wild manner in which Kushaldas' program was being advertised in the streets. Posters of him defaced all the walls, and his adorers conducted campaigns wherever they could find a crowd. They would start somersaulting like circus performers while young and attractive ladies handed out leaflets. They succeeded in convincing the public that not attending the program would be a tremendous loss. They must have spent at least twenty million on newspaper and magazine advertisements alone. But they weren't losing anything. They would have mopped up fifty million at the end of the program thanks to all the gullible attendees.

CHAPTER THREE

The Story of Pakkirisamy

My name is Pakkirisamy. Some months ago my name was splashed across the front page of all the national dailies and I was even something of a celebrity on local and national television. It was an act of mine that led to this fame – or notoriety – call it what you will. No, I didn't win an Olympic medal, nor did I bomb the Parliament House. I just took my own life. Many people commit suicide but their names don't make it to the front page. So why me? Well, I was a minister's close aide, and that minister was mired in one of the biggest ever corruption scandals that shook the country.

But I didn't commit suicide to save the minister's life. I did it to save the lives of two people I loved – my wife and my five-year-old daughter. If I hadn't killed myself, they would have both been murdered. The newspapers described my death as a homicide, but that's not what it was. It was definitely a suicide, but come to think of it, instigating someone to commit suicide is akin to murder. Much worse than murder, in fact.

At one time I used to be a real estate agent whose job was to find tenants for vacant houses. Twenty or thirty years ago, a one-ground plot cost thirty thousand Indian rupees. Today it costs ten million. As house rents rose to stratospheric heights, the commission I made on my deals rose in proportion and the money I made was more than enough for my needs. The house owner and the tenant each had to pay me a month's rent. If the house rent was pegged at fifteen grand, I would earn a commission of thirty grand, and if I sold a house or a plot, the owner would pay me two per cent, and the buyer one per cent. Thus, if I sold a client's house for ten million, I would get three hundred thousand rupees. But if the owner was a gullible sort, I would adopt other tactics. I would negotiate a rate of thirty million for a house that was actually worth sixty. With an advance payment of five million, I would transfer the power of attorney to my name, and after six months, I would sell the house for sixty million, then hand over twenty-five million to the owner.

Life was coasting along smoothly till the day I was asked to suggest a "good bit of property" for a minister who hailed from my area. The mere mention of a minister's name made the owner agree to sell without a murmur. Two grounds constituted the land which belonged to an old Brahmin. The minister was delighted when I managed to negotiate a price of ten million for a property worth one hundred million. Truth be told, any one of his underlings could have rendered him the same service, but a man who extracts honey from a hive will no doubt lick his fingers.

He would have made a commission on the bargain and his boss would have ignored it. But my style was different. I didn't like to make my commission in an underhand manner because my eyes were fixed on the bigger prize. And in the course of time, things worked out the way I wanted them to.

A house built during the British era and located in the heart of Chennai came to my notice. It was a house where three generations had lived at one point, but now, the sole occupant was an elderly lady. A background check revealed that she was the third wife (read "mistress") of her husband. The other two wives had died, and between the three of them, they had produced more than twenty offspring. Though only the old woman remained in the house, all the children had rights over the property. What worked in my favor was that there was no proper will or legal claimant to the property which consisted of six grounds. It was a property under litigation and worth two hundred million at least.

I went to the old woman and told her: "I will give you five million. Put it in a fixed deposit and you will get thirty thousand rupees every month. I will also give you an apartment to live in. Take the apartment and move out of here; it will be more convenient for you. When you die, I will ensure that you have a proper burial. The minister himself will come to honor you. I shall name this street after you and the sons of your husband's other wives who humiliated you will die of jealousy. But if it's someone else, you won't get even the five million I'm willing to offer you." I kept pressuring her until she agreed. I also assured her that if any of her children or other heirs created problems, I would deal with them. It was the minster's writ that ruled in those parts, so nobody would dare open their mouths. Those who had tried in the past had vanished without a trace or had committed suicide. Even a sum of five million was a considerable amount for the old lady. Thus, the property was quietly transferred to the proxy of the minister.

After I pulled off this deal I became a trusted confidant. If the goddess Durga has ten arms, a minister has a thousand. But I became his man Friday only because I had acquired a reputation as a person who got things done efficiently. Since everyone knew I was close to the minister, my work became even easier. There are quite a few *poramboke* lands lying idle in the suburbs of Chennai. There was nothing wrong if the minister decided to put them to use. It was not as if he was amassing all these properties for his own benefit; those who enter politics in this country *need* vast amounts of money. During election season, buying a single vote may take anything from two hundred to two thousand rupees. So, calculate the amount of money it takes to win an election. Grabbing such lands is not easy either. First you have to find out where these lands are located; I got the information at the *tahsildar's* office. As soon as I identified a *poramboke* land, the first thing I did was build a fence around it. Soon, a party flag went up on the spot, followed by a small temple. The title deed was readied as soon as the folks in the *tahsildar's* office were slipped some money, but as I mentioned earlier, it is not as easy as it seems. I began with grounds and slowly graduated to acres with the blessings of the minister.

Over the next five years, my life and lifestyle changed dramatically. Before I met the minister, I had been living and conducting my business in the suburbs of Chennai. Now I was the proud owner of a real estate firm in the heart of the city – the size and swank of which rivaled that of a multinational company. The millions that flowed into the minister's coffers were invested in the company and thus I became a corporate owner. I liked my new life; I mean, who wouldn't? I got everything I wanted at the click of a finger. Money can buy anything for it is Aladdin's magic lamp. And when money is aligned with political power, you can rule the world. The minister's leader was the ruler and we were the lesser lords. Fancy a good time with an actress? Man, just call her directly. If she makes a fuss, there are the police, humble servants who are meant to do your bidding. If the cop in question refuses to play ball, shift him to a place where there isn't enough water to wipe his ass. There is a saying that says you should stay away from evil people if you see them, but we don't do that; instead, we ensure that the evil person is removed to a remote place. Since the actresses have already been "adjusting" to the demands of other actors, producers and directors, why should she refuse to accommodate a politician? Some actresses will come around only if you threaten to book them on charges of prostitution. Some might get married to avoid such problems. One actress tied the knot at the height of her career just to escape my advances. I don't pursue married actresses unless they are willing; every profession has its ethics. That applies even to ganja-smuggling – you shouldn't sell tobacco as ganja; if you do, you don't deserve to live.

Now for the "interesting incident" that happened in my life. It came to my notice that a two-hundred-acre golf course located on prime property in the city had no legal heirs. The company that was managing the property had taken it on lease a century ago. The lease term had expired fifteen years ago and the only remaining member of the family that had leased out the property was old and decrepit. The property was worth ten billion now.

I informed the minister who told his leader, and pressure was exerted on the company. We told them, "We don't want the property. Just give us the ten billion." Finally, a deal was struck at six billion, of which my cut was two hundred million. Though I gave it to the minister, he told me to keep it. I refused. I was the *benami* for the millions of rupees that belonged to him, so what difference did it make whether the money was on my name or his?

This story has an important point and one's life may hinge on it someday. An incident that occurred during the early phase of our friendship bears testimony to this. Once, I saw the minister's henchmen beating up one of their gang members. That night, as we were all drinking together, I asked the minister, "Why did you beat him up? If you had a problem with him, you could have just kicked him out."

The minister told me that he had given the fellow

one million and had asked him to keep the money with him until he asked for it. Ten days later, he demanded the money and the chap returned it. It was for this that he was beaten.

You don't understand? Well, at first, I didn't either. The fact is, the minister had actually given him one million and one hundred thousand, but the fellow assumed there had been an oversight and pocketed the excess.

Suddenly, I felt a chill run down my spine for I too had been given one million on one occasion. When I mentioned this, the minister laughed and said that it had been a test. "But that is not all. When I realized that money would not do the trick, I gave you another test."

One day, an actress had come to see the minister at his guesthouse. I was there along with two other men. But the minister didn't turn up even after many hours. Night had fallen and still there was no sign of him and his phone was also switched off. It was two a.m. and we felt that it was unlikely that he would turn up so late. The two fellows with me winked and nudged me on: "*Anney*, go try your luck," they said, but I refused. I do like women but I had a reason not to take them up on their offer.

The girl in question was a Hindi actress, not very well-known in the industry. She had acted in a few small "art films." When she realized that she would not be able to compete with the big names in the Bollywood film industry, she dared to do something risqué. She attended a couple of film festivals in a mini-skirt without wearing panties. When she uncrossed her legs on stage, everyone caught a glimpse of her "toad" and she became famous overnight. Some other actresses, jealous of her newly-acquired fame, tried to follow her example. Whether she wore panties or not was her business, but what riled me was that when began to star in Tamil films, she got all holier-than-thou, talking about yoga, meditation, martial arts and *bharatanatayam*. Suddenly, she was an expert in all these disciplines and claimed to know twelve languages. I ask you: why would someone, ostensibly so accomplished, need to pull such a cheap stunt to get her big break in the movies?

If I have to thank someone for narrowly escaping the thrashing hands of the minister's men, it is the writer Udhaya. I am so obsessed with things like land and house and *patta* that even in my dreams I see only *patta* and the *tahsildar's* office. I wouldn't have known about this Hindi actress' pussy-flashing stunt had Udhaya not shown me the footage of the same on his laptop. This stunt was why I was not willing to bed her. Look, if you want to be a whore, be straightforward about it. Why pretend you are a paragon of virtue?

If it had been any other actress, I would have been hung up to dry by the minister's men. But paradoxically, it is Udhaya who is also responsible for my suicide. If I had been beaten up by the minister's men that day, I might have parted ways with him for good and I wouldn't have had to commit suicide. What the Hindu religion says is true – that people who die a natural death go straight to the soul world and become one with the eternal soul there, but those who die an unnatural death – suicide, murder, accident – are condemned to wander as ghosts.

I don't know about other religions; but Hinduism talks about reincarnation. According to it, the circumstances of our present life are determined by the good karma accumulated in our previous life. If one becomes a beggar or suffers from leprosy or AIDS, or like me, commits suicide at the age of thirty-five, it is because of our actions in our past life.

I have argued about this at length with Udhaya. Once, we were discussing about our leader, a man who has done so many evil things in this life that committing atrocities was child's play for him. But he led a very comfortable life and never once suffered any deprivation. Udhaya said, "Whenever I think of your leader, I lose the last dregs of faith in God." On hearing this, Socrates, the leader's grandson, pointed to the sky and said, "Good karma from his previous birth." I believe him, but there's a catch. On 9/11, the Twin Towers were attacked and three thousand people died on the same day at the same time. Did they all die because of bad karma from a previous life? Thousands of Tamils were killed in the Sri Lankan civil war. Did they too have bad karma – the whole lot of them? It is rather confusing. Perhaps I will find the answers when I finally leave this world and ascend to the soul world.

Udhaya once told me a story that he had read somewhere. A woman gave birth to four children but all of them died. When she lost her fourth child, she chopped his index finger in half and placed it in the child's grave, vowing to never have another child. But a fifth child was born to her and it survived. However, it had only half an index finger.

I brokered an important business deal and the minister gave a license to someone close to us. And by "close," I mean a person who would give us a bigger commission. It was a huge risk, but the minister was clever. He took care of all those who needed to be taken care of and settled the matter with the utmost secrecy. The money was split between four or five people, the minister got ten billion and my company became the *benami* for the stash. The person who got the license was from the company that supplied vodka to us. The vodka was called diva and it cost one million dollars which was to the tune of fifty million rupees. The bottle was encrusted with Swarovski crystals and diamonds. It was Udhaya who gave me all this information.

"What a waste of money! It will only end up being flushed down the toilet," commented the minister. "*Anney,* do we commit suicide today just because we are destined to die anyway?" I pointed out.

This was the one thing I disliked about him. Despite his multi-millionaire status, he continued to live like a pauper. Some called it simplicity, but I called it niggardliness. I must be careful in case someone's listening. Hey, why should I be afraid now! The minister can't do anything to me because I have already committed suicide. He always wore rubber slippers and a cheap cotton shirt and the stuff he drank was worse than piss. But all said and done, he never interfered with my ways although he put in his two cents from time to time. I drank Chivas Regal and not the ordinary stuff, mind you, but Chivas Regal that had aged a hundred years and cost one hundred thousand a bottle.

"You are going overboard," the minister would caution me, "If you respect money it will stay with you."

I would reply, "With so many millions at your disposal, should you spout such a middle-class philosophy? Ambani built a house worth fifty billion, did his wealth desert him? It is not enough to just be a rich man; you must learn to enjoy your wealth." Most of the rich men I know are people who don't know how to enjoy the money they make. Take our leader, for instance. He will not chase a crow with the hand he has been eating with. Fine, but does he spend at least a pittance on himself? Not at all. He once wanted a cable connection for his TV. When I went to his house, I realized that the TV was of such ancient vintage that the new cable connection would be of no use. I threw the old one out and replaced it with a new model. The very next day, the leader's man came and told me that he wanted a TV just like the old one as he didn't know how to operate the new model.

I went to his house and told him that it was actually quite easy and wrote down the instructions on a piece of paper. But it did no good. Finally, I had to get him the old model he'd asked for.

If I'd told the leader about the expensive Diva vodka that the minister and I had drunk, I am sure he would have had a heart attack.

Of all the people I met on earth, the only one who knew how to live life like it was perpetual celebration was Udhaya. I met him through Socrates. I didn't understand most of the stuff he talked about. He was a pure and unadulterated hedonist but he was not a rich man. He was an ordinary middle-class chap, but if you want to learn about luxury and flamboyance, he is the person to go to. It was he who introduced me to different kinds of liquor. He was a very unpredictable fellow, but that's part of his charm. Once, during summer, he asked me to get a sack of *nungu*. We got hold of four fellows who knew how to collect *nungu* from palm trees and that day we had vodka mixed with the *nungu* juice.

"How is it?" he asked me.

"Terrific," I replied.

"But it lacks one thing."

When I heard what it was, I was shocked and wondered if all writers were such perverts. He said that the vodka-*nungu* juice mix could do with a dash of a woman's... *ugh!* How could one talk of such private matters so unabashedly in public?

A few days before I killed myself, Udhaya introduced me to a single malt called Macallan; it was even richer than Chivas Regal. I asked him why these liquors cost so much. He explained to me that they were made by fermenting grapes in oak barrels for hundreds of years. In our country, the stuff is fermented in iron vessels that don't rust. That explains the staggering price difference between local stuff and imported stuff.

Let me come back to the reasons for my suicide. To the great misfortune of the people concerned, the media got wind of the fact that the person who had got the license at a throwaway price from the government was actually a *benami* for Dawood Ibrahim.

The minister went to prison and I found myself facing the unenviable situation of having to turn approver in the case. Refusing to cooperate with the investigating officers leads to the mental asylum.

But the price of turning approver was a heavy one – my wife and child would lose their lives. The minister and the people behind him were known to carry out their threats. Two other people had already committed suicide with their families in Anna Nagar and K. K. Nagar – suicide or murder, it was hard to say. When the police are controlled by the powers-that-be, who will expose the truth? Both the men were close to the minister, but neither could ask him anything. He loses it completely when someone broaches a subject that is not to his liking. Why should people who commit suicide poison their own children too? Where are those poor innocents at fault? When I ran into the person from Anna Nagar in the spirit world, I asked him about this. But his advice was: "If you go around bearing the burden of your old life's memories, it will hinder the passage to the soul world, so forget about all your earthly ties, trials and tribulations." You can never understand the pain of one condemned to wander around as a ghost. The life of a ghost is worse than that of a stray. The most intense grief flows from memory. Memory is the mother lode of most of our misery.

When you part from a woman you love, you feel sorrow, so it follows that memory and sorrow are one and the same. Don't needle me with counter questions like: is hunger also a memory? Hunger makes you forget everything, I know. It's also a kind of pain, a bodily reaction similar to the pain you feel when someone beats you. One kind of pain is associated with the body while the other is associated with the mind. Since ghosts don't have bodies, memories of our past lives continue to torment us ceaselessly. Here's a story that Udhaya once told me:

Mulla Nasruddin was tossing around in bed one day, unable to sleep. His wife asked him what was troubling him. He said, "I promised our neighbor Abdullah I would return the money that I had borrowed from him tomorrow, but I don't have the money, so I am unable to sleep." "Is that all?" said his wife. "Don't worry. I'll take care of this." She stepped out of the house and called out loudly to the neighbor: "Abdullah, Abdullah!" Abdullah came out of his house, rubbing his eyes sleepily. The mullah's wife told him: "Nasruddin cannot give you the money he owes you tomorrow." Then she went back into her house and told Mulla Nasruddin: "Now Abdullah won't be able to sleep, but you will."

After entering the world, I realized that it is our emotional attachment to things that causes us pain. I realized this when I encountered Silk Smitha's ghost. She was a film star and a sex bomb and at one time, all of South India was at her feet, drooling. But in our country – sorry, I forgot, ghosts have no country, nor do they have a religion, caste, race or anything else that defines human beings. People have many reasons for suffering and die in many ways. But in India, most of the female ghosts are the spirits of women who have been raped. The tales that Noida ghosts tell are especially gruesome – rape, murder, dismemberment, bodies dumped in ditches and drains…

There are also many other spirits commonly found in India – ghosts of businessmen and actresses who committed suicide, ghosts who were once members of our political party but were silenced by those in the top echelons, husbands whose throats were slit by deceitful wives and their illicit lovers while on honeymoon…

Sometimes the ghosts of wives are seen too – for instance, the ghost of the wife who made fun of her husband's dick, saying it was too small. It's really pathetic to hear her sob. "I was just teasing," she says.

There are also spirits of children who die of various causes. They are in a separate league.

My own memories are not so terrible. I didn't have any problems, save the fact that I had to desert my darling wife and beloved daughter on earth to suffer alone. While I was alive I lived like a king. It is difficult to listen to the stories of other trapped spirits. I had no idea people could suffer in so many different ways. When I was alive, I spent all my time thinking of land and property, and when I had some time on my hands, I spent it on booze and babes. Even if I had noticed people's sorrows, I would have ascribed it to their past life karma or something, but now when I hear their stories I feel grief seeping into me.

There is another special category of haunting spirits in India – the spirits of those who die in communal riots. The millions who died in the carnage that followed the partition of the subcontinent in 1947; Sikhs who were killed in the riot that followed Indira Gandhi's death (Udhaya told me many times that he was an eye-witness to that carnage); some three thousand people who had died in the Gujarat riots. The spirits of newborn infants are also part of this list. Some were killed before they were born into this world – cut out of their mother's wombs and set ablaze. I heard that all those babies went back to India soon after landing in the spirit world.

African spirits are numerous. They mostly belong to people who died before their time from hunger and poverty. Though such deaths were neither suicide nor murder, their spirits too couldn't ascend to the soul world because their deaths were not classified as natural deaths.

There are hundred thousand Tamil spirits – the spirits of those killed in the ethnic conflict in Sri Lanka. All of them died untimely deaths and if you listen to their stories, I guarantee you that blood will gush forth from your ears.

Just as there are good people and bad people, there are good spirits and bad spirits among us. I don't have to tell you that the good ones are very rare. I wanted to talk to the Mahatma's spirit, but I heard that it left for the soul world soon after reaching this place. The ghosts of Indira Gandhi and her two sons, Sanjay and Rajiv, are still knocking about here but I am not too keen on meeting them. They are the spirits of people whose party wrecked ours, after all.

Apart from real estate, the only thing, or person rather, who affected me was Udhaya. At times I find myself wondering whether I am the spirit of Pakkirisamy or of Udhaya. Once I reach the soul world, my problem will be resolved. There, one will not be hounded by memories of past lives. The reason why Udhaya had such an effect on me is because we were polar opposites in the lives we led. He was always criticizing our party in his newspaper columns though he liked to hang out with us. Sometimes I would ask him, "Why don't you mingle with people from the other party? That way, neither you nor we will have problems." His reply was, "I could do that, but then they don't know me the way you know me and I know you."

Though he did not really belong in our crowd, there was something attractive about Udhaya. Life was much more fun when he was around. I lack Udhaya's talent for writing for I studied only up to grade ten and my reading was limited to the film advertisements of local newspapers. Even as a child, school was a bitter experience for me. If I tried to read a book my head would spin and I would see bright lights dancing before my eyes. It was only when I met Udhaya that I realized that I hadn't lost anything by not getting an education. Thank God I didn't study further. If I had, I too would have become a beggar like him. He runs a magazine with money borrowed from friends. I doubt anyone is able to understand one word of what is written in it. He was running from pillar to post trying to get advertisements for his magazine. Socrates would tease him about it: "If God appeared before Udhaya and gave him one boon, he would ask for advertisements for his magazine."

Many a time, I heard Udhaya complaining that he was able to get only one advertisement. So one day I asked Socrates whether I should place an advertisement on behalf of our company in Udhaya's magazine. "Sure, but let's wait till he drops by next time. Then we can discuss it with him," he said. And finally that day arrived.

"I was thinking of telling Pakkiri to place an ad in your magazine, Udhaya. But you upset the apple cart when I least expected it," complained Socrates. That week, Udhaya had gone to town criticizing our party in a local magazine.

Udhaya's retort was immediate: "You have been promising this for the past three years, Socrates. You should understand that friendship is one thing and a writer's freedom is another." It was during this time that the minister got entangled in the license issue. He was targeted by everyone in the media and since I was his close aide, the spotlight fell on me too. Socrates called up the company that was releasing advertisements to Udhaya's magazine and made them stop. I didn't like the move Socrates made. The license problem was also spiraling towards a crisis. The minister was cooling his heels in prison while I was spending my time shuttling between the investigating agency and my home. Udhaya stopped meeting me completely during this time. He also started criticizing us in the vilest terms. What the heck! I knew the writer kinds rather well. They didn't have the power or potency to pluck a single strand of my hair, by way of doing any harm.

But what did Socrates gain by blocking the few ads he used to get? Like a dog that had been beaten, Udhaya began to bark even more loudly at us. Should a man who is dealing in millions wage war with a fellow who can barely scrape together ten thousand rupees? Socrates didn't understand this because he was also an educated fellow. All these fellows have useless brains, it seems. It was true that I didn't like what Socrates did to Udhaya but I couldn't say anything about it. When you are dealing with the rich and powerful, you have to keep your profile low and your mouth shut. Otherwise, you will be branded an enemy or a traitor. Once that happens, death will be an act of mercy. After all, who wants to become a beggar on the streets? And that is only the least of things they can do to you.

When Udhaya called me, I tore into him without preamble: "Udhaya, why are you maligning my name? You can write what you want about the license affair. But why do have to attack me personally?"

"But I never make personal attacks, Pakkiri."

"Of course you have, though I haven't read any of it. Socrates told me about it. When have I ever read the trash you write anyway? It was Socrates who read it out to me: 'Pakkirisamy is like his leader; he is used to taking, not giving.' Why did you write such things? I have to face flak from so many quarters for being your friend. Once I sponsored the tea party for everyone at your literary meet because you persuaded me to. It cost five thousand rupees. Now how to I assuage the feelings of the person who sponsored it?"

"Would you stop my bread and butter just because I criticized you? Why did you block the ads for my magazine?"

"I swear upon my child, I would never do anything as contemptible as that!"

"I don't believe you. You are the one behind it. If you do things like this, I will be forced to commit suicide."

Then he hung up. After this conversation, I made some enquiries and realized that it had all been Socrates' doing.

See the insidious connection between me and Udhaya?

He threatened to commit suicide but I was the one who actually went ahead and did it.

CHAPTER FOUR

1 – Death by Fire

Traveling in a car in India is dangerous and unadvisable for a multitude of reasons. One is that a goat, a cow, or a human might suddenly materialize out of nowhere and fancy crossing the road. I remember the night I was returning to Chennai from Tirupati; our car almost swerved off the road due to the ghostly apparition of a huge white pig that was saucily shaking its rump. Next, drunk drivers, like the gods, are ubiquitous. Take a look at the outside of a TASMAC shop around nine in the evening; it's either a motorbike exhibition or a free roadside parking lot. Despite a law banning drunk driving, there are pie-eyed blokes at the wheel. (I mean, there are laws against bribing, rape and murder too, but those don't stop folks from bribing, raping and murdering – just saying…) Hang around at a traffic signal in India for a bit; it will soon become clear to you that four-fifths of the population suffer from serious mental issues. Even when the traffic light is red, there will be a moron – or ten – furiously honking without letup; and half the drivers, in addition to having no mother wit, have no driving license. When Kokkarakko and I were on our way to Bangalore from Chennai, we were on a one-way route when a car, coming from the wrong direction, collided with a truck in front of us. The driver of the car probably fancied taking a U-turn like a boss.

People in Europe have more road sense than their counterparts in India, but there, drivers tend to fall asleep at the wheel as they drive on highways that seem to go on forever. This I witnessed thrice: when I traveled from Paris to Oradour-sur-Glane, again from Paris to Berlin, and on another occasion from Toulouse to Barcelona.

Kumarasamy and Murugan, who accompanied me to Oradour-sur-Glane, were both Sri Lankan Tamils. Train travel would have been my preferred mode of getting there if not for the overpriced ticket fare and the want of a train that went all the way up to Oradour-sur-Glane. I was wary of making the trip by car as Kumarasamy had only recently learned to drive. He got accustomed to driving on the Parisian roads but the road to Oradour-sur-Glane was a highway – no place for turtle races – which meant he had to ride at a perilous speed of 150 kmph. I was relieved when Murugan offered to take the wheel. Bewilderment was writ large on their faces when I first said "Oradour." They confessed it sounded like the name of a Tamil village. Technology then was not as sophisticated and omnipresent as it is today for us to have looked it up.

Kumarasamy dialed his friend Catherine with whom I'd once had an argument at the Amethyst Café when she'd been visiting India. She was my friend Vincent's French girlfriend. It turned out that the conceited Frenchwoman knew sweet Fanny Adams about French writers. Such is the case with Italian tourists in India as well – ask one about Italo Calvino and he'll look at you like you asked him if he knows who the Ashwinikumaras and the Apsaras are. When a trio of my friends went to Goa, they made the acquaintance of a Russian in the bar of the luxury hotel they were staying in. Each man introduced himself – one of my friends was a professor in a medical college, the other was a six-figure earning sales representative of a multinational company, the third worked in the export business. As for the Russian, he was a welder! In Thailand, I asked a Russian streetwalker whether she'd heard of Tarkovsky; she royally snubbed me like I'd asked her to fuck a wild banana and let me film it.

While I was engrossedly discussing Serge Doubrovsky with Vincent, Catherine cut in with some poppycock. When I told her she was misinformed, she got furious. *You dare challenge a French national about something concerning a French writer?* This was what the look on her face said to me. Oh, simmer down, you *belle dame sans merci*! Being French isn't the same thing as being a connoisseur of French literature which I have been for thirty years and counting. Besides, she was trying – and making a court jester of herself in her attempt – to speak the Brahmin variety of Tamil. Why do all whites come to India and act all high and mighty? Anyway, it was this Catherine that Kumarasamy called for information on Oradour. Turns out her knowledge of Oradour was commensurate with her knowledge of French literature. She told Kumarasamy in a snot-nosed way: "If they've come from *Eendia*, tell *zem* to see *ze Tour Eiffel* and be done *wiz eet.*"

It was December and the sky was overcast. When we left Paris behind it began to drizzle. At some point on the highway, we had to pull over to pay a toll. Neither Kumarasamy nor Murugan had two cents to offer and as for me, I'd spent a fortune on gas and vehicle insurance. I was left with just two hundred and fifty francs of which I parted with fifty only to be told that the toll was a hundred.

After being cash-stripped, we traveled fifty kilometers when a strong wind began to blow. It soon became clear to us that we were heading into a storm. I was sitting in the backseat, fumbling with my seatbelt when I heard Murugan murmur, "I think Udhaya's scared shitless." If he'd stopped at that, it would've been fine, but he tossed in the fact that he too was scared stiff. "Every time a truck passes, I feel like I'm a hair's breadth away from death." Now the fear set in. What he said held true for me as well. Those trucks were like sixteen-wheeled monsters next to our ladybug-like car. Their tires mercilessly whipped rainwater onto the windshield and the condensation, aggravated by the keening wind, only worsened the visibility. It was a nerve-wracking experience, but Murugan just wouldn't stop talking.

"It's been two years since I've driven a car."

"Why didn't you drive for two years?"

"An accident. I stopped driving after that."

Kumarasamy immediately started enumerating every

accident he could remember – like accidents were the most comforting things to hear about in our chancy situation. One of his friends had driven down to Pondicherry. When they were on the road, the friend who was driving announced that he hadn't been behind the wheel in a year because of an accident. En route, they met with an accident. The first friend to regain consciousness found the driver slumped over the wheel, quite dead. The rest who managed to not die were seriously injured. Kumarasamy had barely concluded his grim tale when Murugan began to describe, in minute detail and with photographic precision, a freak accident he had witnessed.

Their stories were messing with my head, so I yelled, "Please just stop! Both of you! If you don't, I'll die of a heart attack before the pair of you explode in this car."

Murugan didn't seem to care for my heart or any other part of me, so he dropped another bombshell. "Udhaya, my eyelids are heavy with sleep. At least in Paris there were traffic signs to keep me alert, but on the highway it gets monotonous and I feel drowsy. The only way I can stay awake is if I talk." My chicken-heart was in my mouth by the time he'd said his say. Then he said, "Udhaya, I have often laughed myself silly reading your articles. Why don't you crack some dirty jokes? I'll be less likely to fall asleep then."

I was left without a choice; it was a matter of life and death. So I told them a joke I'd heard many years ago in my village, sitting with my companions under a tree.

A foolish monkey was making whoopee with its female

partner without a break for three hours. The female finally got cheesed off and complained to God on high. God on high ordered a bitch to gather intelligence on the situation, but the bitch had her own complaint: "Lord, he doesn't care how many people are watching. He just jumps on me shamelessly." After hearing similar tales of woe from many other animals, God on high was moved to anger and declared: "All male animals shall remove their organs and hand them over to me and I will give them all tokens in exchange. Each animal can then come to me but thrice a month, hand in their token and collect their organ." The female monkey was delighted. She cocked a snook at her partner and taunted him, saying, "Serves you right!" But the male monkey was not even slightly badgered. When the day came for the animals to hand in their tokens, the male monkey was beside himself with excitement. This puzzled the female monkey until she was told: "I stole the elephant's token and replaced it with mine!"

Oradour-sur-Glane, Saturday, June 10, 1944: A day frozen in time. This little village still bears silent testimony to the extremity of violence of which man the beast is capable. Nazi soldiers segregate the men, ostensibly to check their identities, and line them up at the granary. The women and children are made to endure a torturous wait in a nearby church. The men are shot below the waist and burned alive. Once the men are burned beyond recognition, they lob grenades at the church, killing the women and children. Anyone trying to escape is promptly felled by a machine gun. A woman sees her daughter go down with a bullet. Her name is Rouffanche, Marguerite Rouffanche. The church is ablaze and the air is filled with smoke and is being rent with the piteous screams of the women and children inside it. Madame Rouffanche notices a ladder near the altar behind which there are three windows. She rests the tip of the ladder against the largest window – the one in the center – and starts climbing up. She jumps down nine feet. Another woman with an infant tries to do the same, but both are gunned down by the Nazis whom the child's cries alerted. Rouffanche is injured in the shooting too but somehow manages to crawl into the bushes where she hides until the arrival of the French troops the next morning. The Nazis continue to search for survivors. They stumble upon a child and an old man and burn them alive. Finally, they loot the village and scorch it.

The French have preserved the village just as the Nazis left it. I spotted a mute witness to all the carnage – the burnt shell of the mayor's car. Oradour looked like a ghost town, like a tsunami-ravaged place. There were aged rails on which trams must have plied once; a burnt sewing machine – so many objects, each with its own story. The killers were like us – human beings with hearts, with families. Historical records estimate the death toll of that black day to have been six hundred and forty-two. Nobody has been able to explain why these people had to die in so brutal a manner, why they had to die at all. And it wasn't even an act of revenge; it was just an act of bestiality perpetrated in the name of nationalistic pride.

The same western European countries that were decimating each other's populations during World War

II have now formed the European Union with a single currency for and visa-less travel to all the countries that are part of it. But in India, if you're traveling from one state to another, like in a private hospital, you have to undergo a thousand checks. Before 1947, the land which now goes by the name of Pakistan used to be called India. But today, India and Pakistan are sworn enemies. And it's not just Pakistan. India and China are antagonistic to each other as well. It is not much different with Bangladesh. As for Sri Lanka, the diplomatic relationship is dictated by political necessity to prevent any cozying up to China.

December 25, 1968: I was in grade ten when I heard some elders discuss an incident in a village called Keezhavenmani in Thanjavur where forty-four people had been burnt alive. This village being a rather small one, I'd never heard of it before. My school textbooks had acquainted me with the Jallianwala Bagh Massacre, but this was something different altogether. A landowner had burnt his workers to death for daring to ask for an additional measure of grain as a wage-raise. The men had fled to the forest while the women and children hid themselves in a small hut which was torched by the *zamindar*'s men. Those who ran out when the hut began to burn were speared and pushed back inside to die. We got to hear the news broadcast on the radio that was in the library near the police station. I ran there to listen to the news. Forty-four people had been killed – twenty women and twenty-three children. The elders said that the youngest child was one year old.

A few months later, my uncle apprised me of the circumstances that had led to this incident. Those were days when the landowner's word was law. My friend Siva's father owned a huge tract of farmland and Siva took me there one day. I usually preferred to read a book than to wander around the village purposelessly. But Siva promised to show me more interesting things than books. As it was sowing season, we could ogle at the women who were engaged in scattering seeds. But when I reached the field, I was sorely disappointed for the women were all like dried up prunes who reminded me of my mother. They were not a tad like the women in the movies. They were not even as average-looking as the girls at school. It would have been some consolation had they been like Siva's mother or my aunts. Unwilling to squander more time than I already had, I began pestering Siva to let me return home. Then Siva did something I am yet to forget. He turned to an old woman – she had seen at least three generations from the looks of it – and said, "*Ennadi pakkirey?* What are you gawking at? Get back to work!" I was so embarrassed that it felt like my shorts had slipped down to my ankles. A middle-aged woman who was beside the abused grandmother gently chided Siva. "*Enna thambi?* Must you speak so rudely to an old woman? How could someone your age use the likes of *vaadi, podi* and *ennadi* to her? *Thappu saamy.*" Composing himself, Siva said, "Oh well, whatever! Just do your job." And Siva was fifteen at the time.

Now this was what my uncle told me about the Keezhavenmani massacre: On the evening of the incident, two Dalit farmers from the village, Muthusamy and Ganapathy, were tied up and beaten black and blue by a landlord called Sauriraj Naidu. On hearing this, a group of farmers came to their assistance; they untied the two men and led them away. Following this, another powerful landlord called Gopalakrishna Naidu went to Keezhavenmani with a gun in hand and some henchmen. As soon as the bullets started flying, the men ran for their lives and took cover in the forest. The women and the children... well, you know what happened to them.

The news reached the Keevalur police station at eight p.m. but the police appeared at the scene of the crime only at midnight. A case was filed against Gopalakrishna Naidu, but he went scot-free because of a lack of witnesses.

I don't know if anyone still remembers the village of Keezhavenmani, for when it comes to forgetting history, no one can beat the Tamils.

I was able to obtain a list of the people who were burnt to death that day after a lot of persistence.

1. Sundaram, 45
2. Saroja, 12
3. Madambal, 25
4. Thanakayyan, 5
5. Paappa, 35
6. Chandra, 12
7. Aasai Thambi, 10
8. Chinnapillai, 28

9. Vasuki, 3
10. Karunanidhi, 12
11. Poomayil, 16
12. Karuppayi, 35
13. Vasuki, 5
14. Kunjambal, 35
15. Ranchiyammal, 16
16. Damodaran, 1
17. Jayam, 10
18. Kanakammal, 25
19. Rajendran, 7
20. Suppan, 70
21. Kuppammal, 35
22. Pakkiyam, 35
23. Jothi, 10
24. Rathinam, 35
25. Gurusamy, 15
26. Nadarasan, 5
27. Veerammal, 25
28. Pattu, 46
29. Shanmukam, 13
30. Murugan, 40
31. Aachiyammal, 30
32. Nadarajan, 10
33. Jeyam, 6

34. Selvi, 3

35. Karuppayi, 50

36. Sethu, 26

37. Nadarasan, 6

38. Anjalai, 45

39. Aandal, 20

40. Seenivasan, 40

41. Kaviri, 50

42. Vedavalli, 10

43. Gunasekaran, 1

44. Rani, 4

2 – Sorry Mr. Engels!

After my Oradour trip, the next was from Paris to Berlin in the last week of December, 2001. I wanted to spend the New Year with a friend of mine who lived in the German capital. Three students – James, Alex and Kanthan – whom I had befriended at a literary meet in Paris volunteered to take me there on one condition – that I would spend Christmas with them at Wuppertal. Christmas was the very next day. I promised to be there and we set off. All three were emigrants from Sri Lanka. They lived in Germany with their parents and spoke fluent Tamil.

James and Alex took turns at the wheel on our way to Wuppertal. When it was Alex's turn James would say, "Drive carefully now."

"Don't you worry. I left my derring-do behind in Paris," Alex would retort.

Alex had driven a Mercedes at 200 kmph to attend the literary meet in Paris and was slapped with a goodly fine of five thousand francs.

It snowed all the way to Wuppertal, making driving a difficult task. Several cars that skidded off the snow-covered roads had been abandoned on the highway. Fortunately, there were no major accidents. James said that driving on a snow-blanketed road was like driving on glass. When the snowfall intensified, he took over from Alex. In India, the roads see to it that you feel the speed of the car, be it a Tata Sumo or a Jaguar XF, and that you're always bouncing or banging your head. With James at the wheel we might as well have been on a cruise liner as the car seemed to be gliding across the highway. When I asked him at what speed the car was going, he said, "One-fifty." I was blown. "You don't believe me? Open the window and look out." When I did, I was able to feel the car's actual speed.

It was my dear friend Vincent who had taken care of my every need since my arrival in Paris. For fifteen days, he did all he could do to make my sojourn enjoyable and comfortable, but in so doing he had exhausted all his leave and had to return to work. He washed dishes at a restaurant.

When Vincent went back to work, he entrusted me to Kumarasamy. As luck would have it, Kumarasamy lost his job the day I met him. If you are scratching your head over what luck has to do with it, hear this: In France, if a worker loses his job, his employer has to pay him severance pay until he finds another job. Congratulatory messages for Kumarasamy were pouring in and the phone calls never stopped coming.

But Kumarasamy had filed a lawsuit against his

employer so there was a delay in receiving his wages. He didn't have two coins to rub together and neither did I. In our penniless state, how were we to travel or buy food? While we were at home, Kumarasamy would pull out some fish or pork from the fridge and whip up a tasty dish. But I hadn't come all the way to Paris to feast on homemade fish fry and pork pie, so I would just down a cup of tea in the morning and set out. We couldn't even take the car to the next block because it was not insured. Kumarasamy and I were making a short film on Paris. Though the film was short, the camera was gargantuan and we took turns lugging it. It was December and the biting cold was not merciful to our hungry stomachs.

When I left for Paris Krishna gave me ten thousand rupees, cash. One third out of ten had been spent to host a tea party for my friends in Chennai. The rest of the money I had converted into francs, one thousand or thereabouts. I wonder how Krishna's face will look when I tell him I spent upwards of three hundred francs just to be granted kind admittance into the restrooms. My friends began to worry that I had diabetes. "Nonsense! It's just the zero-degree weather," I told them. An average restroom cost me two francs and a posh one cost me three. I needed to take a leak every thirty minutes.

In Germany, such conveniences were simply not available. There are toilets on every Parisian street, but no matter how much or how hard I searched, I couldn't spot a single one in Germany. It embarrasses me even now to think of the ordeal I had to undergo in Wuppertal, the city where Friedrich Engels had lived. James and I had planned to pay the great dead man's house a visit. The air was frigid and there was a light flurry of snow. We took the hanging train – the city's most unique feature – and reached Engels' home. By the time we reached, I was squirming uncomfortably like a wriggly-worm.

The streets were all deserted because "'tis the season" and all. Engels' house and the nearby factory were locked. "Why are you so restless?" James asked. I told him why. "You'll have to do it right here. You don't really have much of a choice, you know?" Although I was dying to empty my bladder that was threatening to burst, I was afraid to because I was in a country where people with smiling countenances are hard to come by. In this respect, it is starkly different from Paris.

My bladder was starting to grow a mind of its own; I couldn't hold it in for another second. The doorway was the only place that afforded me some privacy so I tinkled there. This abominable deed of mine scarred my mind. Leftists go to Highgate Cemetry to visit Karl Marx's grave, take pictures and share them for all the world to see. And then there was me, a pathetic unfortunate who visited the house of Friedrich Engels to urinate in his doorway.

It is in sticky moments like these that one should expect the unexpected. James was supposed to be keeping a lookout. I told him to warn me if he saw even a dog approaching. My job still unfinished, I saw a woman behind James. I caught her looking at me just as I was zipping my fly. Phew! That was a close call and the thought of her almost catching me in the act makes me shudder even now.

I spent only two days in James' house in Wuppertal. I couldn't suffer myself to hang around there longer. His parents were completely hooked onto the only Tamil channel on cable. Assuming me to be homesick, they invited me to join them.

3 – Om Muruga! Om Muruga!!

My next trip to Paris was in 2005. It was organized by Karuppusamy, one of my readers. He told me one day, "You have written extensively on Paris and so it is my wish to visit that very place with you." I'd experienced the harshness of a European winter on my previous trip, so I felt that it would be more advisable to visit during springtime. I suggested this to Karuppusamy who gave me a deaf ear and insisted on leaving immediately. Glad for his company, I packed my bags and off we went. This was my second visit to Europe in the month of December. Back home, in Ooty, the mercury would dip almost to zero degrees, but a zero-degree European winter is vastly different from a zero-degree Indian winter. Is it because that the European continent hasn't experienced a warmer climate for many centuries? Karuppusamy was from Namakkal and he was, at one point of time, an affluent contractor who owned several trucks. One day, just like that, he lost everything. Time is a great leveler indeed – it can turn a pauper into a prince and a prince into a pauper. The once wealthy landlord now had the appearance of an impoverished farmer. There was not a trace of joy to be found in his face. He wore a pair of old rubber sandals, one of which was held together by a diaper pin, and a wrinkled cotton shirt. Even in an emergency, he never took an auto, preferring to commute by bus at all times. I warned him that he would turn into a block of ice if he went to Paris clothed so scantily. I also pointed out to him that buying shoes in Paris would be an ignorant move as he would have to pay five times the price of the Indian shoe. With the money he saved, he could start putting together a winter wardrobe. I told him he'd need a sweater, woolen socks, gloves, jackets, a muffler and a skullcap. He agreed to buy shoes and a sweater. He settled for the most ordinary pair of shoes and bought no coat, no muffler, no gloves – absolutely nothing. And he was ready for his trip to Paris.

My problem with him began on the plane. Karuppusamy has a bad habit. Even if a person is right beside him, he shouts like he is at the other end of a busy street. He was giving me an earache. A white man, who had endured this ordeal for some time, finally lost his patience and asked Karuppusamy to lower his voice. He tried to talk in a normal voice for a couple of minutes, but normal wasn't exactly his thing.

Embarrassed, I mouthed an apology to the white man. Karuppusamy belligerently said, "Tell him to bugger off! Let him not think he's a lord in our country!"

I wanted to tell him that we were far, far away from Namakkal. We were 30,000 ft up in the air, probably flying over Turkey, but I held my tongue, knowing he'd have a loud response to that as well, and it wouldn't be brief either. So I closed my eyes and feigned sleep, fearing the ear-shattering bombardments that might ensue if I opened them. The few times I sneakily opened my eyes, Karuppusamy pounced on me like a cat on a mouse and he would go on yet another boisterous rant. By this time, he had downed around five rounds of Scotch. I might have given ear to the man had he been an engaging conversationalist but all he did was complain about his wife. The more he complained about her, the more I began to feel a sense of deep respect for the woman. Kudos to her for having lived for as many years as she did with this braying ass.

When we walked out of the airport in Paris, Karuppusamy pulled an object out of my hand-luggage, held it up and said, "Look at this, Udhaya!" It was the blanket that the airline provided its passengers during the flight. Even though it was biting cold in Paris, I broke into a sweat. What if someone caught me with the blanket? I would have been extremely embarrassed, but Karuppusamy, blissfully unaware of the consequences, said that it would help keep us warm.

We took a taxi from the airport to Gare du Nord. This time I had no plans to stay in the houses of friends like Vincent or Kumarasamy as I had burdensome company. The best alternative I could think of was to rent a room in a lodge. But there was a problem – Gare du Nord was a hub for Sri Lankan Tamils and black Muslims from Maghreb. Most of the owners of cheap lodges were Algerians. They took one look at me, and before I had the chance to open my mouth, they began shouting, *"Haram, haram!"* This was because of the ring I wore on my right ear; it had led them to assume we were a gay couple. We finally found a room that was not really to my liking. We took it because the owner was an elderly Frenchwoman. But a new problem cropped up. Karuppusamy was shivering uncontrollably because of the cold and once we entered the room, he refused to step out except for lunch and dinner.

La Chappelle, the locality in which we stayed, was like a mini-Jaffna. There were Tamil-owned shops throughout the place, so finding South Indian food was not a problem, but I hadn't come all the way to Paris to remain confined to my room like a medieval prisoner in a tower and eat rice with *sambar* or curd.

Karuppusamy was a chain smoker and he smoked the cheapest cigarettes. I had a problem with this, but I didn't have enough money to take a separate room. I can overlook this too, but what Karuppusamy did on the train journey from Paris to Toulouse is something I can *never* forgive.

Toulouse had not actually been on our itinerary as my original plan was to celebrate my birthday – December 18 – and Christmas in Paris and return to India. I would have liked to extend the trip till the New Year, but we couldn't afford to overshoot our modest budget, so we booked our return for December 26.

During my stay in Paris, Vincent, who was holidaying in Cuba, sent a young Sri Lankan Tamil to meet me. His name was Edward. He looked twenty-five and was dark and wiry. He sported a Beatles-inspired hairdo and he spoke naïvely, though he was far from being naïf. I could hear inflections of Tamil in his French. He told me that he had been in Paris for three years and that he was well-acquainted with my work.

While still in school, he had joined the guerilla movement and undergone his arms training. Disillusioned by the authoritarianism, he quit the movement only to fall into the clutches of the Lankan army where he was accused of spying. They subjected him to all kinds of torture. Quite unmindful of the fact that we were in public, he lifted his shirt and showed me his back, criss-crossed with scars. I was shocked, as I had come across harrowing scenes of torture only in books and films, but this was visceral. I can see Edward's body in front of my eyes now in all its physicality. When a small nick of the razor or a cut to the finger pad from a kitchen knife can be so painful and so bothersome, can you or I imagine the agony of a person whose skin has been branded with red-hot iron?

"No Udhaya. They bound me hand and foot and took turns to slash my back with a scalpel. 'Tell us the truth! Tell us the truth!' they kept yelling. What truth could I tell when I knew nothing? I had fled from the common enemy myself! If my own people had caught me, they would have killed me as a traitor. I managed a narrow escape from the army and reached Colombo. I paid an agent there for safe passage to Thailand.

"The first thing I did when I reached Bangkok was go to a brothel. Sex had become my only way of eking out a living. Sex was the only way I could forget all the torments I had endured in my country. I met a sex worker called Chimlin during this time. She looked sixteen but was actually twenty-two. We ended up falling in love and I thought of marrying her and finally settling down in Thailand, but she was not willing to quit her work. She made it clear to me that she would continue to sell her body even after we were married and this was something I couldn't understand. She saw prestige in what she did because, after all, it was "work," and it had nothing to do with our love for each other. Even though she hated what she did, her hatred was different from mine. Sex-workers gradually develop a distaste for sex. She had to sleep with half-a-dozen customers in a single day, sometimes even more. 'Day and night, all the time, *boom... boom... boom... BOOM!* You should have seen her say it, face and actions and all. She and I communicated mostly through signs and some broken English. Chimlin knew just fifty words in English and half of them were related to sex and other smut. We tried to understand each other with our gestures and those fifty words as best as we could.

"Believe it or not, Chimlin had become a prostitute for her father's sake. In Thailand, any couple who has a daughter is doubly blessed as daughters revere and worship their parents. For Thai women, one's parents are to be honored more than one's spouse and loved more than one's children. It was in obedience to her father's wishes that Chimlin was doing "boom, boom."

"In the end I realized that we were never going to see eye to eye. I had to end our relationship as the idea of sharing my life with a woman who shared her body with other men was distasteful to me. I joined a gang of car thieves who taught me many ingenious techniques. We mostly targeted women, especially women who drove alone. A car, a motorbike and three men were part of this operation. One man tailed the woman in the car while another gang member and I followed behind. When the woman hit a deserted stretch, the fellow in the car would bump into the woman's vehicle. When she got out to confront the man, one of the bikers would get into her car and speed off. The others would speed off at once. Sounds like something out of a movie, doesn't it? This, my friend, is the greatest way to steal a car. We would then sell it to a car broker at a throwaway price. After a while, I grew tired of what I was doing, so I contacted a travel agent and went to China. I was lying on the Great Wall one day, smoking a *beedi* and thinking about the trajectory of my life. Was my birth as a Sri Lankan Tamil the cause of my misfortunes and my homeless state? Would this have been my fate had I been born Sinhala or Chinese?

"It was a full moon night, and that was probably why I lay awake till dawn like a lunatic, all variety of thoughts rolling in and out of my mind. Who was I? What connection existed between me and this Great Wall? What power was it that brought me here from a place thousands of miles away? Was it destiny? If yes, was it the same destiny that made me carry guns at an age when I should have been carrying books? I could never have imagined back then that one day I'd be lying on the Great Wall of China, smoking a *beedi*.

"From China, I traveled to Russia. It wasn't easy. First, I had to go to Kyrgyzstan and then to Kazakhstan and onward to Russia. Many people in our group had come to Kyrgyzstan directly from Delhi; only a few like me had taken the roundabout route from Thailand to China. We had no plans of staying on in Russia, but it offered the easiest way to smuggle ourselves across the European border. We traveled to Alma-Ata by plane and from there we took a bus to the Russian town of Petropavlovsk. Some folks who come thus far have a regular passport but no entry-visa for the transit countries. Such people have a harrowing ordeal in store for them.

"There were twenty of us in Petropavlovsk, all Sri Lankan refugees. Refugees are usually given a place to stay, but when we reached, there was already another considerable group from Afghanistan. So, we had to spend the first night under the stars. The place was terribly cold. The agent had warned us several times but we paid him no heed. What did we know of minus-ten degree weather? A sweater, a cap and a muffler were simply not enough to withstand the chill. Two people died that night and one man lost his arm. At sunrise, we trudged to a restaurant to find something to eat. One man opened the hot-water tap and put his hand beneath it. His hand went numb and he was told that it would have to be amputated. Later we learned that one's hand should be massaged until it reaches a certain temperature before it is thrust under hot water.

"Finally we reached Moscow where we waited for our next visa. There were five of us and we rented a flat in an apartment complex. People warned us not to carry too much money when we stepped outside because if we were robbed, even the cops wouldn't come to our help. Apparently, even the cops might rob us. There were many like us in Russia – refugees who didn't have a work permit. For this reason, the locals didn't care about us brown-skins. We also got lost once while returning home in the snow. We sighted a police car and asked the cops for directions but they wanted to check our IDs and passports. They pronounced our documents forged and demanded money. We gave them the fifty rubles we had on us but this didn't satisfy them one bit. They patted us down, feeling around our necks and checking our fingers and wrists. We realized they were looking for gold jewelry. Kanthan was wearing a gold ring with the words *Om Muruga* engraved on it. He couldn't remove it when the cops asked him to hand it over. It was stuck. One of the cops casually extracted a pen-knife from his pocket, chopped off Kanthan's finger and put it in an envelope. Then they got back into their vehicle and drove off.

"Two weeks after Kanthan lost his finger, we were out walking when a Russian hooker accosted us. I ignored her advances as I'd had a bizarre experience with a young Russian prostitute just the previous week. The girl, who looked like a goddess, had turned out to be a twelve-year-old boy. That day, my companions had gone to meet some friends who had recently arrived from their country. Finding myself alone, I took a walk and happened to find myself in a *toshka*, a red-light district. It is a stretch of road where hookers stand around soliciting customers. If you pick up a hooker in Russia, she is required to stay with her client till six the next morning. In Paris, they leave immediately after their job has been done. Even Bangkok doesn't offer the clients this facility. Anyway, this young hooker had floored me. She was beautiful, with green glow-in-the-dark eyes that invited you to get lost in them. When I asked her age, the *mamoshki* told me she was sixteen. Only after I brought her to the apartment did I realize that my ravishing "girl" was in fact a twelve-year-old *boy!* He had a long story to tell but I will save it for another day. I can tell you one thing though – he was sold by force. The brand on his thigh said more about his plight than words ever could.

"This is why I didn't want to take the other hooker home. My companions ended up bringing her home. I didn't approach her as I was not interested in having my go at her, like guys taking turns to use the toilet. After they had all used her, she slept in our flat and left the next morning. The same morning at ten, we heard a knock at the door. It was the hooker, and she'd brought company – three burly men carrying sticks. Clearly, they hadn't come to socialize with us. I realized that they were a band of thugs and I fled to the toilet. One of my companions jumped off the balcony and the other three beseeched the thugs to take whatever they wanted but to leave them alone. They took the TV, the tape recorder and practically everything else. They were pathetic; they even took our *lungis*. Vincent said they'd use them as tablecloths. The fellow who jumped had broken an arm and a leg. Thankfully he'd jumped from the first floor or he would have been cold. After taking him to the hospital, we went to the police station. One of the cops in the station was wearing a gold ring inscribed with the words *Om Muruga*."

Edward ended his story by saying, "If possible, go to Lourdes. It is an incredible place."

It was now December 22. My money was soon to be over. What I had left would buy us food for another three days perhaps. I promised myself a trip to Lourdes on my next visit. The day after my encounter with Edward, Karuppusamy and I were standing in front of a Tamil bookshop in La Chappelle when a well-built man of about fifty came up to me and introduced himself in a deep voice. His name was Gunaratnam and he had read my books. He had a receding hairline, thick eyebrows, big eyes and hirsute arms. Gunaratnam invited us to spend a few days with him in his home. He insisted that we postpone our return and promised us food and a car to take us wheresoever we wished. Besides, he had plans to visit Lourdes on Christmas Day. "I am not a believer," he said, "but I do visit the Sanctuary. I'll admit that *St Bernadette* has some power. Whenever I go there, I feel this inexplicable energy and emotion surge through my entire being. Lourdes is not that far from Toulouse. The drive is just a couple of hours. The only problem is that we're going to have to book train tickets to Toulouse which is six hours from Paris."

The next day, the three of us were on our way to Toulouse by train. Karuppusamy had managed to arrange for the tickets. He had told me once that he had bank deposits to the tune of one hundred thousand. But he was very particular about not spending a paisa more than what had been earmarked for the trip. However, tempted by the prospect of lingering another week in France, he finally withdrew some money but it was not much so all three of us had to starve. We woke up at the crack of dawn to catch the six o'clock train. We did not drink a drop of water until we reached Gunaratnam's house at two. Snacks and drinks were being sold on the train but we didn't buy a thing. While I was dying of hunger, Gunaratnam seemed to be enjoying himself thoroughly and Karuppusamy was sleeping soundly. With nothing do to, I glanced out of the train windows and beheld paradise. There is no other way one can describe that breathtaking view – groves of Christmas trees covered in snow. The place looked like a heavenly white forest. Even if only for a minute, my hunger pangs were definitely forgotten. I tried waking up Karuppusamy but hardly did he open his eyes than he fell asleep again. How I pitied him! He'd slept on a ride across paradise.

On Christmas Day, I knelt before the statue of Saint Bernadette of Lourdes. A woman asked me where I was from. When I said I was from India, she enquired about the weather. I told her that the temperature would be about thirty degrees down south.

"Wow!" she said enthusiastically. "That means I wouldn't have to wear a lot of clothes, right?"

Ah, the burden of clothes! Gunaratnam said, "Back

home, if you want to buy a cigarette, you can just throw on a shirt and go to a shop which is a stone's throw away, but here one has to wear underwear, two sets of trousers, a shirt, a sweater, a muffler, a coat, a cap, gloves, socks and boots. The clothes alone weigh thirty kilograms! And you have to take the car as well."

If civil war had not broken out in Lanka, he would have still been a professor at the University of Jaffna, leading a happy and peaceful life, buying handsome gifts of gold for his wife and his three daughters, while watching and reviewing *masala* movies. Once a year he would have visited Chennai to attend a literary festival. But Lanka's contemporary history had dragged him all the way to Toulouse.

He'd been living in France for twenty years. After working at odd jobs all over the place for a decade, his health had suffered, but he was now living a comfortable life thanks to the generous government dole. Since the government had also undertaken to finance the children's education, he had no worries on that front. Still, he was not a happy man. "This place has everything a man could possibly need, but it feels so empty," he said. Assailed by these recurrent feelings of emptiness, he took refuge in liquor. He drank when his friends from Tamil Nadu visited, he drank when his friends from Paris visited, he drank when his friends in Toulouse invited him to parties and he drank when he was home alone. He drank because he could not forget his homeland and the life he'd lived there. It weighed him down, sapped his mind and body of strength, making it difficult even to breathe. Alcohol made his burden a little lighter to bear.

However, drinking was not his biggest problem; he talked like a deranged man. His pictographic memory, his ability to remember things down to the minutest detail inspired me with fear. He would speak as if reading from a book and he would make no errors. He talked continuously from eleven in the morning to midnight. He even talked when he was eating. The only time my ears were given some respite was when he excused himself to use the toilet which, by the way, was decorated with fresh flowers whose freshness the cold weather helped retain. There was a bathtub and even a neatly stacked bookrack. And he thinks he is the most unfortunate man on earth. "To which country do I belong, Udhaya? As a person who cannot cast his vote in any country, can I claim to have a country of my own?"

I was careful not to argue with Gunaratnam, fearing the unending monologue it would trigger.

"Have you seen the refugee camps in Tamil Nadu? The inmates cannot leave the premises and are treated like prisoners serving a life sentence. I've known people who were trapped in the same camp for more than ten years. In terms of "accommodation" from the government, the least those people could get was a dog's kennel and the most they could expect was a cowshed. And the structures are at least twenty years old. The roofs are made of asbestos; some houses just have cardboard. No toilets anywhere, and if one wants to pass urine or defecate, one would have to take a long walk. There were no trees or shrubs in the visible horizon around the Mandapam camp in whose cover women could defecate. They had to walk several more miles to find any foliage that would protect them from the prying eyes and the barbs of the local men. And that journey too came with its own risks. Many women were bitten by snakes in the forest around Mandapam. Drinking water was not available in the camp. Both men and women had to bathe out in the open. Power was in short supply, but that was not something to fret over as the rest of Tamil Nadu also enjoyed electricity for four hours every day."

Gunaratnam, being a Marxist, would hold forth on his research in Marxist ideology. He talked about China's fifty-year-old history and quoted extensively from Edgar Snow's *Red Star over China.* Then he would digress and speak of the caste system in Jaffna. He would recite the names of each caste and deliver a one-hour speech on each of them. Once he tired of that, he would take out old picture albums he had brought with him from Jaffna and show them to me. Each picture would be discussed for half an hour. "See this photo? This is my brother Gunasekaran." Then he would dive into his brother's life story, starting from his birth to his current identity-less life as a refugee in Copenhagen. Then he would point to another picture and say, "This is Gunaseelan; he died in a landmine blast." The next hour would be devoted to Gunaseelan's story. Thus, the people who populated Gunaratnam's world were the shadow figures who filled his picture albums. I don't really remember what Gunaratnam said about any of them. I would just sit and mutely observe his nostalgic face as he spoke.

Perhaps, unable to put up with this, Karuppusamy left on the third day, saying he would meet us in Paris. There was no escape route for me and I was forced to hear more stories from Gunaratnam about love, loss and his longing for his beloved homeland and all the near and dear ones he'd left behind. Intermittently, Gunaratnam's wife would peep in and tell me loudly enough for her husband to hear, "I feel sorry for you." But even this did not dampen his storytelling spirit.

I stayed at his house for four days. There was something that happened on the third night that I am bound to remember with shame for the rest of my days.

I was punch drunk and I needed to pee. My stupor was such that I didn't even know where I was. Sleepy, intoxicated and in a curious semiconscious state, I felt like a stranger to myself.

My urge was great. I stood up clumsily in a haze.

It was dark and there was this unusual heaviness to the darkness that I had never experienced before; it was almost like I could grab a chunk of it in my hands. Then, everything closed in on me and I stumbled and fell.

I must have hit something for I heard a sound. How many hours had passed? However hard I tried to align my senses, I couldn't. I couldn't understand where I was or what I was doing.

Have I been trapped by the fighters who had betrayed me to the army? Am I going to be executed for my treachery? Has the army captured me? What country is this? Who am I? Where am I? What is the name of this language in which I am thinking?

I thought I might pee in my pants.

Please, free me from these walls! I'm a human being with a human urge! I need so desperately to pee! Once I have relieved myself you may shoot me dead if you will. Wait, I am not Pablo. No, I do not wish to die! Please save me from these walls that are closing in on me! I didn't do anything on my own. I'll tell you everything you want to know! Let me go! Isn't it my birthright to live in this world? Please, have mercy on me! Please let me go to the bathroom now! I lie prostrate at your feet. I beg of you. Grant me this one favor, just this one... I swear I've done nothing wrong. I was forced to do the things I did. Forgive me, just this one time, and I will do whatever it is you want me to do. If my writing is sinful in your eyes, I shall never write again. I am not a belligerent; I do not oppose you. I shall live my life, unseen and unknown, in a corner like Little Jack Horner, without causing any trouble for anyone. Please, spare my life! Allow me to urinate now. If you let me, your wish shall henceforth be my command. Just this one time... Just once...

But wait... What is this wetness? Am I dead or alive? But if I'm dead I wouldn't be able to feel the wetness in my pants, would I? Didn't they take me to the kill-room? Did they allow me to escape? Are they the kind of captors who let their captive go scot-free? Or are they testing me?

Perhaps they have intruded on my thoughts with their nodes and their technology. Oh, mind, think well of them! They are good people – revolutionaries who only desire the welfare of the people. They are going to pardon you. From now on you will work for them. Whatever you do – whatever they tell you to do – is for the benefit of the people. They have given you a second chance at life, an opportunity to correct your mistakes. That is why they spared your life…

I wet myself.

I never met Karuppusamy in Paris. When I tried calling him, his phone was switched off. The few common acquaintances we had were also unaware of his whereabouts. I began to worry. Had something happened to him? Was he dead? I returned home without any answers. Sometime later, I heard from Vincent that Karuppusamy had clandestinely slipped from Paris to London and that he was doing quite well for himself.

4 – Bienvenido a Barcelona!

I was walking alone in the neighborhood of El Raval, Barcelona. Ten years ago the Spaniards called this place Barrio Chino (Chinatown) although there was no Chinese presence there. They called it Chinatown because a significant number of Indians and Pakistanis had made home there.

"How do you know so much about Europe, sitting in your rat's corner in India?" María asked me.

"You see Maríalita, that is my problem. France, Spain and the Arabian world and everything related to them seems all too familiar to me. I find myself thinking more of Tangiers and Barcelona than the place where I was born and raised. There's this music composer guy back home in Tamil Nadu. The Tamils worship and adore him much like a God. His music is to them what football is to Latinos. If there's something you should see, it's my peeps back home swaying and swooning and getting maudlin to his music at this Chennai pub every Thursday. But it just doesn't strike a chord with me. Though I write in Tamil and speak in Tamil, and he also writes in Tamil and sings in Tamil, he just doesn't move me. But when I hear the name Umm Kulthum, my pulse quickens. Listening to *"Alf Leila wa Leila"* transports my soul to the highest heaven. The woman has enraptured me. Whenever I hear her voice, I feel that Egypt is my motherland too."

Hers is the kind of music where intoxication and passion rise and rise like froth in a glass of absinthe. *"Alf Leila wa Leila"* should be every human being's love song, regardless of which country he chooses to call home.

María began to sing softly, *"Ya habeebi... ya... habeebi... ya... habeebi...*

"Fi leilate hobi hilwa bi alfi Leila iw Leila iw Leila, alfi Leila iw Leila, alfi Leila iw Leila, alfi Leila iw Leila, alfi Leila iw Leila...

"Bikolli ilomr gowa ilomri Eih, ghair lailah zayyi illeilah zayyi illeilah..."

Dear reader, these words on paper cannot render you intoxicated. Hear them sung from the lips of Umm Kulthum and you will be electrified with passion and gripped by emotion.

Chinatown was also called the "Evil of Barcelona." The air held the smells of the night before. The narrow streets, less than six feet wide, reminded me of Shahjahanabad in old Delhi. But these roads were lifeless unlike the hustling and bustling ones in Shahjahanabad. Now and then, whores leaning down from the balconies would stretch out their arms and call out, "Indoo, Indoo!" They recognized that I was an Indian at first sight. I walked past Chinatown and made my way towards Las Ramblas and the sheer beauty of it filled me with anger and sadness. I wondered why, just why, in every foreign country, only the localities inhabited by the Indians and the Pakistanis were characterized by filth and foul stenches.

In Europe, the walkways are often as wide as the roads and they are a delight. In Las Ramblas, there was a girl with canvas and easel, a man who stood completely still, moving ever so slightly only when someone gave him money. There was yet another fellow sporting huge feathered wings and long curved horns with an owl perched on his forearm. But it was the greasepainted clown who brought my biggest grouse with Indians to the fore. When I review his antics, it was obvious that he was performing his routine within measure, never overstepping certain boundaries. He poked fun at everyone. He walked beside an African and did a ridiculous imitation of a break dance. The African laughed gamely with everyone else instead of launching into a tirade against racist stereotyping. The clown then began to follow a pretty girl who was clueless of his pursuit. When she discovered him, she burst out laughing. Then he approached a car that had stopped at a signal, swung onto the bonnet with a neat sideways movement and blew flirtatious kisses at the couple inside. He took a hat from a bald old man's head and put it on his own. When he was nearing the boundary line, he tossed the hat back to its owner. What he did next was hilarious: he walked up to a young man, jumped onto his chest and pretended to smooch him. If this had happened on a street in India, the police would have been cracking skulls. In Las Ramblas, it was all entertainment. If you kept your cool with the clown and clowned around with him for a bit, then both of you won. But if you were a hotheaded spoilsport, you lost. The clown was clinging to the man like a monkey. Do you know what the other man did? He grasped the clown firmly to his chest, pushed him against the wall, and rocked his hips back and forth like he was making out with him! People were doubled over or on their knees laughing. It saddened me that I wasn't born here and that I couldn't live here. I made my way to Hassan's house. He was the person I'd come all the way to Las Ramblas to meet.

Hassan was from Morocco and was Maria's friend. Before she introduced us, she told me that I'd never meet another specimen like him, like ever. He was a cabaret dancer in a ladies' club. I'd heard of male prostitutes and gigolos, but a male cabaret dancer was something new to me. His routine featured a striptease where he slowly and sensuously peeled off his clothes one by one. Once he was naked, there would be a catfight to rule which of them would get to give him a blowjob. "I don't know how much Viagra he takes. He has to satisfy every last female present there, you know," María said, feeling bad for him.

5 – The Changing and the Unchanging

It had been forty years since my feet had walked the roads of Thanjavur. Forty years is a terribly long time in the life of a human being.

I was twenty; Mekhala was thirteen. She started menstruating shortly after our first kiss. Our physical relationship continued even after that but when I moved to Delhi at the age of twenty-three, I forgot all about her. My life was totally consumed by reading, writing and films.

There was once a wrestler called Urangavilli who was very devoted to his wife, Ponnachi. He held a parasol over her head to shield her from the sun whenever she went out; he never walked beside her as he wished to always behold her face – which meant he walked backwards. He was the laughing stock of the whole town but he couldn't care less.

One day Ramanuja, the Vaishnavite saint, came to town and witnessed this spectacle. When he was informed of Urangavilli's steadfast devotion to his wife, he told his disciples, "I have long been seeking a man like him who will be able to serve me well. Have him brought to me."

When the wrestler was brought before him, Ramanuja asked him, "Why do you do as a slave would do for your wife?"

"If you were in my place," said the wrestler, "you'd do the same. Her eyes are so beautiful. I've never seen a pair of eyes alike to them in beauty."

"What will you do if I were to show you a more beautiful pair of eyes?" asked Ramanuja.

"I shall devote my life to the owner of those eyes," said the wrestler.

Ramanuja showed him the eyes of Lord Vishnu and thence Urangavilli became a devoted servant of Ramanuja.

My story is not very different from Urangavilli's. My mind that had been besotted with Mekhala when I was in Thanjavur was now lustily craving literature and film in which pursuits I spent most of my time, eventually forgetting about Mekhala and Thanjavur.

After some years I met a woman and began living with her. Before this woman, I never once mulled over Mekhala, so why am I swamped with memories of her now? My past life was being resurrected in my memory.

I was amazed to find that not even a signpost had changed in my hometown. It was like I'd returned to the same Thanjavur of my youth. My aunt's house where I had stayed during my college days was located in an alley near the temple. As you entered the street, there was a house belonging to a family that raised cows. It was a tableau preserved down the passage of years, unmolested by the hands of time – the house, the cows, the man at the table with two pails beside him, selling milk. This man was probably the son of the man who'd been selling when I was a youth there.

CHAPTER FIVE

1 – Ohghaaaaaad!

If you do not know where Honduras is, I suggest you dig out your school atlas. Do you know of the things that happen there? Do you know about the lives people lead there? Have you ever heard of Roberto Sosa, the poet? Don't fret if you knew little to nothing. I won't chide you for it. After all, Honduras isn't exactly your ex-lover's bedroom for you to break your head over what goes on there. The army was responsible for treacherous murders during the 80s when they were in power. When Sosa's poetry was declared treasonous, he fled to Nicaragua, fearing assassination. In Tamil Nadu, the situation is worse: it is not really the government that creates problems but the fascist cultural outfits on the fringe.

I adore women and I love talking to them, especially on the internet. It isn't unusual for me to spend hours in the virtual company of women; not only is it pleasurable, but also it doesn't cost a dime. Another perk is that all parties involved can fantasize and masturbate to their hearts' content. I have seen the semen of other men – and left some of my own – on the floors, keyboards and computer screens of internet cafés whose owners take the trouble to print and paste warnings on the walls to folks who log on to adult websites. It is also not unusual, in our day and age, to find men convincingly posing as women to lure women into their lair. Why would a knave like me miss out on such pleasures?

It might interest you – or disgust you – to know that I have written an entire novel based on my escapades in online chatrooms. In my defense, there was an element of social service involved. I have, on at least six occasions, saved ageing spinsters from oleander seeds, their razor blades and the noose. There was this unemployed Tamil woman living in the U. S. of A. Her parents had returned home to India for a month. She stayed behind as she was job-hunting. Twenty-nine, lonely and depressed, she had no outlet for her sexual desires. She was forced to remain intact as the Tamil community would have doused her in gasoline and dropped a match on her if she dared to engage in premarital sex. It would be scandal to even express her desires. Which woman – which Tamil woman – would openly say that she wanted and needed sex? She was in this suffocating situation when we got entangled with each other in the virtual world. I befriended her and it was our frequent chat sessions that kept her from jumping off the ledge. Our chats lasted for five to six hours, sometimes even fifteen without a break. At the end of each day's chat, we would masturbate, looking at each other and pouring our hearts out even then.

I never once met her in person. After she married, I lost touch with her. Our conversations would later become the raw material for my erotic novel. What else could I do to memorialize our short-lived romance? I use my own life as raw material for my writing, so why stew over fairness and ethics when a wiser one than I has said that all is fair in love and war? Writing should be exempt from such moral considerations. Moreover, the woman used me too. She had confessed, however, that if not for all our erotic conversations, she would have lost her wits, fallen to pieces, and ended her life. She talked frequently of suicide. After her, I developed an aversion to online sex chats. Chatrooms are full of all that is superficial and untrue – men and women expressing love and lust in flat, shallow, unimaginative language. There's not really much of a difference between the sex chat of an American man and a Japanese woman, an Eskimo and a pygmy, or a Tamil man and a Tamil woman – it's just "baby" and "sexy" and "dick" and "pussy" and "hot" and "wet" and lots of oohs and aahs, that's all.

There was this other woman from Kerala. Our chats soon got wild with topics like incest and orgies cropping up. But despite all my efforts and my pleas, she refused to part with her phone number. It turned out that she was well-acquainted with my work. Turns out that *she* was a man and also a close friend of mine. Imagine my plight and my embarrassment when I thought of how we'd had virtual sex and spoken of incest. It had all been a masturbatory fantasy and he played along. The bastard had me believing he had boobs and a cunt because he knew how to channel his "inner woman" or whatever his secret was.

Around this time, another woman's messages kept popping up. I've got to say she was persistent. Whenever I booted my laptop, her messages would be at the top. I was impressed. What woman devotes such a ridiculous amount of time to the pursuit of a man she has never met? Either she wanted a human pillow to cry on and blow snot into like the Tamil-American female or she was a con like my male friend had been. Or maybe she had her own motives. She succeeded in getting what she wanted as her relentless pursuit wore me down. I responded to her. At that point in time, I was not in a relationship with Anjali and was living in a state of extreme sexual deprivation. Little did I know that responding to this woman would bring about a tragic denouement.

Once she had me in her thrall, she persuaded me to give her my phone number. I did, and that triggered a barrage of phone calls every five minutes. She begged me to send her an autographed book of mine and sent me her address.

After noticing the startling frequency of the phone calls, Perundevi asked, "Who is this girl?"

"Some deranged maniac."

"How did she get your number?"

"My number isn't that difficult to find."

After a few days, when the phone calls became unbearable, I sent her an angry mail: *Who are you? What right do you have to constantly harass me with calls? Do you think you can take such liberties just because you're a woman? What do you really want from me?*

The woman responded by posting full transcripts of all our online conversations, embellished with outrageous smut that I was supposed to have said. As she was playing innocent victim, she'd edited out many of her own dirty statements so that I appeared all the more degenerate. Was she really a woman? I began to suspect the male friend who had duped me. The several thousand comments that flooded in more or less seemed to say: "He is an obscene pervert who gets a kick out of harassing women; he is a psychopath who should be bound and flogged." Some wished for my death, others threatened to kill me; some wanted me imprisoned, others wanted me exiled. I received at least fifty hate-mails every day. Some of my correspondents, in very colorful language, expressed the desire to mutilate my wife, strip my sister and fuck my mother.

Later there were some people who suggested I should publish my version of events since the girl had seriously disfigured my reputation. How could I? There were two people involved in the affair, but only one person had been exposed for all the world to spit shame on. I didn't even know the name or the face behind the messages. In this shadow play, if both of us had remained shadows, it would have been a mere puppet show, but instead, one person was real and the other was a shadow. How could a real person confront a shadow?

There is so much a nameless, a faceless and a genderless person could do in the virtual world.

One of my notable shortcomings is my inability to be tactful in worldly matters. When Nalini and I separated, I was homeless because of my stupidity. The two properties and a house that I had bought with the money I had saved were in Nalini's name. What's more, I introduced her to Marx, Engels and Bakunin, and then to Hélène Cixous and Julia Kristeva. Like an educated fool, I explained to her how the structure of a family was akin to that of a prison and gave her R. D. Laing's *The Politics of Family* to read. Not much after that, she announced, "I don't need you anymore. In fact, I don't need a man in my life at all. A dildo will suffice." And she divorced me.

I wasn't bothered by the divorce. I too was beyond doubt that a dildo could satisfy Nalini more than my dick ever did. What was of immediate concern was the fact that I was homeless. I asked Nalini to give me one of the three properties. "You won't get two pins from me, you miserable dog! Get out of my sight and out of my house!" she barked. Attempts to speak to her over the phone to resolve the issue only worsened matters. "*Behenchod!* I'll see to it that you rot like a corpse in jail if you dare call me again," she thundered. Slowly, I reconciled myself to the fact that the immovable assets that were once mine were mine no longer.

Now, you may ask how I can be uncertain of a person's gender when I've spoken to them over the phone. Let me tell you, mischief-makers determined to trap someone will move heaven and earth if need be.

One day, I got a call from Balu's phone. "Hello Udhaya," said a very husky female voice that would give any man a boner, "I'm your fan and I'm crazy in love with you." I was casually walking down a busy street. Her voice was so enticing that I hurried to a quiet spot to hear more of it. She told me her name was Mala, a Tamil girl from Goa. She was twenty-four and had met Bala and Kittappa when they drove up there to have some naughty fun. *But how did she get her hands on Balu's phone?* Apparently, the two men had gone down to the beach and she'd chosen to remain in the room, drinking. She'd chanced on my number while fiddling with Balu's phone. It must have been around ten in the morning.

"Do you drink in the morning?" I asked her.

"If it's a holiday…"

"How many rounds so far?"

"Four. Smirnoff."

The conversation jumped from liquor to sex. She was sleeping with both of them.

"If you come and join too… ooh, I'm getting wet just thinking about it! But you know what the problem is? Indians suck at group sex. They pretend they're too shy to look at a bra strap, let alone more than one naked body minus their own. Foreigners are the real deal, man. Once, three men with huge…"

I do not wish for any reader to double over and puke, so I will refrain from writing the rest of what she told me.

It alarmed me that she considered this apt first-conversation material. She must have read my mind because she said, "You think I'm a wench but I'm actually a software engineer."

Who *was* this woman? Was she speaking the truth or was this all bluff and fantasy? And how did she get hold of Balu's phone so easily?

At the end of the conversation, she gave me her phone number and told me she was looking forward to meeting me in Goa. When Balu returned to Chennai, I asked him about Mala. He confirmed everything she'd told me. He also added, "One Mala is equal to a hundred women."

"How so?"

"That's something you can find out only when you meet her in person."

I was drooling. I spoke to her on the phone a couple of times after that and she told me stories that no other woman had ever told me. Hardcore porn films would pale in comparison with some of her stories of her sexual revelries. Every word out of her mouth felt real.

She would wake up my little man by telling me how she loved to give blowjobs, and describing a few she'd given.

One day she said, "My partner once asked me for a blowjob but I couldn't give him one."

"Why not?"

She told me the story of how she was riding a bullet bike. It was her first time at the handlebars and she was piss drunk to boot. Of course, she crashed the bike and lost four teeth. She had no option but to get dentures. Due to gingivitis, that day, she didn't wear her false teeth which was why she was unable to give her partner a blowjob.

All this seemed even better than sexual fantasy but I lost interest in her after a while. I'd never been interested in pen-friends and phone-friends one bit. To me, anything meaningless and purposeless is a waste of time. Besides, my writer's profession does not allow me to waste time on insignificant people and inconsequential things. Truly I tell you: writing excited me more than sex.

Most Tamil writers are only concerned with composition and the process of writing, giving a damn if their writings don't reach far and wide. I greatly admire a poet called Dharmu Sivaramu. Around one-hundred people in Tamil Nadu might be aware of this man's existence. Those one-hundred people are diehard lovers of literature who can only be compared with religious extremists for they don't care about anything if it isn't literature and it doesn't matter to them in the slightest if people read their works or spit on them, or if they understand them or give themselves a headache trying to make sense of them. They frown upon societal recognition and royalty from the public and the publishers. But unlike them, I don't want to die unknown and unsung.

Every assistant film director in Kodambakkam has but one dream – to make it big as a director, no playing second fiddle. If you direct a blockbuster, you will become more famous than Mahatma Gandhi. You can make an address at the UN; you can turn into an overnight expert on counter-terrorism, the moral hollowness of capitalism, sub-Saharan poverty, and social anthropology; you can claim to be able to root out corruption in a day; you can thunder in front of enraptured TV audiences that you would bring peace to the Sri Lankan Tamils and frogmarch the fascist Mahinda Rajapakse naked across the length of Mount Road; you can even launch a political party. All it takes is a hit Tamil movie. Such things happen only in Tamil Nadu.

Mala had been forgotten not very long after. Some days later, Balu and Kittappa went to Masinagudi with a woman called Nisha and I tagged along. There, I was shocked to find Nisha talking on Balu's phone in Mala's tone. I realized then that the three of them were a team. I gathered this was a prank they'd been playing for years. Only now, the intended targets happened to be the new friends they made.

It all begins with honeyed whispers. "*Ma puce, mon chouchou, ma chérie…*" There is nothing like the tenderness of her voice when she says these words to me. In sexual congress, we move like serpents in a mating ritual. It goes on and on, an endless dance. I cover her with kisses from head to toe, smother her in them. I move inside her, unleashing waves of desire. She moans and screams in pleasure and pain. Perched on the edge of emotion, she would keep uttering the words Oh God endlessly as we rode together into an oblivion that we craved more than life.

oghad   oghad   oghad   oghad oghad   oghad oghad   oghad
oghad   oghad oghad   oghad oghad   oghad oghad   oghad
oghad   oghad oghad   oghad oghad   oghad oghad   oghad
oghad   oghad oghad   oghad oghad   oghad oghad   oghad
oghad   oghad oghad   oghad oghad   oghad oghad   oghad
oghad   oghad oghad   oghad oghad   oghad oghad   oghad
oghad   oghad oghad   oghad oghad   oghad oghad   oghad
oghad   oghad oghad   oghad oghad   oghad oghad   oghad
oghad   oghad oghad   oghad oghad   oghad oghad   oghad
oghad   oghad oghad   oghad oghad   oghad oghad   oghad
oghad   oghad oghad   oghad oghad   oghad oghad   oghad
oghad   oghad oghad   oghad oghad   oghad oghad   oghad
oghad   oghad oghad   oghad oghad   oghad oghad   oghad
oghad   oghad oghad   oghad oghad   oghad oghad   oghad
oghad   oghad oghad   oghad oghad   oghad oghad   oghad
oghad   oghad oghad   oghad oghad   oghad oghad   oghad
oghad   oghad oghad   oghad oghad   oghad oghad   oghad
oghad   oghad oghad   oghad oghad   oghad oghad   oghad
oghad   oghad oghad   oghad oghad   oghad oghad   oghad
oghad   oghad oghad   oghad oghad   oghad oghad   oghad
oghad   oghad oghad   oghad oghad   oghad oghad   oghad
oghad   oghad oghad   oghad oghad   oghad oghad   oghad
oghad   oghad oghad   oghad oghad   oghad oghad   oghad
oghad   oghad oghad   oghad oghad   oghad oghad   oghad
oghad   oghad oghad   oghad oghad   oghad oghad   oghad
oghad   oghad oghad   oghad oghad   oghad oghad   oghad
oghad   oghad oghad   oghad oghad   oghad oghad   oghad
oghad   oghad oghad oghad

We writhe in ecstasy. As the pace quickens, she screams, "Fuck me deep, deeper! Tear my pussy!"

"'The pipe is sweet; the lute is sweet!' say those who have not heard the prattle of their own children," says Thiruvalluvar. But to me, the sweetest words I'll ever hear are the ones that issue from her lips when she says, "I'm coming! I'm coming!"

There is more, much more, but if I put it on paper, Tamil culture will be imperiled. It's not that I fear opprobrium. In other countries, transgressive writers are usually thrown into prison or exiled by the government while the wider society stands for them. But in Tamil Nadu, the public would brand the writer a pedophile. Probably with hate-slogans, angry protests and public book-burning, they'd press the government to toss him in prison. The media, which calls the shots, will accuse, try, convict and sentence you. The writer will be remembered for all eternity for being a crazed sex-maniac who sexually tortured an eighteen-year-old girl who tried to say hello to him.

The girl gives her statement to the media. "I said hello to the writer on Facebook. His immediate reply was, 'Will you sleep with me?' I got scared. When I said hello to him the next day, he said, 'Will you let me fuck you?' I was speechless. I've said hello to him ninety times and each time he asked me whether I would consent to sex with him."

"Such things are not new to Udhaya, the psycho writer," says the media. "Our findings tell us that this beast of a man has harassed not one but ninety women. When we contacted him for his statement, he brusquely said, 'I don't have time for chatter.' Thirty of his ninety victims are now undergoing rehabilitation. Should this beast be allowed to live among men?"

This came from the Tamil front. And what about the English media?

'Tamil writer embroiled in sex scandal,' screamed the headline. They concluded with: 'We contacted the writer. All he had to say was, 'I trust in God and my wife trusts me.'

The bombshell followed later.

'The city police commissioner, on enquiry, informed us that no complaint had been registered against the writer, nothing to get him chucked into prison on a trumped-up charge for fifteen years.'

How's that!!!

Have you watched Tom Twyker's *Perfume: The Story of a Murderer*? In it, Grenouille, who has murdered many women, is taken to the gallows. The entire community bays for his blood. It is a striking illustration of the kind of violence that lies dormant within the collective unconscious of the society – a constant urge to kill someone or something. This kind of mindless violence is often seen in India where there are glaring economic disparities and gruesome inner conflicts.

Under such circumstances, how could I possibly include Anjali's love rants in this novel?

I couldn't.

2 – Couscous

I've been craving a Maghrebi dish for quite some time.

"How about preparing some couscous?" I asked Anjali who promptly consulted her cookbooks, flipping through them until she found the recipe.

COUSCOUS

Ingredients:

1 tbsp butter
1 cup onions, coarsely chopped
2 capsicums, coarsely chopped
4 garlic cloves
1 ½ cups water
1 cup couscous, cooked in extra virgin olive oil
Kosher salt
Black pepper, freshly ground

Directions:

Melt the butter in a saucepan and sauté the onions, capsicums and garlic for 5 minutes. Add water and bring to a boil.

Add the couscous, cover the pan, and remove it from the stove.

Add salt and pepper to taste.

As the couscous was cooking, we were dancing to Lara Fabian's *Je t'aime,* Anjali's hand in my hand, her head on my shoulder.

We were so lost in the moment that we'd forgotten about our couscous that had burnt.

Anjali called me out for my inattention to detail later that day when she spied my written record of the dance.

"What have you written, Udhaya? You always get the finer details wrong. When we were dancing, both your hands were around my waist and both of mine were on your shoulders. I was singing the song into your ear and you were repeatedly moaning the title into mine. Remember now?"

I wrote my first French poem that day.

Notre amour est rempli
de bises,
de gouttes de larmes,
de douleur,
d'extase,
de colère,
de conversations douces.

Nous ferons l'amour
durant la journée,
durant la nuit,
sous le soleil,
sous la lune.

Je coupe ton souffle

quand j'entre ton caverne
comme un serpent affamé.

Tes jus jaillissent,
goûtant comme le lait de coco.

Je pense à vous
tout le temps.

Je t'aime,
je t'aime.
Oh, comme je t'aime !

"Has there ever been another who has spoken of love so movingly?" I asked Anjali.

"We'll know once you've read what I've written you."

Je n'ai jamais goûté l'amour jusqu'à ce que
je l'aie goûté avec toi.
Je n'ai jamais rêvé d'amour jusqu'à ce que
j'en aie rêvé avec toi.

Nos souffles sont les mots,
nos mouvements sont la poésie.

Peut-être c'est folie,
Peut-être non.

Ton amour me calme,
ton amour m'agite.

T'es le premier homme
et le dernier homme
qui j'aimerai.

Mon cœur a trouvé, enfin,
un autre cœur à aimer.

Quand je ferme les yeux,

je vois ton visage,
j'écoute ta voix,
je sens ton corps.

Dearest,

I called you in the morning as my schedule and my situation have conspired against me, leaving me with no time or room to breathe for the rest of the day. I just wanted to let you know that you fill my every thought. I am so truly, madly and deeply in love with you, but words are poor conveyors of my love. I want to scream your name in ecstasy; I want to be under the sheets with you – me beside you, you inside me. I am aching for your warmth, for your electrifying touch.

Before you came things were just what they were:
the road precisely a road, the horizon fixed,
the limit of what could be seen,
a glass of wine no more than a glass of wine.

With you the world took on the spectrum
Radiating from your heart: your eyes gold
As they open to me, slate the color
That falls each time I lose all hope.

With your advent roses burst into flame:
you were the artist of dried-up leaves, sorceress
who flicked her wrist to change dust into soot.
You lacquered the night black.

- *Faiz Ahmed Faiz*

Yours always,

Anjali

I crave the warmth of you, the sight of you.

I felt your hands on my shoulders, pushing me down,
I felt hot tears spill from my eyes,
but the pain soon metamorphosed into pleasure.

There was solace in your presence,
warmth in your touch.

You know that it's unlike me to break into verse like people spontaneously break into song in the movies. I am more comfortable with writing than with speaking although I am no grand poet. My heart just opens wider when I write.

Dispel all your fears, let your guard down.

All you ever have to be with me is yourself.

You came into my world with the force of a wind.

You are my mother,
my child,
my saint,
my slut,
my everything.

Give me what you will –
poison or nectar –
and I will take it.

I fuck myself, daydreaming of you in my bed,

and I fuck you, like a dog fucks a bitch, in yours.

I doubt anyone's sex-life is as interesting as mine at this age, Anjali. I am celebrating the best moments of my life. That's probably why they throw slippers, tomatoes and eggs at me.

This thing we share –

it is not love alone,

but bliss,

enlightenment.

Pourquoi suis-je heureuse quand le téléphone indique
ton nom ?
Pourquoi mon cœur sursaute lorsqu'il entend ta voix ?
Pourquoi ta chaleur amène une telle extase qui était
inconnue pour moi ?
Pourquoi suis-je en larmes quand je pense à toi ?
Pourquoi tu n'es pas là, mon cher, pour répondre à
tous mes « pourquoi » ?

CHAPTER SIX

1 – Wholly Screwed by a Holy Screwball

My mailbox is rarely a recipient of publishers' cheques. It's just a receptacle for phone bills, electricity bills, water bills, the faithful correspondence of my haters, and not to mention the occasional legal notice. I felt the need for a spiritual anchor to deal with this scale of derision. Even though I identified as an atheist, I loved having engaging conversations with monks and mystics. And when I became a believer, my curiosity about these men of faith had turned into reverence.

Jymka Saamiyar claimed to be an avatar of God. My friends questioned my sanity when they saw that I believed him. I do not fault them for this, for I am a gullible man.

It wasn't too long before the film on my eyes got peeled off. Jymka was no god; he was a crooked godman. I was decided on this even before a video of an actress giving him head surfaced. It all started when I noticed him trying to filch my wife. He wanted her to join his ashram and renounce the world. Perundevi was easy prey – the ascetic life had appealed to her since her childhood. She was only a few days shy of joining Jymka's fold when the sex scandal popped up. It was not the holy man's sex-life that concerned me. I was livid that Perundevi had swayed under his influence, nearly leaving me behind to disappear into the woods with that serpent. To exact revenge, I wrote a series of critical pieces on Jymka for a leading magazine.

Jymka was no ordinary adversary. He ran a spiritual empire worth several million dollars. And here, I was up against money, muscle and political might. My articles provoked a barrage of legal notices from him and the actress who – shall we euphemize? – was filmed worshipping his Holy Tool. All that said, I was being sued for 100 million for defamation. One legal notice I received ran into almost a thousand pages. I needed a battery of legal eagles just to keep track of the number of such notices. Jymka wanted a public apology. I thought a "fuck off" would suffice.

His sexual shenanigans would not have provoked me in the slightest had he not tried to lure my wife from me. I feel like branding myself in the forehead for respecting – hell, even worshipping – this culprit, believing he was "enlightened."

It was a fine morning when I received a legal summons from the Hyderabad High Court. If I didn't answer it, I would have to cough up 100 million and face criminal charges. I boarded a bus.

In the good times, I'd visit Hyderabad to pub-crawl on Banjara Hills with Kannan. This trip was painful. Bus journeys are tedious especially when an adult male has yet to master the art of bladder control. SPN, the coach firm

I had opted to travel with, operated a vast fleet of Volvo buses. They are, by and large, relatively more comfortable than regular buses. And only last week, an SPN on the same route with thirty-odd passengers skidded off the road and crashed. I hopped onto this one with praying lips.

The bus set off an hour behind schedule. To make up for lost time, the driver drove like he was on trial for a Formula 1 team. Two hours into the brain-rattling journey, he lost control and rammed into a tree. It was a miracle that all of us escaped unhurt. The driver's diagnosis was that his drop in speed from 100 kmph was what led to the accident. A fellow passenger sallied that if that was indeed the case, we'd be having this conversation in heaven or in hell.

Kannan accompanied me to the High Court complex in Madina Circle. This was only my second visit to a court of law. My maiden visit was when I was getting divorced from Nalini.

In the case filed by Jymka, I was the first accused, the magazine editor was the second and the publisher the third. The second and the third accused were no-shows. The editor, who was my friend, told me he would appear the next hearing and had arranged a lawyer for me. The man to whom my defense had been entrusted was vertically challenged, spoke a Telugu-Tamil-English pidgin, and had the manner of a property agent. He seemed keener to part me from my money than to secure my liberty. I was told that I would have to produce proof that I owned property in Hyderabad to post my bail bond. Kannan immediately volunteered to hand over his property documents to me without even consulting his wife. This gesture of his astonished me. My lawyer snatched the three thousand I had on me. A little later, we were told that the judge was on leave. The lawyers swarmed around a clerk who was sitting in the judge's chambers to fix another date for the hearing. At that moment, a sightly woman in a black sheath dress entered the room. She looked around for a few seconds until she found who she was looking for. She came up to me and said, "You must be Udhaya." When I responded in the affirmative, she introduced herself as the godman's lawyer and went over to the clerk along with my lawyer. The clerk fixed a date for the hearing but altered it when she raised an objection. The hearing was adjourned for two months. Even though this didn't resolve anything, it still gave me time to cool my brains.

The publisher accompanied me to the next hearing. The management of the magazine had arranged for a different legal representative. It wasn't easy because none of the competent lawyers in Hyderabad wanted to accept our brief. My editor friend picked up that Jymka had paid off most of them.

Our new lawyer seemed efficient and honest. He took complete charge of the situation. A year passed in adjournments and court vacations, without there being any tangible progress. I felt that Jymka was using this case just to intimidate and harass us with no serious intent of receiving closure. Just when I had begun to lie back, I got a call from Hyderabad on a Friday morning. The caller, with a heavy Telugu accent, informed me that he was a cop. Apparently, the godman had filed a new case against me and the magazine and the Hyderabad police wanted to serve us the summons for which my address was needed. The thought that I could probably be spending the remainder of my life in a dark cell resurfaced. Could it happen tomorrow? Life in jail would be dreadful for two reasons: one, the absence of an air-conditioner and two, a shared toilet. But more immediately, what about my weekend plans?

The bail application could be moved only on Monday. So I decided to perform a vanishing act before the police showed up with tasers and *lathis* at my doorstep. I called up Krishna who was an industrialist of repute in Chennai with an impressive Rolodex that featured influential politicians and high-ranking policemen.

There was a time when Krishna, Balu and I were thick friends and party animals. When I dropped off the radar, Krishna and Balu remained friends for frolic. Krishna said he'd meet me at 10 Downing, a pub every other college girl in Chennai had on her places-to-go-before-I-die list. It is the only pub that uses books as props. They shared space with the expensive china on the racks that lined its inner walls. Fuck you writers...your books are mere ornaments here!

The name 10 Downing brought with it a flood of memories. Three years ago, Krishna, Balu and I were drinking there. We saw a young, handsome couple a few tables away. After downing a couple of mojitos, I made a quick trip to the men's room. When I'd returned, it stunned me to see that the earlier mentioned couple had shifted base to our table. Krishna and Balu were speaking to them like they were long lost friends. "The vodka belongs to Shruti and the beer to Bhaskar," Balu said by way of introduction. I was eager to know how my friends had pulled this off. Of course, it wouldn't be proper for me to ask in the presence of our Shruti and Bhaskar. Balu seemed to hear my thoughts and launched into an explanation. "*Anney*, when you went to take a piss no, I decided to spread some cheer because today is my birthday, no? So I approached our friends and requested the pleasure of their company on this happy occasion. And coincidentally, it is Shruti's birthday too, so we're all happily toasting to long life here." After four pegs, Krishna and Balu excused themselves to go have a smoke. Keen to cull out fact from Balu's fiction, I joined them. This was what had *actually* happened: Balu bet with Krishna that he would get the couple to our table in two minutes flat. At this juncture, I must tell you a few things about Balu. His skin is dark and glowing; he has a penchant for head-turning clothes and shoes; he's forty but looks thirty. He had the manner of a millionaire. He knew nary a word of English, but had turned that into an asset. The three of us were once on a train to Coimbatore. Till about eleven at night, we were covertly enjoying cocktails in a corner of the compartment close to the exit. When the ticket inspector sniffed out our little secret, we poured him a couple of drinks as well. Does any man in India, rich or poor, handsome or ugly, single or married, ever say no to Johnnie Walker? In his drunken state, Balu couldn't quite remember his berth number. He randomly woke up a man and asked, "What is your date of birth?" The unfortunate target who had been fast asleep could scarcely come to grips with this midnight attack. He mumbled something unintelligible when I decided to rescue the situation. "My friend here would like to know your berth number. Sorry to disturb," I said. Not a day of 's life passes without such antics. Now, let us return to 10 Downing.

"All that is fine Balu, but what if the girl didn't fall for your birthday bluff and called the bouncers instead at your invasion of her privacy?"

"Well, in that case I would have said, 'I'm sorry *sister*,' and come back to my table," he said, enacting his folded-handed apology for us. "How will life go on if we allow such trivial things to bother us, *Anney*?"

I told Krishna about the summons from the Hyderabad police.

"Escape to Goa for a few days," he suggested. He made all my travel arrangements that instant. He broke my SIM card in two and threw the unequal halves away so that the cops couldn't trace my whereabouts. He lent me a spare phone he had. The prospect of a life in hiding seemed kind of thrilling, but what the fuck had I done to run and hide? I've criticized several powerful people throughout my writing career but I realized then that taking on a godman was a different ballgame altogether.

In the meantime, Perundevi called to inform me that the Hyderabad cops swung by the house to deliver the summons. Since I wasn't around, they left word that if I failed to show my mug in court at the appointed date and time, they'd swing by again – with an arrest warrant. In panic-mode, I spoke to my lawyer who assured me he'd appear on my behalf. My life in exile was thus postponed until their next visit.

2 – The Pichavaram Carnival

The first time we met was in 2007 in a five-star hotel in Bangalore. We were twenty mouths and stomachs and all our food and drinks were paid for by an ordinary middle-class young man called Guru. I think around five zeros followed the one on the bill. Like any group of male friends meeting after a month or after a year, we discussed music, literature, films, drinks, sex, women and politics.

The following year we met again in Pichavaram.

Now, like a good reader, I'd like you to read this entire list:

LIST OF NECESSITIES
Shamiana (30 x 15) – 1
Chairs – 30
Blankets – 3
Tables – 8
Kerosene – 10 l
Loudspeaker – 1

Generator – 1(as there is no electricity on the island)

CD player – 1

Tube lights – 6

Microphone – 1

~~Bridegroom's chair – 1~~(This was struck out at the last moment as I said none of us really needed it. After all, no one was marrying or remarrying there.)

Water for washing hands, mouth, backside – 15 cans

Drinking water – 15 cans

Buckets – 2

Bathroom mugs – 2

Plastic mugs for drinking – 300

Plastic plates – 100

Meat knife – 1

Vegetable knife – 1

Paper napkins – 6 packets

Candles – 50

Tender coconuts – 100

Banana leaves – 100

Curd – 10 l

Soda – 24 bottles (0.5 l each)

7Up – 4 (2 l each)

Mirinda – 1 (2 l)

Pepsi – 1 (2 l)

Murrel fish – 4 kg

Goat – 1

Chicken – 6

Prawns – 8 kg (I thought this was a ridiculous quantity. Who would have the patience to skin 8 kg of prawns? Was it even possible? Kokkarakko's friend Mani showed us it was. He and his relatives handled the job – while one woman ground the masala for the curry, two others deftly skinned the prawns. Of these two women, one was Mani's sister-in-law, a new bride and a Ph.D. holder.)

Groundnuts – 1 kg

Namkeen – 1 kg

Tapioca chips – 2kg

Moong dal – 2 kg

Orbit chewing gum – 100

Halls mint candies – 100

Tablecloths – 12 m

Adhesive tape – 2

Plastic spoons – 100

Chilies – 2 kg

Coriander – 5 kg

Rice – 25 kg

Idli batter – 5kg

Urad dal – 2 kg

Pepper – 2.5 kg

Cumin – 2.5 kg

Garlic – 2 kg

Oil – 5 l

Mustard oil – 0.5 l

Custard – 10 packets

Cardamom powder – 2 boxes

Appalam – 100

Tandoori appalam – 100

Mustard – 100 g

Fenugreek – 250 g

Turmeric powder – 100 g

Bengal gram– 1 kg

Toor dal – 2 kg

Cashewnuts – 250 g

Cinthol soaps – 4

Dabur Meswak toothpaste – 2

Imported coconut milk – 10 packets (This was needed to make a little-known item called a tender coconut pudding. Since my passion for literature and my passion for cooking are commensurate, I will give you the recipe later.)

Cumin powder – 200 g

Asafetida – 100 g

Tamarind – 1 kg

Salt – 1 kg

Garam masala – 1 packet

Ginger – 2 kg

Small onions – 5 kg

Large onions – 5 kg

Local tomatoes – 5 kg

Bangalore tomatoes – 1kg

Potatoes – 4 kg

Beans – 1 kg

Green chilies – 500 g

Radish – 1 kg

Cucumber – 5 kg

Lemon – 150

Eggplant – 3 kg

Cluster beans – 2 kg

Coriander leaves – 1 bunch

Mango – 2 kg

Coconuts – 10

Curry leaves – 1 bunch

Mint – 2 bunches

Carrot – 4 kg

Coal – 4 kg

Tin – 4

Firewood

King's cigarettes – 10 packets

Gold Flake cigarettes – 5 packets

Ganesh *beedis* – 4 bunches

Pickles – 2 bottles

Matchboxes – 3 packs (10 boxes each)

Boats – 2

Smirnoff – 5

Bacardi – 4

Mansion House – 5

VSOP – 8

Warehouse – 4

McDowell's No. 1 – 2

Old Cask – 2

Royal Challenge – 2

Royal Stag – 2

Rivera – 2

Caesar – 4

Rémy Martin – 2

Tequila – 1

There were some other liquors too, but we drank so much that I can't remember all their names. Forgive me, Kokkarakko.

Now for that recipe I promised you…

TENDER COCONUT PUDDING

Ingredients:

Tender coconut water – 1 cup

China grass – 2 tsp

Nestlé Milkmaid – 1 tin

Milk, boiled and cooled – 0.75 l

Tender coconut slices – 1 cup

Grated coconut – ¼ cup

Sugar – ½ cup

Directions:

Mix the china grass with a cup of water and heat it over a moderate flame.

Once the grass has fully melted, add tender coconut water.

In a thick-bottomed vessel, mix milk, Nestlé Milkmaid and sugar. Heat this over a moderate flame. Stir continuously.

Once the sugar dissolves, add the china grass and tender coconut water mixture and stir well.

Remove the vessel from the flame and add slices of tender coconut to it.

Pour the mixture into a wide glass bowl and allow it to cool before transferring it to the fridge.

Before serving, mix some sugar and grated coconut in a wok and sprinkle it over the pudding.

(Serves 4)

Of all the things that were mentioned, the only thing we lacked in Pichavaram was a fridge. But the pudding turned out exceptionally well. Its taste lingered even after we'd downed five rounds of liquor.

There is an uninhabited island in Pichavaram. It is surrounded by the ocean on one side and the backwaters on the other. A good part of the island is covered by a marshy forest.

My favorite writer is Nikos Kazantzakis. In his book, *Zorba the Greek*, there's this writer who spends a night with the titular character, drinking wine and roasting mutton, the moonlit Mediterranean around them. I often expressed my desire to spend such a night to Kokkarakko, so he chalked out an action plan to fulfill my wish and executed it to perfection. We even planned to roast the mutton barbecue style.

It was for this carnival that the items on that extensive list had to be collected. Kokkarakko had taken a week off work and set up camp in Pichavaram. He and Mani began to collect the provisions from Chidambaram. The liquor was also arranged for. Spoilable items like fish had to be bought on the day of the carnival.

Usually, a literary meeting is an event where ten to fifteen writers congregate in a dirty room in a bookshop and tear into each other until it's time to leave. From experience, I know that people who participate in such meetings suffer from depression and frustration for a week. But Pichavaram meet was a celebration. Fifty of my readers had shown up there for the event, all ignorant of what constitutes and what follows a literary meeting. They were also ignorant of the purpose of the wine and the barbecue, and the whole concept of a carnival, were clueless as to why we were on an island, and were curious to know who the organizer of the whole affair was.

If Kokkarakko declared that he was the organizer, the next question would inevitably be: "Are you related to Udhaya?" to which Kokkarakko would reply, "He is my uncle." One reader asked him, "Will hot water be available on the island? I'll need it for my bath in the morning." Kokkarakko said, "Once, there were roughly 150 fishermen who lived with their families on this island. The tsunami of 2004 took them all. Today, there are probably just a couple of ghosts on that island and a lot of coconut trees under whose shade they can hang around. The island doesn't even afford drinking water which we have to take with us." The reader had no more questions. He didn't turn up for the carnival either.

Some other readers kept asking, "Has Udhaya come yet?" It meant that they would come only after my arrival was confirmed. I reached the island two days before the carnival. Kannan had said he'd be coming from Hyderabad with his girlfriend. As none of the others were bringing girlfriends or wives, expectations were high. I cautioned Kokkarakko. "We are fifty men and Kannan's girlfriend is only one woman. We'll need to be careful."

The carnival was on a Saturday night. Kannan arrived at noon that day but he hadn't brought his girlfriend with him. That was forgivable, but what irritated us was the fact that he'd brought another male friend, Kalaiselvan, "in her place." Talk of anticlimaxes!

Meanwhile, a reader from Madurai asked, "Why didn't you organize this carnival in Madurai?" Immediately, a reader from Tiruppur demanded to know why we didn't organize it in Tiruppur.

"I have spent a six-figure sum to hold it in Pichavaram," an incensed Kokkarakko said, "and I'm not a rich man.

Do you think I'm running a circus to organize shows in different places? If you want to hold it in your town, you make a list of all the things you'll need, spend a fortune getting them and every last ounce of your energy making arrangements and answering stupid questions."

The discussions died and suggestions immediately stopped coming in.

Because many people were not familiar with the island and how to get there, Kokkarakko put up a huge flex board at Chidambaram Bus Stand and posted a couple of volunteers at the spot in case the sign didn't do its job. But most of the readers saw neither the signboard nor the smiling volunteers and kept bombarding us with calls to find out how to get to the island. Telling them where the volunteers were was a herculean task that drained us of our energy. Imagine directing them to the island!

A friend called Prabhu who was working as a chef on a cruise liner had agreed to take charge of the barbecue. We'd readied the goat, the coal, the drum and everything else he'd need.

The island was three kilometers away from Pichavaram. We had to use a motorboat to navigate the backwaters. The water was only three feet deep. We decided to split the group into halves. Kokkarakko, Prabhu and I were in the first group. The second group's boat ran aground due to the low depth and the muddiness of the backwaters. If anyone got into the water to try and push the boat, the blade-like oysters would rip his soles. The motor growled but the boat didn't budge. Their boat had to be tied to ours and pulled out of the mud. It was an hour before all was well again.

Several times, I had told Kokkarakko, and he in turn told Mani, that every single item on the list had to be taken to the island without fail. Forgetting even one item would jeopardize the entire celebration. The second group reached the island late. As soon as they landed, Prabhu ran to them and requested a matchbox. This they had forgotten to bring. There were no matchboxes on our boat either. Instead of another taxing journey back, we luckily managed to borrow some matches from the helpers.

The barbecued goat was so delicious that most of us forgot we were part of a civilized society. Gnanam was gnawing away at an entire goat-shank like a carnivorous beast. The next morning, when he started whining about the meager amount he ate, we showed him a priceless picture of himself battling it out with the goat's leg.

The helpers also partook of the revelry. This took them by surprise, for, on such occasions, they were given the dregs and the spittle. They were so pleased that they took the boats out to sea that night, brought in a good catch and even cooked for us.

The merrymaking lasted till the wee hours of the morning. Gnanam had drunk too much and was lying akimbo on the sand. We were worried because he was lying face down. Four of us shifted him to the tarpaulin, one limb per man, but he rolled back onto the sand again and we left him there.

Kannan, who was sitting in a chair, kept turning to

the left and then to the right, like he was trying to cross a highway. He threw up with each half-turn of his head. He was also asking a question that seemed to be bothering him no end: "Why the bloody hell doesn't Mani Ratnam ever make a good movie?" After he had asked this question maybe a hundred times, he drifted off to sleep.

I must be careful to not spill too much ink about Kokkarakko; he might walk off with the entire novel. But I insist on telling you how we became acquainted with each other. You will never fully understand him if I don't. He was one of the readers who was in attendance at the Bangalore readers' circle meeting. Nothing about the man struck me then. He was just another face in the crowd. It was only the next day I realized that there was something about him that singled him out, that set him apart from the others. He asked Guru and me if we could go to a pub on Brigade Road the following afternoon. We accepted the invitation and gave him our numbers without asking for his.

That night, Guru and I hit the sack late after staying up with friends. As was my wont, I woke up with the birds, but Guru was out like a fused light. I tried in vain to wake him up at ten, then at noon, and then at six, but he didn't stir. Kokkarakko called me at six as well to tell me that Guru wasn't answering his calls. I told him that Guru was playing Sleeping Beauty and we agreed to meet at one of the pubs on Brigade Road at 7. My last attempt to rouse Guru was also in vain. The vodka must have been too strong for him as he was more of a beer person. The drunken spell having run its course, Guru woke up at 9 and had a quick shower after which we were off to Brigade Road. It was 10 by the time we reached.

Kokkarakko told us that he and his friend Natesan had been milling about Brigade Road for three hours, waiting for us to turn up. If I'd left without Guru, I might've ended up in Manipal. The pub was about to close. We managed to order three rounds of drinks before leaving for Natesan's place where we spent the night.

In the morning, when I woke up, Natesan was not home. He'd probably left for his morning walk. Wanting to make some tea, I went to the kitchen. Neither match nor lighter generated a flame. Kokkarakko came into the kitchen after hearing me potter about. When I told him I was trying to light the stove, he said, "You have to open the cylinder valve too." He did so and lit the stove. Immediately, a huge column of fire shot up and Kokkarakko's hair got singed. Kokkarakko didn't panic; he just turned the cylinder valve off. The fire vanished almost instantly. Kokkarakko didn't seem to mind that he'd nearly reduced us both to charcoal. Only after Natesan returned home did we realize what had happened. Natesan, it turned out, was a stickler for cleanliness. After all of us had slept, he'd washed the kitchen clean. To clean the stove, he'd disconnected the tube that connected it to the cylinder. When Kokkarakko opened the valve, the gas had escaped via the tube. I swore to never enter a stranger's kitchen again.

My thoughts keep returning to how he called Guru all day even though he had my number and decided to try me only at six in the evening when we were scheduled to meet in the afternoon.

Months after our meeting in Bangalore, I received an e-mail from him. He had much to say:

Tokyo is the city that outshines both Singapore and Hong Kong. In Hong Kong, the area where the Chinese live is quite filthy (not unlike Indians), but there is no doubt that the city is exciting. Though the whites quit the place ten years ago, it still functions more or less like a colony.

Tokyo is a chunk of paradise on earth. It appears to me that its society is cleaved into two parts. The first part is hostile, purely Japanese, unadulterated. The other part is more welcoming of gajins. Gajins *are the outsiders. It is amusing to watch the faces of the Americans fall when they realize what they are being called. The purely Japanese sect frequents their own bars while the other sect goes to theirs. This is the custom here. As I'm a* gajin, *I go to Roppongi, Japan's Sin City. There are several strip clubs, cabarets and restaurants there. My friends and I decided to go someplace and have an orgy that day. I'd been unwell then, so I was on a diet, but to my luck, the fever subsided, allowing me to relish some authentic Japanese food.*

I stuck to vegetarian food because of my sickness, so I couldn't try the sashimi, *but my friends ate on my behalf and told me how divine it was. I contented myself with a screwdriver.*

Next, these friends of mine took me to Geronimo, a shot bar. This bar serves only liquor, which means you don't get any soda to dilute the stuff with. You just drink it "raw." And in one gulp – no sipping. Here, different liquors are mixed and served under fancy names like "Cracy Phuk," "Slippery Nipple," "Blue Nights," Pink Orgasm," and "Flaming Lamborghini." You drink to cowboy music there. The walls featured metal plates with names and dates inscribed on them – achievement boards of sorts. If you want to see your name feature on these plates, all you have to do is down fifteen shots in one night. You can't drink the same thing twice, and you can't choose what you drink; that privilege is exclusively the bartender's.

I don't know how, when or why I decided to take up the challenge to have my name inscribed on a plate. By 4 a.m., I had downed twelve shots – just three more to go. I told this to the barman. He showed me the menu and asked me to give him the names of the shots I'd already drunk. While naming the shots, I realized that two had been repeated – what a waste! My friends urged the barman to bring the remaining five shots, all of which tasted like acid.

Flaming Lamborghini was one of them. Although I was sipping it with a straw, it felt like fire in my mouth. The last shot was tequila with a large worm in the glass. It was part of the drink, I was told. I had to swallow a worm after being a steadfast vegetarian the whole day! The worm tequila was my seventeenth shot. If you ever happen to go there and if you're sober enough to read, you can try searching for a legend's name on the plates. What you say? It's KOKKARAKKO – 20.08.2007. *I saw it even last week but did not have the presence of mind to take a picture of it.*

They also gave me a t-shirt with the bar's logo as well as the names of the seventeen shots I'd drunk that night.

It was half-past-five by the time we left Geronimo. Outside, the sun was shining brightly. We half-staggered, half-crawled back to our rooms. When I regained consciousness, I heard a scraping at the door like nails on a chalkboard. Opening my eyes as wide as a slit, I looked at my watch – 8:35. The sun was still shining. Was it evening already? Or was it the next morning? If it was indeed the next morning, my flight would have departed! And just then I noticed I'd slept with my shoes on.

I got to my feet. When I tried to walk, I tottered and almost fell face first to the floor. Somehow, I managed to go outside. My colleague – fresh as a fucking daisy because he didn't take seventeen shots – was waiting for me. He told me with a sickly sweet smile to get ready in thirty minutes. I asked for a few minutes and got ready for the "ice cure." Do you know what an "ice cure" is? It's this remedy that fixes a hungover man's fucked up homeostasis. All you have to do is plug your washbasin, dunk several ice cubes into it and fill it with water. Then, you keep your face in the chilly water until it's frozen stiff. Then, you sit in a tub of cold water for fifteen minutes.

The ice cure took care of my hangover. When I resumed the company of my friends, they all greeted me like a returned hero. Nobody could believe that I'd returned to work within three hours after downing seventeen shots.

Now you might understand why I feel that Kokkarakko should come with a 'Beware of Walking Drunk Tank' sign around his neck. They say that even elephants can stumble sometimes. History repeated itself when we were celebrating my birthday in Kodaikanal. Kokkarakko had driven us there from Chennai. He had four pegs of vodka to celebrate our arrival and went off to sleep, exhausted after the drive. I tried slapping him, shaking him and shouting at him to wake up and have a peg for the occasion. He jumped up and gulped down three pegs. He babbled for a bit and fell asleep again only to wake up at 10 p.m. the next day.

3 – Guilt over a Goat

We had a series of meetings in quick succession soon after the Pichavaram Carnival. Most of them were held in Mahabalipuram which was proximate to the sea. I preferred forests and mountains to the ocean, but since we were all middle-class men, we had to keep the costs in mind. Since it cost less to travel to Mahabalipuram, my friends preferred to meet there. However, I nagged them every once in a while to persuade them to choose the mountains sometime.

We eventually settled on a mountain house in Ebbanad.

Ebbanad is a small village nestled in the shadow of a mountain, around fourteen kilometers from Ooty. It has a population of 6000. There is a mountain path in Ebbanad that leads to a house, the only token of human habitation. The owner of this house rents it out to travelers. It was in that very house that the ten of us were planning to stay. The place is not easily accessible at all. The path is rocky and only a jeep can take you there with much ado. If it rains, there is the possibility of the jeep gliding like a bar of slippery soap on a laminate countertop and falling off the ledge.

My friends had put me and all our belongings in a Tavera and sent me on my way. When we were almost halfway there, it began to pour. It was only good fortune that Arul was an ace driver who was determined to convey me to the house. The others had to walk in the rain. No connectivity meant I couldn't even get hold of them on the phone.

Though the journey was fraught with danger, Arul reached the house without incident. The house stood alone in a ravine. Mountains towered behind it like giant sentries. Only the twittering of the birds punctuated the silence. A profound tranquility hung over the area.

Arul unloaded the luggage and got back into the car for the arduous return journey to Ebbanad. In a few hours, my party had arrived, soaked to the bone and dripping all over the place. They were being bled by leeches. The slimy creatures were all over them. My friends began to pull them out and toss them into the fire. Their wounds continued to bleed for several hours. Just then, quite unexpectedly, Arul appeared before us in pretty much the same leech-bitten condition. The Tavera had stalled during the ascent and he came to ask for our help to push the vehicle. My friends groaned in dismay. They had just arrived after a grueling six-kilometer trek through the forest and now they were being called to exert themselves further. Ultimately, five of the sturdiest young men went to help Arul with the Tavera.

There was no electricity in the house. We had come prepared for it, so that wasn't much of a problem. If we wanted light, we could just start a campfire outside the house. Inside, we could use hurricane lamps. But we soon realized that there were other problems in store. There was a cook and a helper in the house. The former had no clue about cooking. When we asked for *sambar*, he served us boiled *dal*. When we asked him if he could make some gravy with the dry fish we'd brought, he said he could whip it up in no time and that it was no big deal. We ended up having to eat fish dunked in boiling water with spices sprinkled on it. Every cup of tea came with a lethal six tablespoons of sugar in it. And like all of this wasn't enough, there was no water in the bathroom. In the style of the villagers, we took some water in plastic bottles and relieved ourselves among the rocks, but this too was dangerous. If you are spotted by a bear or an elephant that starts pursuing you, there's not much you can do to escape with a bottle of water in your hands, a half-full bladder and your pants around your ankles. We discharged in fear and, trembling, hurried back into the house. Hot water for a bath was out of the question. Imagine the plight of having to bathe in cold water in a hill station! Only the braver among us bathed. We were totally severed from the world for three days without electricity, mobile phones, laptops, newspapers and television. Wait, there's more! The rain had drenched all my clothes while I was on my way here, so I couldn't change out of my wet clothes for three days.

But even amidst all these problems, the ravine felt like

heaven. Sometimes the mist obscured the mountains from view. When the mist lifted, I thought I saw a huge boulder at the top of the mountain, but when I looked at it through my binoculars, I realized it was a bison.

Prabhu the chef was also among us. It was he who saved us from the culinary experiments of the house chef. On the first day, he cooked the chickens we'd taken with us. The next day, there was barbecued lamb. Now you must be wondering how we stumbled across a goat in the middle of the forest… That, dear reader, is a story in itself.

After Prabhu had cooked the chickens, we made a campfire and were sitting around it having literary discussions aided by generous helpings of drinks. Around midnight, two young men arrived at the place on a bike. We couldn't believe our eyes.

They were college students from Avinashi. Even they'd wanted to relive the Zorba story. "We brought a goat with us for it," they said. They had biked 80 kilometers to Ebbanad. As they felt the police might suspect them of being goat thieves, they'd been smart enough to get a receipt from the seller. It was a good move for they were indeed pulled over by the cops at a number of places along the way and the receipt was their saving grace. Some cops had even stopped them thinking they were abducting a child. They had the bleating goat to thank for that. With all that, they managed to reach Ebbanad at 10.

It had been one hell of a task to carry the goat and push the bike on the slippery rock-strewn path in the rain. They'd sustained scratches and bruises from their falls (from the bike and the walk). They had the pitch darkness to worry about and the prospects of the goat's bleating attracting a wild animal that would have had a most sumptuous dinner.

The goat had been seated on the lap of the pillion rider. The dark and the strangeness of the journey terrified the goat enough to bite the back of the young man riding the bike. At one point, unable to bear the creature's perilous antics any longer, they tied it to a tree and continued their journey. (The man who had sold them the goat had also furnished them with a rope. What a great sense of business ethics he had!) But what unsettled them was the lurking doubt of where the path they were taking was leading them. They had set out to meet the writer, braving all the odds. They assured themselves that the path would lead them somewhere and they could ask for directions if they got themselves lost.Along with the goat, they'd hidden some bottles of liquor so as to reduce their load. When I heard their story, I was reminded of how Werner Herzog had a steamship transported up a steep mountain for the film *Fitzcarraldo*.

Okay. Now all that was left to do was find the goat and bring it to where we were. Only a while ago, the gang had returned after pushing the Tavera up the mountain. Going back up again was a dismaying prospect but we were infused with vigor when we thought of the impossible feat the young men had achieved. My friends accompanied them into the forest with a torch. They left at midnight and returned at 2 a.m.

The barbecue was to be held the next evening, but our hearts began to melt as the goat kept bleating piteously throughout the day. "Should we take a life to satisfy our hunger?" I asked. A friend replied that if we didn't eat such creatures, the ecological balance would be upset. This is the opinion of Marvin Harris, the American anthropologist. Culture and the environment are related more closely than we think. Can a desert-dwelling Mongolian survive on vegetables? Another friend argued that even plants have life.

An excellent argument indeed! Both plants and cows have life, so there is no difference whether you eat one or the other. Another asked, "In that case, can we eat human beings too?" I replied that Tolkappiyar had given a most remarkable answer to this question. I recited it from memory:

Once the recitation was through, I launched into the explanation.

"Among the animate beings in this world, there are the trees and the plants that are equipped with but a single faculty – touch; then come the snails and the mussels who are bestowed with the additional sense of taste; termites and ants have an olfactory apparatus while wasps and honeybees possess the fourth sense of sight; animals that bear themselves on two or four limbs have five senses; and the human being is endowed with six."

Tolkappiyar had treated of evolutionary theories 3000 years before Charles Darwin. Not to mention that he was only compiling what others had discovered before him. Okay, let's shelve this discussion for later.

ஒன்றறி வதுவே உற்று அறிவதுவே,
இரண்டறி வதுவே அதனொடு நாவே,
மூன்றறி வதுவே அவற்றொடு மூக்கே,
நான்கறி வதுவே அவற்றொடு கண்ணே,
ஐந்தறி வதுவே அவற்றொடு செவியே,
ஆறறி வதுவே அவற்றொடு மனனே,
நேரிதின் உணர்ந்தோர் நெறிப்படுத் தினரே.

புல்லும் மரனும் ஓர் அறிவினவே,
பிறவும் உளவே அக்கிளைப் பிறப்பே;

நந்தும் முரளும் ஈர் அறிவினவே,
பிறவும் உளவே அக்கிளைப் பிறப்பே;

சிதலும் எறும்பும் மூவறி வினவே,
பிறவும் உளவே அக்கிளைப் பிறப்பே;

நண்டும் தும்பியும் நான்கு அறிவினவே,
பிறவும் உளவே அக்கிளைப் பிறப்பே;

மாவும் மாக்களும் ஐ அறிவினவே,
பிறவும் உளவே அக்கிளைப் பிறப்பே;

மக்கள் தாமே ஆறறி வுயிரே,
பிறவும் உளவே அக்கிளைப் பிறப்பே.

Going by Tolkappiyar's distinctions, can one equate the eating of a cow with the eating of a plant? Or can one justify the eating of a cow by a human being? The cow, compared to man, falls short of one sense. Nevertheless, it would have taken cows millions of years to reach the fifth stage in the evolutionary process. And here we are, swallowing all those millions of years along with our beef curry.

Suddenly, I veered off course and asked my friends eagerly, "What will happen to this world if people couldn't feel hunger anymore?"

No response was forthcoming. I declared that the world would be headed towards inevitable destruction.

What would you do, dear reader, if you couldn't feel hunger?

On the night of the barbecue, Prabhu had our undivided attention. With his silver tongue, he began to narrate select events from his life on the ship. At one point, he looked at me and asked, "Which women are the best seducers?" "Brazilian women," I said immediately. "True," he replied, and went on to tell us about the time he met this Brazilian girl who was on the barstool next to his. She was part of the ship's crew. They'd talked for a long time before parting. The next day, Prabhu got a call from the woman who demanded to know why he didn't call her. When a bemused Prabhu asked her what the matter was, she whined, "But yesterday you said, 'See you later!'"

The yackety-yak continued until we were all tired.

While my friends were as calm as still water in their deep and peaceful slumbers, I was tossing and turning like a man with restless legs syndrome. Who knew that thoughts of a goat could rob a man of his night's sleep?

CHAPTER SEVEN

1 – Becoming Music

Sex with Anjali produces two predominant rhythmic states. One is meditativeness; the other, music. Meditativeness is a bite-sized sampler of death. Sex isn't dissimilar. With music, the destruction of self happens a little differently. We lose our sense of self and become one with the other. Anjali is my "other."

Try listening to *Femme adieu* in a silent spot with your eyes closed. You'll hear the voice of God speak to you in Serge Lama's moving prayer.

Beethoven's *Bagatelles* – I've listened to them all and every time they play, I remember Anjali's beautiful neck and the countless kisses I've pressed to it.

Our post-coital routine involves Anjali resting her head on my chest as we listen to Dire Straits' *Sultans of Swing* or Carlos Santana's *While My Guitar Gently Weeps.*

There are many songs and compositions I love, but Anjali, when I enter her, we become music, our bodies harmonizing with each other.

2 – Still Naughty, Twenty Years post Forty

Even if you are about to rip this book in half down the spine and toss it into the gutter, this section, I'm sure, will be your money's worth.

In the Indian society, geezerhood begins at forty. The Indian man who is thirty-nine going on forty begins to believe he's at death's doorstep. He worries himself sick – so sick he gives himself cardiac problems by the time he's fifty. If he's not a heart patient, he's definitely got to be diabetic, and that might cost him an eye, a toe, or even a leg. The loss of a toe would alter a man's gait entirely. Then, he starts popping pills for blood pressure. The repercussions are so dreadful they're almost unspeakable. These nasty little pills boil down his penile vigor. This is something I've experienced. Men and women lothe to talk about it. (After all, what woman would open up about her husband's malfunctioning member?) Middle-age health and wellness as a social issue aside, I had my own two reasons for wanting to retrieve my lost youth. The first reason was, of course, Anjali. Sixty had to be in lockstep with thirty. Second, the society wished death of old age and sickness upon me. Cultural fundamentalists were baying for my blood like a pack of rabid dogs. In the face of such a ferocious attack, a man of my age would drop dead from cardiac failure, or he would throw himself off a cliff. Either outcome would spell victory for my enemies.

To steel myself, I had recourse to two things – ancient Indian herbs and God.

The first thing I did was search out *kaya kalpa* herbs. *Kaya* – the ageing body – was subjected to therapies that brought about rejuvenation – *kalpa*.

Thoothuvalai is one of the most potent *kalpa* herbs. A chutney made of sautéed *thoothuvalai* leaves, black pepper, a few *sambar* shallots and garlic is a great restorer of virility. The flowers of the *thoothuvalai,* when dried in shade, powdered and consumed with milk, can also have the same effect.For Indian remedies to work, you need to follow the routine for a *mandala,* which is forty-eight days.

Consuming nine leaves of black *tulsi* – the Indian basil –, three pods of country garlic, and a half-inch slice of ginger before going to bed reduced my cholesterol levels considerably.

For enhanced sexual pleasure, you can try any of the following concoctions depending on the availability of the ingredients. Try them, and you'll never have to shamefacedly ask the druggist for the blue pill again.

- A tea made with sun-dried hibiscus flowers

- Mahua flowers boiled in milk

- Poppy seeds soaked overnight

- Powdered cumin and wood apple bark sautéed in ghee

- A chutney containing *ponnanganni keerai*, Indian spinach, *agathi keerai*, a pinch of salt and a teaspoon of ghee

I've been taking these herbs *mandala* after *mandala*.

As a rule of thumb, the bitterer the herb, the stronger an aphrodisiac it is.

Chewing betel an hour before intercourse delays your orgasm. You can make a slave of any woman in bed with that kind of an advantage.

3 – Snakes in the Grass

In the Nagore shanty where I grew up, snakes outnumbered the people and ghosts outnumbered the snakes. Every other death there was attributed to ghost attacks or snakebites. The shamans helped with the evil spirits and the *siriya nangai* plant helped with the snakes.

A *siriya nangai* plant at the door is a No Entry sign that snakes heed. It's hardly possible to spy snakes in urban areas these days. Traditional snake-catchers now work as construction laborers. If, perchance, you encounter a snake-catcher, ask him about the primacy of this plant to his now extinct profession. The sight of the *siriya nangai* plant to a snake is like the sight of the switch to a badly behaved child. Without fuss or hiss, the snake would docilely crawl into the snake-catcher's wicker basket. In a fight unto death between a snake and a mongoose, the latter, when badly injured and on the verge of defeat, will scurry to the nearest *siriya nangai* bush, have a good roll and return to emerge victorious.

Of the three thousand odd species of snakes in the

world, India is home to about three hundred of which thirty could be found in Nagore alone. The posh chunk of the town in the east and the *agraharam* in the west were mostly free of snakes. The cremation and the lands skirting it were snake pits. If you found yourself in the crosshairs of the deadly King Cobra, the banded krait, the Russell's viper or the saw-scaled viper, you'd only have to pray they kill you quickly.

When snakes were sighted in our slums, they were not killed; they were worshipped. When a snake entered my house, my mother would speak to it like it were a naughty child. "Now, be a good boy and crawl back home, will you? Are you hungry? Alright, go now, and I'll be with you in a little bit with some eggs and milk." The snake would quietly slink away.

A King Cobra was not called a snake; people called it "the good one." While there were people who admired these noble reptiles, there were also morons who killed them. Mother would attribute the occasional death in the field to the human folly of treating the snake as an enemy. With snakes too, love begets love. My mother firmly believed that snakes attacked only the evil stock. I remember two incidents in our village that validated her belief.

There was a woman named Adilakshmi who was in the illicit liquor and ganja trade. Her husband was a drunkard and her lover, Purushottam, was the operator of a local chit-fund. The affair was common knowledge, but neither did a finger point at nor a tongue wag against it. When the lovers had a violent fallout over finances, tidings of their scrap reached every nook and cranny of the village. Things came to a head when the two enraged lovers tried to gut each other in full public view. The furious woman sought her alcoholic husband's help in her quest for revenge. "If you are indeed a man, bring me Purushottam's head," she said, throwing the gauntlet of manly honor at him. The husband duly discharged his wife's order and triumphantly placed Purushottam's hacked head at her feet. This act of husbandly obedience and "manliness" earned him a lifetime in prison. Adilakshmi helped herself to another moneyman. Shortly, she was found dead, bitten by a snake.

The next incident unfolded in the riverside village of Nalloor where a moneyed youth called Balakrishnan molested Poonkodi, a Dalit girl. A complaint was lodged in the Nagapattinam police station and the village *panchayat* was convened to adjudicate.

It was a time when upper-caste men were able to terrorize Dalit women openly and unrestrictedly. Their crimes against these women went unpunished as the police force too was packed with members of higher castes. However, the superintendent of police, during the time of this incident, was a respectable North Indian man with no stakes in the caste game. He brokered peace, and, keeping the young girl's honor in mind, had Balakrishnan marry her in the police station. The wedding made headlines in the local newspapers. After a week, Balakrishnan took Poonkodi to a farmhouse where a mob of men were waiting to have their turn with her. Poonkodi was held captive there for ten days and gang-raped.

"You complained about me to the police, didn't you? A hundred of us have fucked you over the past ten days. Take a good look at yourself and go name a hundred names to the police now, you whore!" Balakrishnan said.

Battered, bruised and half-dead, Poonkodi returned to her parents' home, told all, and thrust her hand into the snake pit. Shortly afterwards, her parents took their own lives. What happened thereafter has become the stuff of legends in Nalloor.

Incredibly, Balakrishnan was found dead of snakebite in the same farmhouse where the gang-rape took place. Rumor had it that he got his desserts while he was on top of a woman. The next day, his father dropped dead. One by one, all the men who had raped Poonkodi started getting bitten by snakes like it was the destiny of every upper-caste man to die of snakebite. Snakes attacked them in every place you could possibly think of – the cinema hall, the bus station, wardrobes and rivers. One fellow was bitten on his backside while taking a dump. The panic-stricken upper-caste folks began to flee the village. It is believed that the snakes avenged Poonkodi by taking down every single man who had raped her. I must have been fifteen years old then.

The story of Balakrishnan, Poonkodi and the avenging snakes is still told in the village like it happened the day before.

4 – Fear of the Enemy

A snake can send an army into a tizzy, but can go into a tizzy itself at the sight of *siriya nangai* and *vellerukku* plants. *Vellerukku* also has health benefits, but it should not be consumed without professional advice. The plant is like a knife which is useful in the hands of a surgeon and destructive in the hands of a killer. The nature of the plant depends on the nature of the soil in which it takes root. If the plant is found in a place where evil roams, the evil affects the plant as well.

I don't think I need to explain what evil forces are, but if you care for an example, I can damn well give you one. Many Indian politicians are evil forces. Each politician has a death grip on a town or a city, his little fiefdom, where his word is law. Neither collector nor commissioner can function without these puppet-masters. If they ruffle a politician's feathers, they are given a few blows in the face and a transfer to the middle of nowhere. In the worst possible scenario, he gets killed.

There used to be a Man Friday called Bhagavati Balu in

Madurai who was the right hand man of a self-proclaimed leader. He was involved in murders, kangaroo courts and kidnappings. By virtue of his Man Friday status, he had the authorities wrapped around his pinky and was hence immunized against the law.

Once, a government official raped a female employee who was his subordinate. Most women choose to keep their lips sealed when they are sexually assaulted, but this one went to the cops. Meanwhile, the rapist approached Bhagavati Balu – BB – to "take care of" the situation. BB asked one of his second fiddles to make a call to the D2 Police Station. The assistant commissioner there was a North Indian called Srivastava.

"It has come to my knowledge that a woman has come to your station to file a rape case," he said. "You are not to register that complaint. Do you hear me?"

"How do you expect me to do something like that? It's a *rape* case for God's sake and the victim herself has made the complaint. Besides, who are you to tell me how to do my job?" asked the assistant commissioner.

"If you don't do as you're told, I'll slap you with a transfer to some miserable shithole. Do you know who you're messing with? You're just a dog from up north. You dare to defy someone who has pledged his life in this game of local politics? Just do as I say if you know what's good for you. You know what happened to your predecessor, don't you? Or do you need a reminder? If you don't, just do the needful."

Srivastava remained silent once the call was over. He

knew full well what had happened to the assistant commissioner before him. BB had come to the station and slapped him in the presence of his colleagues. Nobody knows what transpired between them after the slap, but the AC and his family had committed suicide by poisoning. The investigation hit a dead end and the case went cold. Several such mysterious deaths had occurred in the town. Srivastava had a young wife and a daughter. After the threatening phone call, he laid low and eventually managed to get transferred back to the north.

BB used to be a vegetable vendor with a pushcart, but his fortunes started to climb once he entered politics. He was an eccentric devotee of Chottanikkara Bhagavati, featuring her name – sometimes more than once – in every sentence of his. He paid the goddess a monthly visit at Chottanikkara. Perhaps it was she who was responsible for his unbelievable rise to power in the political arena.

He was recently arrested on suspicion of terrorist links with a group of Pakistanis, and treason. During his arrest, he tried to win over the police officers.

"*Anney, anney,* you all know that I'm incapable of such things," he said, a note of pleading in his voice.

They were amazed to think that this was the man who had marched into the station like he owned it and slapped the erstwhile assistant commissioner.

As they pushed him into the cop car, he bellowed with fiery eyes, "Chottanikkara Bhagavati will strike down those who have falsely accused me!"

I once sighted BB at Chottanikkara. After going to Sabarimala, I decided to visit Chottanikkara on the advice of Rajan Panickar, an acquaintance and conduct a *Mahishasura Mardini puja* for twenty-one days. The pilgrim need only pay the temple priests who would conduct the *puja* on his behalf. So BB hands over seven hundred and fifteen rupees to the priest and leaves. Performing this *puja* destroys one's foes. I wonder how the goddess chooses who to destroy when the petitioner himself is a *shatru* – an enemy – to all the human beings he wishes destruction upon and more. I'd like to think that his arrest was her design.

CHAPTER EIGHT

Trivial Troubles in Lovers' Paradise

Love is a wondrous thing and an affliction at the same time. It becomes an affliction when the fear of losing it starts taking over your mind. When Anjali is with me, I feel like I am in possession of a priceless treasure. Her absence drives me to sickness and despair.

Morning, at 9, she would send me a *bonjour* over the phone. It would be 5.30 a.m. at Paris. Speaking of a French greeting, what I love most about Paris is the Seine. If you suffix an "ng" sound to the end of the word Seine (pronounced "sen"), you'll turn it into *sein*, the French word for breast. But we digress…

I grew so accustomed to Anjali's morning message that I became restless the day it didn't come even after 11. I rattled my brains and worried myself silly for two hours. I wondered, *Should I call her? Should I text her? But what if someone else picks up the phone or reads my message? Where the fuck was she and what the fuck was she doing that she couldn't send me my morning wish? Was she okay? Was she in trouble?* Questions buzzed in my brain like a billion bees.

My anger reached a fever pitch. I was only ten seconds shy of exploding when her *bonjour* arrived. It was 12. I slowly cooled down and regained my sanity, but only temporarily.

"Why the delay?" I queried.

It emerged that her cousin Venkat had come visiting and had been toying with her phone.

"He'll be gone tomorrow," Anjali assured me.

She'd mentioned this accursed cousin Venkat in the past. Her explanation roused my anger. So, all it took to delay her message was an insignificant relative? Motherfucker.

Anjali's circumstantially enforced state of silence scrambled my brains albeit it was just for a few hours. I could focus on nothing during those wretched hours. That period of non-correspondence was new and frightful.

Every time I fell in love, I managed to write a novel. I cannot claim with any certainty that it was a mere coincidence, or that a romance-creativity causality was at work. However, the completion of each novel was unerringly succeeded by the beginning of a real-life tragedy. Some fuck-up or the other over the course of writing the novel would put a full stop to my relationship. But this novel, I am pretty sure, will have a happy ending. Moreover, my romances of the yesteryears, when considered in retrospect, seem like amateur stage productions with the most farcical scripts when in comparison with my relationship with Anjali. What Anjali and I had was true love – an absolute union of mind and soul.

Hey there! It's Kokkarakko. Rremember me? Of course you do. I'm plotting my entry – an invasion of sorts – here. I hope I don't disturb the furniture too much. But I'll spice things up, trust me. Udhaya, who knows as much about compartmentalizing his writing as an ass knows about the scriptures, is a trainwreck waiting to happen. I've seen him tie himself up in knots when readers ask him about his writing style and his lifestyle at literary fests. Many of his readers find his high-pitched explanations radically convincing. But he can't hoodwink me. I shall return for comic relief at the same juncture in his next novel when he holds forth on true love and creativity. Let me beat a retreat for now.

I cursed myself for acting like an attention-seeking teenager and working myself into a frenzy over a delayed text message. Dickheadery of the highest order! And this was only a few hours. Imagine what would become of me if the non-communication lasted longer than a day. Some more self-loathing followed. Had I turned into a gutless idiot who overanalyzed and feared the future?

I had managed to delude myself that love, true love, produced unrivaled contentment. But love is just torment in a convincing pink and red disguise. This hard truth hit me like a hot blast from a furnace. I held back my urge to call Anjali. Why did I have to? (And that wasn't my ego speaking. I have none when it comes to her.) Oh, how I despised that Venkat – the devil who caused this kerfuffle!

Finally, at five in the evening, she texted me to ask if we

could talk. How stupid of her to be so formal by troubling to ask! But we'd mutually agreed to speak over the phone only after ensuring each other that the coast was clear through text messages. I didn't answer.

Rattled by the non-response, she called me. I didn't answer her calls either. She persisted. I thought I was punishing her, but holding myself back was nothing but an act of self-flagellation. I wondered how I'd feel if Anjali were me and if I were Anjali. I sent her a message enquiring who she was. I also added that I don't talk to strangers. She explained that an army of relatives had suddenly descended upon her house. "I've only just managed to get them out the door. They haven't even reached the bottom of the staircase yet, and here I am trying to call you." I couldn't keep the faux-fences of my anger standing any longer. She tore them down, but not completely.

"So, we can't talk if your cousin's around? Do I become insignificant when they're around you? From now on, you needn't trouble to send me a morning greeting. Even if you do, don't you ever expect me to reply." I continued to pick her apart for quite some time and finally fell asleep angry at myself for behaving the way I did.

The next morning, my anger had completely vanished and I was back to normal. In spite of all my resolve to never acknowledge her greetings, it was I who ended up sending her a *bonjour*. There was no reply. My anger possessed me again. Who the fuck was visiting her today? She would usually slink into the bathroom to chat with me when there were eyes and ears other than her own about her house.

When she finally did call me, it was 11. When I heard what she had to say, my anger turned on me. She'd been reading late into the night and had woken up just then. As it was a holiday, she'd switched off the alarm and gone to bed. I wept when I heard her explain in her mesmerizing voice. It was a public place and I'd attracted quite a few stares. I sent her a message that said: "I feel so ashamed. I don't even have a handkerchief." She replied: "I've never known a man who loved so much my entire life. Are we a dream or are we real?"

CHAPTER NINE

1 – Wicked Women

Nature is always conversing with us, but we never stop or hush ourselves to listen.

I met Rajan Panicker in Mettupalayam. The man rolled cowry shells. People have been telling fortunes with these shells for centuries. This form of astrology has a history of practice in many parts of the world. Ancient religion *Obi* of Africa practiced cowry shell astrology. In Kerala, an astrologer rolls 16 cowry shells twice and counts the number of shells facing upwards and downwards, calculates 256 formations and evaluate a man's life. It is beyond me to grasp how a man can roll a set of cowry shells, analyze the formations and tell you about your past, present and future like he's lived them with you. Now I reckon that *paramapadham*, played with cowry shells, is more than just a game. It is a signifier of the fortune of the players. One unlucky formation and the even the man who has climbed the highest ladder can be dragged down by a snake. This is life.

Perundevi rubbished all these beliefs and practices as mere superstition. Of course, a spiritual woman like her would be inclined to think so. I had recourse to God as I wanted to be safeguarded from the snares of my enemies, my fellow human beings. If astrology is a superstition, then God should be one too. But I am not interested in proving that argument. Anyone else in my wretched place with crazy lying chits and vulturous journalists would have died of a heart attack or thrown himself off the LIC Building. I explained to Perundevi that I was banking on these superstitious beliefs and practices to keep myself alive.

The forest in which Bhadrakali *amman* resides is situated at about 5 kilometres from Mettupalayam. The river Bhavani flows near her temple. Close at hand is the lush Nelli mountain. After the customary ablution in the Bhavani, I implored the mother goddess to spare me from the rabid jackals who were hounding me.

As a child, I'd come across Mettupalayam's Vanabhadra Kaliamman Temple in the stories of Mahabharata. Later, I encountered the poet Pukazhenthi's story of Aravalli and Suravalli.

Nellurupattinam in southern Andhra Pradesh was ruled by seven sisters, all unconquerable magicians and sorceresses. Aravalli, Suravalli and Veeravalli were the oldest sisters and anyone who opposed this all-powerful trio was either gored on the battlefield or cast into a dungeon.

Having vanquished several kings, the sisters set their sights on the Pandavas whom they wished to enslave. They sent a cockerel to them with a message that beckoned them to the land of the women. "You can all have a good life there. All you have to do is chant Aravalli's name and beg for food."

"I will not return until I have destroyed that woman!" Bhima declared.

Yudhishthira tried to deter Bhima by warning him of the dangers of miring himself in a web of dark magic, but Bhima was firmly resolved to go, unafraid of losing his life or his limbs.

It turned out that he was no match for the Aravalli sisters. They defeated him with the dark arts. It was not a straight fight at all.

He did not know who he was having a sex chat with. The newspapers seemed to know more than he did.

Bhima was imprisoned but he managed to escape and went running to Yudhishthira.

Aravalli wrote a letter to Bhima. It said, "You lost the war to three women and we even took you prisoner. You even escaped from prison like a thief. Do you think you're in any fit state to deserve a kingdom?"

On reading the letter, Yudhishthira was enraged. He summoned his brother Sahadeva who was an expert astrologer.

"I want to raze Nellurupattinam to the ground and destroy the Aravalli sisters completely," said the former. "I want you to read the stars and tell me what lies in store for us all."

Sahadeva said they'd be better off consulting their nephew, Allimuthu, on the subject of their futures. Allimuthu prayed to Vanabhadra Kali.

This incident unfolded in days of yore when Mettupalayam did not exist. It was to this very same goddess that I – a so-called postmodern writer – came running, seeking succor and boons. And what was the boon, you ask? To defeat a couple of twenty-first century hardcore feminist sisters who made a living hell out of my life with their threats. I do not know whether the boon will be granted or not. We shall know my plight – and that of the feminazis – by the time I finish this novel.

I – sorry – Allimuthu accepted the sacred ash and sword that Vanabhadra Kali gave him and made his way to the Aravalli sisters' palace, successfully countering the dark magic and sorcery they'd used to thwart him. He was only too clever for all the tests the sisters put him through.

What tests? They stole his password and cooked up a steamy sex chat that was one part real and nine parts bullshit. As Allimuthu fancied women, they lured him again and again and again and again and again into sex chatrooms and phone sex. These were the tests they'd created to destroy him.

As we already know, I am a fool. Unlike Allimuthu, I didn't go to Vanabhadra Kali before the war began; I went to her only when I'd almost lost everything.

It came to me as a rude shock when some of my readers who held my writings in acclaim ventured to ask me whether "it" was true. Whether *what* was true? There was a man and there was a woman, both of whom started sexting each other. I told you that much, so why come around asking if it's true?

The Aravalli sisters ask pardon from Allimuthu. They also promise him the hand of one of their daughters, Palvarisai.

Allimuthu was in no hurry to accept the offer.

"You are all sorceresses," he said. "The apple can't have fallen far from the tree."

"Our daughter was raised in a dungeon," they replied. "She is yet to set eyes on a man."

On his way back to the kingdom with Palvarisai, Allimuthu misplaced Vanabhadra Kali's sacred ash. He is overcome by thirst during the journey and he faints. Palvarisai immediately squeezed a lemon and fed the juice to Allimuthu. The juice from the lemon, given to her by her mother, kills Allimuthu instead of reviving him. Palvarisai knew nothing of the poisoned lemon.

When news of Allimuthu's death reached the Pandavas, they declared war with the Aravalli sisters.

In the meanwhile, a saddened Arjuna went all the way up to heaven and retrieved Allimuthu's soul from Indra. He kept it in a box, returned with it to earth, and restored it to Allimuthu's body. Allimuthu was back from the dead.

The Pandavas fiercely attacked Aravallipattinam which later became known as Nellurupattinam. They emerged victorious as they'd sought Vanabhadra Kali's blessings before the war. They imprisoned six of the Aravalli sisters. The seventh escaped to Kerala where she became Kambalathu Bhagavati.

2 – Warning: Thou Shalt *Not* Masturbate on a Pilgrimage

One fine day, on a whim, I decided to make a pilgrimage to the Ayyappa temple in Sabarimala, and began to practice the rituals and observe the austerities the pilgrimage prescribes. My friends openly howled and laughed at my decision. "I know of all your antics, but this one takes the cake!" Kokkarakko opined. "This is your biggest sham yet!"

I've often toyed with the idea of going on a pilgrimage to the shrine of the bachelor god Ayyappa in the past, but the thought of complete abstinence from sensory pleasures for forty-eight whole days in preparation for the trek of faith deterred me. I was convinced I lacked the will to do it. Moreover, I have accustomed myself to comfort. I can't walk barefoot at home for a day, let alone going about shoeless for seven weeks. Perhaps not being able to afford passable footwear till I was eighteen had something to do with it. Going barefooted was only one of the austerities to Ayyappa the devotees had to observe. That aside, they had to perform *puja* twice a day after a cold-water bath – one before dawn and one after sunset. I couldn't even begin to contemplate this enforced but voluntary forty-eight-day celibacy. I could probably survive without sex, but without masturbation? The hell I couldn't!

When Kokkarakko told me about the calamitous aftermath of breaking the rules, I was panic-stricken. Kokkarakko had been making the pilgrimage for four consecutive years. In the fifth year, he was overcome by an urge to shag himself. He walked up the mountain, praying to Ayyappa for forgiveness. He took the forty-eight mile route through the forest. Born into a Vaishnavite family, Kokkarakko was blessed with a well-chiseled physique and was cast-iron. A trek he'd completed with consummate ease on four occasions was not even close to good in the fifth year. No matter how carefully he climbed, he slipped and fell several times, sustaining bloody injuries. When he finally managed to reach the sanctum sanctorum in one piece, prepared for the highest point of his penance – the *darshan* of Lord Ayyappa – one of the Namboodri priests was shielding his view of the idol. His pleas to the priest to move aside were in vain as his shouts did not travel in the din. With thousands of devotees in waiting, the *darshan* time was barely a few seconds. Kokkarakko's time was up. He was tossed out by the wildly advancing throng.

He spent the night sleeping on the temple floor and recounting his misfortune to a security guard who was stationed there. What came over the guard we do not know, but he whisked Kokkarakko into the sanctum sanctorum for his *darshan*.

After his bitter experience the fifth time around, Kokkarakko decided to never undertake the pilgrimage again.

"People like you and I can never stay true to the vows prescribed by Ayyappa. Forget it, buddy," he said, smirking. It was difficult not to agree with him, but I felt that things had sufficiently fallen into place then to make the pilgrimage. After I'd met Anjali, I had eyes for no other woman. "Even Anjali will never believe this," my friends taunted. When I asked Anjali to introduce me to one of her female friends who was a Lara Fabian fan, she jabbed my forehead with her index finger like it was the mouth of a pistol and said, "I'm fucking *warning* you." However hard I tried, I just could *not* make her understand (or maybe she just pretends not to understand) that I would have no one but her.

She once accompanied me to a news conference in Chennai. Usually, when I'm in her company, she oozes sexy passion and her body does all the talking. Fortunately, she was able to put all her sexiness and lust on a leash at the media event. I had to compliment her on her supreme acting skills and her self-control.

"You're in the news – again. Why should I create a new scandal? Besides, most of the journalists in attendance were women. If I didn't keep a poker face, they could have told I was undressing you and fucking you in my head. We wouldn't want their imaginations running wild, so there wasn't so much as a twinkle of the eye or the twitch of a lip when I looked at you. It was tough, I'll admit, but not impossible," she said.

For the first time in my life, I didn't feel like an infidel. In the Indian context, fidelity is synonymous with monogamy. An *ekapatnivrata* is a man who is committed under oath to one woman alone. A man's fidelity was not more important than a woman's chastity. Sangam literature is replete with paeans to chastity, describing the conduct of a chaste woman in these terms: when the man of the house returns from the abode of his mistress upon hearing that his wife has given birth, the chaste wife of impeccable upbringing lets on no displeasure whatsoever and welcomes her lord and master with the pleasantest demeanor.

I detest the word *vrata* as it suggests that formal and external oaths and vows tie a man and a woman to each other. In my case, nothing external tied me to Anjali; it was all a matter of the union of minds, hearts and souls.

3 – Affairs: Both Real and Imaginary

My friend Vettukkili has a wife and three girlfriends and is always on the lookout for more. Most of his time and energy is spent on expanding his harem. I envied him once. He never found the woman who would end his quest. He prowls around like an eternally hungry beast. I can only pity him now. Why, even Kokkarakko sails in the same boat as Vettukkili! By Kokkarakko's own admission, his wife gives him no reason to complain. Yet, he has four lovers – Manju, Andrea, Abinaya and Ranjani – all of whom he met through Facebook.

Manju, 21, is a college student. She was going steady with her boyfriend whom she had plans to marry. The boyfriend was a thorn in her flesh, an overtly possessive chap who wanted to micromanage Manju's life. He wanted to control who she met, what she ate, the girth of her smile when she greeted other men, how high the waistband of her jeans should be – stuff like that. They hadn't even kissed once in their two-year relationship.

Kokkarakko had known her for three months.

"Screwed her yet?" I queried.

"Willy-nilly."

"What's that supposed to mean?"

This requires some explanation. In Tamil Nadu, there are no safe houses where consenting adults can have sex. Even five-star hotel rooms are not free from police raids. But Kokkarakko is a smart bastard who can thread an elephant through a needle.

There's a government-run tourist resort near Mahabalipuram. Government-owned hotels offer many advantages. One, not many people know they exist; two, the police would never enter a state-run establishment. This resort, located on the seafront and complete with a swimming pool, was frequented by bureaucrats who were keen on cutting shady deals over drinks. Kokkarakko zeroed in on it.

Expressing a desire so early in the piece, to get into her churidar, carries the risk of a girl as young as Manju wanting to eject out of the conversation. Subtlety and patience are vital in such an operation. 'The city is too hot and noisy. Let's head to a tranquil spot. I know of one by the sea,' suggested Kokkarako masking malice. Kokkarakko booked a room at the resort, picked up the girl and drove there. They spent time talking in a leaf-carpeted corner of the beach. Manju, like most women, wanted to get her feet wet. She stood on the shore and enjoyed the feel of the sun-warmed waves lapping at her ankles. When all the seaside fun was over and her *salwar-kameez* had been soaked into transparency, under the pretext of having a fresh water wash, Kokkarakko ushered her into the pre-booked room. There were two doors to the suite, one over looking the pool and other the sea. He kept both open while Manju was in the washroom. The conversation continued. After a while Manju locked both the doors because the cool air of the air conditioner was going waste.

Kokkarakko showed me a picture of Manju. Describing my friend's girlfriend here would be inappropriate and detrimental for a multitude of reasons which I do not care to enumerate. Suffice it to say that she was a dusky beauty like the women in the great epics.

"Did you fuck her?" I asked.

"No, no, I didn't," he said. "She'd have a poor opinion of me if I did."

"You brainless asshole."

Do you know why these women refuse to have sex before marriage? It is because he would think that she was chaste and that he had chosen the right girl. Otherwise, the marriage might not even take place. And men's dicks start growing moralizing consciences during periods of inevitable marital fiction. "Weren't you the one who had no compunctions about bedding a man before marriage?" the husband retorts. How well he occupies that dubious piece of real estate called the moral high ground!

Now coming back to Kokkarakko, while he never did manage to unhook Manju's bra or slide down her panties, he did flaunt his tonsil hockey and sleight of hand skills. But Manju was still unspoiled. The slightest touch goose-pimpled her skin and had her gasping. "Oh my sweet fucking goodness," was Kokkarakko's response to her reaction.

The Manju-Kokkarakko love affair eventually ripened to the point that Manju was ready to dump her boyfriend. She had fallen for Kokkarakko, and she had fallen hard. She started pestering him to marry her. That, according to Kokkarakko, was one of the reasons why he was evading sex with her.

One day, Kokkarakko showed me a text message from Manju. It read: "*Poda MP!*" So Manju had graduated to overt smut-speak. She was calling her lover *mutta pundai* - a stupid cunt. I was gobsmacked.

"You've turned me into a dirty little bitch," she told him. "I surprised myself when I mouthed and typed the word 'MP.'"

"Hah, but you've only used the word in abbreviation and that too in a text message. Let's hear you say it out loud," Kokkarakko teased. Manju couldn't say it.

"Us men worship *pundai* and never pass up the opportunity to use the word every chance we get," Kokkarakko informed her. "*Pundai*, for us, conveys every human emotion."

A person who talks meaninglessly is a *pechchu pundai* (a blabbering cunt). Is someone staring at us? *Vedikkai pundaya, poda...*(watching us, cunt, get lost). A fellow who shows attitude is a *kozhuppu pundai*(arrogant cunt). Someone from a bank calls and tells you to take a loan, you say, '*oru thevai pundaiyum illa, un velai pundaiya parthuttu podi* '(don't bother cunt, mind your own business). And if some other bank fellow calls up to remind you about late payments, *enakku vantha koduma pundaiya paaru...* (what a fucking cunt I'm). Someone goes on talking about America's greatness, *periya athisaya pundai* (What cunt greatness?)

Once I was supposed to meet Udhaya at six p.m. but when I reached the appointed place, it was eight. He asked me angrily, 'Is this six p.m.?' 'Bloody time *pundai... poda...* you are enjoying yourself here... but I had to make my way here in Madras traffic... Take that brandy *pundai,* let's drink,' I said. Kumar and Sekar were also supposed to join us that day but they didn't turn up. Then I said, 'That Kumar *pundai* and Sekar *pundai* didn't come...' Like this, we use the word *pundai* to refer to people too. The word is used to express class distinctions as well, like,'he is a bloody rich *pundai* '. If the communists had used this technique, they wouldn't have failed internationally. We even refer to literature as *ilakkiya pundai (literature cunt)*. There is a noble Tamil writer who thinks it is a sin to drink and lust after other men's wives. So I call him 'virtuous *pundai*'.

One of Udhaya's readers wrote something he called a novel, made a present of it to Udhaya and asked him to write the foreword. He frankly told him, "You've written a novel *pundai*. Take your *pundai* rag and get out of my sight, *mutta pundai*." There are some who reckon that "novel *pundai*" is the highest *pundai*-expression.

When we worship *pundai*, why are the very creatures

with *pundai* so ashamed of that word? God shouldn't have given all you females genitals if the whole lot of you are so repelled by the sound of *pundai.*

"Alright Kokkarakko. I'm so sorry to have to push you out of the spotlight for few minutes. I'm just curious. When this novel is translated into English, how will the translator translate *pundai?* Will she leave *pundai* as it is? Will that be alright?"

Kokkarakko said, "Oh Udhaya! What a justice-seeking *pundai* you are! Retain *pundai* so that the English-speaking *pundais* will have a chance to enrich their vocabulary. What is the *pundai* problem in it?"

When a woman falls in love, she gives in to her lover's wishes and changes in so many ways, but her lover doesn't change at all. He just pretends to. Kokkarakko later said that women don't affect men the way men affect women.

Andrea was twenty-nine years of age. She was as fair as day and her face reddened at the slightest touch. Upper middle class. Married with a five-year-old child. Her husband, another Suresh, approaches her only once in three months. He has no energy to pump or thrust as he works all day and returns home at midnight. When there's a holiday, he and his laptop are inseparable.

"He might as well be married to his laptop," she told Kokkarakko. "Are all these IT guys the same? I don't even remember the last time he touched me."

"Have you screwed her, Kokkarakko?"

"Well, it's complicated because, you see, she feels she's

doing something wrong. She says that her obsession with me is hindering her from focusing on her daughter. She wants to go see a shrink. I told her I'd counsel her myself."

Once, Kokkarakko and I were sharing a room when we'd gone on a trip. I overheard his phone conversation with Andrea. It surprised me to hear him talk to her the same way I talked to Anjali.

Kokkarakko: Can I kiss your cunt?

Andrea: [moans]

Kokkarakko: Lift it.

Andrea: Oh, come on! I can't do that. Stop it!

Kokkarakko: Why? Is your cunt temporarily unavailable? How can I kiss it unless you lift it?

The dialogue continued in this vein for a good thirty minutes. Since Kokkarakko had a cheap Chinese phone, I could hear both sides of the conversation loud and clear.

"At last!" he sighed after the call was over. Then he said, "Udhaya, how do you manage to talk to Anjali with such intense passion? When she doesn't call you, you call her. I simply can't fathom how you do it. The biggest problem with women is that they expect you to keep making small talk with them for hours. I've never known any woman to be an exception to that."

Abinaya, twenty-seven, fiery rebel and activist infused with all the traits of a revolutionary, non-believer in marriage, does not consider sex a taboo act or subject, takes off all of a sudden to carry out extensive research on *adivasis* and write newspaper articles about them, travels all the way to Delhi to protest against the government, rides pillion with Kokkarakko on his motorbike, aware that Kokkarakko has multiple girlfriends, doesn't give a shit.

Ranjani, twenty-four, software engineer with film-star looks. Love has freshly blossomed between her and Kokkarakko and it is very interesting to think of how it came about. They used to chat and slowly got around to meeting for coffee, and then one day, she called him in a very agitated state, saying that an auto driver had squeezed her butt as she was walking down the road. She has noted the number of his vehicle and wanted him punished.

It is common knowledge that the public hates and fears cops more than it hates and fears thieves. If you lodge a complaint with the police, they will harass you and call you at brothel hours and you will *never* go to them again – ever! However, Kokkarakko thinks that the problem lies with the public who don't know how to approach these exemplary law-upholding men who have a tiresome eighteen-hour workday.

Kokkarakko instructed her in talking to the cops. The most important thing, he said, was to use a decent mix of both Tamil and English. On entering the station, she was to wish the cops respectfully (this would create a good first impression as no one bothered to do this) and say that someone – anyone, even her wastrel uncle – had sent her (the cops always approved of women who were sent by someone). Then, she was to say, "I need your help, sir, but you look busy. You must have a tight schedule. I can come tomorrow." This, according to Kokkarakko, was all it took to become the honeybunch in the police station.

After one visit from Ranjani, the auto-driver was cooling his heels in prison and she was more in love with Kokkarakko than she had ever been. This sounds very much like the plot of every Tamil movie. But Kokkarakko added, "The poor girl doesn't know that within a month, I'll squeeze her butt harder than the auto-driver did."

When I told Anjali all about Kokkarakko's love-life, she said, "Why does he want to stop at just four when he can have a whole harem of forty? He is such a desirable, appealing man. It's no wonder women are queuing up for him. Tell him he has my blessings."

"Sure, and I'll just look at his harem and sigh."

"I swear I'll fucking *kill* you! Come *straight* to Paris or move here for good!"

"Oh darling! This is what I love most about you – how fucking possessive you are of me."

(I first drafted this novel in 2011. I am rewriting it now, three years later. It looks like Anjali's blessings are really working. Kokkarakko now has fifteen lovers and fifteen girlfriends!)

A little more than a decade separates the present from the events I am about to narrate.

I speak of a time when my friends Gopalakrishnan, Krishna and I made monthly jaunts to Salem where Krishna had a farmhouse.

Now, in order for you to appreciate what is to follow, I must acquaint you with Gopalakrishnan, the friend who reminds me of Kokkarakko. He was the kind of man who did not necessarily fall short in terms of physical desirability. He was well-proportioned, standing tall at six feet, and was the possessor of a smile that hardly ever ceased to be. He was a holder of government office by profession and a hockey player by passion – fortes that caused his desirability to take on new dimensions.

He was slow to anger – in fact, if my memory serves me right, I do not recall the man ever being angry. However, flaws are just. They spare no one. Gopalakrishnan comes from the mold of a Jane Austen character – a much-hated one, the autocratic Lady Catherine de Bourgh. And where there is a high-and-mighty De Bourgh, there ought to be a servile Mr. Collins, and what a perfect Mr. Collins Gopalakrishnan found in Krishna!

Friends contented themselves with frowning upon the master-slave dialect, while one of Krishna's girlfriends contented herself with a verbal lashing: "Those two, so questionably attached at the hip! Has Gopalakrishnan twisted a nerve in Krishna's brain or made jelly of the whole thing? Whenever I try to make an arrangement with Krishna, he is engaged with Gopalakrishnan. Urgent affairs, he tells me."

Verbal lashings, however, struck Gopalakrishnan with the force of a domestic cat's tail.

It was during one of our customary morning walks on the Marina Beach that I tried to diplomatically cut him to size. In the end, I had earned writers a low blow delivered in the guise of a joke. Not quite what I was hoping to achieve.

I will be leaving you with only a half-portrait of Gopalakrishnan if I do not address his libertine lifestyle.

His preferences in terms of women were quite peculiar – they were mostly prostitutes whom he euphemized as "lovers." He nosedived into numerous risqué relationships, but deftly sidestepped commitment in all its forms.

One day, I ventured to ask, "Say, how many 'girlfriends' do you have?"

The word had the effect of sour cream in his mouth.

He said, "They are merely 'lovers,' Udhaya. Flings."

I played along.

"If you say so. How many 'lovers' have you had, then?"

Gopalakrishnan's face was at its contemplative best.

At long last he answered, "A hundred or thereabouts."

I allowed myself some amusement at the thought of Gopalakrishnan trying to arrive at a convincing number.

It so happened that our Casanova one day launched into the details of his encounter with a village prostitute in his home state of Andhra Pradesh.

"A friend and I were repairing to a lodge when we saw a most mesmerizing woman approach, fire in her eyes and the wind in her hair. She was possessed with something divine, ethereal, something that almost brought me to my knees. And then, with the gesture of a hand, she beckoned us. My pansy-friend stayed put, sheepishly refusing to approach.

"Her voice effused all the warmth and familiarity of a long lost childhood playmate with whom you were once accustomed to sharing table and bed with when she told me, 'I have a room available. Why do you want to pay here?'

"We ended up boarding at her place for three days. She performed equally well in the kitchen and in the bedroom. Our appetites for food and lovemaking were greatly satisfied."

Gopalakrishnan described his sexual adventures in Andhra Pradesh with the mien of a soldier describing his war adventures in Afghanistan.

"There was another woman in Chennai," he recommenced, and I wasn't surprised. Truly, I wouldn't have been if he'd told me he'd spilled his seed in a backroom in each of the twenty-eight states. "It was her time of the month when I went. So I just slept in her bed the whole night and in the morning she refused to take money from me. However, I thrust the money in her hand when she asked for my phone number. I gave and I dismissed it from my mind."

"Two weeks thence, she touched base. When I went to see her, she mentioned that she'd never had a 'client' treat her as well as I did. She went red in the face when it occurred to her that she might have given offense and was profound in her apologies.

"Then she bashfully told me that it was her birthday.

"I bought her a saree and treated her to dinner, after which I dropped her home. I didn't spend the night with her."

"How come?" I asked, knowing full well that his ego was wounded by the girl who called him a 'client,' not a dashing Romeo, not her soulmate – a 'client,' a man with a weakness for prostitutes.

"I was in no mood for sex," he said quite simply like he was stating a universal fact. "Just so you know, she's been my 'lover' for five years now. She's smitten with me."

Truth be told, the man had the pride of a peacock and the brain of a bathroom flea.

At nine the next morning, we – now a group of four, courtesy of Aditya's company – left for Coimbatore in Krishna's Cielo which Gopalakrishnan was driving. I was accorded the honor of riding shotgun.

Not long after we hit the road, Gopalakrishnan's phone started ringing. He shot a glance at the number and tossed the phone to me.

"Hello?" I said testily.

I was greeted by a cloying female voice.

"Is Gopalakrishnan around?" she asked.

I shot him a look and he shook his head in the negative. In that moment, he reminded me of a wet dog shaking itself dry.

"When will he return?" she asked.

"I wouldn't know."

"Where has he gone?"

"He never told me."

"And who might you be?"

"The manservant."

"Manservant?"

"Yes, I work at his house. I cook and clean his bedroom."

The woman hung up. My witty closing statement earned me a clap on the shoulder from Krishna and a round of applause from Aditya.

Gopalakrishnan's phone rang again at half-past-nine. He urged me to answer in his stead once more.

I exchanged hellos with the same woman who had called earlier.

"Is Gopalakrishanan back yet?"

"I wish he was for your sake, but unfortunately, he has urgent affairs to tend to."

The line went dead.

The woman was maniacal. She placed calls incessantly.

As for me, I had to play the part of secretary cum manservant cum unhelpful telephone operator.

She tried new numbers and new voices and when her patience was worn thin, around the time of the thirtieth call, she resorted to expletives.

Pangs of jealously gnawed at us. The ardor in that

woman's voice haunted me. She *was* smitten with Gopalakrishnan after all.

Gopalakrishnan was once more behind the wheel for the following drive when history decided to repeat itself.

The phone announced the woman's call, and I realized that Gopalakrishnan did not plan to relieve me of my middleman duty.

I greeted her with thirteen syllables instead of the customary, clichéd two: "Please don't hang up with expletives like the other day."

She wasted no time in informing me of the intelligence she'd gathered.

"You're not the servant. Gopi told me who you are."

"Gopi?"

"Go-pa-la-krish-nan," she said, stretching every vowel out for a good two seconds. "Where is he?"

"Still out of town."

"Your game's up trickster. I know you're within kissing distance of each other. You have a way with words. You're both smooth operators, you know?"

"Lady, put the weapons down. Someone with a voice as beautiful as yours shouldn't be spitting poison darts like grape seeds."

"For the last time, where is Gopi?"

Gopalakrishnan, her Gopi, bid me come closer. I did.

"Tell her you love her," he whispered into my ear.

I replied that I already had a bad reputation and was not willing to compromise it further.

"What does he say?"

"Lady, I've lost count of how many times I've told you. He's not here."

There was venom and resignation in her voice when she spoke next.

"You should be ashamed of yourself, whoever you are. I hope life screws you over."

"There, there! Why are you so generous with curses, you beauty?"

"Oh, who told you I'm beautiful? Gopi?"

"Nope."

"Who then?"

"Your voice suggests you have a beautiful face, you know?"

"Oh, so you fancy my sick voice? I have a cold."

"You want to know a good remedy for a cold?"

"What is it?"

"Brandy!"

"Brandy? There's *no* way in hell I'm drinking brandy."

"Why?"

"I don't like brandy, simple."

"How about beer and wine?"

"Of course not! I don't even drink sherbet."

"So you don't drink brandy, whiskey and wine even with Gopalakrishnan?"

"*Chi!* He drinks that bilge but I don't even *touch* it."

"How can you hate something you haven't tasted?"

"I don't know, but I won't drink. I'll get into big trouble at home."

"Home?"

"Yes, home. Do you think I live in the jungle?"

"No, I mean… Who are you afraid of at home? Your husband?"

"*Husband?* You think I'm an old crone?"

"Yes – no wait! I mean no."

"You are just *too* much!"

"Why?"

"Never mind why. Forget it."

"Well, okay then."

"You're quick to surrender."

"That's because everything I say ruffles your feathers. If I tease you, you can't handle it. If I compliment you, you can't handle it either."

"Okay, but do I sound like an old crone to you?"

"No, you sound like a very sweet little teenage girl."

"I'm not a teenager anymore, not since last month. I'm twenty, okay? I'm doing my masters."

"Is that so?"

"What, you don't believe me?"

"No, but if you're a twenty-year-old student, how come you're involved with Gopi?"

"I don't understand what you're getting at."

"Won't your family be furious?"

"Do you think I'm stupid to tell them when I'm going to Neelankarai with him?"

"Oh, so you go there with him?"

"Yes I do."

"Long journey, isn't it?"

"Well, I begin from home at eight in the morning and return in the evening. It's just like a college day. Now, for the last time: are you going to hand over the phone to Gopi or not?"

"Which part of 'Gopi is not here' do you not understand?"

"Oh, to hell with you!"

"Hey, hey, hey! You don't need to curse me!"

"Alright, have a good life then."

There phone never rang again.

When Gopalakrishnan got his head back into the game, he realized that he'd reached Karukkurichi instead of Pudukudi. Pudukudi is a place that is perched in between Kutralam and Karukkurichi. "Pudukudi," meaning "new settlement" was a misnomer as the 250-acre expanse did have historical mileage. Krishna's estate was situated there, bordered by the Western Ghats and speckled with five-thousand odd infirm coconut trees.

A second car arrived moments later. The man who emerged from the steel and glass, Pichappa, was going to have a fortune fall into his lap.

"We used to swim and play in the lake," Krishna reminisced and Pichappa listened. "There was water in it then." His voice was heavy with sadness when he said, "My grandfather bought this land, but it's been uncared for. In a year, with maintenance, this tract could yield ten lakhs, but in Chennai, I can make the same amount in a mere ten days."

Pichappa and Krishna surveyed the land before them.

"The entire tract is yours for fifty lakhs," Krishna said, and a royal realm was sold for chickenfeed. He returned to his friends. "Once upon a time, this place teemed with snakes by the thousands, but now, you won't find even one."

"Why?" I asked.

Krishna extended his hand. I looked in the indicated direction and behold! There was a pride of about a hundred peacocks.

The males strutted about with their lofty gait, tails fanned out, while the peahens, like silly little girls seduced by the rich sight, pursued them.

Krishna's smile was tinged with sarcasm. He had seen this before.

Boys of five usually play with trucks and roll in sand-pits. I was an anomalous child. I was different. When *I* was five, I began to masturbate regularly. I didn't know that there was a word for rubbing your genitals. "It was only when I entered college that I realized it was a *bad* word, that it was not something you speak of in polite society," I told Anjali.

"It was the same with me," Anjali said. "Until I went to college, I never had any idea about self-pleasure. I thought it had something to do with experiencing God. Do you know when I finally figured out what masturbation was all about? The boys had nicknamed our institution 'Brinjal College.' I didn't get what brinjals had to do with anything. Then, one of my friends told me that a girl in the college hostel had tried to pleasure herself using a brinjal that got stuck inside her love-tunnel when the stalk broke. She needed to go to a doctor to get the thing out."

"Every women's college has its own share of dirty stories, sweetheart," I told her. "During my freshman year in EVR Periyar College in Trichy, I'd heard that one of the girls masturbated with a test tube that broke inside her vagina and tore it. Everyone with a dick in Trichy came to know this story. But for all you know, the story was probably cooked up by some depraved youth who'd been binge-reading porn.

"There is no dearth of stories, Anjali. After failing my pre-university tests, I wandered aimlessly like a nomad for two whole years, doing re-sits in April and October for the exams I'd flunked. I'd flunked five exams – Tamil, English, Math, Physics and Chemistry. I passed Tamil that October. The next year, I got through English in April and the dreaded trio of Math, Physics and Chemistry in October.

"It was during my wandering years that I got initiated into drinking, whoring and all else. But hold your imagination right there! The prohibition law was in effect in Tamil Nadu then, but once you crossed Vettar and there is Vanjur from where Pondicherry Union started. In Vanjur, toddy, arrack and wine shops operated and flourished without the slightest hitch and in large numbers. There was this chap called Robert from Vanjur. He was a huge volleyball player who made me look like a pygmy, but he was harmless. Robert's father was a wealthy man and the owner of a wine shop. He had built his son a cottage in Vanjur. It was in this cottage that Siva and I had downed our maiden bottles of beer. Robert brought two bottles – one for himself and the other for Siva and me to share as it was our first time. He promised to buy us another bottle if we liked it. I despised it, so Robert and Siva finished the bottle between themselves. Another time, Robert asked us if we would like to try opium. It was the color of tar. You had to take a cherry-sized amount, press it against the roof of your mouth and wait for it to dissolve, drinking tea all the while. Even a bitter gourd was mild when compared to this! I was introduced to *nilavembu kashayam* much later in life, but opium was by far the bitterest drug I had ever done. For three whole days, I lay in Robert's cottage, lost to the world. After that incident, I abandoned my experiments with intoxicants. It was only in Delhi that I got reacquainted with liquor, but I steered clear of opium and LSD. I did smoke ganja for a few days, but that toxic trip did not agree with me. At times, I would feel like I'd lost an arm, and if I tried to walk, I felt like I was walking on air. One day, a fellow smoker told me, 'It's nice to eat a little sugar after smoking ganja.' Some of the sugar fell to the floor when I took a pinch. Each crystal seemed to shine like a polished diamond. Ganja really magnifies and exaggerates your sensory perceptions. A person who smokes it timidly screams in terror and whoever smokes it confidently starts guffawing like a madman. A sad smoker will wail like an infant and a happy one will lapse into a profound graveyard silence. It's like being demonically possessed. That's why I stopped using."

I had a friend called Ganesh who told me the most interesting stories when he returned home from Jamal Mohammed College. All his stories were picaresque love and lust stories. All of his stories involved Stella, a seventeen year old Anglo-Indian girl who wore skirts.

(Just so you know, women in the shanties of Tamil Nadu don't bother to wear panties. When we first saw underclothes on display in shops, Siva informed me that only hookers wore them. Village women don't wear bras either. I asked a village man why this was the state of affairs and he told me that any man would ask a woman who wanted to wear a bra who she wanted to impress with her figure. If this was their take on bras, I wonder what they would have to say for panties. This happened in 2014, but Stella's story belongs to the '70s.)

This is what Ganesh told me.

"Stella was fair like a daisy. Her thighs were so smooth that your hand would just slip on them."

"Where? Up? Down?"

"Every which way, Udhaya. They'd go to that sweet spot between her thighs too. There was no love, it was all sex. She was a little nymphomaniac."

"At seventeen?"

"Age is of no import in such matters. She had no father and lived with her mother who had the hots for me. Mother and daughter looked like sisters. The mother often went out of town, and when she did, I would bolt to her house. She would receive me stark naked at the door and embrace and kiss me. For her, doing it in the 69 position was like playing kitchen. We took long baths together in the tub and even made love in it. One day, she wanted me to piss all over her face…"

"What the *fuck* are you even on about?"

"There's nothing I consider taboo in sex. There was only one problem. She was not satisfied with me alone and wanted at least two other men to have sex with."

One day, when Siva and I went to meet Ganesh in Trichy, we checked ourselves into a lodge in Palakkarai before heading to his hostel. He wasn't too pleased to see us. When we enquired about Stella, he brushed us off.

"Stella is not the same person she used to be," he complained. "She's acting all strange and she barely speaks ten words to me."

"But you were telling me that everything was going great last week!" I said. "Sixty-nine and doggy-style and all…"

The cat was out of the bag when Ganesh's hostel mates

told us that Stella was only a figment of Ganesh's overactive imagination. He'd tried to feed them all his Stella-stories but none of them bought his crap. One day, Ganesh said he needed a room urgently to have sex with Stella as her pussy was on fire.

"Why all these days it happened only at her house. Now what?"

"Stella's mother isn't moving anywhere and we need a room urgently."

A group of students who had rented a house let him have it for a few hours. Among the students in that particular group was a boy like Kokkarakko. While the rest of his housemates went for a matinee show, this fellow hid on the terrace of a shop in front of the house. From two to six, Ganesh was alone in the house, jacking off to Sarojadevi romances. No Stella came to see him and the poor spy baked in the sun like a brick for four hours. When the housemates returned, Ganesh started entertaining them with unbelievable stories about his session with Stella that afternoon, but the spy chimed in with the truth and poor shamefaced Ganesh had to face their wrath for taking them for a ride.

We were *so* disappointed when we realized that Ganesh had lied and that Stella had never existed. We'd traveled all the way from Nagore to Trichy just to meet an imaginary person. Siva recommended we go to Thanjavur since the *devadasis* had lived there during the Maratha period. Although the *pottukattu* ceremony had been abolished in 1947, they still lived there, clinging to the remnants of their past. The next problem was how to identify a *devadasi's* house. Well, you just needed a *rickshawala*. Let's go!

We got to Thanjavur by bus. It was 9 p.m. when we reached. Siva briefed a sixty-something shoeless *rickshawala* who didn't seem to care that his *lungi* had been tied to expose his knee-length underwear.

Since Siva was stout, the *rickshawala* was able to drive his vehicle only by jumping on his seat and pressing down hard on the pedal.

He stopped outside a hut and I was stunned to see four or five people in a queue outside it.

"Don't worry about all these old geezers," said the *rickshawala*. "They won't take very long. All of them will be done in no more than an hour. Take your time. I'll wait for you both."

I was flabbergasted. I had to wait in a queue to have my first sex?

"Siva," I hissed. "I don't feel good about this. Let's just go."

Siva followed me back to the rickshaw where he made more enquiries about the *dasis*.

"Alright," the *rickshawala* said. "I'll take you to a *dasi*, but I hope your purse is as big as your hopes."

Siva had enough money on him.

He parked his *rikshaw* at the mouth of a street and demanded his share.

"Knock the fifth door on the right," he said, "and enter paradise."

Siva padded to the door like a cat and knocked softly. No one answered. He knocked louder and a terrifying male voice boomed, "Who on earth is it? Do you know what time it is?" We galloped like madmen from that street to the bus stand. During our mad dash, we'd also noticed that the *rickshawala* had taken off.

It was Anjali who put an end to my endless quest which began at that young age. When all you need is available around the corner, why go searching elsewhere? When you have eaten your fill, why force yourself to eat more? Why pour into a cup that is already filled to the brim? Only those men who have not tasted nectar like Anjali's will settle for dishwater. If every man found the woman of his dreams, then the fashion industry, yellow magazines and brothels would vanish overnight.

(Even if you eat to your heart's content, you take ginger juice to digest it, don't you? My lovers are like ginger juice.

Kokkarakko)

4 – How Kokkarakko Spends his Nights

Kokkarakko sleeps only after 1 a.m., after drinking booze and sexting women. This usually happens when he's outside Chennai. In under two minutes, he would go from "hello baby" to "suck your nipples" and "lick your cunt." He was guaranteed a sweet slumber only after two solid hours of raw talk. When one of his babes calls him the next day, he doesn't give a rat's ass about her or her call. The poor woman will make at least fifty-something calls before giving up. That night, alone again, he finds himself another woman.

"They just keep coming to me," he says, "and all in ten minutes or less. I feel sorry for them, you know?"

I couldn't help thinking of the rich man in Charlie Chaplin's *City Lights*.

CHAPTER TEN

All This Talk of Sex

"I challenge you to write a novel with no sex in it," Anjali told me one day. How is that even possible? How can I, a depraved man for the better part of my life, not write about sex? During my womanless days, when masturbation was my only recourse, I thought of the Nereis worm.

Nereis worms live in the deepest part of the ocean. Every month, on full-moon nights, the penetrating moonlight draws the worms to the surface where they mate. The fish linger just below the surface, lying in wait for their food. On such nights, you'd find the seagulls hovering above the ocean, anticipating a hearty feed of fish. Fishermen, more than delighted to see the entire round face of the moon, gaily take their boats and nets out to sea. Another interesting point to note is that the Nereis worms, when they ascend to the surface to mate, form a circle that is one whole kilometer in circumference. I have often climaxed visualizing these creatures fabricating themselves into a circle in order to mate.

We, the great human species, talk about time and space

like we are so conscious of them, but we are not seasonal breeders concerned about where we play the mating game. Animals always mate in particular seasons and they don't do it just anywhere. Cranes travel from Yakutia to China to mate. Now tell me, will a man come to India all the way from Australia just to mate? A person once trapped a hundred birds – fifty males and fifty females – to study their breeding habits. During breeding season, he kept them caged, but there was no mating as the cage was a cramped, non-ideal place for mating. In a desperate effort to escape the cage, the birds kept flinging their bodies against it until all their feathers fell out, until their strength gave out and they died.

The women I bed enjoy multiple orgasms and they can't seem to get enough of my love-muscle. *Nithya Karma Vidhi* made it possible.As a young boy, I learned it from Somasundaram who was a devotee of Vallalar.

Vallalar wrote a book in which he explains what and what not a man should eat, what he should use to clean his teeth, how he should shit, how he should sleep and how he should conduct himself. With maybe a couple of exceptions, I follow his every injunction. For instance, I wake up before sunrise to meditate, and that is the equal of two hours of sleep; it energizes and ensures longevity.

Vallalar asserts that ejaculation can be delayed through a certain technique of breath-control where the person neither suppresses his breath nor releases it in short puffs, but inhales deeply and allows his breath to "flow in the middle." This way, he can guarantee himself satisfactory sex all the time. (If there's aught else you want to know about the best way to breathe when having sex, there's Thirumoolar the saint to help you).

All my knowledge of sex, however, was futile as it didn't help me with stubborn Perundevi who closed her legs after a few years.

I think Vallalar, who said that sex once in four days is "excessive," should be blamed for Perundevi's abstinence as I fucked her close to four times a day. Vallalar, I'm sure, indoctrinated her against sex itself and influenced her to start living like a *sanyasin*.

In Anjali's case, I didn't feel sated even when we had twice the amount of sex I had with Perundevi. Every time I touched her, I never felt the same thing. She felt new, fresh and different every single time and I felt like a badly starved beast – and a badly starved beast digs right in without an ounce of concern for table etiquette. In other less cryptic words, I got down to business without any foreplay. I realized that Anjali seemed to want it that way too. When she saw me, she would spread her arms like an angel to embrace me and spread her legs shortly after like an impish little slut to let me in. My lips would brush her earlobes and from there travel to the nape of her neck. When I kissed her there, she gasped, a tremor running through her body. This, I discovered, was one of her erogenous zones.

I usually took her unawares, kissing her sweet spot when she was cooking in the kitchen or pottering in the bedroom. Desire would well up between her legs like rainclouds in a clear sky. Before she had the chance to get two words out of her mouth, I would start working around her love-tunnel, kissing her furiously. How she would cry out, begging me to stop! I would show no mercy, continuing wildly till she climaxed, screaming my name.

Kissing her lips, I'd carry her to the bed. If I hadn't exhausted her, she would tell me how dirty and depraved she thought I was and squabble with me. But during our crescendo, she would feast on my lips that smelled and tasted of her juices. Once we were done, I'd ask her, "So, how do you like the way you smell and taste down there?" She would feign incomprehension to draw out an explanation only to chastise me for it. Sex with Anjali never palls.

She has a bath every evening, but one evening, she didn't. When I asked her why, she said, "Your smell is still lingering on my body even though you touched me in the morning. I don't feel like washing it off."

***

Gnanam, Raja and I went to the restaurant Pelita one day. Over a dinner of fish head curry, we started to speak of health and that broad topic narrowed itself down to the bypass surgery I'd undergone ten years earlier.

"People who've undergone heart surgeries are so scared of even a *bajji*," said Gnanam, "but *you* are still eating like a king, drinking like a sailor and womanizing like Don Juan."

I retorted, "I can make merry, I can eat, I can drink, I can fuck, but I can't lift a woman."

Although I am, by admission, an extreme Francophile, I still live in Tamil Nadu. Tamil cinema has always been a big part of my life, wielding a massive influence over me even after my exposure to European film in my later years. I have watched Tamil actors carry women with such effortless ease since my childhood. In Tamil cinema, carrying a woman is a man's highest expression of love. I had become a piano enthusiast thanks to Sivaji Ganesan. He made the playing of the instrument a class act. When he played, I was not captivated so much by the movement of his fingers across the keys as I was by the expressions on his face – his lips, his mouth, his jowls – when he played sadly at his lovers' wedding receptions... Even Marlon Brando would never have been able to surpass Sivaji in a scene involving a piano and the playing of it. I can't pretend to even have a scrap of Sivaji's talent in acting, but I don't think I need to master acting to master the piano.

Raghav, my friend, a film director, convinced me to slap on the greasepaint when he promised me the role of a musician in one of his movies. When he told me I'd be playing a musician, I was reminded of Jamie Foxx's Oscar-winning portrayal of Ray Charles. I aspired to act with the same fervor. Only after the shooting commenced did I realize I was only a harmonium player and was quite disappointed. If a piano could be compared to the Everest, a harmonium would be an anthill. It just did *not* have the same cachet that the piano and the saxophone had. But Raghav flattered me, saying, "Work those nimble fingers,

Udhaya!" I wanted to swear at him so bad, but then I remembered I was going on a pilgrimage to Sabarimala shortly, so I couldn't even think or write bad words, let alone yell them at the top of my voice. I'm good with fingering only when it comes to a woman's cunt. Maybe I could have thought of a piano as a woman's cunt and played my part to the tee, but there wasn't much "fingering" one could do with a harmonium. And Raghav was not even willing to let go of me. He was a voracious reader of world literature and a fan of world cinema and used to tell me about Andrej Wajda's *The Conductor*, a movie that was very much to my liking because you never just heard the music in it, you felt every note, every beat in your fingers. I started to firmly believe that I could make the same magic with my fingers, but my hopes were shattered on account of Georges Bataille. Let me tell you how.

A great admirer of Bataille, Raghav gifted me *Story of the Eye*. I happened to have written a novel called *Midnight Stories* in Bataille's bizarre erotic style, but Raghav, in a magazine interview damned it for being nothing but third-rate porn. This ruptured our friendship and as a consequence, my fingers were given a mere fifteen seconds of screen-time in the movie, putting an end to all my hopes and dreams of making a memorable debut in the industry.

All the Tamil movies I'd seen made me desperate to lift women. In Nagore, it is customary for the groom to carry his bride into the bridal chamber. It was a custom that made the grooms highly nervous as they were forbidden from seeing their brides before the marriage to "size them up." My desire to carry a woman remained unfulfilled until I met Anjali, a woman who needed a thousand reasons to be kissed. Do all Tamil girls fancy a kiss to be some intangible thing or a mere brushing of the lips for a split second? I can never forget the day I kissed Anjali tenderly on the cheek, two days after we'd first met. Now don't start moralizing! I did it because I felt we'd known each other for years. When we were talking about it after a few days, I asked her, "What do you see in me? You're thirty and you look twenty and I'm sixty. What made you fall for me?"

She sent me a long e-mail in response to the burning question:

"Honey, you showed me what love is… I thought I was destined to never find someone who would love me truly – the way you love me. I learned to live with what I had, but I never did imagine that my noir days were numbered. I realized what had been missing all along when I found you.

Initially I thought this would be a risky nosedive, I thought I was expecting too much. I was desperate. I didn't want to listen to that voice inside me that kept crying out for love, love, love – something I never knew about.

You made me feel love in a mere handclasp, a smile, a peck on the cheek, a hug… My heart and soul are gravitating towards you. I can't seem to control them any longer. Even though I saw you three times today, I'm not satisfied. It just wasn't enough! My God, am I actually starting to fall in love?

After you walked into my life, you turned everything inside-out. You pulled me out of the deep, suffocating waters; now, I can breathe again. I feel light; I feel free; I feel saved. You are the first and the only person to take away my loneliness, to warm my heart which had frozen. Now, my heart flutters like an excited butterfly when I see you. I don't ever want you out of my sight even for a minute. I know, I know I have to take it slow…

Also, you asked me why I've started praying. I'm praying now because I want this to go on forever. I love you, I love you so much!"

Anjali became acquainted with my writing only accidentally when she had accompanied one of her friends to the Tamil bookshop in La Chapelle where she found one of my books. Attracted by the blurb, she picked it up. The considerable sprinkling of French words and expressions in my book interested her. That was the beginning.

She said that my book had terrified her. Her reading had been limited to Hugo and Maupassant. My novel was unlike anything she'd ever read before. She later told me that my writing had penetrated her all the way to her soul. Little did she think that destiny and coincidence had conspired to bring her face to face with the man whose book she was holding in the La Chapelle bookshop. Once we met, our lives were never the same. The moment our lives became intertwined was one we've relived together several times.

"*Coup de foudre*," she said. Love at first sight.

When I asked her about it on another occasion, she said, "It was magic; it was a miracle. I don't know how else to explain it."

On the third day, we met in a café. On the fourth, we met in my hotel room.

"This is the fourth time we're meeting and we haven't kissed yet," I told her.

"You did kiss me," she said.

She'd been living in Paris for ten years. French kissing there was as common a sight as public urination here. You'd see plenty of couples kissing, oblivious to the world, in parks, metros, buses, pretty much anywhere. Was Anjali referring to that feather-light brush of my lips as a *kiss*?

"Is your son your own, or is he adopted?"

"Why do you ask? That's how Suresh kisses me."

When I cut to the action, she didn't protest.

I was fifty when I had to undergo heart surgery. That was when I'd given up my desire to lift a woman as I was told that people who had gone under the knife aren't supposed to lift anyone or anything that's heavy. So, could I ever have imagined doing what I'd always wanted to do at the age of sixty? I might have told my friends that I couldn't ever lift a woman, but you know what? I lifted Anjali, and you can't even imagine how satisfied and accomplished I felt when I did.

"Anjali, my seductress, my lusty lady! Yours is a body that has been made wholly and solely for sex. How is it that you think so lowly of the body that turns me into an animal in bed – that body which makes me do it like I'm twenty instead of sixty?"

"Suresh doesn't love me. Hell, he doesn't even lust after

me. I masturbate from time to time, but even that gives me no gratification."

One day, after having had sex for two hours, neither of us climaxed. At one point, she began to scream and bite the pillow.

"I thought we'd be doing it until the ambulance arrived," she said afterwards, laughing. "I've never experienced such ecstasy even in my wildest dreams."

"But you didn't climax," I said.

"Who needs to climax when you're having sex like this? If we climax, it will be the end of the experience. Today was like a day without end. Think Udhaya, what would it be like if we were able to transcend death? I felt like I did. I wonder if there's anyone else who's done it. As far as I've known, from books and from experience, you can climax in five minutes – ten, tops. But us, we've been at it for *two* hours! Who would believe that? We were *so* tantalizingly close to our climax. It was like coming this close to a fire –" she showed me how close with her thumb and her forefinger "– and not falling into it. My goodness, what a man you are! The greatest fucker in the world! But Udhaya, answer me honestly. You've been with many women. Was it the same for them too?"

"Sex has more to do with the mind than with the body, honey," I said. "I convince many women to let me screw them with my falsehood and my charm, but they are never satisfied with what I give them in bed and they leave. They tell me I don't make myself desirable to them. Here's the thing: I can't "provide" desire. I can't make myself desirable for them. You can't be passive in bed. It doesn't work that way. It takes two to tango. Our lovemaking is so fulfilling because we are each other's missing pieces."

"I tried to suppress my lust for you by working hard. I wanted to push you out of my head. I worked to the point of exhaustion every day and then I'd come home and go straight to bed. There was this chap in the dance class who wanted to sleep with me. He was handsome and he was committed to someone, but he still fell for me and he begged me to do it with him "just once." Do you know how disturbed I felt after this? I stopped going to classes. Thought of switching over to another job. But you know what? I did consider taking him up on his offer. I didn't see what was wrong in it. I'd been married for ten years and had never experienced thrill or desire even once. My life was desert-dry. I'd forgotten what sex was. I'd considered his offer several times. *Just once.* But I couldn't do it. I was scared of the aftermath. Then I thought of becoming a monk, but I realized that renunciation would be a greater pain than this would ever be. I didn't want to escape from my body."

"I get it, Anjali. In the movie *Dead Man Walking*, Sister Helen confesses that she chose to become a nun just to escape interaction, she wanted to sever all her ties with the world. Such is the resolve and the clear-sightedness one would require to become a renunciate. It isn't right to choose renunciation as an escape."

"I had a friend called Nina from Pondicherry who became a monk. I wasn't proud of her. I disapproved, in fact, because I know she chose that path out of hatred. My mind feels heavy when I think of her. Our choices in life must be dictated by love, but hatred influenced Nina to choose the path of renunciation. The same thing happened to me, albeit in a different way. It would most certainly not be fair to compare Nina's life with mine, but like her life, even mine was like a parched desert, devoid of love, affection and desire. There was also this other friend called Anuthama whose husband, Sundaram, was Suresh's college mate. Anu and Sundaram have only agreed to disagree on everything since they were married. They fought when they were alone, they fought in the presence of friends and in the presence of strangers too, but they haven't separated although Anu would tell me that death was preferable to living with her disgusting husband. She confessed to me that she was staying with him only because nobody could beat him in bed. You should see her eyes widen when she says that. I never did understand their passion for sex. But now, I see in my own eyes the very same passion."

CHAPTER ELEVEN

1 – Metamorphosis: When Siva Became Amba

When I look back on my time in Nagore, I am led to the especial remembrance of one friend who distinguished himself from the rest of the pack.

His name was Siva.

It was during our stint as students at Arignar Anna Arts College that his interest in numerology was born. He soon became slave to his newborn passion, obsessively informing himself about it, going so far as to peruse tomes in both Tamil and English on the subject and applying himself to painstaking research.

Soon, he was so gripped by the subject that it became the sole occupant of his thoughts. He was convinced that numerology held the answer to every unanswered question. He claimed that numerology had helped him deduce why India was eclipsed by European nations, why the Pandavas were relegated to a life of exile in the forest and notably, why he was obsessed with sex.

The more deeply he immersed himself in numerology, the more convinced he became that he had attained

samadhi. This notion led him to style himself Balayogi–
the all-knowing youth.

He shed his old identity like a snakeskin. He would
fly into a fit of fury if anyone addressed him by his given
name, Siva. He was so crazed that he would deliver
sermons exceeding the two-hour mark on the wonders of
numerology to hapless fellows.

He went on to publish his change of name in the gazette
and performed elaborate *pujas*, prayers and rituals that he
believed would render his name powerful.

He then went abroad – to one of the Gulf countries –
where he lived for three years.

Siva's family was in fortunate circumstances, financially.
His father practiced law and was regarded with general
disfavor as he, in cahoots with affluent businessmen and
cops with greased palms, banished the peasants from
their own land in order to help the businessmen erect and
establish a new company. He earned a lot of money in this
deal.

Siva had a strained relationship with his father as he did
not subject himself to his old man's will.

I remember Siva telling me how he was so flat broke
that he couldn't scrape together the money to buy himself
a spare set of underclothes. And I don't think numerology
held the solutions to such problems. Siva soon understood
that his father, who could not spare him an allowance
for underwear, would not even entertain the thought of
settling him through marriage. Thus, at the age of twenty

and seven, he set out to the Gulf on borrowed money, and there eked out his living as a garbage collector. The wretched job had him working two shifts.

In his bitterness, he wrote me a letter, describing in vivid sensory detail the filth he was suffered to handle – ill-disposed, bloody sanitary napkins, goat innards, offal and putrid food. He was plagued by these smells that lingered like indelible bad memories. Even a dozen baths in succession would not render him stench-free. His letter would not be complete if not for his assertion that he had not abandoned numerology.

Give or take some time, and Siva had met Ashwini, a beauty from Thrissur. Ashwini's story shares certain pathetic elements with Siva's. When she was of legal age, she was married off to a man in Palakkad, bearing him a son and a daughter within the bracket of two years. Her husband conceived suspicions of her infidelity and in that respect, her beauty soon turned out to be a scourge, as it only intensified his misbegotten feelings. For close to a decade, she allowed herself to be battered and tortured by him. When he finally left her for an older woman, she returned to her parents' home. Her father had died and she had two younger sisters – dependents.

As if by a stroke of luck, an agent promised her a job abroad. After six months of uncertainty, she ended up in Qatar on a visitor's visa. As for work, she was forced into the whorehouse. And the only remotely good thing that came out of whoring was that it was a job – though an illegal one – that helped her convert her visitor's visa into a work visa.

Once she parted with whoring, which was eight years since her arrival in Qatar, she found work as a nanny and raked in fifty grand a month. Her earnings sufficed to marry off her sisters and erect a small house back home.

I chanced to meet Ashwini when I attended a conference addressing the rights of sex-workers in Thrissur. We ended up talking in a bar from dawn to dusk. We spoke mostly on the subject of my work – my novel and my essays, most of which she had read.

Alcohol is assistive in loosening even a mute man's tongue. After four rounds, I declared my love which she happily accepted. We ended up going to my room and, instead of having sex, had a discourse on it. We also discussed our respective lives and families, and Qatar. And at some point in our conversation, numerology reared its head like a jack-in-the-box, and it was discovered to me that Siva was no stranger to her.

What strangely marvelous designs was fate responsible for!

You see, Anjali, Siva had gone to her once. He made enquiries about her name and date of birth and then proceeded to make some calculations. At long last, he told her that a slight modification of spelling would bring good fortune in its wake.

He rewrote her name as "Auschweenee," and that respelled name bore eerie resemblance to that Polish concentration camp.

"So, did you end up changing the way you spelled your name?" I asked her.

She responded in the negative, adding that he gave her ridiculous instructions to follow that involved her waking up at the crack of dawn, taking a bath and writing her "new name" one hundred and eight times in a notebook. This was to be done for a month.

On hearing that Siva was my friend, she expressed her surprise. She did not exercise an ounce of moderation when she spoke of him.

"He must be completely mad now," she said.

I requested a little insight.

She told me that he, during his brief interaction with her, had remarked that she, a goddess in the flesh, had no place in the sex industry.

"Goddess-ing," she knew full well, would not keep her afloat.

When she expressed her dislike of pointless flattery to Siva, he raised the roof and threatened to have her handed over.

Ashwini, whose temper was on a leash, could restrain it no longer.

"You son-of-a-bitch!" she yelled in his face. "Did your numerology ever tell you that a whore would show you the door?"

Ashwini and I never met post that encounter. No, I never loved her, Anjali. Never take a drunk man or a sober numerologist seriously.

Siva returned to India, but he never went home. Instead, he started a business in Tiruppur. I got wind of his having got into some trouble, the nature of which I will not pretend to know, for which he served time in prison. After his sentence, he returned home. No misfortune in life had succeeded in dulling his interest in numerology. He added astrology to his repertoire and soon after, he adopted the lifestyle of a monk. It wasn't long before he changed his name to Amba, a woman's name.

I did ask him what prompted the change of name.

"The life of a woman is the life I was destined to live, not the life of a man."

He was far from being a man of few words. He launched into a numerological and astrological explanation of his decision that endured for hours. He then sought to interest me with his collection of books.

As I was examining them with piqued interest, he said, "Udhaya, Mercury is exalted in your horoscope. I have taken that and several other parameters into consideration and have concluded that you will see greatness face to face if you apply yourself to the study of astrology."

The idea actually did resonate with sense, because, you see, as a writer, I'm always strapped for cash. I was starting to think better of all the astrologers I'd regarded with a jaundiced eye. I could never hope to be their equal in riches, but at least I could guarantee myself a stocked refrigerator and pantry.

"You know I have the memory of a ninety-year-old," I said in jest.

"Everyday, eat the leaves of the *brahmi* plant," he advised me, "and watch your memory improve exponentially."

"You are intelligent, so intelligent in fact, and yet the world sees you as a half-wit," I told him.

He showed me a little gleaming silvery bead on a thread that encircled his wrist.

"The *rasa mani*," he said reverentially. "*Rasam* is mercury, Lord Shiva's. It channels the *vata, pitta* and *kapha* energies, orders them, thereby helping man achieve whatever he seeks to achieve. I have found the *gyanam* I have long sought. A rationalist, a writer, a rationalistic writer like you would never believe what a saint says.

"I hope you understand someday, Udhaya. This *rasa mani* was bestowed on me by my guru, an alchemist. I intend to advance it into *kekana gulikai*, the *rasa mani*'s superior in power that allows the wearer to experience the transcendental. A man engaged in such an arduous, demanding effort is above the invectives of common men.

"My guru transmutated tin into gold, made solid beads out of liquid mercury."

Siva put a poem of Konkanavar to tune. The poem treated of alchemy.

"It's not magic," he said.

What inevitably followed was a long-drawn-out lecture on the liaison between chemistry and alchemy by my friend Siva, in a chrome yellow silk saree and a blouse with elbow-length sleeves.

He is Amba now. She is Siva no longer.

2 – Homeward

Every human being has a special niche in his heart for his hometown. It will never be easy for him to reconcile himself to change in its appearance or functioning.

I was in an auto riding in a narrow street of Mylapore. The driver, Murali, told me that there used to be weavers' looms on that stree thirty years ago. Now, they had all vanished without a trace. I could hear an ache in his voice when he spoke of the Mylapore of the yesteryears, the Mylapore he knew as a youth.

Besides Nagore, there are at least a hundred towns that evoke nostalgia in me – and many of these towns I have never seen. When I read Dostoevsky, I feel like St. Petersburg is my home; when I read Mario Vargas Llosa, I feel like I know the towns and streets of Peru like the back of my hand. I wonder, can a writer lay claim to a city or a country? Two millennia ago, the Tamil poet Kaniyan Poongundranar wrote: யாதும் ஊரே ; யாவரும் கேளிர் . All the world is my world, all humanity is my fraternity.

Pattinacheri, an age-old fisherman's hamlet, was situated

along the banks of the Vettar where the tributary met the sea. It was to this place that Shahul Hameed, the Sufi mystic, came some five centuries ago from Uttar Pradesh. When he died in Nagore, a magnificent *dargah* was erected to commemorate him.

When I was a boy, there used to sit a eunuch near the *dargah* at the corner of Kunjali Maraikkar Street – a street named for the man who opposed and fought the Portuguese. The eunuch sold fried *vaadas* that I hogged with great relish. I only got to eat *vaadas* like his thirty-five years later on a visit to Malaysia. *Vaadas* are made with *urad dal* batter. The eunuch's were filled with delicious shrimp.

Nagore's intercourse with Malaysia goes back many centuries. Nowhere else did I find anything similar to the meats served in Nagore, except Malaysia, in Penang. Dining there at Tajudeen Hussain Nasi Kandar took me back in time.

In Penang, where I'm sure no one has ever heard of Nagore, one can find a street named after the South Indian town. I'm not surprised they don't know anything about Nagore because I wouldn't think people who live in Chennai's Armenian Street know its history. There wasn't a soul from Nagore on Nagore Street. Near the street stood a *dargah*, a miniature replication of the one at Nagore.

I've visited Malaysia and Thailand during their summers. Summers there did not melt or burn people. While Tamil Nadu experienced eight to eighteen-hour-long power outages, the Government of Malaysia saw to it that its citizens remained oblivious of the meaning of load-shedding.

On a day when the sun beat down mercilessly, I went to the *dargah* in Nagore Street. There, only an old man who was somewhere between sleep and wakefulness was present. I sat myself down next to him and said, "I'm from Nagore too." But he didn't even deign to look at me. I doubt he'd even heard what I said. From there I went to the tomb and made a wish and left the place.

If the Vettar is crossed by boat, you will reach a small village called Melavanjur. A little beyond Melavanjur lies Keezhavanjur, and a little beyond Keezhavanjur lies Thirumalairayanpattinam, another tiny village with a hundred and eight ponds in with an abundance of water lilies and lotuses. When I visited in 2010, the ponds were replete with water.

Between 1453 and 1468 A.D., a representative of the Vijayanagar Empire,Vitharana Raman, better known as Thirumalairayan, created the village of Thirumalai and built a palace there. When his daughter fell ill, he made a pledge to the goddess and she survived. To honor his pledge, he dug one hundred and eight ponds, one of which he named after himself and another of which he named after his wife.

There were around fifty ponds in Nagore too, but we knew nothing of the people who dug them, not even a name. There were a dozen ponds on my street itself. There was another pond in the palm grove in National High School where I studied. I remember bathing and playing in it. The streets where poor people lived had no plumbing and they relied on the public tap at the end of the street.

The clay pots would be deposited at the tap in the night. In the morning, you'd see women there, tearing each other's hair and pulling each other's *sarees*. Sometimes, they'd end up rolling on the ground. I've heard that the Punjabi language contains the highest number of dirty words, but only people who are unfamiliar with my writing will say so. I owe a debt to the scrappy women in the neighborhood, for it is from them that I learned how to swear. Their words and their volumes could have made ears bleed. They fought with ten times more rage than WWF contestants. But towards the evening of the same day, the same women who'd beat each other bloody in the morning would be seen picking lice out of each other's hair.

The palm grove was the site of Nagore's famous football matches, the most important of which pitted Nagore's National High School against Mannargudi's National High School. It was probably because of the Muslim majority that football was the main sport, but our sports instructor, Kannayyan *Saar,* did all he could to popularize volleyball. In the thirties and the forties, the name Vaduvur was associated with Tamil's foremost detective fiction writer, Vaduvur Duraisamy Iyengar, but I'd heard only of Vaduvur Ramamoorthy, the volleyball champion of Thanjavur. There was such intensity in the air when he and Kannayyan *Saar* played volleyball. As I was very slight and frail, I was excluded from participating in games. My playmates were the girls who lived in my street with whom I played dice, *pallaankuzhi* and *paandi.* I am quite the expert at dice even today.

Besides Kannayyan *Saar*, the Tamil teacher, Seeni Shanmugam *Saar*, was an unforgettable character whose classes were a riot as he was a quick-witted debater who engaged everyone. After being my class teacher for three consecutive years, he went to Karanthattankudy to pursue higher studies in Tamil literature. He returned as my Tamil teacher in the ninth grade.

Another local hero was B.A. Kaakka. Kaakka is one way of saying "elder brother," and the man was always shown off for being the first person in our town to obtain a bachelor's degree. And another one was Farid Kaakka, who was an expert stuntman who went on to work in a number of Tamil movies.

When I visited Nagore recently, I saw – to my utter horror – that the seashore was no longer a sea shore but a garbage dump. Food was the only thing that appealed to my senses there. Nagore's *parottas* and *dumroot*, a kind of *halwa*, are to die for. However, Nagore's *dumroot* is not as famous as Tirunelveli's *iruttukadai halwa*.

Vellore is famous for its *idlis* which are served with *vadai* curry. In Nagore, you can enjoy delicious, soft, fluffy *idlis* in the Sethurama Iyer Hotel that serves delightful tiffin.

Sports and cinema were the two greatest obsessions of the youth in the days I speak of. In Nagore, movies were screened for six months in a theatre people called "Dooring Talkies" which was actually a licensed tent. In 1943, when *Sivakavi* was released, it ran for six months when other movies could barely run for a week due to Nagore's sparse population. After *Sivakavi*, the owner of the theater, whose name was unknown to us, was dubbed Sivakavi Iyer.

Another striking aspect of Nagore was the ghostly silence that pervaded the western part of the town – much like the eerie calm of the cemetery. After forty long years, the silence still reigned supreme, lending the place an air of antiquity.

In Ray Bradbury's short story, *The Pedestrian*, the protagonist, Leonard Mead, is taking a walk through the deserted city streets one night. He gets picked up by the cops and gets incarcerated in a mental asylum. Bradbury wrote: "Mead is the only person to be out in a city where no one else is out of doors, ergo, he is mad." I too, like Mead, traipsed the streets of Nagore at night but the cops never bothered to bother me. The streets were completely empty. The abandoned rice mill near the post office looked like it had been frozen in time. Time hadn't changed it a bit. Nagore was often devastated by cyclones but remarkably, even the chimneys of the mill were intact.

A good number of houses in Nagore have the same decrepit look they have had for the past two hundred years, and these houses I speak of are not to be found only in some murky alley; they stand like old rotten teeth on the main street itself.

Traveling on foot in Nagore gave me a better understanding of the theory of relativity. As a boy, I'd have to walk from my house in Kosatheru to Perumal South Street, turn left onto Perumal East Street and take the first right onto Pidari Kovil Street where my school was. At the end of this walk, I used to feel like I'd traversed the length and breadth of an entire city.

When I failed to pass my pre-university course, I decided to learn shorthand for which I had to take the train to Nagapattinam. Although I was eighteen then, the walk from my house in Kosatheru to the railway station felt like a tiresome journey from the North Pole to the South Pole. Till today, Nagore's roads – its arteries and veins – and its landscape as they had been remain fresh in my memory. However, when I returned twenty-five years later, my hometown didn't seem as big as used to be. It was like a forty-foot giant had shrunken into a four-foot dwarf.

I was ten when my Uncle Subbiah came to visit us after twenty-five years. He remarked that not even a brick had changed. Looking at the tin plate on the wall of a house on which the name of the street was engraved, he said, "The British left this a century ago and it's still here, just a little faded due to the sun and the rain."

Apart from Siva, I had other friends in Nagore. One of them was called Chandran and he looked like a Hawaiian. He had a strong and sinewy body and worked as a welder. When I enquired after him after thirty five years of non-communication due to my being away, no one seemed to have any idea of who I was talking about. Finally someone said, "Chandran, you mean Naina, don't you?" and gave me the directions to his place. He was delighted to see me and said that he often saw me on television and that his daughter-in-law held my works in high esteem.

Vijayan was another friend who was doing business.

I managed to find his telephone number and call him. "Come to the big minaret of the *dargah*," he said. When I reached the place, I saw him stringing up lights for the upcoming *Gandoori* festival. We were meeting after thirty-five long years. Though he was hoary, he was still fit as a fiddle. "Come, let's go up and talk," he said casually, like he'd been seeing me every day all those years. He bounded up the narrow staircase like a mountain goat. He probably had enough energy to run a hundred laps after climbing three flights when I felt exhausted on the first level itself. I stood there panting and he came back down to look for me. We stood there talking for a while. I could see the main gate of the *dargah* from where I was. If I went up further, I would have been able to see the sea and the seashore but I wasn't feeling up to it. Chandran and Vijayan were in good shape, both physically and mentally. They were not well-educated, but were dedicated and capable physical laborers. Siva was educated but had the reputation of a madman. As for me, too much introspection has scrambled my mind. So, which should I blame for turning into a psycho – introspection or education? Maybe the people would have been more sympathetic towards me and not considered me a psycho had I been uneducated like them.

After leaving Vijayan, I went to the *dargah* where I'd spent the better part of my youth and prayed to the *ejamaan*. I held my face over the pot of incense after which I felt like sitting on the cool *mandapam* for old times' sake, but I couldn't as it was crowded with heavyweights.

Once I'd finished praying to the *ejamaan*, I made my

way to the western part of the village where I'd lived as a child. My friends who had lived on this street were the sole testimony of time's relentless passage. Though they were only sixty years old, they looked like they were eighty and some looked like they were on death's doorstep.

Kandaswamy was one of my schoolmates. I will never know how he managed to identify me after all these years. He rushed to me and enveloped me in a warm hug. He made his living rolling cigars and had a son who was working in Singapore. Moving to Singapore or Malaysia is considered to be the greatest achievement of a Hindu in Nagore.

A dilapidated Draupadi *amman* temple stands at the end of the street. Once in a while, someone would light a lamp there. I have observed that religious fervor has increased among the people the same way the statistics of murders and rapes have. As a sign of their rekindled faith, the townsfolk had the temple renovated. I remember how much time I'd spent alone in that temple, refusing to talk to people, preferring my own company. People used to frighten my mother saying I'd become a *sanyasi.*

I made my way to the street where Chettiar's house was. It was another place where I'd spent many happy hours as a boy. Chettiar had passed on but his son, my school friend, had taken his father's place. The magnificent Siva Temple Pond was situated behind the house. The men and women stood in the steps of the pond bathing and washing the clothes.

After leaving Nagore, I headed to Thanjavur which

was not much different than the former. Only the areas that were given a facelift reeked of modernity; the western parts had remained the way they were at the time of the Naickers. Only the occasional scooter served to remind one that it was the twenty-first century. Here too, there are several streets and places that take you back in time – Rani Vaykkal Lane, *Naalukaal Mandapam* and Venkatesa Perumal Street. There are several people who glorify the beauty of India. Just pay a courtesy visit to the places I've mentioned. You will be promptly greeted by the sight and smell of shit and urine that flow in the open gutters around houses that lack underground sewers.

Think about this: Thanjavur's population is 2,500,000 and roughly 500,000 people live in the western part of town. We are human beings who eat thrice a day and expel whatever we eat at a later time. With no underground sewers and no proper sanitation, do you think people are going to worry if they turn the ruins of a temple into a toilet? I don't know which whiz-king was responsible for building Thanjavur. The western part is like a maze with one street intersecting ten or twenty others. You can't even begin to guess where these streets lead to. At most, two people can walk abreast of each other in the narrow lanes. If you were on a bike, pedestrians had to pin themselves to the walls to avoid being knocked into the gutter.

When I was studying in Serfoji College, I used to spend most of my time in Saraswati Mahal Library. King Serfoji (1777 – 1832) was a polyglot who knew Tamil, Telugu, Sanskrit, Urdu, English, French, German, Danish, Greek,

Dutch and Latin. He dispatched emissaries to every corner of the globe to bring back books for his library. I have seen his numerous notations in English in several books here. He was well-versed on the subjects of medicine, architecture, astrology, music, dance, theatre and food. I doubt there was ever another ruler so adored and loved by his subjects. It is said that he built an underground sewerage in Thanjavur, but I'll never know how it disappeared and where to. I wonder what poor King Serfoji thinks when he sees his domain – now an open-air toilet – from wherever he is.

Standing in *Naalukal Mandapam*, I thought of Mekhala. Forty years had gone by – where would she be now? In her eyes, I was nothing but a deceiver. I don't know what had come over me that I'd started to ruminate over the past all of a sudden.

I entered a lane hoping to find my way to West Street. I had to repeatedly ask for directions. People would tell me to turn this way or that, but I always wound up in front of somebody's house or at a dead end. I pressed on and managed to find another lane that led to West Street where the Kamakshi Amman Temple was.

When I lived with my aunt – my mother's older sister – in Venkatesa Perumal Kovil Lane, I used to accompany her to the *amman* temple daily. My aunt, like the goddess, was called Kamakshi and she spent a good deal of time at the temple, but her devotion to the goddess did not win her any succor or relief from the misery the two feckless men in her life – her drunken, unemployed son and her untrue, uncaring husband – caused her. She eked out a living by working by a maid in four houses. She regarded me as her son and I looked upon her as my mother and was very devoted to her. Every Saturday, she would give me an oil bath, train the smoke of the incense on her *puja* tray on my face, and feed me a sumptuous lunch of rice and mutton curry. I had never been as fond of my own mother who, to be honest, I'd barely touched. My aunt continued to give me oil baths even when I began going to college. She frequently asked me to massage her legs and press her feet when she was tired and soap her back when she was bathing. I remember how my hand used to slip down her marble-smooth back. It felt strangely good to touch her, and it saddened me that a beautiful woman like her was unloved. Before I left, she held me close to her bosom and stroked my head. "You won't forget this mother of yours when you go to Delhi, will you?" she asked me. While I loved my aunt, my mother despised her. She would tell me she used her fair skin to seduce men.

I'd told my aunt about Mekhala, but telling someone about her had not unburdened me. I was restless in Thanjavur, so, when I landed a job in Delhi while I was still in college, I slipped away in the night without a second thought or a word to anyone. I'd always dreamed of going to Delhi and once I got there, I forgot all about Mekhala, but my aunt, even though I never thought about her much, I felt guilty whenever she crossed my mind. Perhaps I could have eased my conscience by sending her some money, but my income could not sustain me if I sanctioned a share for her as three hundred rupees of my salary of five hundred and sixty had to be sent to my father. He'd taken a loan from his brother to marry my sister and the unfortunate task of repaying the loan, interest and all, had fallen to my lot.

Within a year of getting married, my sister delivered a baby girl and my father promptly wrote me a letter saying he needed money for the child's ear-piercing ceremony in Tirupati. He reminded me that, as the maternal uncle, it was my duty to buy the child a pair of gold earrings. I sent him an obscene letter. This was the gist:

At my age, you were a father of two children, but at the age of twenty-seven, I still have to pleasure myself as I am still single. If my brother-in-law fucked my sister and gave her a child, why must I be burdened with meaningless expenses? You have two other daughters who are younger than me. Do you expect me to pay a fortune for their weddings, but gold for their offspring and get relegated to a street corner while they happily fuck their husbands? By the time I think of getting married, my dick will have shriveled and fallen off like a dead leaf.

After my letter had been read, my family concluded I was crazy.

Almost everyone you know has come to the same conclusion that it doesn't even surprise me anymore.

After my explicit letter had reached them, I heard not another word from them.

I was twenty-four when I last saw my aunt, just before I

left for Delhi. Although I was tight for money, I don't think I was justified in not sparing a portion of my earnings for her. I could have at least paid her an annual visit. I didn't. To this day, my heart aches when I think of the way I abandoned her. How could I have been so ungrateful to the woman who loved me more than my birth mother?

Exactly thirty-six years later, I found myself weeping bitter tears before Bangaru Kamakshi *amman*. I silently asked her, "What grievous sin did that woman commit? All her life she's been most faithfully devoted to you yet she is visited only by sorrow. Where is your mercy? People look to you for justice. Is this your twisted notion of justice? But what are you to do, poor thing? After all, you were carried here to safety from Kanchipuram because the Brahmins wanted to save you from the Mughal ruler who would have melted you in the furnace and made ornaments out of your golden body to adorn the bodies of his concubines.

In the year 1786, the Mughal army was marching towards Kanchipuram. The people of Kanchipuram feared that the soldiers would loot the golden Kamakshi idol, so it was clandestinely moved to Udayarpalayam where it was hidden. The Maratha ruler of Thanjavur did not want the goddess lying unworshipped in Udayarpalayam, so he invited the Kanchipuram Brahmins to install her in Thanjavur itself.

CHAPTER TWELVE

The Story of a Tamil Family

Aunt Kamakshi had been married off when my grandmother's coffers were still full. Her husband, Kandasamy, was a port officer in Chennai. My aunt's beauty was divine like the goddess who was her namesake. Like Kamakshi Amman, Aunt Kamakshi shone like she was dusted with gold; when she walked, her feet were like little birds that never seemed to touch the ground; her skin was as fair and as smooth as the inside of a seashell. Kandasamy, in stark contrast, was the color of soot; he had a lopsided face and rodent-like front teeth. He was a sight to behold in the bridal chamber, I was told.

One year of conjugal life had not infused any love into the marriage. Kandasamy never once took Kamakshi out, and at home, they lived like strangers under the same roof. He always had his nose in a book during the day and the evenings would find him in a club where he played table-tennis. On his ten o'clock return, he would resume his reading. This was the unchanged tune of his life.

Within a year of marriage, Kandasamy kissed his job goodbye, saying that it was futile to slog for a foolish wife.

He packed them both off to Villupuram soon after. There, he began privately tutoring college students, but his income was a pittance. It wasn't enough to make ends meet.

In the meanwhile, Aunt Kamakshi gave birth to a son who was named Natesan. The birth of the child, a third mouth to feed, reduced the family to dire straits. Kandasamy was as affected as a stone. His life was comprised solely of reading, tuitions and evening games. After he had relocated to Villupuram, his sports preferences shifted from table-tennis to volleyball, something that had his interest and devotion.

As Kandasamy chose not to work and Kamakshi had no choice to work, food was scarce or lacking altogether in the household, and when Kandasamy heard that his wife had begun to borrow provisions from the neighbors, he thrashed her for having brought dishonor upon him. Kamakshi's life had begun to take on a familiar pattern of hunger, neglect and beatings. Kandasamy did not have to fear for his fare as he had several well-stocked friends in town.

Kandasamy and Kamakshi's son, Natesan, was bright-complexioned and handsome – everything his father was not. His good-looking son gave him cause to suspect his wife's fidelity. He reasoned that she'd been frequenting the neighbors' houses, even after being barred from so doing, for more than just rice, tamarind and chilies. She soon became a prisoner within her own four walls. She was forbidden from showing a sliver of her face to her husband's tutees.

As Kandasamy's overbearingness intensified, Kamakshi's endurance was wearing thin. When the last portion of her tolerance had evaporated, she packed herself and her son off to her mother Pappathy Ammal's place. However, the mother was neither a rock nor a relief to her ill-used daughter. Pappathy's petulant raves made up for Kandasamy's indifferent silence.

Finally, like she had done once before, she packed her chattels and quit the place.

The next person on whose doorstep Kamakshi found herself was Umayal's.

Umayal was Kamakshi's older sister and the two shared the feeling of sororal warmth, but Pappathy popped up frequently like a fly in the milk to pick fights with Kamakshi. What her husband had suspected her of, her own mother had accused her of. Pappathy alleged that Kandasamy was not Natesan's father. On hearing this, Kamakshi flew into a fiery rage and accused Pappathy of killing her husband, Umayal and Kamakshi's father, just so she could roll around with other men.

Pappathy Ammal said no more. She just repaired to Servarayan Temple and hexed Kamakshi, her own flesh and blood.

Within a week, Natesan's stomach tumefied and he died.

Umayal's husband, Ramasamy, was the owner of six acres of land and two houses, and the father of four sons.

The firstborn, Azhaguvel, completed his education up

to the elementary level. He associated his memories of father with the sound of a thwack. The abuse made him bitter and despondent; he became a smoker and a drifter. He pinched money from the house to go to the movies, and, at the age of twenty, acquired a mistress, whose bed he found more comfortable than the sweet-nothing he slept on in his father's house.

The second-born, Murugavel, had a singular passion, dedication and devotion towards film. While in the eighth grade, he played around with the idea of writing a film script that would be a game changer, and finally, he ended up writing one instead of studying for his exams. Not surprisingly, he failed, but this was no matter of great sorrow, for the young man did not wish to attend school any longer.

The third son was called Gnanavel. He played truant from school in order to go and play in the tamarind grove. This went on for a year before his father was acquainted with the information. From then on, Ramasamy took it upon himself to drop Gnanavel off at school, and, as a sign of rebellion, the son soiled his shorts in class every day. Unable to bear with Gnanavel's shenanigans, the principal summoned Ramasamy and boxed his ears. Following this humiliating incident, Ramasamy stopped forcing his son to attend school and Gnanavel eventually dropped out.

Rajavel, the fourth son, was akin to his brother Murugavel in many aspects – he watched movies everyday and wrote scripts, but he soon realized that direction was a more intelligent exercise than screenwriting. *Is the leader of the ship the captain or the engineer?* he loved to ask. Rajavel was of the opinion that Murugavel's understanding of cinema was faulty, and he became the sharpest critic of his brother's works. The two had lengthy, heated discussions, debates and arguments on Tamil cinema all day long. At times, Murugavel, chastised by his younger brother's sharpness, would beat him up, but he couldn't be beaten out of his belief that he was a know-all where film was concerned. He would criticize flaws in song-lyrics, even if they were penned by the legendary likes of Kannadasan. He was generous in his unsparing criticisms: "Fool! Can't you say something I haven't heard a hundred times before just in a hundred different ways?" He would constantly boast of his game-changer film that was still to come.

In Kamakshi's absence, her husband had an affair with a nurse from Pondicherry. After Natesan's death, Kandasamy came to drag his wife back to Villupuram. He blamed the child's death on her. The nurse was still an active force in Kandasamy's life. He was most willing to set Kamakshi aside and marry her, but she would not hear of it.

Kamakshi would go on to have a second son, Dhanapal, whom she loved very little and sometimes not at all, due to his striking resemblance to the man she hated.

Though Umayal had borne Ramasamy four sons, she had a strained relationship with him because of his sexual indiscretion and misconduct. I realized this many years later from the broad hints Umayal dropped during our conversations.

"Your uncle is a scoundrel," she said. "He binds a woman's mouth and hands to have his way with her."

Once, when she had returned home from the border of the lake with her load of washed clothes, she found Ramasamy forcing himself on the maid who was gagged and bound like a goat taken to slaughter. Shocked out of her senses, Umayal ran to the maid and untied her. She forcefully pushed Ramasamy to the ground.

Ramasamy casually put on his *veshti* and left the house, not a word said. He returned home late at night and went to bed in silence.

Silence, however, wasn't there to stay for long.

The next morning, Ramasamy rushed to his wife who was sitting cross-legged on the kitchen floor, cutting vegetables.

"From whose seed were your brood of four conceived, you whore?" he bellowed like a madman and kicked her in the face. He planted his foot on her neck in an attempt to suffocate her. Arms and legs flailing wildly, like a writhing animal, Umayal managed to wrap her fingers around the *arivaalmanai*. She brought it down hard on Ramasamy's foot.

She ripped her *mangal sutra* off her neck and hurled it at him, hitting him in the face.

She smeared her head and body with the blood of her husband that she had spilled. She said vehemently, "Even upon my deathbed, I do not wish for a fleeting glimpse of you, you beastly bastard!"

This having been said, she left for Villupuram.

One day, it so happened that two of Ramasamy's sons left home – Murugavel left for Chennai, and Azhagavel ran away.

Murugavel, on his way to Chennai, decided to call on his aunt, Kamakshi Ammal, in Villupuram. He visited her and she bid him stay for a week which extended itself to a month which further extended itself into a year. He was moved to tearful sorrow when he observed the manner in which his aunt was being treated. His sympathy soon mutated into something else, a feeling that was strong but undefined, blurred around the edges. It could have been affection; it could have been love; it could have been both; it could have been neither.

Murugavel spent most of his time writing, a job nothing – not even the apocalypse – could pry him from. However, the sight of his aunt in the kitchen would prompt him to abandon all else to rinse a cup or wash a potato.

The frequency of Kandasamy's visits decreased. His tuitions stopped, and so did his marital obligations with a money order for fifty rupees.

Murugavel was thinking of taking up a job, but Umayal told him that paying jobs were hard to come by in Villuppuram, so the family migrated to Thanjavur.

Being uneducated and unaccustomed to working, Murugavel was clueless about what occupation would best suit him. He felt that his was supposed to be the life of an artiste, rubbing shoulders with the rich and shaking hands with the famous, but in reality, he was but a luckless smalltown chap with big dreams who would have to crate vegetables and heave rice sacks for a living.

He was torn between his lust for the film industry and his love for Kamakshi. He tried to coax her into accompanying him to Chennai, but she was steadfast in her refusal, reasoning that her presence would only be an inconvenience; it could offer him no security. She told him he was free to leave, should he want to.

There was not a grain of rice or a pinch of salt to be come by in the miserable house, so Umayal, audacious and resourceful as she was, began to smuggle booze from Pondicherry into other districts. Consequently, there was an inrush of money, money of a quantity their eyes were unused to seeing. After the first barnburner, they went in a horse carriage to movies. Emboldened by the fruits of her craftiness, Umayal would undertake her next trip.

A year after they had migrated to Thanjavur, Kandasamy had stopped visiting them completely. Kamakshi gave birth to a third son named Kamalanathan, a replica of her nephew Murugavel. Their lives were going on smoothly until misfortune caught up with them once more.

Umayal was preparing to leave on yet another trip to sell contraband liquor when Kamakshi's son Dhanapal insisted he tag along. Murugavel's response was to lock his junior cousin and stepson in a room whereupon he began to raise a ruckus. Kamakshi could not abide the treatment her lover had meted out to her son and she intervened.

"Would you dare to treat Dhanapal as you just did if he was your own?"

Incensed, Murugavel retorted, "I have no place in this whoring house!"

Umayal, who had witnessed all and knew all, went ballistic.

"Selfish demons!" she screamed, and dragging them roughly towards a carton, she shouted, "Let me see if you two have the wherewithal to deliver it to the address I give you." In the end, she set about the task herself, taking Dhanapal with her.

It was on the selfsame occasion that Umayal got apprehended for the first time. She was thrown into prison and Dhanapal into a correctional facility for juveniles. With Umayal in prison, the family was out of funds. Murugavel felt hopeless. None of the stories he sent out to magazines gave him his big break. However, rejection did not dissuade him; his high hopes and pipe dreams had not completely deserted him. He devoted his efforts to writing film scripts. He had planned to leave for Chennai as soon as Umayal was released from prison.

Kamakshi began to sell the utensils one by one. When they had all been sold, other things in the house began to vanish. A collection of Kalki's novels, Murugavel's dearest treasures, were bartered for rice. Although she got a trifling sum for all that she sold, she cooked only the most expensive variety of basmati rice. Finally, when there was naught to sell, she began to borrow money.

Six months later, when Umayal returned from prison with Dhanapal in tow, she was shocked to find Kamaskhi with child again. Both she and Murugavel were in fine fettle although there was a mountain of debt waiting to be repaid. During her stint in prison, she had resolved to nevermore peddle liquor, but the food at home tasted worse than the worm-infested gruel she suffered herself to spoon and swallow in prison because it had been bought with borrowed money. She left Kamakshi's food untouched. On borrowed money – ironically – she set off for Karaikal the next day with some glass bottles tied to her stomach with a length of cloth. She returned with money and blisters in galore. The bottles, so tightly strapped as they were, lacerated the skin on her stomach. The sight of festering and bleeding blisters moved elicited animalistic wails from Kamakshi who applied a salve to her sister's wounds and waited on her.

This happened several times; I saw it with my own eyes whenever I visited Thanjavur as a boy. Even with the passage of years, the memory of this pathetic scene remains fresh.

Murugavel's dream to go to Chennai remained a dream. Umayal was still peddling liquor and would see the entrails of some prison every now and then. She started to wear a full-sleeved white vest so as to strap the bottles to her person without inconvenience or injury. Her stints in prison had introduced and habituated her to smoking and cussing, but her acquisitions did not cost her a cubic inch of her respect. She presented a formidable appearance with her white vest, her ash-smeared forehead and her top-knot, which became something of an insignia. The day she hurled her *mangal sutra* in Ramasamy's face was the day she wiped off the *kumkum* on her forehead, nullifying her wifehood. She no longer wore her hair in a braid or a bun. Whether it was on account of her unusual appearance or her natural tendency for tough love, she enjoyed a lot of goodwill both in prison and in the hood.

Whenever Umayal was in prison, the house was overcast with gloom.

After Kamalanathan, Kamakshi had a daughter called Suganthi. In the meanwhile, Dhanapal, like Umayal, had acquired the habit of smoking and had also experimented with gay sex from reformatory school. He never studied, choosing instead to play at cards and pull all-nighters with his friends. On days when he returned home late, he would serve himself a bit of supper, eat it, and sleep, but on occasion, he would perform a vanishing act and would not appear until a week later. Once, Murugavel asked him sternly, "What do you fancy this house to be, you little scoundrel?" When Dhanapal threw the question back at him, Murugavel tried to manhandle him and got kicked by his stepson. Dhanapal was fourteen when this happened.

Thenceforth, no one dared to raise his voice, his hand or his warning finger to Dhanapal. The only person he feared was Umayal, but bringing him to heel seemed beyond her natural capacity. How could she? Dhanapal gently stroked the welts on her stomach that were as large as shoe-impressions in mud. He bought her new vests when her old ones tore and massaged her callused feet to palliate the ache; he bought her the imported cigarettes she loved to puff. He was the only person who understood her needs and satisfied them without being asked and without being compensated. For these reasons, he was exempted from Umayal's bad graces. She knew that the boy would be able to brave the world somehow.

When Dhanapal was sixteen, he met a landlord called Vasu who lived near Thanjavur. Dhanapal soon won his confidence and became his right hand man. Within a couple of years, Vasu reached a stage where he couldn't function independently from Dhanapal, be it in drinking or even whoring. Dhanapal was not remunerated for his services, but his patron ensured that he and his kin were well-kept. Once, Vasu sent two sacks of rice to Dhanapal's house and the latter angrily told him that he would sever all ties with him should he do it again. Vasu did not, knowing full well that Dhanapal was a man of his word.

Vasu was a political figure of some importance and Dhanapal became associated by default with the party he belonged to. During poll season, they slogged in their attempt to bring the party to attention.

At the age of forty-five, Vasu died of a heart-attack, leaving Dhanapal shattered.

It was Dhanapal, then thirty, who made me discover my sexuality to when he introduced me to masturbation. The correctional facility had fashioned a sex-expert out of him. It became a custom for us to seek sexual pleasure from each other through fondling and stroking. The idols perched on the courtyards and seated cross-legged in their niches of the Brihadeeswarar Temple were mute witnesses to our sexual escapades. Apart from sex, I used to frequent the temple to read in the shade of the courtyard, propped against its cool walls.

It was at Brihadeeswarar that I had chanced to meet Somasundaram, a companionable man around forty. A devotee of Vallalar, his house was like a shrine to him – the walls were lined with Vallalar's pictures and Somasundaram spoke of him every time, all the time. He gave me food and had sex with me. I objected to neither. In retrospect, I wonder at how such an impassioned devotee of Vallalar had no second thoughts about having sex with a mite of a youth like myself.

Kamalanathan shared all of his father's traits. Films were the central axis around which his life revolved. He flunked his school examinations, had several romances and dalliances to his credit, and planned to become a playback singer.

Umayal was growing tired and worked less frequently than she would have liked to. Now that the prohibition on liquor had been lifted, it became easily available, so she began to smuggle ganja which landed her in prison for two years. She left prison a walking corpse and returned home to realize how far behind they were on the rent. The landlord gave them a tongue-lashing in full view of the street which led to a loss of face.

They vacated and began to pay forty a month for a rathole on Venkatesa Perumal Koil Street. It was to this shack that Dhanapal would return punch-drunk in the middle of the night and retch all over the place.

Life bore down on Umayal too heavily. It soon reduced her to a wreck.

Age was catching up with Ramasamy. Gnanavel had installed himself in his mistress' house. Azhaguvel, who had flown the coop years ago, suddenly materialized out of nowhere with tuberculosis. He found himself a job as a cinema operator, worked late nights and early mornings, and returned home coughing up bloody phlegm. Rajavel spent every waking hour in gambling dens. Without the knowledge of his brothers, he gambled away half his father's money. He was generally not heard from or heard of.

One day, as fate would have it, Rajavel ran into his brothers and engaged them in serious conversation. He suggested they sell their father's land and migrate to Chennai with Umayal. He had Ramasamy give his concession to said proposal, but Murugavel laid down a single condition: Kamakshi and the two children should be allowed to come along. Rajavel did not contend his brother as he already knew that Kamakshi would refuse. She did, adding that she'd much rather starve to death in Thanjavur than move to Chennai. When Rajavel came to fetch Umayal, she growled with the little strength that inhabited her, "If only this body had more strength than it is possessed with right now, I would meet your father with the broom-handle and take a swing at him!"

After selling both house and land, Ramasamy and his four sons left for Chennai.

Around this time, Vasu's friend, a landlord, hired Dhanapal to do odd jobs. Dhanapal would do whatever the man bud him do as he was dependent on his funding to buy liquor. This man, unlike his late friend, was a teetotaler who made sure Dhanapal knew his place.

Once, he asked a favor of Dhanapal. As his far-flung village lacked a good school, he wanted Dhanapal to put up his son Rasu at his place in so that he could attend school in Thanjavur. In return for his help, he would send as many sacks as was needed for Dhanapal's family. Dhanapal's situation was so pathetic that he couldn't refuse.

Rasu was enrolled in the fifth grade. The family put up with his antics because his father's rice kept their stomachs from ballooning with gas. On one occasion, however, Rasu crossed the line and Dhanapal acquainted his father with his misbehavior. The man snapped, "If the midget causes trouble, beat him up! I will not question you even if he dies." When the next complaint about Rasu came, Dhanapal hit him, for the complaint was not of a trivial sort. The boy had snitched the teacher's money.

One day Rasu had an idea which he shared with Kamakshi and the others: if they could nick coconuts from the trees behind their house, they could enjoy them, couldn't they? They certainly could, for all they were subsisting on was rice with neither condiment nor curry, and besides, the landlord kept hiking the rent. Kamakshi have her consent, but who would bell the cat? What if the neighbors spied them? Rasu assured them that he was an expert climber and since he planned to do the deed at night, no one would know.

At midnight, the boy deftly climbed the chosen tree with a sickle strapped to his waist. He then did the unexpected. Instead of plucking the coconuts stealthily, he shook the tree and created a racket that was loud enough to shake the sleep out of the entire neighborhood, which it undoubtedly did. Kamakshi and the others ran for cover to their shack.

The neighbors emerged from their houses with flaming torches. Rasu climbed down the tree and told everyone that it was Kamakshi who had masterminded the whole plan of stealing the coconuts.

When Dhanapal notified the landlord of this incident, Rasu was taken back home. The landlord would rather his son lose a year of education than share a living space with thieves. He dismissed Dhanapal with whom he wished to have naught more to do in the future.

Dhanapal stopped drinking and gave himself up to drugs. He found his drug-dependency to be of the same obsessive-compulsive nature as Murugavel and Kamalanathan's dependency on daily films. He would suffer immensely if he did not have his daily ration of dope. By then, the consensus was that he had twisted every single nerve in his brain.

There was no one to finance Kamalanathan's tickets to the movies, so stealing from the neighbors became his recourse. When that failed to satisfy him, he stole on a larger scale from shops and bartered his booty for money. In so doing, he continued to indulge in his most dearly beloved pleasure.

Suganthi, who was born after Kamalanathan, inherited a life of hunger and poverty, but she was proud of her comely appearance and had hope for the future. She was sure that her prince would come someday in a chariot and spirit her off to a good life, to a world where hunger and starvation were unknown and unheard of; a world where she would not have to wash mountains of her brothers' soiled clothes; where her loins were not chafed by the stiff rags she was forced to wear when she bled, where she was not taunted by a mother who asked her who she was thinking of when she slept on her stomach, or who told her she was not old enough to have sex when she slept on her back; where she did not have to run away in tears – humiliated – from the roofless toilet into which lecherous men would peer through the gaps in the thatch; where it was not expected of her to clean the rancid vomit of her drunken brother; where there would be no mother to kick her in fits of misdirected anger; where there were no older brothers who fought with her mother, cursing the misfortune of their birth and the inauspicious time at which their father decided to fuck her; where she would not have to endure the shame of calling her father her older brother; where she would not have to hear the animal sounds her mother made at night as she rolled around with that same older brother; where she would not have to go to school pinching her nose to avoid the stench-waves while passing defecating children on the streets.

In the world she had imagined, flowers would rain on her when bathroom taps were opened; a mere thought would cause savory food and drink to materialize before her eyes; there would be flower beds to romp and lie in; a lover would come and whisper in honeyed tones of passion; servants would wait on her; she would have adorable pet dogs to frolic with – everything would be possible and everything would be beautiful. Someday a man would come who would fall headlong for her charms.

When I went to visit my aunt during the holidays, I had to relieve myself in her roofless toilet. In Nagore, most houses lacked toilets and I sometimes found myself having to make water out in the open when the toilet was in use. In Thanjavur, the toilets were a little more than buckets and a thatched roof. In Nagore, the river-banks and the thickets, where *karuvelam* trees grew in abundance, offered some degree of privacy. These places were usually deserted, so one needn't fear prying eyes. Any balcony or terrace served as a vantage point from where one could get a fairly good look into the roofless toilet in Aunt Kamakshi's house.

The public toilet was a dry latrine with no running water. A low-caste woman had to clean the night soil in the morning.

The house, a hut to be exact, never had a bathroom. One had to hoist buckets of water from the well behind the house to wash or bathe. To preserve their dignity, Aunt Kamakshi and Suganthi chose to bathe in the kitchen.

Within a few days of reaching Chennai, Azhaguvel succumbed to his illness. Murugavel and Rajavel were unlikely to get acknowledged by Kodambakkam. The money from the sale of the house and the land was petering out. Realizing that the day when the four of them would be reduced to scraps was not far off, Rajavel opened a rice shop and charged Gnanavel with it. After many a great effort, Murugavel and Rajavel managed to find work as assistant directors, but their film projects stalled midway. Even if by some miracle as film was released, it ran for no more than a week.

Ramasamy was worrying himself sick over not having married off his sons – who were still virgins, he believed – to carry on the family legacy. Azhaguvel was no more, Murugavel and Gnanavel had started to gray at the roots. But couldn't he at least find them a couple of poor girls? He couldn't, because no girl, however poor, was willing to marry his ill-reputed sons. Only Rajavel preferred marriage over a mistress, but his notoriety made his prospects bleaker than his brothers'. Wherever and whenever his father sought an alliance for him, he was met with cutting rebuke and humiliation.

Eight years separated me and Rajavel in birth. One day, on my return from school, I was confronted with a sight most alarming. Rajavel was being mercilessly thrashed with sticks by a group of four men. A crowd had gathered to witness the spectacle and watched it like a film. Frightened, my friends and I climbed into a house and watched from the porch. Rajavel's underwear was his last scrap of dignity, but it too was soon gone. The posse continued to rain blows. Bleating like a lamb being castrated, Rajavel ducked between a pair of bony thighs and escaped. The four men followed in hot pursuit.

Later, we learned the circumstance that had warranted the sound licking – Rajavel had given a love-letter to my classmate's mother.

Post this incident, a disgraced Rajavel skipped town for a year. He resurfaced like a hero, swaggering in the streets wearing sunglasses.

Once I left Thanjavur, I lost contact with this motley brood of first cousins.

CHAPTER THIRTEEN

Kingdom Plantae

More than the ocean, I feel drawn to the mountains and the forest. There is a reason for this. The Sangam era Tamils classified the land into five geo-spaces – *kurinji* (the hills), *mullai* (the forest), *marutham* (agricultural land), *neythal* (the coastal region) and *palai* (the desert or the wastelands). There is no actual desert in Tamil Nadu, so the term is applied to the agricultural lands and the coastal regions when summer parched them almost dry. Each geo-space had its characteristic flora and fauna and even its own deity. Nagore, my hometown, is a coastal region with no mountains, so, just as a person who lives in the mountains and who has never seen the ocean dreams of it, I who lived near the ocean dreamt of the mountains and the forests.

Every place has its own language – its own way of speaking to you. In the Nagore *dargah*, you'd always hear the cooing of thousands of pigeons on the minarets with the sound of the waves. The Bay of Bengal was known for its restless temperament in Nagore. On full moon and new moon nights, the waves roared deafeningly and they would rise up to thirty feet before subsiding. In my youth, I was surrounded by the sound of the ocean as much as I was surrounded by air. Nagapattinam was on the coast too, but the sound of the ocean there was muted by the blaring noise of vehicle horns.

I lived in Delhi from 1978 to 1990. For two years, I lived on Mall Road in the northern part of the city where there was a shrubby mound called Majnu-ka-Tilla that was part of the Delhi Ridge. For someone coming from a region whose terrain was as flat as a *dosa*, even a thicket seemed like *Dandakaranya*. I used to frequent the place and on my excursions, I discovered that the forest too had its own orchestra of sounds, its own distinctive language. The forest is populated with an abundance of creatures. There is a place called Silent Valley in Kerala where you will not hear a single cricket screeching. The silence there is to be felt, not spoken of as it is beyond description. When I entered the deepest part of Silent Valley to climb the mountain, I stumbled upon a considerable number of discarded condoms.

Back in the day when there was no such thing as the computer, a number of Malayalam movies with explicit titles like *The Father-in-Law's Lust, The Passion of the Sister-in-Law* and *Miss Malini's Dirty Little Lessons* found their way into Tamil Nadu's cinema halls where they ran to jam-packed houses. Tamil Nadu used to suffer from a sex drought that movies such as these served to rectify. In fact, you got odd stares from folks if you mentioned you were going to watch a Malayalam movie. The wave created by these movies was big enough and strong enough to sweep away John Abraham, Adoor Gopalakrishnan and Aravindan who made internationally acclaimed films. Erotic Malayalam movies lost their cachet in the nineties with the advent of the computer and the mushrooming of porn sites.

The curious sexual tastes of Tamils who watched these movies astounded me. The women of their dreams were barrel-sized with birthday-balloon boobs, beach-ball buttocks and elephantine thighs. I used to see posters of these women with their legs apart, their nipples and privates were covered with no more than ribbons.

While the tastes of the men made me wonder, the antics of feminists made me anxious. Armed with tins of tar, they would blacken the breasts and the thighs of the Amazonian women in the posters. Sometimes the parts of the posters featuring the nipples and cunts would be torn by the sex starved men. May be they would have thought that they could see the real parts by tearing the papers. I used to wonder if these feminists who rubbed tar on boobs and cunts in posters with rage were any different from the men who torn the posters.

(Kokkarakko claims that women have been devising ways and means over the years to make their figures look more appealing. One day, he visited a lingerie shop in Chennai and began to wonder if he had mistakenly walked into the hardware store. Some bras looked more like breastplates – and he was told they were called underwire bras – while other bras looked like they were designed to cover butt-cheeks rather than boobs.)

Twenty-five years ago, I was invited to a feminist conference. My speech featured a few lines from Germaine Greer's essay, *Lady, Love Your Cunt*. The feminists took umbrage at my speech and there was a huge uproar that resulted in my being unceremoniously evicted from the place.

The following incident was narrated to me by Santhanam. It occurred in June 2014. Santhanam and his brother were returning home from their walk in Nageshwara Rao Park in an auto when his brother decided he wanted to buy the day's newspaper. As his brother was walking to the shop, Santhanam noticed someone up to something odd in front of the O Kadey's Restaurant. A tall, strapping young six-footer with an ID card suggesting he was employed in a software company and a leather bag dangling from one shoulder was busy shagging. Santhanam was shocked. He looked around and spotted a man talking on the phone. "Sir! Look at what that fellow is doing in public!" he spluttered. The man on the phone thought Santhanam was asking for directions and signalled him to wait. The young man was wanking off furiously. Santhanam yelled in his direction. "*Dei!* What the devil do you think you're doing?" The man climaxed that very instant, zipped up and casually walked away. Perhaps he was only urinating, Santhanam thought as he walked up to the spot to examine the ground. But he wasn't urinating. Santhanam was smart enough to tell semen from piss.

I wanted to see this place for myself, so Santhanam took me. There are many places where a person can jerk off.

You can even do it in the middle of the road and pretend you're peeing. After peeing, it is socially acceptable for a man to hold his dick and give it a little shake to prevent residual drops from wetting his underwear – or his pants if he did not fancy underwear – and this can be mistaken for masturbation. So, it is certainly not impossible for someone to masturbate in the middle of the road. But what Santhanam told me did not add up. The fellow, according to him, was standing in the middle of the road and masturbating with his erect penis in his hand. "Was he facing the wall or the road?" I asked. I was doubtful as the spot where the incident supposedly unfolded is so congested that one would find it hard to even spit. The Parvathy Bhavan Restaurant, the New India Assurance Building and the O Kadey's Restaurant all formed the street-front. Beyond the street-front, there were petty shops selling newspapers, cigarettes and snacks. Where could the man have been standing and wanking off? He could have afforded to do it where Santhanam said he did it because it was 8:45 on a Sunday morning, but the place Santhanam kept insisting he did it was the entrance of the New India Assurance Building. What was even more incredible was that the man wasn't facing the wall; he was jerking off facing the busy road.

My confusion persisted. If he was so desperate to jerk off, he could have gone to one of the restaurants and done it in the toilet. Maybe public masturbation gave him a thrill. That was most likely it. Porn sites these days feature videos of sex in public places wherein couples copulate on the sidewalk in broad daylight and crowds surround them to gape or to film the act.

Santhanam also informed me about another interesting incident. His eighteen-year-old daughter, Divya, was a fresher in an engineering college. One day, she brought home a friend called Rekha who was studying in another engineering college in Thanjavur. The girls were discussing various colleges and Santhanam and his wife joined the conversation. When Santhanam enquired about Rekha's college, the girl said that it was a shithole.

"Why?" Santhanam asked.

"Vellore is the best," she said.

"And why is that?"

"There is no maternity hospital near our college, but it's always easy to find one in Vellore. Lucky girls who study there!"

"What does the proximity to a maternity hospital have to do with your opinion of the college?"

"Oh, come on, Uncle! Don't act like you don't get what I'm implying. In Vellore, if you want to have an abortion, you don't need to go far."

Santhanam and his wife were deeply shocked to hear this from a girl who came from an orthodox Vaishnavite family.

After she'd left, Divya asked her father, "*Appa*, did you hear what she said? Don't imagine that today's youngsters are saints and angels."

The most appealing sights in Majnu-ka-Tilla were the hundreds of *kondrai* trees. These trees earned themselves the name "golden shower" as they appear golden when in flower. There are hardly any Sangam poems in which flowers are not mentioned. The golden shower was a favorite of the Sangam poets who did were generous in their praise of nature. Whenever I see a golden shower, I remember a song from the *Kurunthogai* that I'd learned as a child:

> These fat cassia trees
>
> are gullible:
>
> the season of rains
>
> that he spoke of
>
> when he went through the stones
>
> of the desert
>
> is not yet here
>
> though these trees
>
> mistaking the untimely rains
>
> have put out
>
> long arrangements of flowers
>
> on their twigs
>
> as if for a proper monsoon.
>
> (Kurunthogai 66*)

My lifelong interest in trees and flowers developed when I started reading Sangam literature, especially the works of Kapilar. In Kuninjipattu, Kabilar has mentioned the names of ninety-nine flowers in his Kurinjippaattu.

*Translated by A.K. Ramanujan

The flowers which are named in this song are:

1. Kantal Malabar - Glory lily or Indian Coral tree or Scarlet Bahunia.
2. Aampal - White water Lily
3. Anicham - Blue Pimpernel / Scarlet Pimpernel
4. Kuvalai - Fragrant water lily
5. Kurinchi - Square–branched conehead
6. Vetchi - Scarlet ixora
7. Senkoduveri - Rosy–flowered leadwort
8. Tema - Sweet mango
9. Manichikai - Purple Heart Glory
10. Unthoozh - Large bamboo
11. Koovlilam - Bael
12. Erruzh - Paper flower climber
13. Chulli - Porcupine flower
14. Kooviram - sacred garlic pear
15. Vatavanam - Shri Tulsi, Ram Tulsi
16. Vaakai - Sirissa/women's tounge
17. Kutacham - Indrajao
18. Eruvai - Small Bulrush
19. Seruvilai - White–flowered mussell–shell creeper
20. Karuvilam - Mussell–shell creeper
21. Payini - Indian Copal Tree
22. Vaani - Spindle Tree
23. Kuravam - Asiratic Terenna
24. Pasumpidi - Mysore gamboge
25. Vakulam - Pointed–leaved ape–flower
26. Kaya - Ironwood tree
27. Avirai - Tanner's senna

28. Veral - Nilgiri Bamboo
29. Sooral - Wild Jujube
30. Sirupoolai - Mountain Knot Grass
31. Kurunarunkanni - Crab's eye
32. Kurukilai - White Fig
33. Marutam - Indian Laurel
34. Konkam - Golden silk cotton tree
35. Ponkam - Horse–eye beans
36. Tilakam - Red–wood
37. Patiri - Yellow–flowered fragrant trumpet–flower tree
38. Cerunti - Panicled golden–blossomed pear tree
39. Atiral - Hog–creeper
40. Chenpakam - Champak
41. Karantai - east Indian globe thistle
42. Kulavi - Indian cork–Millingtonia hortensis or Patchouli
43. Pulima - Wild variety of Mango
44. Tillai - Blinding tree
45. Palai - Pala indigo plant, wongai plum
46. Mullai - Arabian jasmine, Juhi
47. Kanchankullai - Indian Hemp
48. Piitavam - Bedaly emetic–nut
49. Chenkarunkaali - Red catechu,
50. Vaazhai - Plantain
51. Valli - Yam, Five leagf yam
52. Neytal - Red–blue water–lily,
53. Thazhai - Coconut Spathe of the coconut tree
54. Thalavam - Red jasmine, pink jasmine
55. Taamarai - Lotus

56. Njaazhal - Orange cup–calyxed brasiletto–climber wagaty
57. Mauval - Poet's Jasmine
58. Kokudi - Indian jasmine
59. Chetal - Night–flowering jasmine, coral jasmine
60. Chemmal - Spanish Jasmin
61. Chirusenkurali - A mountain creeper Water Chestnut
62. Kotal - Malabar glory lily White species of Malabar glory lily Yellow glory lilly
63. Kaitai - Fragrant screw-pine
64. Vazhai - Long–leaved two–sepalled gamboge, Surangi
65. Kanchi - River portia, False White Teak
66. Karunkuvalai - Red Water Lily
67. Paankar - Tooth brush tree
68. Maraam - Lac tree–Shorea talura
69. Thanakkam - Whirling Nut, Helicopter Tree
70. Eenkai - Twisted acacia
71. Ilavam - Red–flowered silk–cotton tree
72. Konrai - Indian laburnum
73. Atumpu - Hare leaf, Goat's foot vine
74. Aathi - Maloo Creeper, Yellow Orchid Tree
75. Avarai - Field–bean
76. Pakanrai - Indian jalap
77. Palaasam - Palastree, Flame of the Forest
78. Pinti - Asoka tree
79. Vanchi - Rattan Palm
80. Pithikam - Wild Jasmine
81. Sintuvaram - Five–leaved Chaste tree
82. Thumpai - Bitter toombay, a common weed

83. Thulay - Sacred basil, Krishna Tulsi
84. Thondri - Malabar glory lily
85. Nanthi - Indian rosebay, Crape Jasmine
86. Naravam - Indian lavanga
87. Punnaakam - Poon
88. Paaram - Indian cotton–plant,
89. Peeram - Sponge gourd, strainer–vine
90. Kurukkathi - Common delight of the woods, Helicopter Flower
91. Aaram - Sandalwood tree
92. Kaazhvai - Eagle–wood
93. Punnai - Mast–wood
94. Narantham - Malabar Lemon Grass
95. Nagappoo - Ironwood of Ceylon
96. Nallirunaai - Iruvatchi Jasmine
97. Kururuntham - Wild lime–Indian Atalantia
98. Venkai - East Indian kino tree
99. Puzhaku - Crown Flower

Of the ninety-nine flowers he mentioned, I have spotted and identified at least fifty in Nagore. Whenever my eyes alighted upon a new flower, I would feel elated beyond words and I would immediately set about finding its botanical name. Even in the forest, I am always on the lookout for new flowers. The scarlet ixora is one of my favorites.

In Nagore, most of the trees grew near the Vettar. The most common tree was, of course, the beautiful golden shower that came into full bloom during the autumn. The pollen of the flowers was like gold dust. Whenever my friends and I came across a golden shower, we would peel the skin off the firm fruits and remove their neatly arranged seeds. Sometimes we'd perforate the lobes and make the seeds rattle. At other times, we'd make a long hole through the tubular fruit, remove all the seeds and blow. This would produce a loud whistling noise capable of waking up the entire village. This noise, to us, was music.

When I went to Nagore last year, I was rudely shocked to see that there were now a number of huts where the golden showers used to be. The trees were all gone. Not a single one was left.

Once a month, we would walk all the way to Velipalayam to watch movies at Star Theatre. We were familiar with the names of most of the trees along the way. The gulmohar tree with its bunches of scarlet flowers was, like the golden shower, another favorite of mine. On Tuesday nights, my mother observed a fast in honor of Pillaiyar. Only women keep this fast and men are traditionally forbidden to be present at the *puja*.

According to legend, there once lived a poor peasant who had seven sons and one daughter. The grains brought home by the sons in lieu of wages were full of husk and chaff, so the family was unable to have a proper meal. One day, the poetess Avvaiyar knocked at their door for alms. The daughter wept, saying that they had only husk and chaff to eat. On hearing her plight, Avvaiyar, moved by compassion, gave her some rice grains. She instructed the girl to make an offering of them to Pillaiyar and begin a fast that would rid her of her poverty and bring happiness into her life.

The girl took Avvaiyar's advice and began her fast on a Tuesday and ended it with a *puja* at night after her brothers had fallen asleep. As there was no fire, the girl went out to see if there was one still burning and saw a mast tree and a tamarind tree standing alongside each other. Planting one foot on either tree, she climbed. Craning her neck, she spotted a fire burning at a distance. When she made her way to the location of the fire, she realized that it was a cremation ground. When the *vettiyan* espied her, he asked whether she was a woman or a ghost. She explained her situation to him whereupon he asked her to pray for him as well and he gave her a cake of dung and some burning coals. Upon returning home, she broke some twigs from the mast and tamarind trees and made some dumplings with the leaves, arranged them in the form of two human beings – the *vettiyan* and the corpse from whose pyre she obtained the burning coals – and offered them to Pillaiyar. Within a few days, the family began to prosper as Avvaiyar had said it would.

Ever since, women have observed the Tuesday fast. The ritual demands that the men of the house should not hear the women's chants and prayers or taste the dumplings even after they are offered. So, the women choose a house where there are no men. The rice grains brought by each woman are ground and mixed with tender coconut water to form a dough. *Adais* are made out of this dough and they are steamed. Pillaiyar is fashioned out of the dung cake of a calf and the *adais* are offered to it. Once the offering is made, the women eat the rest of the *adais* as they cannot be taken home. Before dawn, the dung-idol of Pillaiyar is submerged in the nearby river with the mast and tamarind twigs, hay and flowers.

During the months of *Aadi* and *Thai*, I was tasked with fetching the mast twigs for my mother every Tuesday. As there was no mast wood tree near our house, I had to go all the way to the cremation ground. I refrained from collecting tamarind twigs as ghosts – who supposedly targeted the oldest child of the house – were said to dwell in tamarind trees. As I was the oldest child in my house, I steered clear of tamarind trees.

I always associate tamarind trees with the images of hanging women, most of whom took their lives following a nasty fight with their husbands. In Nagore, men don't commit suicide; they head to the toddy shops. If women too had the option of drowning in toddy, most of them wouldn't have committed suicide. The ghosts of all the dead women took up residence in the tamarind trees. I do not doubt this as I have seen many a man vomit blood and die under them. These ghosts do not kill women, but tend to possess them. The fact that several women had committed suicide meant that there were several ghosts looking for bodies to possess. This became a grave problem as the number of possessed women in Nagore only kept increasing. Crazy, possessed women were probably one of my reasons for fleeing Nagore. Even today, I'm afraid of the dark.

As boys, we knew that the ghosts would leave us alone if we went in a group in broad daylight, so we would all go together and pluck the fruit of the tamarind tree. If the fruit was ripe, the flesh inside would separate from the outer shell; you could tell if there was a rattle when you shook it. We used to break off a small piece of the shell, pour some water into the hole and shake it vigorously to obtain a delicious drink.

Now, when I see a mast tree, I think of my mother's Tuesday fast. I remember people pressing oil from the seed of the tree's fruit. Bats usually make their homes on mast trees; they eat the fruit and drop the seed husk. If the seed husks are dried in the sun, they can be cracked open easily. The seeds, once taken out, are dried again for ten days after which they are pressed to yield oil. One kilogram of mast seeds can yield 0.75 liter of oil. A mere half-liter of this oil can be used to run a HP diesel motor for an hour.

I have befriended and spoken to a number of trees in Nagore. When I spotted an Arjuna tree in Odisha, near the Puri Jaganath Temple, I just ran to it and hugged it. Hugging that tree did not feel much different than hugging my mother.

In the 172nd poem in the book *Nattrinai*, the poet writes of a hero who goes to his beloved's house. He takes her to the mast wood tree under which she tells him, "Since my childhood days, I have nurtured this *punnai* tree with great love and affection. On seeing this, my mother told me that it is my twin sister. So I feel shy to talk to you under this tree. If you wish, we can find a shady spot elsewhere."

The mast tree is the *sthala vruksham* of the Kapaleeswarar Temple in Mylapore where I now live. Legend has it that when Ambal prayed to Siva, he appeared before her standing under a mast tree.

In the seventh century, there was a man called Sivanesan who lived in Mylapore with his daughter Poompavai. Sivanesan was keen on marrying his daughter to Gnanasampanthar, a great devotee of Shiva. However, before his plans of marriage could materialize, Poompavai died of snakebite. Sivanesan kept her bones and ashes in an urn which he presented to Gnanasampanthar along with an explanation upon his return to Chennai. Gnanasampanthar meditated on Kapaleeswarar and sang eleven sonnets. When he had finished the last sonnet, the urn exploded and Poompavai emerged from the ashes. Sivanesan lowered his head and fell on his knees in gratitude to Gnanasampanthar and requested him to take Poompavai as his wife, but he was met with refusal. Gnanasampanthar reasoned that he, by virtue of having given her life, was a father to her. Poompavai remained unmarried and spent the rest of her days serving Lord Shiva.

There was a *ya* tree in Nagore's palm grove. *Ya's* delicate barks that the elephants strip and eat due to their high moisture content. Though the *ya* has a life span of seventy years, it flowers but once in its lifetime; the flower is quite large and can be smelled from afar. Most *ya* trees are *ardhanarishvara* – androgynous.

Durga is the presiding deity of *palai* and her flower is the *payini*, the flower of the *ya*. There is a poem in the *Kurunthogai (37)* in which there is mention of *ya*.

The heroine who is worried that her lover has not returned to her is consoled by her friend: 'During his journey he will see a male elephant stripping the bark of a *ya* tree so that the hungry female elephant can drink from it. On seeing this won't your love's heart be touched? Then he will remember you and come running to your side.'

Seven years ago, we moved into the house we are now living in. It was rather old when we got it, but we could have got worse. There were a number of trees around the house, a portia and a gulmohar among them. I was thrilled to have these two trees growing outside my house as I was seeing them after twenty whole years (I last saw them in Ngaore). I remember my mother using the steamed leaves of the gulmohar to ameliorate knee pain and backaches. To me, the tree looked like a peacock with its tail fanned out. As for the portia, if you stood under its broad shade, you wouldn't feel the heat on a hot summer's afternoon. Inside our premises, we had a jackfruit tree, two mango trees, a guava tree, a hibiscus plant, a coconut tree, a curry leaf tree, a papaya tree and a few neem trees. Monkeys would sometimes come over and treat themselves to a few mangoes. A considerable population of squirrels, bats, parrots and cuckoos also lived with us. But fate is vagarious; I was forced to cut down my two most dearly beloved trees – the portia and the gulmohar. Let me digress a bit before I tell you why.

A Chinese girl who was my classmate at Alliance Française had her phone robbed one day. She was certain she had it when she entered the building, so it had definitely been stolen by someone within the premises. She told me that it wasn't the loss of the phone that upset her as much as the fact that someone had taken something which did not belong to them.

Even when there is a traffic accident, there are slimebags who make off with the dead person's purse, cellphone, jewels and other valuables before the cops arrive on the scene. So, if the accident badly disfigured the person's face, identification would be a task. What breed of scumbags do such things? And just so you know, the folks who steal at the scene of an accident are not always poor.

Now consider this incident. In Toulouse, Gunaratnam, his daughter Dharmini and I were returning to his home after an outing when we spotted a bulging purse lying on the road. Inside it were wads of cash, a keychain, several bank receipts and a passbook. Clearly, this purse belonged to someone who'd just recently been to the bank and withdrawn money. We took the purse to the bank and were told by an officer that an elderly woman had come to him a little while ago to enquire if her purse had been seen. We decided to wait at the bank until she returned.

The old woman came back shortly afterwards and was delighted to get her purse back. Out of gratitude, she took out a hundred franc note from her purse and offered it to Dharmini. Confused, Dharmini refused it. Throughout our journey home, Dharmini kept asking us why the old woman had offered her money when we'd just returned to her what was rightfully hers.

Here in India young boys kidnap their own friends for ransom just so they can buy themselves a pair of Adidas shoes, a geared bicycle, an iPhone or an iPad. Consumerism has made maniacs and fools of a lot of people. Santhanam told me that he'd gone to the hospital when his sister-in-law delivered. When he entered her room, the television was on full blast and the woman was engrossed in a Velukkudi Krishnan speech. The woman was so proud that her twelve-hour-old infant was listening to *Bhagavata Upanyasam.* This is how our poor Indian children become addicted to and enslaved by the television.

Okay, now I shall tell you the story behind the felling of the portia and the gulmohar. As the tress cast an expansive shade, auto and taxi drivers would park their vehicles underneath them and take a nap. I could tolerate sleeping and snoring, but they got bolder with time – they'd bring bottles of cheap liquor, drink and break the bottles under the trees before leaving. This worked up Perundevi who stopped attending to the housework to keep vigil. She had sharp ears and whenever she heard the sound of a vehicle, she would go to the door and shout at the driver. When I asked her why she was so obsessed with trying to ensure propriety, she said, "Try picking up shards of glass and you'll know why." I felt sorry for her. Some drivers paid heed to her while some retorted. "This is government land," they'd say. "Who the hell are you to complain?" She used to call the police a lot and this earned her the nickname "Crime Branch." There were some fellows who parked their cars under the trees overnight. The car provided a convenient cover for them to drink and the darkness for them to defecate.

The stench of their shit defied description. Although I grew up in the midst of the odor of other people's waste, I was left nauseated. These drivers eat truckloads of food and leave behind mountains of shit. If my fulminations have got you thinking I'm a discriminator, you're dead wrong. The food one eats is responsible for the smell of one's body and, of course, one's shit. If you eat a plate of beef and a pot of rice all cooked in rancid oil, your shit will out-stink sewage. Cow dung doesn't stink because it's just grass and cotton seeds.

I've heard a number of Indians ridicule the ass-cleaning practice of the westerners as Indians who travel abroad have a personal problem with the use of toilet paper to wipe the filth off their backsides. As they eat food with an over abundance of *masala*, they will find it harder to clean their asses, and they will need bucketsful of water.

Perundevi's first task in the morning was to dispose of the mountains of shit in front of the house after covering them with mud.

One day, unable to bear the sight of her cleaning up what had come out of another person's hole, I told her, "Just cover it with mud and leave it there, won't you?"

"Okay, but what about the glass shards? Won't my feet get cut when I draw the *kolam*?"

I said no more.

Santhanam told me he'd fixed a plastic *kolam* at the

entrance of his house. While this is a convenient solution for people living in apartment houses, it wasn't for us because we had the road in front of our place and Perundevi had crows to feed.

She finally came up with a solution to stop the drivers from using our place to defecate once and for all. The trees had to be felled. Once there was no longer any shade in that spot, no driver would want to park his vehicle. So, I chopped the trees and ever since I did, no motherfucker has dared to shit in front of our house.

No amount of explanation will make the sordid ways of Indians comprehensible to Westerners. When I visited Kutralam recently, I discovered that the mountain path to Shenbaga Devi stream had been closed off to tourists and could only be accessed with permission from the government. The path was closed because the visitors usually ran amok. No amount of police surveillance could stop people from drinking there and littering the place with bottles. The sage Agathiyar lived on the mountain that was being profaned with litter because no wino gives a flying fuck about a sage. Although the path to the stream had been closed, the temple below the stream was still open. To visit the temple, many young men would tie yellow *dhotis* around their waists and climb the mountain. Their hysterical shouts make the entire forest shudder. I will never understand the logic behind screaming like a lunatic monster to express enthusiasm. They piped down after a warning and a sermon from a cop. One of the cops told me that the rule was imposed to prevent the deaths of drunk people who often lost their footing and fell into the stream.

CHAPTER FOURTEEN

Hum Tum Ek Kamre Mein Bandh Ho

Johnny Mera Naam starring Dev Anand and Hema Malini; *Sachcha Jhoota* starring Rajesh Khanna and Mumtaz; *Kati Patang* and *Aan Milo Sajna* starring Rajesh Khanna and Asha Parekh; *Purab aur Paschim* starring Manoj Kumar and Saira Banu; *Safar* starring Rajesh Khanna and Sharmila Tagore; *Kab, Kyon aur Kahan* starring Dharmendra and Babita Kapoor; *Dastak* starring Sanjeev Kumar and Rehana Sultan... and this '70s litany, like Rose's heart in *Titanic,* could go "on and on," with the infinite permutations and combinations of hero and heroine, lover and beloved, Romeo and Juliet, and... I think you get the picture.

Another thing you should "get" is the fact that these Hindi films usurped the throne of popularity down south with the likes of *Aradhana, Kati Patang* and *Bobby* riding high on celebrity and running to full houses. And what could this upsurge of Hindi cinema's popular appeal be attributed to if not the dwindling appeal of Tamil cinema? The '60s and the '70s saw the lure of homegrown films hit an all-time low. The brightest stars in Tamil Nadu's thespian-galaxy, M. G. Ramachandran and Sivaji Ganesan, were beginning to lose their luster.

M.G.R.'s *Ulagam Sutrum Vaaliban* received more ridicule than relish on its silver jubilee as the spectacle of an old geezer (miscast in the role of a young Romeo) prancing around with a young lass in full bloom was far from being amusing in the slightest.

Following the dissolution of the partnership of music duo Vishwanathan and Ramamurthy in 1965, Tamil cinema was relegated to such a sorry place that folks would rather walk out for a smoke than suffer through a song.

The most unforgettable year of the '70s for me was 1973 – the year *Bobby* hit the screen. At that point in time, the number of films I'd seen was exceeded by the number of film songs I'd listened to. *Bobby*, unlike its inferior cousins, was not a film to be watched just once. The hype over the film spread like a contagion, and my peers and I happened to be among the affected. We would faithfully attend screenings of *Bobby* like Sunday services. Friends of mine from whose barrels no paisa could be scraped would stand outside the theater during the shows.

In *Bobby*'s glory-days, a 29 paise ticket got you a bench with no back, a 58 paise ticket afforded you a seat with comfort guaranteed to both your back and your backside. Much like the modern-day college, entries and exits were proceduralized. It would have been ticket for out-pass if you wanted to get out, and out-pass for ticket if you wanted to get back in. The early birds got the best perches in terms of seats.

Bobby's maiden screening was at Aruna Theater in Trichy. After having run there for a staggering 175 days, it was picked up by Gaiety. *Yaadon ki Bharat* was also abreast of *Bobby* in terms of popularity, having enjoyed a year-long run in the latter.

It was customary to keep the windows open so that the dialogues could reach the masses assembled outside the theater. I remember being among them.

The playground of Bishop Heber School – sadly a playground no more – is another space I associate with the *Bobby* craze as the songs of the film were a staple during the school's football matches.

The chief of several reasons behind the film's popularity was eye-candy in the person of Dimple Kapadia. Her first appearance in the film had her clad in such a manner that very little was left to the hyperactive male imagination. Folks would flock in droves to the theater just to catch a glimpse of her well-displayed assets.

Another topic of great interest, aside from the eye-popping, jaw-dropping shape of Dimple Kapadia's body, was the color of Rishi Kapoor's lips slash lipstick. How red were his lips? How red weren't they? And this man's curious lips – that had people swooning – incited debates that ran into hours.

Popular films yield popular songs as is the case with *Bobby* and *Mujhe Kuch Kehna Hai*, where we see that Dimple Kapadia has graduated from short skirts to bikinis. Toying with the assumption that your 20-something-year-old '70s South-Indian boy was an inexperienced virgin with no knowledge of the *Kama Sutra*, one can only imagine how Dimple Kapadia's boobs and Aruna Irani's back would have jerked his dormant libido awake. Wait, during the song *Beshak Mandir*, Dimple was shown gloomily lying in bed, one leg folded and in a slightly inclined position. There were many boys among us who saw that movie 16 times just to see if anything more could be seen under the skirt that rode up her thighs.

From all that has been said, we can very well understand how Kapadia and Irani contributed to the furthering of the young man's knowledge of the female body (Boobs? Check. Butt? Check) and his vocabulary thereof (Panties? Check. Bra? Check.).

The music and the visuals shared a point of similarity in that they could both be described as having been "stirring," though each in its own peculiar way. Narendra Chanchal's *Beshak Mandir* was one such "stirring" song that caught on in Tamil Nadu, and it went on to become a much-performed number, surprisingly by people who couldn't speak Hindi. Hindi was unknown in entire Tamil Nadu. In 1965, students had set themselves on fire to oppose the imposition of Hindi. But a mere eight years later, Hindi movies were given a rousing welcome.

Translating the songs as a service to my friends proved to be an interesting task as they were keen on speculating the meanings of words and overanalyzing metaphors. Take for instance the line, *"Hum Tum Ek Kamre Mein Bandh Ho/ Aur Chchabi Kho Jaye."* I would tell them that *kamra* meant "room" and *chchabi* meant "key," and they would claim that these were just symbols and that there was an underlying sexual innuendo to them.

We ended up deifying R. D. Burman and assigned divine status to Laxmikant-Pyarelal too for their soundtrack par excellence to the *Bobby* film.

Yaadon ki Bharat was full of music and relatively empty of aphrodisiacal visuals, featuring pieces by names such as Lata Mangeshkar, Kishore Kumar, Asha Bhonsle and R. D. Burman. Every aspect of the music seemed to be of semiotic import, exemplifying free-spiritedness, revolt and revolution. The rollicking song *Aapke Kamre Mein Koi Rehta Hai* turned the theater into a dance floor. Dance and music had such a liberating effect. We would sway and jump for ten minutes as the song played. Tariq and his manic guitar-playing exemplified freedom for us. Burman's booming voice and Tariq's frenzied tickling of the fretboard were like a revolt against narrow convention. Once *Dum Maro Dum* concluded, we'd leave the theater in ecstasy. At this juncture, I invite you to think of the role and the reception of these movies and songs at a time when there were hardly any pubs in Tamil Nadu.

R. D. Burman injected western-ness into Indian music and became a craze among the '70s youth. His music helped me understand and appreciate western musical forms like jazz and blues.

The beautiful Dimple who had every man slobbering over her did not appear in any more movies. It was my friend Naseem who told us that Dimple had married Rajesh Khanna even before the release of *Bobby*, and that Khanna had forbidden her to act thereafter. Our fury boiled over when we heard that Dimple was all of sixteen when she tied the knot with then thirty-year-old Khanna. We felt a murderous fury towards the man. We were sorrowful to know that her first movie was to be her last. Nobody could replace her in our affections whether it was Asha Parekh, Rakhee or Mumtaz.

Sharmila Tagore's name was the first to appear in the titles in most Hindi movies of the '70s, before Rajesh Khanna's. I don't know if any other Indian actress could boast of having her name appear before that of the "first superstar" of Indian cinema. It was in 1975 in the film *Chupke Chupke* that the names of both Dharmendra and Sharmila Tagore were equally billed, but I doubted even Sharmila Tagore could fill Dimple's shoes as the former's movies were mostly tearjerkers – *Aradhana* being a typical example. Khanna's character, Arun Varma, falls in love with Tagore's character, Vandana. Not very long after they fall in love, Varma dies in a plane crash, leaving Vandana with child. Vandana now has the reputation of a loose woman and has to face humiliation from Varma's aunt. Varma expressed to Vandana that should the child be a boy, he should follow his father's footsteps and join the Air Force. The white-clad widowed Vandana goes on to work as a housemaid. Prem Chopra, like in most of his movies, played the villain whose main task is to rape the female lead. Vandana kills Chopra when he tries to force himself on her and she goes to jail. She is sentenced to fourteen years but is released in twelve for good conduct. Though the movie is a sappy tearjerker from start to finish, R. D. Burman's excellent score made the film worth watching.

In *Daag*, Khanna escapes from prison after murdering Prem Chopra who attempted to rape Tagore. After his escape from prison, Khanna disguises himself by sporting a drooping moustache.

No male member in Santhanam's family grew a moustache, so he, in his eighteenth year, began sporting one, ignoring the remonstrations of his family members. He was obsessed with Rajesh Khanna's moustache in the movie *Daag*. However, his moustache was short-lived, for his wife-to-be made it known to him on the day of the *janavasam* that she would like his moustache removed. So, his wedding day saw the end of his whisker-days.

Santhanam showed me pictures of his *janavasam*. His moustache was an exact replica of Khanna's *Daag* moustache and if only he hadn't shaved it off at his fiancée's behest, he might have been spared an encounter with Yama several years later.

Santhanam used to live in the postal staff quarters in Teynampet, which, like all government quarters, resembled a filthy slum. One day, when he was returning from his walk in Nageshwara Rao Park, he saw a man lifting his *veshti* and urinating in front of his house, his black dick in full view. Little did Santhanam know that the man with the black dick was Lord Yama come in person. He was angry. *What kind of bastard urinates in front of somebody's house, holding his black dick for all the world to see?* he thought.

"Sir, would you mind doing your business somewhere

else?" he shouted, but the man with the black dick didn't seem to hear, so he clapped his hands and raised his voice. "*Saar*, don't pee there!"

By this time, Lord Yama had finished peeing and turned to face Santhanam.

"You fucking Brahmin! I could finish you *right* now, but today is my birthday and I'm off to see my leader, so I'm sparing you. Just remember you'd be dead meat by now if not for this happy occasion," Lord Yama bellowed.

Santhanam began to tremble like a naked man at the top of a mountain and his heart was pounding furiously against his ribcage.

"W-what d-did I s-say?" he asked. "I only asked you to go urinate someplace else."

"You fucking Brahmin! No motherfucker has ever tried to get my attention by clapping hands and addressing me like a lowlife."

So saying, Lord Yama left the place. When he did, Santhanam's eyes fell on a poster. Lord Yama was telling the truth. He was a VIP in a political party. The posters, all featuring his smiling mug, wished him a happy fortieth birthday and a long life.

"It would have been the day of my death if it hadn't been the day of his birth!" Santhanam said. "But I don't understand how he knew I was a Brahmin, Udhaya."

"If you'd been sporting a moustache, Santhanam, he wouldn't have known."

It took me a whole month to write about the '70s in

Hindi film. If Rajesh Khanna hadn't been sporting that weird moustache in *Daag*, and if Santhanam, who hailed from a family where it was unheard of men to have moustaches, did not decide to sport one, I would never have written this section.

While we were talking, Santhanam happened to mention *Amar Prem*, a movie I'd never seen, but whose songs I adored. My favorite song in the movie is Kishore Kumar's *Kuch to Log Kahenge*. *Amar Prem* was adapted from a Bengali story written by Bhubhutibhushan Bandopadhyay about a woman whose circumstances force her into prostitution.

In the sorrow of Bandopadhyay's woman, Pushpa, I glimpsed the sorrow of every Indian woman. I felt the sorrows of every Indian woman become my own when Kishore Kumar sang *Kuch to Log Kahenge*.

I listened to this song over and over when I was writing this chapter. When I told Anjali the next day about it and sent her the video of the song.

"So, you were under Sharmila Tagore's spell the whole of yesterday?" she asked me. "Is her dimple a black hole for men like you?"

In the month it took me to write this chapter, I began to live in the 1970s. I thought about Rajesh Khanna and Dimple Kapadia a lot. I would often speak about Kishore and R. D. Burman to Kannan as he was a fanatic of Hindi film songs. Kannan was a generation younger than Santhanam and me. Just as we'd listened to Burman on our radios in the 70s, Kannan watched his songs on television in the 80s. Despite his late start, Kannan was miles ahead of me in Kishore Kumar trivia. There was nothing he didn't know about the man. He gave me this little nugget once: when Kishore was a popular actor in the 50s, Mohammad Rafi once lent his voice to a song that was mouthed by Kishore. The song was *Aja Bhai Dastan Teri Ye Zindagi* from the movie *Shararat*. Kannan even sang it for me. I only know a bit about Hindi movie soundtracks from the 70s. I was scarcely acquainted with Bollywood's output from the late 70s to the 90s. In 1990, I returned to Chennai from Delhi. Shortly thereafter, I worked in Vellore for four years. In undertaking the daily six-hour commute from Vellore to Chennai, I'd completely lost touch with the world. It was in the trains that I'd pored over Latin-American literature.

I struck up a friendship with Krishna when I was subsequently posted back to Chennai. Unfailingly, we would meet at the Lighthouse on Thursdays and converse for hours. Krishna's friends would be there too. One day, I noticed a dark, sticky man in the group. Krishna introduced us, but only perfunctorily. For the sake of conversation, I asked the man where he worked. Krishna pulled me aside and gave me an earful. "I know you're a stupid cunt, but you don't want folks thinking you're three sheets to the wind and making fun of the guy. That's Goundamani, currently the most popular comedian in Tamil cinema."

To remedy my three-decade Bollywood blind spot, I'd bombarded Kannan the film whiz with a series of questions: "What's Tariq, the *Yaadon Ki Bharat,* heartthrob doing now? What became of Neetu Singh who performed a sexy number in the same movie? How's the Khanna-Dimple relationship going?"

His answers were shocking to say the least. Khanna and Dimple had split after eight years of marriage. Dimple, after retiring from Bollywood post her marriage to Khanna, made a comeback in the 80s as a sex-symbol. In the 90s, she dabbled in art-house film.

Having heard everything about everyone, I spent quite some time thinking of Rajesh Khanna. He was considered to be the first superstar of Hindi cinema. Indian women went bonkers at the sight of him. According to Kannan, several women supposedly had near-orgasmic experiences merely listening to his voice in *Aradhana*. There were apparently a good number who seriously contemplated suicide when he and Dimple split. When he visited Chennai, there were some five hundred girls hanging around his hotel till wee hours just to catch a glimpse of him – and all of them were ready to jump in bed with him, just so you know. This in mind, why the fuss over a man wanking at the thought of a sexy woman when a woman too takes a male superstar for her fantasy mate? Anyone care to tell me what the big deal is?

There was another thing I failed to understand. How does a superstar like Rajesh Khanna, every woman's heartthrob, fail as a husband to one of the most beautiful women in the world? Dimple is reported to have said that she lost all her happiness the day she married Rajesh. He could give her no happiness, but he was a source of pleasure to countless Indian women. What sweet irony!

Kannan asked me if I'd watched *Khel Khel Mein*. The film was trashy, but I loved the song *Khullam Khulla Pyar Karen*. "How's that movie's star Rakesh Roshan doing? He of the hazel eyes…" I queried like blind old Dhritarashtra who was seeking an eyewitness account of the war from his charioteer.

"That was exactly what I was coming to," Kannan said. "Rakesh's son Hrithik has become the man whose body every woman thinks of when she fingers herself."

Bloody hell! So *this* was the divine-eyed bastard Anjali had told me about, the one she said she thought of when she was jacking off recently.

"Ranbir Kapoor is one of the most popular men these days," Kannan said.

I'd known of Randhir Kapoor, but who the fuck was Ranbir now?

Kannan apprised me that Prithiviraj Kapoor's scions had made a mass-entry into the film industry and had become well-known faces in the country.

"What about Tariq?" I asked again.

"Tariq acted in merely eleven movies between '73 and '95. Disillusioned, he quit film and started working as a manager in a logistics company. I'm sure you're not as ignorant to not know that Tariq's cousin Aamir Khan has become a superstar himself."

In the present day and age, the youth have sophisticated technology that gives them access to porn and sex chatrooms. Oh, the conveniences of technological advancement! It has enabled couples separated by physical distance to masturbate while looking at each other's naked bodies on video chat. Newspapers have reported that hundreds of condoms were found in the toilet of a call center in Chennai. Now let me tell you something that's going to shock you. In the 70s, it was highly unlikely that a young man of twenty would have spoken to a woman who wasn't his mother or his sister.

Hindi movies were the only available source of entertainment. When I was discussing this with Santhanam, who was only a couple of years younger than me, he said that his mania for Hindi films and songs had ruined his life. Apparently, he used to listen to Hindi music for at least six hours a day like a possessed madman. *Vividh Bharati*, Ceylon Radio's competitor, used to air Hindi movie songs from nine in the morning to eleven in the night. Santhanam was able to listen to *Vividh Bharati* as he was studying in Chennai while I only had access to Ceylon Radio.

It is quite something to be able to listen to songs on a tin-box radio that even a scrap-dealer wouldn't touch. Most of the time, the white noise and the crackling were louder than the music. To pick up a signal properly, the transistor needed someone to grip it the right way. If the battery ran out of juice, we had to wait an entire week to get a replacement. We simply couldn't afford an electric radio. Did you know we needed a license to have a radio at home? We used to have to visit the post office quarterly to renew the license. Santhanam surprised me when he said that there was a license called *villai* that one needed to possess in order to own a cycle. But transistors, unlike radios, needed no license. Santhanam had the luck of being able to listen to music being played on a gramophone in Srivilliputhur. Every music aficionado knew and loved the HMV logo in those days.

Santhanam says that there have been only two grand experiences in his life thus far. His first one was getting laid on his first night; the second great thing happened in '71. He'd skipped college to go to Safire and catch a morning show. That was his first time watching a movie in an air-conditioned hall. On a huge screen, with a quality of sound he didn't know existed, he watched Shashi Kapoor's *Sharmilee*.

"Udhaya, do you remember the song *Khilte Hain Gul Yahan* that Kishore Kumar sang to Burman's music? My body and soul tingled when I heard that song in the theatre. I can still feel it. It was just so divine! Rakhee's feline eyes, her otherworldly beauty, Lata Mangeshkar's spellbinding voice!" Santhanam gushed. *O Meri Sharmilee* was another intoxicating song from that movie that I must have listened to more times than I care to remember on my tin-box transistor. Fortunately, Naseem had a Sony tape-recorder his father had sent him from Singapore that was a blessing to us Hindi music maniacs.

I made Kokkarakko read the chapter I've just finished. When he was done, he sat motionless like a rock.

"So, how was it?"

"Terrible. There's not a jot of excitement here. You've

lost your way and your head reading too much Tarun Tejpal."

That was his terse verdict.

CHAPTER FIFTEEN

A Capital Experience – Delhi Diaries

With the exception of Delhi, I have never, at any point in my life, been emotionally tethered to any place. Mandi House and the surrounding libraries and theatres were the sanctuaries in which I became acquainted with and eventually became a culture hog. It was in one of those theaters that I first got introduced to Uday Shankar through his film *Kalpana*, who looked like Lord Shiva. The man Uday Shankar is the reason art has such a great impact on me today.

Between 1978 and 1990, when I was living in Delhi, I used to keep a diary. It runs into thousands of pages. It would make absolutely no sense to squeeze its contents between the covers of this book, so I'll just accommodate a few snippets alongwith comments that surged while transcribing the diary for the novel.

February 6, 1980

In Mandi House, Ramabadran and I were watching the play *Madhyama Vyayoga* which was enacted by a troupe of actors from Kerala who were called *Thiruvarangam.*

The word "*madhyama*" means "middle." In the play, it refers to the middle child of Kunti, Bhima and the middle son of a Brahmin called Keshavadasa. Keshavadasa was making his way through a forest with his wife and his three sons when the Ghatotkacha, the son of Bhima and Hidimba, started to chase him through the forest, asking him for one of his sons. His reason for wanting one of them? Just so his mother could break her fast by eating a crunchy human being. The flabbergasted Brahmin immediately said that he would never give up his eldest son while his wife held on to the youngest son. So, the middle son volunteered himself as food. "Madhyama, Madhyama," Ghatotkacha says, "get ready." On hearing this, Bhima, who was exercising in a clearing, thought he was being summoned – as he was also a middle son – and went thither.

The old Brahmin beseeched Bhima to save his son. When Bhima told Ghatotkacha to spare the youth's life, Ghatotkacha replied that he had to return to his mother with a human being in tow. (His mother was an ogress). Bhima then offered himself up in the place of the Brahmin's son. Ghatotkacha agreed to take him in his stead. However, Bhima laid down a condition. "If you want me to come with you, you must beat me in a duel." Bhima won the duel after a protracted fight. Ghatotkacha still requested Bhima to accompany him to his mother's house.

Bhima's personality was an equal mix of *rajasam* and *tamasam*. This is why Bhasa describes him as having honey-colored eyes as well as a set of fangs. *Madhyama Vyayog* is a one-of-a-kind play for the manner in which it presents the predicament of a man in the middle, who finds himself suffocated and pressed against from two sides. Bhima and Keshavadasa's son had to endure this suffocation and at the same time, a sort of emptiness. As the father is disposed to love the eldest son and the mother the youngest, the middle son learns that there is no one to love him. This is why Ghatotkacha came forward and said to Bhima, 'I like you but I have the responsibility to keep my mother's stomach happy.'

Everyone ended up going to Hidimba and it was finally revealed that it was all just a ploy to bring Bhima to her.

The dialogue at this point in the play is stellar.

Bhima asks Hidimba, pointing at Ghatotkacha, "What is this, Hidimba?"

Hidimba then reveals Ghatotkacha's parentage to Bhima. He is Ghatotkacha's father.

(I skipped work the next day and went to the Central Secretariat Library to read the play in the original Sanskrit along with the English translation.)

The Civil Supplies Department in Delhi where I worked was a den of corruption. My colleagues were only too happy that I didn't show up to work on most days. (I used to spend almost all my time at the Central Secretariat Library). They were happy because my absence meant one less set of fingers to share the grease with. It was a mutually convenient arrangement. I would be in the library from the morning till six in the evening, taking only a short late-afternoon break for a plate of *kachori*. I still have with me a small mountain of handwritten notes I took in the library.

Now, let me share with you another slice of my journal.

February 13, 1980

It's a gloriously happy day today because I beat my colleague Bhilai in an arm-wrestling match. The Rajasthani chap is a skinny midget, only five feet off the ground, but he's as tough as nails.

I once engaged Bhilai in an arm-wrestling match. He had me pinned before I could blink. Chastened by the lightning-quick knockout, I vowed to beat him within three months. The very next day, at the crack of dawn, I was at the Delhi University ground to begin a fitness regime. Rain, hail or shine, I ran every morning. I told myself that I would have to stop shagging (or at least bring down the frequency) and eat before I slept.

I remember going to bed dinnerless a lot in Delhi. Every day, there used to be a minimum of three cultural events worth attending. My first preference was cinema, my second was music and dance and my third was theatre. The events usually wound up at nine and I would reach home an hour later. Delhi is a city of pen-pushers who lock themselves in by eight. When I'd ring the bell at ten, Menon, the landlord, would open the door and give me a dirty look like I'd pulled him out of bed at midnight or when he was at it with his wife. He would let me in and give a deaf ear to my apologies, slamming his door shut hard so as to register his annoyance and disapproval.

I started schooling in the '50s at a government-run primary school located near the Perumal Temple in Nagore. In my school days, getting trashed by a teacher was a routine affair. Sometimes, their punishments would be so brutal that the boys would return home bruised and even bleeding. Unfinished homework got them kneeling-time under the baking hot sun. Some students would piss their pants when a caning was administered; there were others who crapped their trousers. As a shy child who constantly feared embarrassment, I would always alert my teachers by holding up my little finger when I needed to pee. A raised thumb for water, index finger and middle finger for the big job. The teacher would send me out immediately because if she didn't, she'd have to scrub shit off the floor. Strangely, all through my eleven years at school, I'd never seen a girl issue such signals for a toilet break.

Vomiting was also a common phenomenon. Post lunch, some kid or the other would throw up due to indigestion. For some reason, the unenviable task of cleaning up the mess always fell to the girls.

The story of the rise of Seeni Shanmugam *Saar* is the story of the rise of the *Dravida Munnetra Kazhagam*. The rise of the DMK party as a political force resulted in a newfound respect and demand for Tamil pundits and scholars. A purer form of Tamil began edging out of the heavily Sanskritized version of the language that was known as *manipravalam*. It was a time when statues of Maraimalai Adigal, the man who made it his life's mission to de-Sanskritize Tamil – were being erected in every nook of the state.

In those fervid times, my father thought it right for me to have a fashionably pure Tamil name. He changed my name from Udhaya – the name my mother had chosen for me – to Arivazhagan.

DMK supporters began to replace the Brahmins at the apex of the society. E. V. Ramasamy – Periyar – the founder of the *Dravidar Kazhagam*, held that if you encountered a Brahmin and a snake at the same time, it would be better for you if you thrashed the Brahmin first. Fortunately, India did not witness a genocide of the kind Europe witnessed under the Nazis, but the unmistakable stench of Brahmin-hatred hung in the air and kept getting stronger with each passing day.

In pursuit of a degree in Tamil, Seeni Shanmugam enrolled in Karanthai Tamil University. Around this time, a format of public debating called *patti mandram* had begun to weave itself into the state's cultural fabric. Speakers split into two opposing teams would debate on questions like: "Who was the chaster heroine in the epic, Kannagi or Madhavi?", "Tirukural excels in ethics or politics?", etc;

Like most teachers of Tamil, Seeni Shanmugam was a DMK sympathizer. The DMK realized that the most efficient way to gain power was to stoke the people's passion for Tamil while strongly opposing Hindi. The anti-Hindi protests intensified in 1965. The DMK ordered that the Republic Day of 1965 be observed as a black day. School and college students protested in large numbers. The ruling Congress party that favored Hindi was blackballed as an enemy of the Tamils. The protests lasted for a few months. The police sprayed bullets and swung batons at the protesters. Two policemen and seventy people were killed in the riots. Some students set themselves on fire. It was then that self-immolation as a means of protest had incorporated itself into the political culture of the state.

Since the better part of Nagore's population was Muslim, the anti-Hindi protests found little traction there. However, the situation next door in Nagapattinam was dire. Battalions of student-protestors would walk all the way from there to Nagore to enlist the services of the students there to help with the blackening of billboards and signposts that bore Hindi words. The protestors were convinced that the spread of Hindi would push Tamil into oblivion. I saw in the eyes of those students the kind of inflamed zeal one might find in those trying to fight off marauding invaders who were trying to rape their mothers. The riots were quelled when prime minister Lal Bahadur Shastri assured the non-Hindi-speaking states that their languages were not endangered by Hindi and that they could use English as the official language.

The anti-Hindi protests had two key social consequences for Tamil Nadu. One, the Tamils remained completely illiterate of Hindi; two, the DMK had a smooth ride to power in 1967.

(I find it ironical that in the Tamil Nadu of today, a student can finish school and college without knowing any Tamil at all. It is fashionable for the folks of the upper middle class to claim they don't know Tamil at all while the folks of the lower classes know little to nothing when it comes to reading or writing. There is a disgracefully small number of people in Tamil Nadu who have a zeal for Tamil these days.

It is ridiculous to see schools with names like Oxford Matriculation or Cambridge Primary operating under thatched roofs in tiny villages. What is even more ridiculous than the names of the schools is the fact that the teachers there know neither Tamil nor English. It was in one such school in Kumbakonam that 94 children were roasted alive in a fire accident in 2004.

The fact that an entire generation is growing up without proper knowledge of its mother tongue is one of the least concerns of the Tamils. But we have mastered the art of hollow chauvinism. Notwithstanding the inability of most people to read or write Tamil, all public events of the state kick off only after the recitation of an invocation to Tamil, the Mother Goddess.)

In 1968, C. N. Annadurai, the erstwhile chief minister of Tamil Nadu, decided to hold the Second World Tamil Conference. My father had come to Tamil Nadu from Andhra Pradesh, but he was an ardent supporter of the DMK. It is interesting to note that migrants from Andhra Pradesh to Tamil Nadu were passionate about Tamil though they continued to speak Telugu at home. Sociological experts have also observed that those who migrate to a new place are more attached to it than those who have lived there for generations. This attitude is also observable in people who have converted to a different religion.

I suffered much on account of my change of name.

"Who is this Arivazhagan?" the teacher would ask during the roll call. When I stood up, he'd scrutinize me from head to toe. Then he'd say with a smirk, "He has *azhagu*, but let's see if he has *arivu*." And for the next three quarters of an hour, he would test me to see if I possessed any *arivu* and how much. The teacher was a Brahmin who probably saw Periyar of the famous Brahmin-snake quote in me.

As a young boy with a complex, I couldn't help but notice the mocking smiles of the girls when they heard my name. In Delhi, where the /zha/ sound is non-existent, my plight was even worse. On the first day of my job in the Civil Supplies department, the administrative officer had a major problem pronouncing my mouthful of a name.

"What? Ari? Hari? No… Aa-ree-va-la-gan." He was exhausted. "*Bapre!* How*do* you pronounce it? Angam Jangam? What do your folks call you at home?"

When I told him I was called Udhaya, he was relieved to have something common and disyllabic to call me. In the twelve years that I worked there, nobody knew that my name was Arivazhagan.

My father's devotion to the DMK led him to bring his entire family to Chennai to attend the World Tamil Conference. It was the first time seeing the city. People were flocking there by the thousands. The WTC was more like a huge Urs Festival. Every year in my town, there was an Urs for which huge crowds would gather. I think the desire to be a writer at a later age, was sowed earlier at the World Tamil Conference, when I saw the tableaux procession of the Tamil literary greats of the yore - Avvaiyar, Thiruvalluvar, Kambar and Ilango Adigal.

For some inexplicable reason, after the conference, I developed a disaffection for the DMK. But I never became a Congress sympathizer either for I never liked the party at all. I started buying books like *Learn Hindi in 30 Days* and began to teach myself Hindi. This was because I'd begun to despise whatever Tamils took pride in.

Seeni Shanmugam proudly claimed that the Chola kings had crossed the seas and made a name for the Tamils in places like Cambodia, Java, Sumatra, Malaysia and the Maldives, but I placed the Tamils on par with the colonizing Europeans. If anyone claimed that Tamil was the oldest of all the world languages, I would taunt them with Pudumaipithan's words: "So, was the world's first monkey a Tamil monkey?"

Until the eleventh grade, I did fairly well in my studies and stood first in class. I used to go home for lunch and return to school. This meant that I made four trips daily – barefoot, as it was not feasible for my parents to buy six pairs of slippers for their six children. Because I had no slippers, I had blisters on the soles of my feet from walking in the hot sun. I remember how I'd walk only in shaded places just to avoid the scorching roads which were luckily not tarred. When I enrolled in Arignar Anna Government Arts College in Karaikal to study Pre-University Course and medium of instruction was English. As I never understood a single word, I began failing in every subject. Disillusioned, I never made any efforts to study Tamil either. Though I'd learned butler English in school for eleven years, I was unable to keep up with the standard in college. When the physics teacher said, "Let us consider...," the only word that registered was "us."

I was very shy even as a youth. I could never stand beside another boy and take a leak. So, I would control my bladder until I returned home. Once I was home, I'd change into a *lungi* and squat in the yard. Even now, I cannot urinate if there's someone standing beside me. In some cinemas, there is no barrier between the urinals which means you can see the dick of the bloke standing next to you. To avoid the sight of another man's member, I'd use the individual stalls that were meant for people who wanted to defecate.

Since I performed well in school, the family elders suggested I choose the first group that included math, physics and chemistry – MPC. Of the ninety students in the first group, ten came from convent schools and we had nothing to do with them whatsoever. They conversed only in English and answered every question they were asked correctly. Not one of them was seen in the Tamil class and I'd learned this was because they'd chosen French as their optional language. All those who wanted to pursue medicine chose the second group that included the subjects of physics, chemistry and biology. The third group was for the dullards and had subjects like history, geography and commerce. This group was a happy place to be in. Many years after I'd finished college, I realized that a lot of the boys who had chosen the third group had gone on to become professors.

Apart from math, physics and chemistry, I had to study

English and Tamil. All three groups came together for these two subjects. The Tamil teacher stood in stark contrast to Seeni Shanmugam *Saar* and the lessons were nothing but hogwash. As we reached a higher level, we were forced to study stories, plays and poems written by other inferior Tamil professors whose junk passed for "contemporary literature." The classes became a bitter experience for us. Since the professor was no good, we named him *Pandaara Vadai*. Every class was like the Sepoy Mutiny on a smaller scale. There was no such problem when it came to the English class as the teacher looked like a goddess. We did not pay attention to what she taught as our minds were too busy spinning wicked fantasies as we disrobed her with our eyes. There were rumors that the boys in the back benches used to masturbate when she was in the class. This was believable as even I used to get a boner when I looked at her, but I couldn't jerk off because I never got a chance to sit in the back row.

Math, physics and chemistry classes were like torture camps. The antics of the professors who taught us these subjects were comparable, in their unspeakable cruelty, to torture methods like nail-pulling, stretching on the rack, the water cure and the passing of current through a man's dick. There was a torture that went by the name "record notebook." We had to copy from our textbooks in handwriting that resembled print, draw all the pictures and finally submit the book to the teacher. And if the teacher was not happy with it for whatever reason, he'd hurl the pillow-sized book to the ground or, worse still, at the unfortunate student. We had to wordlessly endure their murderous rages. Looking back, I wonder if they behaved like sadist psychos because their sex lives were unsatisfactory. The fact that the students were powerless made them even bolder. Internal assessments carried twenty-five marks out of the total hundred. If the professor disliked a student, he could destroy his life by giving him a zero. Another weapon in the teachers' arsenal was the Conduct Certificate that was issued by the Principal at the time of leaving. If it did not have the word "good" in it, the student's future would be over before it began. He would be doomed to be a cowpoke for the rest of his life as no other college or organization would accept him. And if the teacher complained about you to the principal, you were finished.

Despite the fact that the teachers enjoyed so much power, we were able to have our way with *Pandaara Vadai*. The reason behind this was that Tamil teachers were not a very respected lot and they did not score internal assessments. One of the many insulting things we did in *Pandaara Vadai*'s class was cupping our mouths with our hands and howling like wolves.

We traveled by bus from Nagore to Karaikal. The Nagore bus stand was near the market and the police station. We would loiter near the Thennavan Tea Stall in front of the bus stand. (Thennavan was a schoolmate of mine who started working in his father's tea shop after finishing with school). As soon as the bus came, we'd sprint across the road like lunatics to board it.

Around this time, a young police inspector had come to

Nagore. Now because he was young, he was eager to prove his mettle and conducted several raids in shops and huts where sex was being peddled. One day, Maraikka Vaappa, a friend who commuted with me in the bus, howled when he saw the inspector who, infuriated, gave us all a taste of his *lathi*. I was the first to flee, but duck-footed Maraikka Vaappa couldn't. Never in my life will I forget his agonizing screams.

Luckily, there was a man called Ramalingam at the bus stand who, like Ramalinga Adigal, had shorn his head and covered it with a cloth. He was blind and gyrated slowly, chanting Adigal's verses. I never once saw him sitting or lying down. When a bus arrived, he would stop singing and tell the people exactly which bus it was and where it was headed. It was he who managed to calm the inspector down. Otherwise, Mariakka Vaapa's skull would have been bashed on that day.

It took me three years to pass my pre-university exams which I should have passed in one year. I could have continued my education in Karaikal but difficulties cropped up all on account of a particular girl.

I had passed the lower and higher levels in English typewriting at the typists' training institute in Nagore; they also taught shorthand, but with no success which was why I began to train under a teacher called Thanikachalam in Nagapattinam. He worked as a stenographer in the Velippalayam court and taught in the evenings. Most of the people who trained under him passed, not in the first attempt, but in the second or the third. People flocked to him because institutes were no good. There were three levels in English shorthand – lower, intermediate and higher. People usually passed exam for lower level but not for the other two. You had to transcribe eighty words per minute for lower, one hundred for intermediate and one hundred and twenty for higher.

Thanikachalam was dark, potbellied and hirsute and he gave dictation very clearly. I used to practice hard at home and was able to take the exam after three months of training. He thought that I'd already learned shorthand and refused to believe me when I told him I would practice six hours a day at home. When he saw that there wasn't a single mistake in my shorthand notes – the others would have at least fifty – he would accuse me of having read the passages beforehand. One day, he dictated the contents of the Hindu editorial and I made only three mistakes. "You don't need me. You can appear for the exams without my help," he declared. He didn't tell me this nicely, but angrily, as he was under the impression that I was somehow cheating.

To attend Thanikachalam's classes, I had to catch the 4:10 Thanjavur Passenger train that reached Nagapattinam at 5. It would take 50 minutes by the steam train to cover the travel distance of 6 kilometers. There would be two bare-bodied drivers in the engine's cabin at the front and they would shovel coal into the furnace from time to time. With rivulets of sweat streaming down their bodies it just was not practical for them to wear shirts. They would sport a bandana on their head and have their trouser legs rolled upto their knees. Their bodies would shimmer in the fiery glow of the furnace and sheen of their sweat making it appear as though they were carved out of anthracite. It would seem to me then that a train driver's job was the most difficult one on earth. The main downside with the steam engines was you could not enjoy a window seat. Coal cinders would fly into your eyes and cause acute discomfort.

During one of those train journeys I met a girl to whom I slipped a love letter. She gave me one in reply. The people who witnessed this exchange decided to thrash me because this girl was a Muslim. When I learned of their plans, I fled to my uncle's house in Golden Rock near Trichy. As I'd passed college, I enrolled in E. V. R. Arts College's undergraduate English Literature course. After failing my intermediate exams, I roamed around for two years and learned a bit of English. Two people – R. K. Karanjia and Baburao Patel – were responsible for this. The tidbits of movie dialogues that appeared in Karanjia's *Blitz* and Baburao Patel's questions and answers helped me to learn English to some small degree.

My uncle was an even more ardent follower of the DMK than my father. He always wore a *veshti* with a black and red border – the colors of the DMK – and he wore it in such a way that everyone who looked could see his striped drawers. His house was also painted black and red. I used to wonder if his stools were also black and red.

I couldn't live in my uncle's house for long, again because of a woman. My cousin Kamali – my mother's sister's daughter – lived in Golden Rock and I would often go across to see her. I was nineteen then and Kamali was five years older. Her husband was forty and looked more like her father. After lunch, Kamali would lie back in bed and say, "My feet are hurting. Could you press them a little while?" I would press her feet and slowly advance up to her knees but I lacked the courage to go beyond. Finally, one day, I decided to risk it and went all the way up to her privates. When she felt my hand there, she woke up and angrily struck it away.

One day, Kamali asked me if we could drink some whiskey. But I couldn't do any of the things I'd imagined and planned doing with her as we both fell asleep after a few swallows. A short while later, her brother-in-law arrived at the house and knocked on the door. When no one answered, he jumped over the back wall and entered, only to find the two of us in what he thought was a "compromising position." There was no one who would have believed us even if we swore upon every God that nothing had happened. The news reached my uncle's ears and it became clear that I was no longer welcome in his house. However, it is said that when one door closes, nine others open. It was just after this event that my aunt Kamakshi approached my mother and said, "I will send Udhaya to college." My mother was not excited about my aunt's offer, but in the end, it was my decision to go and stay with her.

I joined the Bachelor of Physics course in Serfoji College. The reason why I switched from English Literature is a huge story.

There was an aged Christian man called Saamy who lived in front of my house and I am, in a way, indebted to him. It was he who introduced me to English Literature. He started me off on Daniel Defoe and we slowly moved on to Geoffrey Chaucer, Charles Dickens and Thomas Hardy. I was unable to get past the first line of a play of Shakespeare, so he suggested I read Charles and Mary Lamb's simplified version of Shakespeare first. After I did, he made me read the originals. He was also responsible for my becoming a stenographer instead of a professor. He told my father that studying literature would ruin my life and he convinced me to switch over to physics.

Saamy lived alone. He had no family and no relatives ever sought him out. He cooked his own food and earned a lot by way of tuitions. As he charged a hefty sum, only Muslim boys from rich families went to him. He walked with a stoop he said was the result of an injury while serving in the army. Other than this, he spoke nothing else of his personal life. He would often call me and my brother to the house to talk to us.

One day, a boy who had studied in the same school as I did came up to me and asked, "Whatever is the problem between Saamy and your family?" I couldn't understand what he was talking about.

"Saamy *saar* is a good family friend," I told him, puzzled.

My friend then revealed that Saamy would rant about my family for at least an hour to all the boys who went to his house for lessons. I also learned that some boys had stopped going to him because they couldn't stand the annoyingly boring tirades he'd unleash against my family.

For the first time in my twenty years, I experienced the pain of betrayal. Saamy was the one who used to call me and my younger brother to his house to talk. He used to ask my mother to give him some gravy to accompany his meals and he would have lengthy conversations with my father. While we considered him to be a family friend, he was busy badmouthing us to everyone. Seething with rage, I went to his house and gave him a bashing. My mother came and dragged me home before anything untoward happened.

Saamy filed a police complaint. Luckily, the police inspector was a nice chap. (The one who'd beaten up Maraikka Vaapa had been transferred to some godforsaken desert after a few months). The inspector told me that once a police case was filed, I wouldn't be able to find employment anywhere and my name would be added to the list of rowdies. So, he didn't file any case and let me off the hook.

In Serfoji College in Thanjavur, I didn't attend even a single class. I never wrote a single exam either. I spent all my time in the library. Oscar Wilde was one of my favorite writers then. I affixed bold and bright posters with his quotes to the outer walls of the hut on Venkatesa Perumal Koil Street – the one with the roofless toilet.

I would change the quotes every week. If it was "The happiness of a married man depends on the people he has not married" one week, it would be "Women were created to be loved; not to be understood" the next week.

I hadn't outgrown my shyness so I was still friendless. Most of my waking hours were spent at the college library, the Brihadeeswarar Temple, the government library across the temple and the Saraswati Mahal Library inside the palace. I'll let you in on a little secret. I took refuge in Wilde and in the libraries only to escape from women. But ironically, Wilde's writings, instead of helping me keep women locked out of my mind, kept my thoughts fixated on them and triggered my interest in them.

People usually have many devices like friends, gossip, games and studies to keep loneliness at bay. I had no one and I had nothing. All I had was faithful loneliness that accompanied me wherever I went. I was confused about the idea of love, and women. I was too shy to approach a girl and talk to her, but at the same time, I was eager to fall in love with all the girls I met. My mind started spinning out of control.

To free my mind from its demons, I frequented the temple. The Venkatesa Perumal Temple was just across the street from my aunt's house and I used to go and sit there for hours on end. But even that didn't help. Even as I stood before the idol of the god, I could feel lust raging through me like a fire, threatening to devour me. I decided I needed to purify my mind if I were to continue visiting the temple.

A little later, I befriended a girl called Bhuvana quite unexpectedly. At the end of the college year, there was an inter-collegiate elocution competition in Thanjavur and I decided to register in the English category as I was desperate to try something different, something I'd never done before. But after submitting my name, I felt rather foolish. I'd always won at elocution competitions wherein I had to make my speech in Tamil. I wasn't sure I'd be able to pull off a speech in English. I'd heard that it was a girl called Bhuvana who always bagged the first prize in the English category. It probably had to do with the fact that she was a student of English Literature in a women's college. We'd never met before and I had no idea of how good a speaker she was. I reconciled myself to the possibility of a fiasco and remained indifferent about the final outcome.

We had to speak on the suitability of a democratic form of government in India. I firmly believed that it was not suitable, but I knew full well that only those who argued the opposite would win. When I heard that Bhuvana had taken the opposite stand I'd taken, I was surprised. Why was Bhuvana, who always walked away with the first prize, unaware that her stand would threaten her victory this time around?

A small spark of hope flickered in me, but what would I do without knowing English? Then, I had an idea. I wrote down my arguments in Tamil and asked a friend who was fluent in both Tamil and English to translate them for me. Then, I learned the speech by heart.

Another surprise lay in waiting. It concerned the identity of Bhuvana. She turned out to be the beauty who lived down my street. I'd seen her countless times and desperately yearned for a jiffy's glance or a tiny smile from her. I tried a few attention-grabbing stunts, but she never once noticed me. Her skin glowed like cream satin in the moonlight and she was perfectly and amply proportioned. She had a mesmerizing gaze and the sight of her moist lips could inflame any man's passions. She was a girl who ruined the sleep of many young men like myself.

Now I became determined to win the contest for I couldn't afford to fail or make a clown of myself before someone I was madly in love with and desired so intensely. I rendered my speech in such a manner that obscured the fact that I'd simply memorized it. I had everyone believing I was speaking extempore. I spoke with perfect pitch and modulation; I never faltered even once. When I walked off the stage after finishing, Bhuvana came running to me excitedly like a child and shook my hand.

"What an excellent speech that was!" she exclaimed. "Where have you been hiding yourself?"

"At the Hanuman temple near your house."

Her peals of laughter reminded me of the tinkling of silver coins.

"I've seen you around a lot," she said. "That El Par shirt suits you well."

"I thought of talking to you many times but I lacked the courage," I confessed. "I was afraid that such a beautiful girl might not want to talk to someone like me."

"Oh my!" she said shyly.

"What?"

"You sure have what it takes to sweep a girl off her feet! And your performance in the competition was nothing short of brilliant."

I was surprised she noticed I was wearing an El Par shirt more than anything else. It was quite the rage among young men in the '70s.

We continued to talk to each other in a corner of the room. I confessed to her that I wasn't fluent in English and that I'd memorized my speech. This was how a friendship sprung up between the two of us. The very next day, I told her I was deeply in love with her only to hear that she was in love with someone else. She still said we could be good friends. Till the end, she never accepted my proposals and I never found out who her lover was.

The Central Government used to recruit employees through the Staff Selection Commission. Passing the exam could get you a job in Delhi's local administration. The shorthand exams weren't as tough as the exams conducted by the other recruitment agencies. All you needed was a typewriter. A North Indian would dictate a passage for ten minutes. This passage had to be typed within a certain time period. I cleared the exam on my first attempt and got a job when I was still in college.

(Don't assume that passing the exam guaranteed you the job of your dreams. Take Santhanam, for instance. A clever and knowledgeable man like him did not deserve to be languishing as a postal clerk. When I asked him if he'd taken the UPSC exams, he told me that his life had gone off the rails as he couldn't get hold of a typewriter in Bangalore. After passing the written component of the UPSC exam, he had to type ten sentences. The examination center did not provide typewriters which meant that the candidates had to bring their own. Santhanam managed to get hold of a small portable typewriter with his brother's help, but he was used to typing on a bigger one. The handlebar of the portable typewriter didn't function properly and he was unable to type even a single sentence correctly. In my case, I faced no problems, thanks to Bhuvana. She went to an institute in our part of Thanjavur and asked for a typewriter. Who could refuse a beautiful girl like her? The owner of the institute personally brought the typewriter to the examination center and collected it himself when the exam was over!

I told Santhanam that he would have been a deputy secretary in the Central Government if only he'd been able to get a functional typewriter.

Santhanam then asked me if I'd watched the movie *Sliding Doors*. It's a movie about a woman who goes to the station to catch a train. We are shown two versions of events – one where she catches the train and one where she misses it.

In the "caught-train timeline," the woman gets hit by a vehicle after declaring her love to a man and dies. However, in the "missed-train timeline," she has it rough for some time but ultimately ends up happy. It's always better to be alive, no matter the circumstances.

Now we return to Santhanam's life.

I was permanently being shunted from the house of one relative to another when I was studying in West Mambalam High School. After the DMK came into power, my school was rechristened. It came to be known as Anjugam High

School because Anjugam was the name of the mother of M. Karunanidhi, the head of the DMK who was also the chief minister of the state at that time.

At one point in time, I was staying with an aunt who lived near my school when I was in the seventh grade. There lived a boy called Sadagopan in the neighboring house. He regularly failed his exams and was constantly scolded by his parents for it. He was street smart though. I was always among the top three in my class whether I exerted myself or not. Anyway, Sadagopan and I became friends during a game of gilli-danda with the neighborhood boys. It was my first time playing the game and my first time playing with these boys as I was new to the neighborhood. We were playing on Rajagopala Iyengar Street, a barren wasteland. It was a Brahmin ghetto like Nanganallur.

I was intently watching the game. When Sadagopan took his turn to bat, he accidentally hit me on the forehead. The wound started bleeding and he rushed to my side, apologizing profusely.

"I'm really so sorry. I didn't do it on purpose."

I replied, "We're neighbors, and there's nothing to feel sorry about. You didn't do it deliberately."

"Please don't tell anyone. I already have more problems than I can handle at home."

"Forget it. I'm not going to tell anyone."

He was still panicky.

"But how are you going to explain the bruise?"

"Well, I'll just say I tripped and fell. That's believable."

After that incident, we became good friends.

Fifteen years later, I'd gone to visit my aunt. I'd left her house and began walking when a car pulled up next to me. When I saw who the driver was, I was stunned. It was Sadagopan! He told me he was the owner of a printing press called Kittambi Press. I felt bad when I heard this. Life is so unfair. How do you explain the fact that Sadagopan, a failure and a dunce in school, was now the owner of his own press while I, a top ranker, was languishing in a musty government office in a dead-end job? I might as well have been like Sadagopan, failing every exam.

Five years later, there was a chess competition in our office for which many contestants had come from different places. I became acquainted with a great player. When we discovered that we were both from West Mambalam, we began asking each other whether we knew this man or that lady.

"Do you know Sadagopan?" I asked him. "How is he now?"

"Was Sadagopan your friend?" he asked me.

"Yes."

"Really?"

"Yes. Why are you doing a double-check?"

"Your friend Sadagopan died two years ago. His obituary was in the papers. How is it you didn't come to pay your last respects? Were you really his friend?"

Sadagopan had gone to Ahobila Mutt with his family. His son fell into a river and Sadagopan jumped in to save him. Both father and son lost their lives.

And now I think of how stupid I'd been to envy him when

he had a printing press and a car. With neither printing press nor car to my name, I am more fortunate than him because I'm still alive.

If I'd caught the train to Delhi, I could have landed up in prison or died. But I missed that train and I'm still around, still walking, still breathing. And I think that's a good thing.

But let us return to the reality – to the story of the person who caught the train to Delhi.)

My departure to Delhi was motivated purely by the desire to flee from the Tamils. I would have no trouble getting around in Delhi because I knew Hindi. A major reason why Tamils fail to pass the shorthand examination is their lack of familiarity with the North Indian English accent. If the dictator says "vokkayyen," he is a Punjabi and the word is "occasion." If he says "Jo kaaj noteej waaj ijood," he is a Bihari and he means "Show cause notice was issued." As I had taken pains to absorb the peculiarities of every version of Indian English, passing the test had been a cakewalk.

But knowing Hindi and every version of Indian English was not going to get me a roof above my head in Delhi. I knew no one there. When I told Bhuvana this, she told me that she would speak to her cousin Raman who lived in Delhi. She assured me that he would help me in every which way he could and that he would even accommodate me. Raman turned out to be as nice as Bhuvana had made him out to be. The Grand Trunk Express took me to Delhi and when I alighted at the station, Raman was there to receive me and take me to his home where I stayed for a few days. Raman's father was not too pleased about having a stranger under his roof. He was a bigot who told Raman in my presence, "I will not dine with this *shudra*. You people eat first. I will eat later."

His attitude towards my caste did not bother me as much as the *babu's* English he used when he spoke to me.

One reason why I didn't take the caste-discrimination too seriously was that it was quite common even in the civil supplies office where I worked. For instance, the jealousy and resentment that people of other states felt towards Punjabis who had left Pakistan during the partition and settled down in Delhi were very obvious. There was a young Punjabi employee called Akash in my department. Whenever he was not around, the others would sit and discuss the traits of Punjabis. They would go on and on about how Punjabis were a money-minded lot. But for some reason, I liked Punjabis. Unlike the Tamils who couldn't even bring themselves to smile, the Punjabis were a jolly bunch who believed in living life to the fullest. Their *khao, piyo, aish karo* philosophy greatly appealed to me.

Like most Punjabis, Akash was also a merry person. Hang on, did I just call him by his name? Now, had I been in Chennai, I would have to address other government employees as "A2," "B2," et cetera, for in Chennai, a government employee's number – not his name – is his identity in the organization. Also, it is disrespectful in Tamil culture to call a person by his or her given name. I realized this when I was working as a prison clerk in Chennai. A person who is below the stenographer in rank would call him "Steno *saar*" while the person above him would merely call him "Steno." This is a peculiar mannerism of the Tamils. For instance, if a Tamil has a driver, he calls him "Driver." Similarly, if there is a watchman outside his apartment complex, he calls him "Watchman." It is believed that your prestige will take a knock if you use these people's names.

In Delhi, I was delighted to hear people properly addressing each other. Everyone's name was suffixed with "*ji.*" People would therefore be called Sharmaji, Varmaji, Guptaji, Anandji and so on. In the case of a superior, the "*ji*" was replaced with a "*saab.*"

As a result of convent education, Akash spoke fluent English. When I asked him what a convent-educated young man like him was doing working as a *babu*, he pointed to the sky. When I told him about the stereotypes concerning the Punjabis, he said they were all true. Punjabis had been affluent landowners in Pakistan, but after the Partition displaced them, they were reduced to paupers and refugees.

"They are driven to recapture what they've lost. It's that drive you see in them," he explained. "Besides, it wasn't just replaceable earthly possessions they lost during the Partition. So many loved ones had been lost too. That sense of loss made us want to obsessively pursue money. Have you ever seen a Punjabi beggar?"

"No, why aren't there any?"

"While it is true that Punjabis are all about money, it is also true that they work hard to earn it. Everything is money, money, money. We don't know anything else, *yaar.*"

"In that case, what do you think of the Tamils in Delhi?"

"You mean the *Madrasis*?"

Before I could tell him that there was no such thing as a *Madrasi*, he said, "Yes, yes, I know. Andhraites, Keralites, Kannadigas, Tamils... What's the difference between them, *bhai*? I know nothing about those Andhraites, but when they say "*randi, randi*" in Telugu, it sounds rather obscene. I believe "*randi*" means "come" in Telugu. What a language, *yaar*!" Keralites are total ruffians. Kannadigas? I don't know. Tamils are numero uno when it comes to *chamchagiri*. But you don't seem to be like that..."

"I'm not a Brahmin, that's why."

"Oh, is that so?"

"Being a Tamil and being a Brahmin are not the same thing, you know. What about the folks from U. P.?"

"Lazy, good-for-nothing fellows."

"Biharis?"

"The filthy guys who are a century behind everyone else."

"Bengalis?"

"Egoistic *chutiyas*, but they're lookers."

Akash's opinion was not at variance with the general opinion. The stereotypes weren't a big deal at all then.

Raman's house was in Sarojini Nagar which was one of the *addas* of Delhi's Tamil population. One kilometer from the market behind the house was Chanakyapuri, a plush locality where you could find an embassy for almost every country on the map. Raman and I used to go there to watch movies at the Chanakya Theater.

The Delhi *babus* usually made some extra cash by renting out a room – the birdcage "accommodation" the government put them up in – to the *Madrasi babus*." Raman approached one of the Delhi *babus* and found me a room in the house of a Garhwali in Netaji Nagar. If Sarojini Nagar was a middle class locality, then Netaji Nagar was definitely lower class. While Sarojini Nagar was full of *babus*, Netaji Nagar was full of *chaprasis*. I lived there for a year. The Garhwali family had four children – two girls and two boys. The boys were permanently in my room. In the mornings, the head of the family would also while away his time with me. I suffered his company for the sake of his wife's ginger tea.

During my twelve-year stay in Delhi, the city and its inhabitants never ceased to amaze me. In the eyes of a smalltown chap like me, everything about the place seemed so extraordinary.

However, I did have my fair share of difficulties there. For instance, finding and boarding the right bus was a confusing affair. In Tamil Nadu, the buses had huge boards on which their point of origin and point of destination were printed in big, bold letters. Above this, in smaller print, you'd find the names of certain connecting stops. The buses in Delhi just had this information scrawled in chalk in Hindi on a cardboard. Though I could read Hindi to some extent, the writing wasn't always legible. The problem was that the same bus plied different routes at different times. By simply rubbing out "R. K. Puram – Tiz Hazari" with spittle, you could chalk in the new route – "Tiz Hazari – Shalimar Bagh." Just when you're thinking that things couldn't have been any worse, let me tell you that they used Hindi numerals instead of Hindu-Arabic numerals.

Government buses were still better; the private buses started rolling only when it was replete and bursting with people. The mini buses were moving hell. They stopped the bus not only in the bus stops but wherever they wished to. The private bus drivers and conductors were not paid a monthly salary but paid according to the number of people they took in.

Sarojini Nagar and Netaji Nagar were both in South Delhi whereas my office was in the North on Under Hill Road. To get to my office from Netaji Nagar, I could either catch the Mudrika bus from Ring Road which went all the way around Delhi or I could make my way to the Secretariat and catch the 220 or the 240 to Delhi University. I chose the second route even though it took more time. Both the 220 and the 240 were like heaven's chariots as the young goddesses who studied in Indra Prastha College and in Delhi University mostly traveled by these two buses. I would admire them all as one can't pick out a single rain drop when rain falls in torrents.

The sari-clad women who had no qualms about showing-off their breasts were Delhi's curiosities. Never had I seen breasts as large as these women's, not even in my wildest imaginings. They were more concerned with covering their heads, wearing their *sarees* like a sacred thread between their breasts. In an anthropological magazine, I'd read that certain South American tribeswomen go about naked while the men wear a penis sheath. After looking at pictures of these tribals, I pondered over how culture reflects the diversity of the human race.

These women also wore a blinding shade of red lipstick. I would occasionally get lipstick smears on my shirt after a long bus journey and this became a subject of jest among my colleagues. Akash used to joke about the Punjabis' addiction to lipstick. (I've never met anyone who could poke fun at his own culture the way Akash did).

"Punjabi women put on lipstick as soon as they wake up," he said, "even before they brush their teeth. If you marry a Punjabi girl, you'll spend your month's earnings just buying her lipstick tube after lipstick tube."

"I'd rather marry a Punjabi girl, Akash," I said. "If I marry a *Madrasi* girl, I will be a little more than a glorified servant, fetching and carrying for her. Moreover, Tamil girls are more aggressive you know..."

"It's rather rare for Punjabi girls to marry *Madrasis*. They look down on your lot – your height, your brownish complexion, your thick moustaches. And besides, they think you boys don't have enough muscle."

"*Arrey gandoo*! You think your potbelly is muscle? Stamina is what is *below* it."

"You're a different sort of *Madrasi*, man, not like the other *chutiyas*."

After Netaji Nagar, I lived in Ramabhadran's house in R. K. Puram. He was a senior Tamil writer. I first met him at a meeting held by the Delhi Tamil Sangam. When he heard where I was staying, he invited me to be his guest for as long as I wanted. Only after moving into his house did I realize that it was worse than the Garhwalis' place. Though he worked for the central government, he was ruled by his nagging, money-hungry wife. One of the three bedrooms in their house was already let out to a student. The second bedroom was given to me. The writer, his wife and their nine-year-old son occupied the third room.

(Owing to the lack of space in Indian households, the entire family has to sleep in a single room and you will often find the husband, the wife and two or three children sleeping on an eight by ten bed. If I ask someone how, under such circumstances, the couple manages to have sex, the person would rebuke me for being a dirty-minded bastard. You will see a similar arrangement and adjustment on a two-wheeler. The husband drives it with two children sitting in front of him with his wife and an infant child at the back. There was also a fellow who managed to accommodate a Great Dane.

A friend of mine told me that her entire family – husband and wife, a sixteen-year-old son and a twelve-year-old daughter – sleeps in the same bed. Is this obscene or is it just my gutter-brain? My friend confessed that this sleeping arrangement was making her increasingly uneasy.

In a recent Tamil movie, the main actors kissed – lightly, *very* lightly – on the lips. The theater immediately erupted in deafening applause. The same thing happened twenty-five years ago when Kamal Haasan acted out the first ever kiss in Tamil cinema. This makes me wonder: haven't Tamils learned to kiss for real yet?

When Jackie Chan leaps from one cliff to another, people clap because he is performing an impossible stunt. So, if Tamils clap when they witness an onscreen kiss, does it mean that kissing is such a daring, adventurous and near-impossible act?

An actor participated in a television show. The anchor asked the audience if any of them had any desires that only the actor could fulfill. At once, a middle-aged woman rose and said that she would like to kiss him.

In Europe, kissing in public is nothing uncommon and nothing to be ashamed of, but in Tamil Nadu, even husbands and wives are reluctant to kiss each other. So, it's something out of this world when, on a TV show with thousands of people watching, an Indian woman asks to kiss an actor. And what if I tell you she actually got to do it? But don't drop your jaws. Keep them closed. It was only a peck on the cheek. After getting a kiss from the actor she so desperately wanted, the woman was interviewed. She said, "When I got up to kiss him, I asked my husband to leave the room." Like, what the *fuck*? Thousands of people can watch her kiss an actor but not her husband? These dynamics of marriage are unique to Tamil culture.

Recently, there was some gossip about the love affair between the daughter of an actor and an assistant director created a big stir. There wasn't a single jockey who wasn't talking about it on the radio. The girl's father, a sixty-year-old, had acquired the sobriquet Casanova for the kinds of things he did onscreen to acquire a woman. More importantly, the objects of his love were always the daughters of rowdies who terrorized people. In one movie, he falls in love with the daughter of a Pakistani terrorist. As proof of his heroism, he is shown to survive a spray of bullets from multiple machine guns without sustaining so much as a scratch. Sorry to disappoint all those of you who assumed he must have been wearing a bulletproof vest. His somersaults were responsible for saving him from getting punctured.

As he was someone who would do the craziest and the most devilish things imaginable for love – in films – the fact that he opposed his daughter's real-life relationship became a conundrum for all Tamil people. When a journalist asked him about this, he said curtly, "That is *reel* and this is *real*." Even this aristocrat was no different than the average Tamil when it came to sleeping arrangements. (He slept in the same bedroom as his wife and two daughters).

So, if a Tamil actor can sleep in the same bed with his wife and children in the same room on the same bed, I don't see why a Tamil writer and his family would think of sleeping any differently.

Once, when that actor and I ran into each other by chance, he told me, laughing, "I bought your novels, but as I have daughters, I have to hide them and read them in secret."

Inwardly I retorted, "My books aren't going to corrupt your daughters any more than your movies already have."

Though he was a protective father, he couldn't control who his daughter fell in love with. She'd even gone so far as to approach the commissioner of police to seek protection for her lover as she feared her father might kill him.

Of course, the tabloids were thrilled with this gold nugget of information. The news became the main headline of every paper, relegating everything else to the sidelines – the deaths of five soldiers in border skirmishes, a seventy-billion-rupee corruption scandal, the eighteen-hour load-shedding and juicy tales of women who had conspired with their paramours to murder their husbands. The media circus camped outside the actor's house.

"I'm no murderer. My villainy is restricted to the movies I act in. In real life, I wouldn't even swat a fly. That assistant director is just too old and too married for my daughter," said the actor in an attempt at damage-control.

The media circus immediately rushed to a small street in Vadapalani. The assistant director, the daughter's lover, was thirty-two years of age and, like the actor said, had been married twice already. He was in the habit of marrying for money. He got his ass thrown in jail. This incident set me thinking: how could the daughter of a dignified father – who did not even allow her to look at my novels – have wanted to marry a scoundrel? But then I also considered this: the actor had been playing the role of a scoundrel in movies for over thirty years. In his films, the lead actress – the daughter of a villainous *crorepati* – would fall in love with him and the *crorepati* father would become even more villainous. Finally, our actor, the scoundrel, would either kill the *crorepati* villain or reform him and marry his daughter. The scoundrel might also commit rapes and the female lead whom he raped would marry him in order to reform him. He might also indulge in petty thievery and fistfights, but his one weakness was his mother who he loved intensely although he didn't lift a finger to help her. He would get drunk, come home and retch all over the place, and his mother would patiently and uncomplainingly clean up his vomit because deep down inside, she knew that she was responsible for her son's becoming a scoundrel. Once the scoundrel married the *crorepati* villan's daughter, the mother would die.)

As Ramabhadran and I had similar tastes, we used to attend at least one cultural program every day and return home late. This is how it went. Around five in the evening, I would catch route No.110, relieving from office. The bus would crawl in the horrifying traffic of Saddar Bazar. Not wanting to wait till it reaches the New Delhi Railway Station, I would alight from the bus and run a kilometre towards the Maharashtra Rangayan cinema hall, panting for breath. Even then, I could reach only five minutes after the film has begun. Ramabadran would be waiting for me smoking his favourite Ganesh beedi. There would be no time to question my late-coming. We would dart into the theatre and struggle to find our seats in the dark. Ramabhadran would ask about the nine o'clock show at the India International Centre and we would run there. We would try to make time for a cup of tea between laps. The two rotis I had for lunch would not keep me up, all this time.

A Fassbinder or a Fellini would be playing. After the movie, at around 12 in the night, we'd walk to R. K. Puram.

Now, why should Ramabhadran feel obliged to wait for me? Film buff that he was, he wouldn't be too happy to miss five precious minutes of a serious movie like Fellini's. Why couldn't I just hit the theaters alone? The coveted film society in which Ramabhadran was a member was born in the early '60s, and since its inception, membership was open to six hundred people, no more, no less. A serious film lover would have to wait for one or a couple of members to die in order to join this exclusive society. Seniority factored into determining who filled the vacant seats. (It was rumored that even Indira Gandhi, erstwhile prime minister of India, was in the waiting list.) As Ramabhadran was one of the founding members of this elite club, I piggybacked on him. Not every member enjoyed certain privileges I was privy to. As he was a large-hearted person who worked with the Intelligence Agency, he was well-respected. Okay, you might be wondering what's so special about this film society. Are there no other film societies in Delhi? There were many, in fact. But *this* society screened many international movies when compared to others. One would imagine that the Delhi of the '80s had many takers of serious cinema. It did, and it was because we had a zero-chance of watching steamy movies then. These serious international movies came with sex scenes. Moreover, they were never censored when screened in these film societies. I also observed that most of the members of these societies were in their late forties or fifties. One look at the title of the movie and I'd be able to predict the number of people in the audience. If it is Dona Flor and Her Two Husbands, work would have to do without me for a day as I'd have to rush to the theater before the seats ran out.

One day, during a heated fight with her husband Ramabhadran, the mistress of the house accused us of being homosexuals. I lost my temper and lashed out at her. Things became messy and I moved out of their house and into West Delhi where I rented a room in a residential quarter, stayed there for three months, and then moved out and into another room. This continued until I found a decent place on Lancer Road.

When Gupta, the bloke who shared the first floor with Menon and me, bought a motorbike, my late-night habits only served to get me into trouble. The new motorbike was parked downstairs. Menon told me that Gupta's previous motorbike had been stolen two years ago. To prevent another theft, the latter had a strong gate erected at the entrance.

The gate was locked from the inside and both Menon and Gupta had keys. Gupta would lock the door at nine and I would return at ten and shout for Menon. As all the glass windows were shut, I might as well have been shouting at the moon like a madman. After I'd shouted myself hoarse, Menon would open the gate for me and lock it once I was in.

One day I went to a music concert at Azad Bhavan that wrapped up at ten. It was biting cold outside. Most of the people who came to attend had their own vehicles. I was at the mercy of public transport. After waiting at the bus stop for an hour, I caught the midnight service bus and reached home. I shouted for Menon to come down for ten minutes but received no response. Frustrated and unable to wait out in the cold any longer, I dropped the "mister" and shouted, "Hey Menon!" I was worried. What if he wasn't there? Where would I sleep? Had it been summer, I wouldn't have bothered to return home.I would have just curled up under a tree or something. Finally, I decided to force the gate open. I threw myself against it once, twice, thrice. The fourth time, I heard the latch give way. Emboldened, I hauled myself at the gate a few times more. I must have made a racket loud enough to wake the dead. When I saw a light come on in Gupta's house, I stopped my exertions.

Gupta opened the gate for me.

"Sorry," I said as politely as I could.

"Better get your ass home by nine. Tomorrow, you'll have to sleep on the road," he said curtly.

"I'll come when I wish," I retorted. "I never asked you to pull your weak bones out of bed."

"If you break open the gate and my motorbike gets stolen, then I'll hold you and Menon responsible," he warned me before he returned to his house, banging the door after him.

Determined to have the last word, I rapped at his door. When he opened it, he looked like he was ready to pick me up and fling me to kingdom come.

"Listen man, I'm not the one who's going to be held responsible if your bike gets stolen."

"*Saala Madrasi behenchod,*" he muttered, raising his hand to strike me but I fended him off with my left arm and drove my right fist into his face. Menon's wife opened the door in time to see the blood trickling down Gupta's split lip. When Gupta realized I had bled him, he yelled like a maniac and ran to his house, returning with a knife.

Menon's wife was standing and watching fun. I thrust her aside and ran up the stairs to find myself a weapon. My eyes fell upon an ancient Kerala sword near the shoe rack. I grabbed it.

"*Saala*, I will have your blood for this!" Gupta yelled, rushing at me like a bull seeing red. His wife stood between the pair of us, trying to calm her husband down. In the meanwhile, Menon had been rudely awakened. He came out tying his *lungi*. People in the neighboring apartments had formed a small assembly outside the gate. A few men came and dragged the seething Gupta downstairs. I followed them, leaving the sword in a corner. Gupta straddled his motorbike and declared that he was off to the police station. The people who had come to help and those who had come to watch tried to dissuade him, telling him that it was illegal to construct a gate outside government quarters. By the time things were sorted out, it was two in the morning.

The next day, I asked Menon to fix a call bell on the gate. He refused, saying that children would give him hell by pressing it all day. I thought of looking out for another place but I knew that things wouldn't be any different if I moved out. Here, at least, I had a room to myself. In some places, you had to share one sleeping area and one toilet with eleven other people.

Before I moved into Menon's house, I'd been staying in a nice, convenient place where I was happy. One day, when I was listening to *qirat* on Radio Kuwait, the house owner dropped in to ask whether I was a Muslim. When I told him I wasn't, he wished to know why I was listening to "all that Mussulman stuff." I explained to him that I came from a town that was sacred to Muslims, like Ajmer. At the end of the month, when I went to him with the rent, he told me that a relative's son was coming to Delhi for college and he asked me to vacate my room and added that I shouldn't misunderstand him.

I moved into another room where a good bit of my money did the vanishing act.

Accommodation proved to be my biggest problem in Delhi. I wasn't able to stay in one place for more than a year, so I was in a quandary, wondering whether or not it would be wise to move from Menon's house. My problem was solved when Gupta got a transfer, but I still had to skip dinner most nights.

It was during that summer that I'd begun running in the morning after Bhilai had trounced me in the arm-wrestling match. The cultural programs were few and far between in the summer so I was able to have a proper dinner and get home on time. Mornings and evenings, I skipped rope. The only downside to my regimen was that it drained me too much to even think of staying up late and reading.

When I felt I was ready, I approached Bhilai and

challenged him. The arm-wrestling match took place in Chandan Singh's tea stall near Indra Prastha College. Chandan Singh and his tea stall had become a part of me in my Delhi life. All those twelve years I worked in Civil Supplies, Chandan's tea shop was where I had my breakfast –toasted bread and channa. Still that taste lingers in my tongue. Unlike many moustache-less North Indians, Chandan sported a big Nietzsche moustache. When I went to Delhi few years back, I visited Chandan Singh's stall one evening and drank just tea as he made channa only for breakfast. I observed that age had made Chandan languid and the tea he gave me was too sweet. I thought I should have told him *'Cheeni Kum'* when ordering, but while I contemplated about this I also thought that the amount of sugar in the tea was perfect in the eighties.

All the girls who were standing nearby began to take notice. For a whole thirty seconds, our arms remained gridlocked. Summoning all my strength, I pushed hard and I won.

"You looked like a ghost getting anal raped," Bhilai commented after his defeat.

When I was staying in Menon's house, I always used to have my dinner at Chawla's. It was there that I met Misra. I'd been searching for Sartre's *Critique of Dialectical Reason* in several libraries but never found it until Misra walked into Chawla's with it. My friendship with Misra began over a conversation about that book.

"Don't waste your time reading it," he told me. "It's lousy as fuck."

I started appraising *Being and Nothingness* only to discover he hated that as well.

"I will accept no one but Heidegger as a philosopher," he said. "That cockeyed Sartre said he'd prefer a third-rate crime novel to Wittgensten's works and people call *him* a philosopher?"

The next time I ran into Misra, he was sporting a two-week-old beard that made him look like a completely different man.

"Now this is a mug I haven't seen in a long time. What happened?" I asked.

He told me he'd been having problems with his father and had subsequently cut off all ties with his family.

"You still have another year of college to go," I said. "What will you do?"

Misra was in the first year of his postgraduate philosophy course.

"Mridula will help me," he said.

He'd mentioned his girlfriend a few times and I was curious to know more.

After that encounter, we ran into each other again after five months in the university stadium.

"How many laps do you run?" he asked me.

"Eight," I answered.

He said he ran ten. I was astonished as the circumference of the stadium was one whole kilometer.

Though he was living of Mridula, he didn't seem to be cutting back on his expenses. He was still staying in Madhuvan, paying three hundred rupees by way of rent for a room. He was wearing a new pair of Avis corduroys and I asked him where he bought them from.

"Oh, Mridula bought them for me," he said. "They're very durable. I haven't introduced you to her yet, have I? Come with me."

He took me to the bus stop on Mall Road. She'd agreed to meet us there. Seeing the four heavy books he was carrying, I asked him, "Doesn't it bother you to carry your books like this? Why don't you get a bag?"

"I don't carry my books. Mridula does."

"I see."

Misra laughed. "Now don't go on a rant about female slavery and male chauvinism and all that bullcrap. I don't like her doing it either, but since she's happy to do it for me, why should I spoil her happiness?"

When I heard this, I became even more curious to see Mridula, but when I finally saw her, I was disappointed. She hardly wore any clothes. After the introductions were made, she offered me a cigarette.

"Don't spoil him," Misra said. "He's a runner too. Needs a healthy body and a healthy mind and whatnot."

Misra always traveled by bus. He never bought a bus ticket and had no student's pass either. When I asked him about getting caught, he said nonchalantly, "In the event of getting caught, I can always come up with some excuse or the other, but I've never been caught, not even once."

Misra liked to tease me by comparing me to film actors. Once, when I fought with the owner of the Chawla Restaurant on behalf of a young waiter, he compared me to M. G. R. and taunted me. Another time, when a mutual friend wished to meet me urgently and asked him my whereabouts, he replied, "It's easy to find Udhaya – he will be wandering on Mall Road in a Bruce Lee t-shirt." He meant to say that, unlike a bearded *kurta*-donning intellectual, I was an average Joe in a Bruce Lee t-shirt.

One day, Misra came to my office looking for me. I usually never liked meeting people at my workplace, so I took him to the canteen. I was anticipating a critical comment about my office environment but he didn't say a thing.

At the canteen, we ordered an omelet and sat down to talk. The man seated across from us looked like Van Gogh. When he looked at us and smiled, I smiled back. He wasn't a familiar face.

After some time, he said, "I'm hungry but I have no money. Can you buy me a cup of tea?"

Just the day before, a peon who worked in the department came up to me and stooped low, revealing a crooked set of butter-colored teeth. He asked me to give him two rupees. He showed me the three rupees in his hand and said, "*Dada*, I need to give five rupees to a poor old man."

Later, when I'd gone to get myself a cup of tea, I heard the canteen proprietor tell the peon, "Chalk it up to *Dada*'s account." The peon looked at me with his repulsive toothy smile. I said nothing to him then, but the next time he demanded money for the old man, I refused.

Misra seemed to have taken a fancy to Van Gogh and began talking to him. The man told him that he'd been a peon in the office and had gone to prison for illicit cement procurement.

Misra, who'd been listening to him calmly, suddenly started yelling.

"*Steal,* don't *beg!* What you want now is a cup of tea. Why are you begging for it? Order a cup! It will come. Drink the tea and walk off. Do you think people will care to come after you for three rupees in this crowd? Even if they do, so what? Tell them you have no money. If you get hit, hit back and hit harder than you got hit. If four people gang up against you, take a stone and knock them all out. They might hand you over to the cops. Let them. Go to prison again and once you're out, don't go and steal a cup of tea again. Steal something more valuable! Pick pockets, snatch women's gold chains, and if you get caught, don't be afraid to try again!"

After this insane incident, I didn't see Misra for a long time. When I went to Madhuvan and asked around, I was told he vacated his room. One day, as if by chance, I met Mridula at the university library and she said she wanted to speak to me. We found a shady nook under a tree and she told me everything about her relationship with Misra, starting from the time she got married to him. I was shocked to hear that Misra had tried to strangle her when she talked to him about having a baby. Luckily, her brother came to her rescue.

"Where is Misra now?"

"Prison," she informed me.

"Prison?"

"Yes, for something I feel ashamed to speak about. On G. B. Road, he and his friend got into an argument with a prostitute over money. The woman beat the friend and Misra attacked her. She died from the blunt force trauma of the blow."

I went to see Misra in prison. There was something in his eyes – regret, maybe.

After a long silence, I said, "I went to Madhuvan several times in search of you."

He mumbled something and fell silent again.

"Do you want me to get you anything from outside?"

"No."

The rest of the visitors' hour passed in silence.

"Is there something you're angry with me about?"

"Stop asking absurd questions, will you?"

Mridula had asked me to meet her after meeting Misra in prison. When I went to her house, I was amazed to learn that she was from a very wealthy family.

On hearing that he'd refused to speak to me, she said, "At least he agreed to meet you. He didn't wish to meet me at all."

A few days later, I heard from Mridula that Misra had committed suicide in prison.

Kiran was driving the car at 120 kmph. With Outer Ring Road void of traffic and mortal bodies, it felt like we were whizzing across strange universes. The unreality of the situation made me feel like a consciousness floating in space outside the snakeskin of my corporealness. I don't know how long the maniacal drive lasted. When Kiran shook me awake, I realized we'd reached Vasant Vihar. As usual, Malhotra, Kiran's father, was not home – he was either in office or out of town on office work. His wife was a Tamil. He'd gone against his family's wishes when he married her. After fifteen years, she left him for another man and returned to Chennai, leaving him alone. Kiran was not fond of Chennai, so she'd chosen to remain in Delhi with her father. There were also several other things that were not to her liking. In fact, I'd call it deep hatred as it was many shades darker and angrier than mere dislike. Reckless driving seems to be the only thing in the world she doesn't hate.

I first met her when I'd gone for a run in the university stadium. It was very early in the morning and still very dark. There were only two other people in the stadium performing yoga. I saw Kiran seated on the stairs in a corner. She had a schoolgirl's face. Every time I ran past her, she smiled at me. Drawn by her beauty, I finished my run and walked over. "Aren't *you* planning to go for a run?" I asked her.

"No, fancy a walk?" She told me I resembled a Tamil actor whose name she'd forgotten.

"Kamal Haasan?"

"Yes! Kamal Hassan."

"It's *Haa*-san," I said, "not Hassan. Oh nevermind! You don't know Tamil. But still, you look like a Tamil girl."

"My mother's a Tamil."

We walked in silence for a while. People had started trickling into the stadium for their daily run. She suggested we go out and we began walking on the University road that was deserted at that time. At the entrance of the University, we saw several monkeys creating a commotion. On seeing them, she got scared and clutched my arm.

"Shall we go back?" she asked me nervously.

"They won't harm us," I assured her. "Come on, let's keep walking."

She was clutching my shoulder now. We took a left and entered the Khyber Pass.

"So, it's monkeys you're afraid of, not human beings?"

"Why do you ask?"

"Well, because here you are walking in a lonesome forest with a complete stranger."

"Nah, I'm not scared. What's the worst thing you can do to me? Rape me? I won't fight you; I'll enjoy it. You don't seem like a lowlife rapist anyway."

I was flabbergasted.

And just when I thought she couldn't shock me more, she pulled out a handgun from her pocket. I'd never seen a handgun in real life before. We talked for a long time in the woods and then returned to the tea stall at the entrance of the university.

Before she left, she told me she loved going for long early-morning drives which was why she'd come here all the way from Vasant Vihar. I passed the rest of the day in a dreamlike state. I couldn't wait to see her the next morning.

I went to the stadium earlier than usual, but my heart sank when I saw the empty stairs. I ran several laps, hoping all the while that I'd find Kiran around by sheer chance. When I'd tired myself out on every level, I slumped down on the steps, panting like a dog, feeling a dull melancholic ache. When I looked up, I saw a beautiful vision approaching me – Kiran. My heart jumped with joy.

She sat down beside me.

"I thought I gave you such a case of the creeps to make you never want to come here again," I told her, giving her a friendly pat on the shoulder.

"Nah, I just slept in. So I came here late. I was on the other side of the stadium and I saw you looking for me."

She invited me home and I happily accepted. We would go on to become close friends.

I introduced Kiran to Misra but they didn't take to each other. Misra, to her, was a male chauvinist pig.

"He's a madman," she confided to me. "Reminds me of a hungry Doberman."

As for Misra, he summed her up as a typical personality-lacking bourgeois who was also deficient of individuality and empathy; a weak and foolish girl with arrogance that comes from being rich. After a couple of encounters, they never met each other again.

Kiran was home alone most of the time. Her father irked me. Though he knew that Kiran's mother was carrying on with someone else, he still referred to her as his wife and made frequent trips to Chennai to visit her. When I asked Kiran why he was yet to divorce her, she laughed and said that he had a reputation to maintain. If he divorced her, then the whole town would come to know of how his wife trashed him for someone else, and he would lose face. I realized that she had been deprived of love and friendship right from her childhood. I began to love her like a daughter and she often called me "dad." But I will admit that I felt a little uneasy when she did because my feelings towards her were beginning to get dirty. Her beauty was making me lose my senses and every time I jerked off to the thought of her, I was guilt-ridden, but I rationalized my sexual feelings in a few days.

One day, I was sitting in her room and doling out some fatherly advice. She was suddenly possessed with an urge that made her thrust herself at me and start kissing me.

"Fuck me, Dad!" she said, squeezing me tight.

I began to stay over at her house and indulge her sexual fantasies.

There was no one in the house apart from Malhotra and a maid and since neither of them ever came near Kiran's room, we didn't have to fear getting caught in the act. In her room, we were mostly naked and when we felt an urge, we fucked each other like animals. Being naked felt so natural to me, but in my clothes, I felt like I was playing a role, a very hypocritical one.

One day, after a few glasses too many of wine, I started kissing her posterior.

"Woman, you've made me understand the greatest truths of life!" I declared ecstatically. "My salutations to you."

"I doubt you understand the greatest truths of life, Udhaya," she dully replied.

"Mind explaining that?"

"Sometimes you look only at the surface of things and other times you see what lies beneath but you pretend you see nothing. If the first half of my statement is true, you are shallow; if the second half is true, you are a hypocrite."

I was offended that she had such a low opinion of me despite having known me intimately. I got dressed and left the room in a huff. I didn't bother to meet her for ten days after that. However, once my temper had dropped a few degrees, I went to her house and knocked on the door.

"Who is it?" Kiran asked from inside.

At the sound of her voice, my heart began to beat faster. How I missed her during those ten days! I just wanted to wrap her up in a tight embrace.

When she opened the door, before I noticed her, I noticed a nude man sitting in the sofa. A real slap in the face.

"Hi Dad, how are you?" Kiran asked with an uppity air.

She took my hand in hers, but I didn't know how to react. Like an idiot, I muttered that I'd come later.

"Why later? Why don't you join us now?"

"No, I can't. I'm sorry."

"Do you understand now why I said that you don't understand anything? You will never understand the greatest truths of life, Dad. Go find yourself a nice, virtuous, educated beautiful woman who knows how to cook and marry her. Write essays on Germaine Greer's *Madwoman's Underclothes* for magazines."

My face flushed with humiliation, I left.

On the way home, I spotted a hornbill perched on a golden shower in Majnu-ka-Tilla. It brought back vivid memories of a conversation we once had about the bird's breeding habits.

The female hornbill takes fifty days to hatch her eggs and it never leaves the nest during this time. It is the male of the species that must hunt for food to bring to the nest for both the female and the fledglings. After three months, when the chicks are bigger, the female breaks the nest open and comes out. She leaves only a tiny opening for the passing of food. After the mother leaves the nest, the chicks remain for another three months.

"Do you know what the female does if something happens to the male and it is unable to return to the nest with food?" Kiran asked me.

"It will wait for its mate and eventually starve to death," I replied.

"Is that true?"

"Sometimes the truth is stranger than fiction."

I quoted the words of the 57th song of the *Kurunthogai* that were written by Siraikkudi Aanthaiyaar:

When the makandril birds which live in water swim as a pair, they feel pain even if a flower comes between them, for they feel as if they have been separated by several years. Without my lover, I too feel the same pain and I feel death is better, says the woman.

When she heard, she had a merry laugh.

"Your Tamil poets are such big liars," she said.

After reading all that I have written of my relationship with Kiran, I started to think that even birds and beasts enjoy better lives than human beings. A recent article in the newspaper bore that out.

Boopathy (33) was from the village of Sinthalavadampatti near Palani. One day, he went to a Tasmac shop. As the side dish he ordered were late in coming, he helped himself to those of a certain Ganesan (35) from Kaalipatti. This led to an argument between them. When the men sitting around them tried to intervene, Boopathy attacked them all with a beer bottle, and in the ensuing melee, Ganesan, Perumal (50), Gnanasekhar (29), Muthusamy (53), Subramoni (45) and Manian (45) from Manjanayakkampatti were injured. The others eventually managed to calm Boopathy down and sent him on his way, but Ganesan and his friends pursued, waylaid and attacked him. Boopathy stabbed them with his knife and Ganesan's gang assaulted Boopathy with a sword. Both Boopathy and Ganesan suffered major injuries and were hospitalized. Boopathy succumbed to his injuries and died. The pair never knew each other before the fateful Tasmac fight.

In Tamil Nadu, most of the Sikhs own automobile shops while most of the Jains from Rajasthan were pawnbrokers. In Delhi, most Brahmins from Tamil Nadu work as government clerks. They seem to have been born for this job that seems to exist only for them. Although the Tamils are efficient employees, due to their lack of fluency in Hindi, there are only a handful of them in the Delhi administration. There was a Tamil who was appointed deputy commissioner in my office. My friend Sugata Kumar was his stenographer.

One day, Suagta came to me and asked, "Why does this deputy commissioner dude always ask his wife to prepare curd-rice for him? Don't you people eat anything else?"

Though Sugata was a Malayali, he'd grown up in Delhi, and hence never knew much about the Tamils. It was quite possible that the deputy commissioner and I were the first Tamils he'd met.

To answer his question, I had to launch into a long explanation.

"Being a Brahmin and being a Tamil are not the same thing. Non-Brahmin Tamils and Brahmin Tamils have different preferences as regards dress and food. I am a thirty-two year old Tamil and I have never eaten curd-rice."

I worked in the civil supplies department for seven

years. Not many people lasted long there. I was left alone as there was a shortage of stenographers and because I never once received an under-the-table payment. During my years of service, I was heavily influenced by one Mr. S. K. Khanna, an officer. He had an imposing height, a handsome nose and a rosy complexion, and he loved women. Who doesn't? What made Khanna different was his open and uninhibited display of interest.

Under every deputy commissioner was a lower division clerk, an upper division clerk, a stenographer and a *chaprasi*, but in Khanna's branch, there were three clerks, all of whom were lower division. Had there been an upper division clerk, the deputy commissioner would have had to dance to his tune. I thought it was rather clever of Khanna to not include an upper division clerk in his posse. As far as I'd known, none of the other officers had been able to alter their teams.

My fondness for Khanna had a lot to do with his initiative to build a restroom for the five hundred people who worked in the civil supplies headquarters. Our office was housed in a very ancient, jerry-built building that the Big Bad Wolf could have blown down with a huff and a puff. It must have been an Englishman's stable – or his pigsty – some two centuries ago. The building consisted of small dark corridors whose walls were lined with small dark cubbyholes. It was in these cubbyholes that we worked. If there was a power outage, the place would be as dark as a closed coffin, and the darkness had a suffocating heaviness to it. The women always came prepared with candles and matchboxes for these hours of darkness.

There were five hundred staff who had to handle upward of a thousand visitors daily. Now, these one thousand five hundred people had to make use of one single toilet which was in a dilapidated state of affairs. There were only a couple of urinals. The officers, of course, had separate toilets, and better ones too. The top honcho, the commissioner, had a toilet attached to his room, and I wouldn't be surprised if it was marble-tiled with a Jacuzzi and bath salts.

The toilet with the two urinals, in addition to not having facilities to defecate, had no door except for the women's toilet. It was just three cement walls and a tin roof. Two people could stand shoulder to shoulder and take a piss. You also had to endure the leaking roof and the leaking pipes. It was hard to stay dry in that miserable smelly armpit of a place. And, like it was the main attraction, the toilet was situated right in the middle of the building.

Before Khanna, I had to perform clumsy – sometimes disastrous – acrobatics to relieve myself. With the arrival of Khanna, the toilet was revamped into a neat space where a person could piss and defecate leisurely and comfortably.

Every year, when the budget was presented in the Parliament, a few hundred thousands were set apart for the amelioration of the civil supplies department. The administration would spend only a few thousands and return the balance to the government. It was not possible to spend the entire amount in just two months February and March. The accounts had to be balanced by the end of March but our officers were not capable of this. Khanna was the only officer who took a substantial part of the money that had been earmarked for us and spent it without worrying even slightly about the consequences.

"We must be careful to submit proper accounts," he would say, "And by accounts, I mean bills, and for bills, we will just have to make an irresistible deal with the suppliers, that's all."

It was with this money that he bought Sushma a refrigerator and a washing machine during one financial year.

There were three women in Khanna's personal branch – Mini, Baljit and Sushma. I was part of the team only because the department had no female stenographers. Mini was too shy for Khanna – she was a Malayali who didn't know a word of Hindi and who was too diffident to speak English. Baljit, being a *sardarni*, was bold as brass, and Khanna lacked the courage to make advances to her.

Which left Sushma. She liked Khanna and Khanna liked her. Both of them were married with children. Their romance became irksome for me as Khanna would call me as soon as I arrived in the morning and enquire about my health and well-being like he hadn't seen me in months. At the end of the conversation, he would casually ask if Sushma had come. When I answered in the positive, Sushma would look at me and press her index finger to her ample bosom so as to say, "Is he asking about me?" Then, she'd pout with her painted lips and give me a wink.

The wink was understandable, but not the pout.

I would nod my head in affirmation to her gesture. Khanna would ask me to send her to his office.

When I told Sushma she was wanted, she'd apply another coat of lipstick and give her face another layer of compact. After tucking her *saree* in properly, she'd catwalk to Khanna's room. Mini would lower her head coyly and Baljit would snigger. I had to follow her to latch Khanna's door from the outside once Sushma was in so that they could get on with their "important business" without any disturbances.

Roughly two hours later, the buzzer would sound.

"Udhayji, please unlatch the door."

During those two hours, I would have to take his calls. Around ten of these callers would be women. I would tell them all the same thing: "Khanna *saab* has gone out for inspection."

Some women would mutter, "Bloody inspection" and hang up. Others, thinking I was lying, would unleash curses on me. Can you believe that, when he was with Sushma, even his wife and the lieutenant governor had to be lied to?

One day, a higher official came to see Khanna. He saw Khanna's door locked from the outside and asked me where he was. I gave him the standard reply. And just then, unfortunately Khanna buzzed me. I picked up the phone and said, "Yes sir?"

The officer glanced at Sushma's empty seat and understood everything.

"*Arrey, Madrasi babu,* you are doing a *good* job. You will make your way up in the department very soon," he said sarcastically and left.

Khanna tended to his office work only on Sundays as he was busy with Sushma during the week. He asked me to come to work on alternate Sundays to give him a hand. If I refused, Nalini wouldn't be able to visit her mother in Chennai. She insisted on seeing her mother at least once a year but that depended on Khanna. If I refused to work on Sundays, he wouldn't sanction my annual leave and Nalini wouldn't hear of going to Chennai alone.

We couldn't absent ourselves to work without permission. In most government offices, there are usually ten people to do one person's job, but in my office, there was one person to do ten people's jobs. The department rarely recruited new employees as most of them thrived on fat payolas. They'd work hard for five years, buy a house and a car, get a license – in some relative's name – to run a ration shop and quit.

Almost every day, Mini, Baljit and Sushma got all their work done in an hour while the stenographers and those employees in the cement division had a heavy workload. Mini had the time to sit in her cubicle and read Malayalam novels – she told me she'd read Asokamithran in translation – while Baljit and Sushma sat around with Surender Mohan Pathak's crime novels.

I never took any bribes, but it had nothing to do with principles. Even without taking bribes, I felt like a pimp. So if I took a bribe, it would have been equal to selling myself.

One day, I returned home late at night from work when Khanna called me, asking me to go back to the office as there was some work that needed to be done urgently. I drank a glass of water, cursed Khanna using every swear word I knew and left. This was one reason I hated the fact that my house was close to my workplace.

"What is with this LG *saab*, Udhayji?" he said. "I had to leave home as soon as he summoned me."

Khanna was a man of refined habits. Even in his anger, he wouldn't resort to cussing. I'd never heard him use words like *behenchod* or *chutiya* even once.

Underneath the irritation in Khanna's voice, I heard a note of gladness for it's not every day that the lieutenant general summons you and gives you a personal chore to handle. There was going to be a function at the lieutenant governor's house for which he urgently needed a hundred liters of pure cow's milk. We knew it wasn't so easy to procure such a ridiculous quantity of cow's milk in Delhi on such short notice. It might be got by traveling forty kilometers to Chaudhary's farm in Gurgaon.

Chaudhary was a close friend of Khanna. He greeted us warmly and served us hot *jalebis* and big cups of milk – around three-fourth of a liter. Khanna emptied his cup in a few gulps while I ate only the *jalebis*. I refused the milk as even one small pint would give me the runs. The milk Chaudhary offered us looked like colostrum – thick and creamy.

I'd once seen Chaudhary in the office. He carried himself with the dignity and pride of a typical Jat villager. He had a thick, curled moustache and a strong, firm body that looked like it was wrought of iron. He always wore a *dhoti* in the style of the villagers.

Even though they are vegetarians, Haranvis are strong-bodied. When I asked Khanna how this was so, he said, "Even elephants are vegetarians. They may be strong but they don't know how to enjoy life. If they are elephants, then we are lions, you know? *Sher-e-Punjab.*"

Chaudhary didn't take a paisa for the milk.

"What is this, Khanna *saab*? You are the *maalik* of the Delhi administration and I am duty-bound to give you even a thousand liters if you ask. No, I will have no talk of money."

After this friendly reprimand, he put the milk into cans which he loaded onto a box truck.

On the way back, Khanna told me, "Chaudhary is very shrewd. I would have paid him one thousand for the milk, but just you wait and see how he will come by one of these days and ask for a favor that would cost us more."

When the milk was delivered to the lieutenant general, he praised Khanna lavishly. "I entrusted the job to you for I knew you'd do it well."

Then, he asked who I was.

"My secretary, a *Madrasi*," said Khanna. "A very dependable young man."

"No doubt," said the lieutenant general. "There is none more dependable than a *Madrasi*. But this boy doesn't look like a *Madrasi*. I thought he was from our parts."

On our return, Khanna told me, "The LG himself has

said it. What more do you want? You know, if *Madrasis* are the most dependable men, then *sardarnis* are the most beautiful women. I think Baljit is very close to you?"

I faked coyness.

"I'm tired of working all day," he said. "Shall we have a beer?"

We drank beer and talked for an hour. All our talk revolved around sex, but he was careful to not drop Sushma's name.

Khanna was truly an unforgettable man. When he left the department upon being transferred, he invited me and another South Indian home for a big feast. His wife had made all the food and she served us several pegs of Scotch whiskey; she even had a few drinks herself. But what made Khanna memorable to me was his gesture of dropping me home in his car in the middle of the night.

There is yet another unforgettable personality I remember but whose name I'll never know. When I was in Possangipur, I used to take a chartered bus to my office. For two years, I noticed this man who used to board the bus at Janakpuri. He looked like an officer in his sharp suit and he carried a briefcase. He avoided sitting with men and always preferred to sit with women even if the entire row of seats was empty.

When I returned to Chennai, I began working for the postal department. Once, someone from a magazine asked me what my occupation was.

"Pimping," I said.

The reporters made news out of my answer.

"This is how one employee of the postal department refers to the job he holds," they wrote, and all the other stenographers who worked with me were seething with anger.

But I never felt there was anything wrong about what I'd said.

If my boss had called me a fool, I'd have to take his insult, mouth and all other openings firmly closed. Though I have written a novel on this, I am going to tell you something here that I failed to mention there.

Many of the officers were like escapees from a lunatic asylum, but there was one man, a Malayali called Thomas, who was a particularly hopeless case.

Traditionally, when a transferred officer arrives, his subordinate in the new office has to go to the railway station to receive him. Thomas was working as the director in Chennai. He'd returned to resume his duties after a long leave of absence. All the officers in his division had been promoted to the rank of postmaster general, while he was still director. This was not because of his leave of absence, but because of the adverse remarks written by all his superiors in his confidential report. He was despised for his nasty habit of constantly needling not only the people who worked under him – both junior officers and stenographers – but also his higher-ups.

Manjula, a section officer who could be described as his twin when it came to torturing people, was to go to the railway station to receive Thomas. She reached the station at four in the morning. The train was running an hour late and Manjula waited in a state of tension although there was nothing she could have done to speed up the train.

In general, postal employees refer to their superiors only with their titles even when speaking directly to them. If they are addressing the post master general – the PMG – they'd say, "I have done what the PMG *saar* told me." They'd be screwed big time if they had the temerity to say, "I have done what *you* told me." They'd probably get chucked into a desert, or worse, get a damning remark in their confidential report. There was this one time a North Indian was appointed PMG at the headquarters of the Chennai Postal Department. One of the officers told him, "I have done what the PMG *saar* told me."

"Which PMG?" he asked him, as there was more than one PMG in the same office, and he didn't understand that the officer was referring to him.

The train finally arrived at half past six. As soon as she saw Thomas, Manjula ran to him with a big plastic smile and started pouring out greetings: "Good morning, *saar*. Welcome to Tamil Nadu, *saar*." All Thomas did was pick up his suitcase and walk off hurriedly, ignoring her.

On reaching the office at ten, the junior officers gathered in his room to greet him. Thomas was informed of this. He yelled on the phone, "Tell them all to get to their seats! It is only because of this *chamchagiri* that work never gets done here. I never asked for anyone to come and see me. Have they begun their antics on the day of my arrival itself? I know how to deal with them!"

When the stenographer conveyed his response verbatim, the officers nearly shat their pants. But that was not the end of it. After they left, he summoned the stenographer to his room and made him draw up a list of all those who had *not* come, snarling that he would show them who he was. If this is not the behavior of a psychopath, then what is?

This incident was narrated to me by one of the stenographers by name Subramoni. Apparently, Thomas had said, "To come and pay your respects is your duty and to chase you away is my right. But if you don't come to see me, then you are mincemeat." This was Thomas the Psychopath's philosophy.

"Bastard," I told Subramoni. "Someone should give him electroshock in his dick."

"Then you'll need to start a concentration camp," Subramoni said. "He's not the only one who'll need it."

Now tell me, was I wrong in saying I was a pimp?

Within two weeks of giving the interview, I resigned my job at the postal department and called up the magazine office to inform them that I quit my pimping job there. The editor published that as well.

October 10, 1983

It took the bus thirty minutes to get to I.T.O. from Mayur Vihar and from I.T.O., it was a ten-minute walk to catch the Mudrika. It took another half-hour to reach my office. As the Mudrika buses kept circling Delhi Ring

Road, they were always jam-packed. It involved a load of effort to push through the crowd when fellows busy pressing their dicks against female passengers' buttocks were blocking the way. Finally, bathed in sweat, I fell out of the bus at the other end, squeezed and squashed like an insect, and then got up and did a half-run to the office to sign the attendance register on time.

Once I reached the office, I was desperate for a cup of tea but I only had enough money for my return bus trip in the evening. Sugatan normally stood the tea, but he'd been transferred a week ago, and I couldn't ask Akash because I already owed him ten rupees.

A few days ago, Madasamy came to the office all the way from Janakpuri to see me. I couldn't just see him and send him on his way without giving him so much as a cup of tea. I'd asked Akash for one rupee, but he gave me ten, saying he had no change.

A year ago, when both of us were staying on Mall Road, Madasamy and I would meet daily. He was staying in Jubilee Hall and was doing his Ph.D. Jubilee Hall was Delhi University's biggest hostel where only research scholars stayed. Each student had his own room there. Every Sunday, the resident scholars were allowed to bring one friend to the canteen. I was that one friend Madasamy picked to lunch with him. The non-vegetarian items there were mouthwatering, especially the mutton curry. Madasamy and I lost touch after he got married. It was my fault as he kept calling me over, but I didn't accept his invitation even once.

He'd married a woman from a wealthy family. The girl's brother had been visiting at the time. Madasamy told me he'd gone to the market on the morning to buy mutton especially for me. However, I didn't come across even one teeny-tiny piece of mutton in the gravy. He then called his brother-in-law to eat. The brother-in-law said that he'd already eaten. Seeing me trawling through the curry for a piece of mutton, Madasamy volunteered to serve me.

"I think the meat got overcooked and crumbled," he said, embarrassed.

His brother-in-law said, "There were only two pieces of mutton in the gravy and I ate them."

Then, Madasamy said to no one in particular, "I made a mistake. I should have bought more mutton."

I always have shit luck with mutton. Once, I went to my friend Bala's brother's wedding. He told me they'd be serving mutton *biryani* for the feast. As soon as the *biryani* landed on my leaf, I began to search for the mutton, but to my shock, there wasn't even a single piece. I slyly glanced at the leaves next to mine. There was no mutton on them either. What the fuck? Was this supposed to be mutton *biryani* or *guska*? I called the server and told him in an authoritarian manner to serve me a few pieces. He said he would be back soon and went into hiding. I cursed my fate and ate the *guska*. Then, I went in search of my friend, Bala, to complain about the mutton-less "mutton *biryani*." I found him in the middle of a heated argument with the man who was in charge of the catering.

"Everyone is complaining that there wasn't a *single* piece of mutton!" Bala was shouting. "Is this your idea of mutton *biryani*?"

"*Saar*, wait! Look, there is mutton in the *biryani*!" the head-caterer said, showing him the pieces.

"Well, well, well! If there *was* mutton, why did you go into hiding when I asked you for some?" I asked caustically and left the place, resolving to never attend weddings where non-vegetarian food is served.

I remembered the countless *biryanis* I'd eaten at weddings and *sunnat* ceremonies in Nagore. There would be four people sitting around one large plate. Got it? Four people and one large plate. It's called *sahan sappadu*.

This is still practiced in places like Koothanallur and Muthupet in Tiruvarur, Keezhakarai in Ramanathapuram, and Kayalpatnam in Thoothukudi. *Sahan sappadu* is a meal of rice with five curries. It also goes by the names *nei soru* and *thalichcha soru* and is a 450-year-old tradition in Nagore. You had *dal* and *kalia* in the first round, brinjal *pachadi* in the second, *thanikkari* (meat) in the third, *korma* in the fourth and milk rice in the fifth.

THALICHA

Ingredients:

Toor dal – 1cup
Mutton – 0.25 kg
Ginger-garlic paste – 2 tsp
Curd – 2tsp
Raw banana – 1
Potatoes – 2
Green chilies – 2
Carrots – 1
Tomato – 100 g
Onion – 2
Brinjal – 2
Cloves – 2
Cardamom – 2
Turmeric
Chili powder
Coriander powder
Tamarind
Coconut paste
Cinnamon – 1 piece
A few sprigs of coriander
A few sprigs of mint
A few curry leaves
A mixture of oil and ghee

Directions:

Cook the *toor dal*. Marinate the mutton with curd, ginger-garlic paste and salt for 15 minutes.

Heat a frying pan over the stove. When it is hot, add three tablespoons of the oil-ghee mixture and drop in the cardamom, cinnamon and cloves. Add the chopped onions, tomatoes and green chilies with the coriander and mint leaves and sauté.

Once the contents of the pan have been sautéed, add 1 ½ tbsp chili powder and 1 tbsp ginger-garlic paste and fry well.

Add the marinated mutton and stir so that it gets coated with the masala. Cover and cook for 10 minutes.

In another vessel, take 1 ½ tbsp curry masala powder, 2 tbsp coriander powder and 1 tbsp turmeric powder and mix well with 2 cups of water. Pour this mixture on the mutton in the pan. Close the pan and allow the mutton to boil.

When the mutton is half cooked, add the cooked *tur dal*, tamarind water, potato, raw banana, brinjal, carrot and coconut paste and mix well. Lower the flame and boil for 20 minutes. Lower the flame and boil for another 20 minutes.

Add some curry leaves and keep the dish covered.

The *thalicha* will be ready to eat in 5 minutes.

One important thing you should know is that people from Nagore never consume oil unless it is mixed with *ghee*. This is probably why I love *ghee*. I buy it pure from Srivilliputhur as you get cow's *ghee* there which is fat-free.

I was surprised with the extremely opposite culture of

Nagore's eating and drinking customs and the habits of conservative Brahmins where the drumstick has to be eaten by keeping it on a plate and scooping out the flesh with your finger. Water has to be drunk looking skywards – it's no big deal if the water gets into your nose and you die. You must cook only after you've bathed,etc;

I described the *sahan sappadu* to Anjali in all its excruciating detail – how, in the end, the tomato *pachadi*, the *seenithova* and the plantain are all mashed and doused with *phirni*.

Anjali gagged and wanted to throw up.

Let's go back to Madasamy.

The last time I saw him was the day we were searching for pieces of mutton in the gravy in his house. Three years had passed since then.

"Why have you become so aloof after your marriage?" he asked. "You don't write in the magazines like you used to. I smiled without answering his questions.

Madasamy was confused. He didn't stop probing. Since I had married for love, he suspected something was wrong.

"Did you come to your senses once your desire and passion were spent? How's your domestic life? Do you have any problems?"

Though I kept mum for his first two questions, I vehemently answered the last one in the negative.

I didn't return the balance to Akash. That morning, we'd run out of kerosene but somehow, Nalini and I had managed to finish the cooking. I used the ten rupees I owed Akash to buy kerosene.

Akash is very particular about money (who isn't?) so I thought he'd demand the balance in a day or two, but he didn't mention the ten rupees for many days. One day, he remembered and said, "It's real damn difficult to find one and two rupee notes these days, isn't it?" I nodded in agreement.

I was able to repay him only when I got my salary. I approached Ram Singh and asked him to lend me one rupee, promising to return it the next day, but he said he didn't have one rupee to give me. Then, I asked him to spare eight *annas*, promising to return it the same afternoon, but he said he didn't have eight *annas* to give me either.

"I have only thirty *paise*," he told me.

My urge to drink tea had intensified. I thought of asking Dogra a cup of tea then and I would pay later but lacked the courage to do so as I already had to pay him last month's due.

Once I realized I wouldn't be able to borrow money from anyone that day, I decided to make some on my own and went in search of my customers and I found Bhatnagar.

"Anything I can do?" I asked him.

"Can you get me a signed 'Issue Today' permit?" he asked in return.

It usually wasn't easy to procure an 'Issue Today.' If a person required five bags of cement, he had to show his ration card to the assistant commissioner and submit an application following which he was given a permit stamped with 'Issue five bags.' On receiving this, the permit section would accept his application, but he would have to wait in queue along with several others. His number would be called after a month and a half. However, if the application came from a well-connected person, the assistant commissioner would give him a permit stamped with 'Issue five bags today' and the person could collect his bags the very same day.

At any given time, there were a hundred people or more standing in line to see the clerk who issued the permit – women with squealing babies, men chewing betel, men smoking *beedis* and so on. A VIP couldn't possibly stand in this queue full of riffraffs, so it was the assistant commissioner's task to send one of his *chamchas* to the counter with the VIP applications and get the clerk sitting at the counter to issue their permits immediately. If an applicant somehow had private audience with the permit clerk in his room, the chances of him getting his head torn from his body by the folks standing outside was high. This is because the common folk are subjected to all kinds of exhausting formalities. They must walk long distances, stand for long hours in several queues and wait patiently for months to get five bags of cement. This was why there were riots when someone jumped the queue.

The previous day, I was taking notes from assistant commissioner Pandey when Gupta (one of his *chamchas*) entered the room and said, "Anand is refusing to issue permits for the applications *saab* sent. Please summon him and speak to him." Gupta sat down. Pandey immediately sent a *chaprasi* to summon Anand.

"*Janaab*, you can call me and hand the applications to me directly. I will do the job. But I don't trust this man," Anand said, pointing to Gupta.

Pandey's face fell and he sent Anand away. It wasn't possible to hand the applications directly to Anand as the clerk cannot leave the counter when the permits are being issued.

Unlike most others, Anand refused to make money through dishonest means. This also meant that he did not abet with people who made money dishonestly. At the other counters, the clerks themselves would write on certain permits, *Discussed with AC. Issue five bags today,* and sign them. One needs a good deal of cunning, efficiency and skill to hoodwink the people standing in line in front of you to pull this off. While writing a permit for the person standing in front of you, you have to simultaneously write another and it should be done in such a way that the person in the queue should not suspect that you are making him wait because you are busy getting somebody else's work done. You also have to keep an eye on the side door. Pandey's *chamcha* might walk in with more applications. Say you need to pee, get up and covertly take the applications and hide them in your pocket. Being a permit clerk sure takes a lot of skill, doesn't it?

After Gupta left, Pandey summoned Anand again and pleaded with him saying, "So many VIPs come here. It is to get their work done quickly that I send Gupta to you. Why can't you just issue the permits? Look Anand, only if we understand each other and cooperate in a friendly manner will things go smoothly. Otherwise, nothing good will happen."

"Okay, how many applications did you send with Gupta yesterday?" Anand asked.

"Eight."

"Gupta gave me fifteen and your signature was on eight of them. The rest had *'Discussed with AC. Issue today'* written on them and they were signed by Gupta.

"Is it? I shall ask Gupta about this. But Anand, you shouldn't have told me in front of Gupta that you don't trust him. If you wanted to say something like that about him, you could have said it to me privately. After this, will Gupta be willing to run around when I ask him to for the VIPs?"

Pandey summoned Gupta again and when Gupta came, he sent me away. They were probably going to discuss how to deal with Anand.

Here in the cement branch, the AC and the *babu* were on back-slapping terms. They smoked together and even ate from the same plate. *Babus* made ten rupees per bag of cement which to them was a well-deserved reward for talent, not corruption. This was how they did it: While sending cement from the factories to the market, they would put three blue stripes on certain sacks containing controlled-rate cement; the sacks without these stripes were meant for open market.

An official of the cement company often came to Gupta saying, "*Bhaiya,* as the workers are illiterate, they have inadvertently put blue stripes on 3000 sacks meant for open market. Would you kindly allow them to be sold in open markets?"

Gupta would go to Pandey with their request and would come back with Pandey's assent. This meant the duo made a profit of thirty rupees per sack of which ten rupees went into Gupta's pocket. Thirty thousand rupees for the man in a single stroke! But Gupta couldn't take the entire amount as it had to be shared with everyone in the cement branch. So, a clerk in our branch would earn five thousand per day. And what about Pandey? I was told he earned six-figure sums.

In the other departments, a person might come to an officer with a request to operate his own granary. The red tape he was given translated to six months waiting time which meant he had to pay a rent of one hundred thousand rupees to the owner of a warehouse. Greasing an officer's palm would clear the file in a week.

I worked in another division where I couldn't afford to become a "liability" to the assistant commissioner's affection. How was I to go to him with Bhatnakar's request when I'd already gone to him once already that month? Before he granted me the 'Issue Today' permit, I had to answer a barrage of questions. "Who's the applicant? Is he known to you? Is he here now?" I doubted he'd concede if I approached him a second time. He might just write 'Issue five bags' which would be of no use.

I decided to chance it. I was overwhelmed with the desire to drink a cup of tea and was willing to go to any lengths, no matter how ridiculous, for it.

"Fine, bring me your application form," I told Bhatnakar.

He left saying, "I'll be back in a jiffy." After ten minutes, he still didn't appear.

My desire for tea was driving me crazy. If I couldn't get money, I'd have to spend my bus fare and resort to ticketless travel. I'd traveled without a ticket once when I was broke.

The next day was payday and I had to show up at work, but I couldn't think of any way to get eighty paise for my morning trip to work. Even the old newspapers had been sold for scrap. I ended up traveling ticketless to office. Ticket inspections often happened at the ITO Overbridge stop so I decided to get off at the previous stop, but the bus didn't stop there and I got afraid. When the bus stopped at the next signal, I alighted and walked back to ITO and boarded a bus that was engorged with people. Still afraid, I kept an eye out for the inspector, resolving that if a khaki-clad person got on the bus through the front entrance, I would get out through the back and vice-versa. But what if two inspectors boarded, one from the front and one from the back? How many days' imprisonment would I have to endure? I decided not to beg them for mercy in case I got caught.

Thankfully, I didn't get caught. I casually got off the bus when it slowed down before crossing the exchange store, not waiting for it to halt at the bus stop.

Though I didn't ever want to endure a similar ordeal again, that too for a cup of tea, I found myself involuntarily walking to the tea shop. I saw Bhatnakar standing outside the entrance to the office and called out to him.

"The application is almost ready," he said. "I'll bring it to you."

I took him aside and cadged a one rupee note from him. Then I went and had my tea in peace.

Note: There are no dates for the passages that follow. They must have been written before October 1984 as there is mention of Indira Gandhi in them.

I could not think of Delhi as a single city because of the vast disconnect between so many areas. Nangloi, Najafgarh, Chirag Dilli, Gulabi Bagh, Lajpat Nagar, Karol Bagh, Darya Ganj, Vasant Kunj, Timarpur, Shalimar Bagh, Janakpuri, Lutyens' Delhi and Chandni Chowk did not seem like areas that belonged to one and same city. (There was no place in Delhi I hadn't seen as I delivered ration cards.) Some sights, however, were common everywhere: gentlemen in business attire munching on peeled radishes in winter, women knitting woolen sweaters, the smell of piping hot *moongphali*, barbers giving haircuts under the trees and the ear-experts under the same shade, digging out the dirt in people's ears with metal ear-cleaners. In summer, pushcarts selling *nimboo paani* are visible everywhere.

From Timarpur, I moved to Kalyanvas in a corner of East Delhi where the government quarters for *chaprasis* of the Delhi administration were located. I later moved to Kalyanpuri and from there to Mayur Vihar. I often wondered about Khichripur, Shakarpur, Shahdara, Patparganj and Chanakyapuri. To me, Delhi seemed like a very curious mix of slums, villages and urban centers.

Ever since my friend, the poet Thirugnanam told me, "It's a must-see, don't miss it," I began to seriously consider visiting the Mughal Gardens. The garden was open to the public only in December. I was bent on visiting the gardens, but I began to have second thoughts: I had only one day off in the week, so should that one day be spent at home or wandering outside? If I decided to spend it in the gardens, pending chores would have to be put on hold. But when Nalini herself expressed a desire to visit the Mughal Gardens, I couldn't refuse. Maybe I should have kept my trap shut. Though it felt like a punishment for me to go out on a Sunday, Nalini looked forward to it.

I spent a whole Saturday thinking about whether or not to go on Sunday. For the past five weekends, we had been busy running around with work and consequently, some personal tasks were left undone. I hadn't been able to read the Sunday newspapers which had accumulated and if we decided to go to the Mughal Gardens the next day, another paper would join the pile, but even that wasn't too big a deal. I'd been writing a novel that was near completion and I felt I could use a Sunday to write a few more chapters. I didn't know which task to postpone. Maybe I could ask Nalini to excuse me from helping her cook the evening meal, but it was unconscionable to expect a woman who came home tired from work in the evening to do the cooking, the cleaning and the laundry all by herself while her husband sits and reads the papers or writes a novel.

When I woke up the next morning, I was hoping Nalini would forget about the Mughal Gardens. For the past few days, neither of us had brought it up.

I made some tea and woke her up.

As she drank her tea, she said, "Let's not go today. I don't feel well. I'll feel much better once I take an oil bath."

How relieving! I gathered up all the newspapers to catch up on my reading. When the fish vendor arrived at ten, I couldn't resist buying a kilo of fish from him even though I was short on cash.

"Half a kilo will do!" Nalini insisted.

"Never mind," I said. "We hardly buy fish. Today we can eat to our heart's content."

Out of the fifty rupees I had set aside for my monthly expenses, I took twenty rupees and gave it to the fish vendor. Then I headed to the kitchen and chopped some vegetables and in my good mood, I attended to a few other chores as well.

At two, Nalini went to take her afternoon nap. When she woke up at five, she made tea and we went for a little walk. I would have preferred to finish that book I'd borrowed from the Central Secretariat Library. They'd already cancelled two of my cards and if this, the third one, got cancelled as well, Nalini wouldn't hear of giving me another. (They were all her cards.)

The next Saturday, Nalini unexpectedly announced that she wanted to visit the gardens. Seeing how anxious she was to go, I couldn't refuse her. Also, the gardens were closing in three days, so I couldn't suggest deferring the visit.

When I got up to make our tea the next morning, I was

shocked out of my wits to find the damn stove missing. I looked for it everywhere – in the living room, in the bedroom, even in the bathroom. Where on earth could it have gone? Completely baffled, I went and woke up Nalini.

"The neighbors asked for it," she told me groggily.

I didn't really feel like knocking on their door so early in the morning to ask for our stove back, but when I saw that their child was up, so I called the little girl and asked her to inform her parents that we needed our stove. *Shit!* That was idiotic of me. What if they sent the little girl back with the stove? I went to their house to ask for it myself.

I couldn't even think of why people with a gas stove and two cylinders would want to borrow a kerosene stove.

"Thank you *ji*," said the woman of the house as she returned the stove to me with a sheepish smile. "We had to borrow your stove yesterday because our gas cylinder wasn't working."

After she shut the door, I realized that I was holding a lit stove! What a bloody imbecile that woman was! Who gave a man a lit stove? Did she want me to explode? "Housewife burnt to death after stove bursts" was a headline that appeared with depressing regularity in the newspapers. Not only was the stove burning, but it was also coated with a thick black substance. When I turned the wick up, enough smoke to suffocate two people issued from it. It was only after examining the wick did I realize it was burnt. There was no kerosene in the tank either. They'd left the stove burning all night!

I shouted, "Nalini, the stove is not burning. It's burnt. Get up and come here!"

Nalini came and explained to me that the neighbor had come and asked for the stove at eight the previous night. Since Nalini was done with the cooking, she gave it to her. The woman conveniently didn't return it and Nalini had forgotten all about it. I'd come home late after watching a movie at the Hungarian Center. Had I known that our stove was in someone else's house, I would have gone and got it back even if I had to bang on their door in the middle of the night. This was a Nutan stove which we'd bought with great difficulty. It had served us well all this while and now, it was ruined.

The stove in her lap, Nalini tried to draw out the wick, but it had burnt all the way down, so it was impossible.

"Why did you have to lend our stove to that woman in the first place? Don't you remember how you suffered with that old stove? It frustrated you so much that you cried you'd hang yourself!" I yelled at her.

I didn't think the neighbors were deserving of our charity. They were not do-gooders. Because our landlord rented out two portions to two separate parties (excluding us), the custody of the keys became a problem. One winter day, I returned home early from work as I was under the weather but I had to wait outside the house till six-thirty in the evening in the freezing cold. After this terrible experience, I asked the neighbor who worked for Godrej, if he could make me a couple of duplicate keys. I didn't feel reluctant to ask him to do this for me as he was always asking if his guests could park their vehicles on my veranda.

After two days, he gave me the keys and a bill. As I had no change, I said I'd pay him in the morning.

"But I have to leave early for work tomorrow," he whined.

"Oh, you work early on Sundays too?" I asked. "Fine. I'll see how I can get some change and pay you."

He'd been talking to me in English. As soon as I told him I'd pay him later, he switched to Hindi and said irritatedly, *"Arrey, nahi bhaiya. Mujhe saat bajhe jaana hoga."*

"Teek! Ab dhe dhoonga," I mumbled angrily, going to a shopkeeper to get change.

"Why did you give the stove to those *chutiyas*?" I asked. "If you'd borrowed her stove and ruined it, wouldn't she yell at you? Call her here and show her what she's done. She didn't even have the courtesy to come and return the stove in the morning. I had to go and ask for it!"

The *chutiya* neighbors were Punjabis who thought that *Madrasis* are *bewakoofs*. Poor things! They have no idea of the wrath of a Tamil man. When I first came to Delhi, some Punjabis, assuming that I was a *bewakoof*, started mocking me.

"Keeya halley jee? Teeeeeek hooo?" they asked me.

"Oye, *mere ko chutiya bana rahe ho, kya? Behenchod!"* I nasally retorted and silenced them.

Most of the Tamils in Delhi are Brahmins. In general,

they keep a low profile to stay out of trouble, but the North Indians take this for fear and try to bullyrag them.

When Periyar would come to our town and preach his famous Brahmin and snake sermon on the erected stage opposite the *agraharam* near the Perumal temple, his black shirts would go to the *agraharam* houses and ask for water and the Brahmins would warmly offer them even a potful.

The *Delhiwalas* have encountered only the Tamil Brahmins.

Within a few days of arriving in Delhi, Pasricha, a colleague, asked me quite seriously, "You Madrasis are so short. How the hell do you manage to do... it?"

To help me understand what "it" was, he curled the fingers of his right hand, brought them near his navel and started moving them up and down.

I didn't get rattled or offended. I decided to play the game.

I asked him in return, "How long has it been since you last bent and looked at your dick with your own eyes? With a potbelly like yours, I'm assuming you have to pull your drawers down in front of the mirror and look at it. If you can do it with such a big potbelly, what makes you think I might not be able to do it?"

Pasricha's face deflated like a pricked balloon. To take the sting out of my retort, I told him a story.

"Once upon a time, there was an orphan called Subramoni. He was so frail that one thought he would get blown away if you sneezed near him. He was very short too. He would go wherever he was summoned and do whatever he was asked and eat whatever he was given. At night, he would curl up in the Pillaiyar temple.

"One day, a bus traveling at top speed on the highway ran over a male from the village and crushed his face beyond recognition. A little boy who had witnessed the accident rushed to the village to break the news.

"'I couldn't identify him, but his penis was as long as a donkey's,' he said.

"On hearing this, all the women in the village started wailing, '*Ayyo*, our Subramoni is dead!' and they all ran to the site of the accident."

Parischa laughed out loud, his potbelly bouncing.

Nalini tried again with the wick of the Nutan stove. She was struggling.

"I can't seem to get this one wick out," she said. "Why don't you try?"

Despite my best efforts, I couldn't do it. She persisted and eventually succeeded. Her fingers were all blistered.

Still, the stove continued to smoke and did not emit a blue flame like it used to.

When I saw the blisters on Nalini's fingers, I was reminded of my mother who had never set eyes on a kerosene stove. Her life was spent beside a firewood stove. The *karuvelam* trees in Nagore were felled for firewood. These trees were thorny, so the branches had to be carefully cut and chopped into smaller pieces. A dark brown liquid would ooze when the wood was burning. Even if the twigs were dry, one's eyes would sting. Cakes of dung were also used with the wood to fuel the stove. Smoke would fill the house and my mother would divert it with a blowpipe. Her eyes would sting, redden and water.

We were a family of eight and my mother had to serve us three meals daily. She had to grind a large amount of *idli* batter and then go to the pond to wash all our clothes. Then, she had to fetch water in pots from the taps for household needs and for the women's baths. She, and all village wives, had hard lives.

My thoughts were broken by Nalini's voice.

"We needn't go to the Mughal Gardens today," she said. However, I insisted we go for if we didn't, we'd have to wait another year.

The gardens were as expansive as a city. There were some residential quarters hither and thither for the *chaprasis* who worked in the President's mansion.

"These people get proper gas connections," Nalini told me. "And not just gas. All their basic needs in life are properly met."

Even our needs would have been met if only I'd grabbed the opportunity that had presented itself three years ago when I was working under Khanna as a stenographer. The notes that the lieutenant governor received from the deputy commissioners were laden with so many errors that reading them was an unimaginable ordeal. This was because most of the stenographers hailed from villages and were only familiar with the English alphabet, nothing else. My typewritten notes to the lieutenant governor, unlike theirs, were perfect.

One day, Khanna called me and said, "Congratulations!"

"Why?"

"The LG wants to meet you."

If the LG wanted to meet me, it could only mean that he wanted me to be his stenographer.

"Do you know what a quantum leap this is for a stenographer?" Khanna asked. "The LG's notes go straight to Indira *ji* and that woman knows ability when she sees it. If you work as Indira *ji's* secretary for some time, she will make you a Member of Parliament and from there, it's a cakewalk to ministership. Udhay *ji*, you are going to become a minister soon, mark my words! Go see the LG at once!"

Instead of feeling excited when he told me all of this, my heart sank as I was not at all an ambitious man. All I ever wanted was to be known as a writer.

What will become of me if I become the LG's steno? I thought. *Should I sacrifice my writing for the sake of a gas connection and government quarters in Baba Kharag Singh Margh in the heart of Delhi?*

I went to see the LG in his chambers and he repeated what Khanna said.

With folded hands, I told him, "Forgive me, sir! I am only a poor writer and a wanderer in Mandi House. I work here only to support myself financially."

The LG understood. People of his station don't have the time or the energy to persuade people like me to do something they were clearly not interested in doing. All because I'd refused that opportunity that was served to me on a gold platter, Nalini had to struggle with the Nutan stove. I looked at her fingers and sighed. She made a big mistake when she married a writer.

There were as many cops as there were flowers in the Mughal Gardens but they must have been napping or on leave when the President's grandson shot and killed the migratory birds that were visiting. The newspapers had reported that hundreds of dead birds littered the footpaths of the Parliament House.

The lawns were well manicured. Prize-winning rose bushes flanked the footpath. One plant, that was just an inch off the ground, had a bloom the size of a human head. Most of the plants had no leaves but only thick stems. To me, the stems appeared like skeletons of dead mongrel dogs. In another place, two fountains sprung from a flower vase on a huge plate. On either side of the fountain was a walkway paved with red stones. If a person stepped onto the grass, screeching whistles immediately rent the air. A young woman struck a pose near the fountain for a photograph. A policeman rushed to her side and said, *"Behenji, aisa nahin hai.* Grass *mein mat aana."* The woman, who had been smiling for the photograph, frowned and went back to her husband.

The place was crowded and the people seemed to be moving at a snail's pace because of the picture-snapping folks. After an eternal wait, we were able to view the fountain. It had five tiers, each one adorned with flowers of a particular color with paper-textured petals. Beyond the fountain, there was a forest clearing where more quarters stood and the clearing was followed by the exit.

On the way back, I noticed that every house in the clearing had its own garden. I took a look and was amused to see a cauliflower plant and some slender shoots that, Nalini told me, were garlic plants.

After I returned home, I was plunged into deep thought about my life on Mall Road. I remembered the Majnu-ka-Tilla forest where there were no manicured lawns, whistles or neat rows of roses, but only free-living trees, shrubs, thorny thickets and flowers. Could the Mughal Gardens, in all their perfect manmade symmetry, ever compare to that wild forest?

When I lived on Mall Road, Sugatan and I used to visit Majnu-ka-Tilla's Tibetan refugee camp and have *tang* and buffalo meat. *Tang* is a Tibetan wine made from barley. It got its name from Princess Wencheng of the Tang dynasty. It is customarily served by beautiful Tibetan women.

Note: The following notes were written in the November of 1984. None of the events narrated and described here are fictitious or exaggerated.

The house in Mayur Vihar, Delhi, was the eighth house I lived in. Every house I lived in presented its own problem. None of them were independent houses, they were all sub-let and most of the owners lived in the same building. One of the owners was a devoted *Ram bhakt*. He would wake up every morning – hail, rain or apocalypse – and sing *bhajans* to Ram. During winter, all the glass windows would be closed which meant his loud chants – *Om Jagadeesa Hari! Swami Jaya Jagadeesa Hari!* – would echo off the walls. Like his robotic chanting voice was not irritating enough, there was musical accompaniment too – his wife played the *dholak* and echoed his *bhajans*. The moment he started, we the entire residential body would wake up with a jolt and submit our helpless ears to this cacophonous torture. The weather rendered it impossible for us to escape by slipping out of the premises.

In another house, there was a problem with the way the toilet smelled because the house owner and his wife did not pour enough water in the toilet bowl. (But they were very particular about washing their hands clean.) I approached the owner and told him that the stink was overpowering and unbearable. I requested him to pour more water in the toilet.

"Toilets stink, shit stinks" he replied indifferently. "What's so surprising about that?"

Then, he went on to give me a painfully long lecture about the scarcity of water in villages whose dwellers suffer immensely while the urban lot was busy wasting water by the gallon.

I realized that he and his wife were determined to not clean up after themselves which meant that the sorry task of getting rid of the shit out of two arrogant *chutiyas'* posteriors was mine.

During our search for a suitable house, one of my friends who was going abroad for a couple of years suggested we move into his house. That was all very kind and good of him, but his house was in Jamuna Bagh, a locality synonymous with atrocities like rape, murder, kidnappings and robberies. My problem with Jamuna Bagh, however, was its poor connectivity. There were only two overbridges connecting urban Delhi to the eastern suburbs where there should have been ten. Due to the number of vehicles and constant harassment from the police, the traffic crawled agonizingly slowly. Some drivers who tried to overtake other vehicles created a bottleneck that would take hours to clear, and to make bad matters worse, the blaring horns sounded worse than a band of screaming banshees. All the noise and confusion would make one want to jump out of his car and off the bridge to his death (which, I assume, would be less painful). Every time I crossed that bridge, I regretted the move to Jamuna Bagh.

Nalini's heart was heavy with its own worries. She witnessed the kidnapping of a young girl by an auto driver in broad daylight. The girl had been walking with her parents when the driver forcibly dragged her into the auto and drove off.

There was yet another bloodcurdling incident. A woman heard a knock on her door at eleven in the morning. Through the peephole, she saw a trio of well-built men. She enquired who they had come for. They said they'd been sent by the Delhi Electric Supply Undertaking following a complaint about a defective electricity meter.

When the woman open the door, the trio barged in, gang-raped her and killed her.

Nalini was greatly perturbed when accounts of these incidents appeared in the papers.

"We just have to be careful. What else can we do?" I said.

I tried to reassure her by showing her how secure and comfortable our house was. As it was on the ground level, we didn't have to face any of the problems that accompanied sub-letting. We had ample rooms, two entrances and space for a small garden. Above all, the rent didn't burn a hole in our pockets. I pleaded with her to adjust.

I was befriended by Rekhi, a twelve-year-old Sikh boy as soon as we'd arrived.

"Are you the new tenant in this house, uncle?" he asked me. "What's your name?"

"Why don't you tell me your name first?" I asked.

"I'm Rekhi. I live on the other side of the road, near the gurudwara. My house is in Block 27."

Looking at Nalini, I said in Tamil, "This one here seems to be a *chutti paiyan.*"

Rekhi asked immediately, "*Apdinna enna,* uncle? *Chutti paiyan?*" in chaste Tamil.

My eyebrows shot up.

"How do you know Tamil?" I asked.

"I study in a Tamil school, uncle," he said. "All my friends are Tamils too. But what does *'chutti paiyan'* mean?"

"It means 'intelligent lad.' Where does your father work?"

His face underwent a sudden change. It was like watching a light burst and go out.

"I'll tell you my story some other day, uncle," he said.

Story? A twelve-year-old with a story? I assumed his story would be a sad one.

I made some enquiries about Rekhi's school. It was on Lodhi Road, quite a distance from his house, but Rekhi told me he commuted in the school bus. As I was planning to admit my daughter Kalpana there, I was pleased to know this, and very relieved.

Rekhi spent most of his time in our house, as a result of which Kalpana grew attached to him. He left only when it was dark, when his mother came to fetch him.

I held myself back from asking him what his "story" was as I was afraid of upsetting him. Not seeing the father whose occupation I'd enquired about niggled my mind.

One day, Kalpana said, "It's been long since we went out, *Appa*. Take me out somewhere."

"Are you coming Rekhi? Will your father allow it?" I asked him.

After some deliberation, the boy said, "Okay Uncle, I think I'll tell you my story now."

Rekhi's father, Sardar Sucha Singh, had been a soldier in the Indian Army and had won several bravery medals. Three months ago, he'd been sent to Punjab as part of a special contingent to control militancy in the troubled state. He was one of the heroes who'd sacrificed his life in the fierce fight between the army and the militants. The aim of the operation was the elimination of Sant Bhindranwale who had vowed to plant the Khalistan flag on Lal Quila. Sardar Sucha Singh was posthumously honored for his bravery and the nation, as an act of gratitude, gave his widow, Harpreet Kaur, a government job. However, being uneducated, she got the job of a *chaprasi*.

When Rekhi had finished his story, I fished out the pile of old newspapers and began to pore over them. As I read and took in the details, Operation Blue Star did not seem like a mere sensational news item. This boy's story – his father's – had now become a part of my life. The report stated that 83 soldiers had lost their lives, 248 had been wounded and 30 people – including terrorists, women and 5 children – had died. The pictures of the war-ravaged Darbar Sahib affected me differently after Rekhi had told me his story.

Those terrible numbers began to acquire flesh, blood and faces. Their deaths must have hit so many loved ones so hard.

I couldn't put the newspapers down. I feverishly and meticulously read every word of every article there was. I read about the terrorists, the caches of gunpowder and modern weapons they'd been in possession of, the subterranean tunnels, the warehouses, the gunning down of the soldiers who were advancing towards the Akal Takht, the government's promise to rebuild it through a *kar seva*. I was completely engrossed.

The Akal Takht – the timeless man's throne – was the product of the efforts of so many mortals to achieve timelessness! The *kar seva* might have been able to rebuild the throne of the eternal one, but would it have been able to restore the forcefully snatched lives of the soldiers? Could it have returned them to the earth that should have been theirs longer?

Rekhi was sitting beside me, staring at the papers. My affection for the boy had deepened.

"Where do you want to go, Rekhi? Get your mother's permission and come home this Sunday. You and Kalpana can decide where we go," I said.

Kalpana and Rekhi spoke to each other in hushed tones in Punjabi. Kalpana had become fluent in Punjabi after all the time she'd spent with Rekhi.

"Let's go to Lal Quila, uncle," Rekhi said.

"Lal Quila? You'll get bored and tired there with all the walking you'll have to do. Why not Connaught Place or Palika Bazaar? It'll be a lot more fun and we can shop too."

"It was because Bhindranwale said he'd fly the Khalistan flag at Lal Quila that there was a war, and because there was a war, my father died," he said. "That's why I want to see Lal Quila."

As we talked, I realized that Rekhi had never been to the theater to watch a movie. We decided we'd go on an outing every month. Lal Quila, Connaught Place, Palika Bazaar, a cinema and a Chinese restaurant were on the itinerary.

Kalpana, Rekhi and I went to Lal Quila. Nalini, who

wished to have an oil bath, stayed behind. The children had immense fun; they jumped and ran all over the place with so much life and spirit, playing games around the Diwani Aam and the Diwani Khas. They gazed upon the glass marvels of the Sheesh Mahal with awe. They stood before the plaque bearing the inscription: *The peacock throne, made of gold, inlaid with diamonds, rested here,* and wondered anxiously who had taken away the throne.

As we were leaving the place, we came across an army camp. I thought Rekhi might say something but he didn't. He and Kalpana were in the middle of an animated conversation. With her rapid Punjabi chatter and her top-knot, nobody would take her for a Tamil child. People cast curious stares our way. We were indeed a strange threesome – two Punjabi-speaking children and a Tamil man.

At seven in the evening, the sun was still in the summer sky. As the children were exhausted, I felt it would be a good idea to go to a Chinese restaurant in Connaught Place instead of catching a bus and going home. Rekhi and Kalpana were excited when they heard my plan.

The inside of the restaurant felt like the inside of a dream with all the translucent lanterns on the ceiling, the waiters with their long hats, the fancy tableware and the soft oriental music.

"I've never been to a place like this with my father," Rekhi said without the slightest tinge of sadness.

I couldn't read the menu in the dim light, so I told the waiter to bring three bowls of chicken soup first.

After discussing and debating over *chole bhatura, palak*

paneer, kofta, naan, channa masala and *aloo* fry, we decided to share two plates of chicken noodles.

"We've come to a restaurant that serves exotic food and you two want to settle for chicken noodles?" I asked them, surprised.

"What I eat here is not important, uncle," Rekhi said. "I'm lucky to just *be* here. My mother is a good cook, but I've never had the chance to come to a place like this with my parents. When he was working, he was always so busy and no matter how many times my mother told him he'd go off his head, he wouldn't listen. He bought me whatever I asked for or he would give the money to Ma and ask her to buy it for me. Oh, and I love the soup, uncle. It's delicious. Once, we went to see the Taj Mahal. Papa didn't come with us, so we went with *chachi* who was visiting then. Every time I tried to make plans with Papa to go out somewhere, he would try to wriggle out of them. I pestered him until one day he agreed to take us to Darbar Sahib.

"But before we could go, he was sent on the mission from which he never returned. He told us, 'When I come back, we'll all go together.' But he never returned."

A few weeks after Sardar Sucha Singh's death, the government would have called Rekhi's mother to give her a medal and the man who had cut a fine and a dashing figure in his military uniform would have his name engraved on a metal plaque.

After our trip to Lal Quila, we visited Connaught Place, Palika Bazaar and Pragati Maidan but we were unable to plan a trip to the movies as the children could not agree on a movie. The movie I was interested in seeing was not something suitable for the eyes, the ears and the heads of children. We finally decided to go to Connaught Place and watch whichever movie we could get tickets for.

Rekhi and Kalpana were eagerly looking forward to their day at the movies on Sunday, but on Wednesday, at around ten in the morning, the whole country was rocked by the news of the assassination of Indira Gandhi. I stayed home that day because of a mild fever and Nalini had stayed back to nurse me. As the *Puja* holidays were on, Kalpana was supposed to have been at the crèche, but since we were both at home, we didn't send her.

At first, we thought that the prime minister's death was just a nasty rumor, but we soon realized that the story was true. When I stepped out of the house, I was confronted with the sight of hordes of charged people shouting slogans in trucks and vans. I was told they were all heading to AIIMS where Indira Gandhi's body was. Some frenzied people were torching DTC buses that hadn't made it to their respective depots quickly enough.

Rekhi didn't come to our house that day. I thought of going and checking on him, but as I was unwell and tired, I decided to go the next day.

We had no idea how long it would take for the situation to normalize. There was no milk for Kalpana and no way to get any. I didn't know if there was enough rice. If there was some *atta*, we wouldn't have to starve. I didn't know how long Kalpana could go without milk, but I trusted we could get by with what we had – water, power and some rice. I fervently hoped that riots would not break out. The assassins were Sikhs – her own bodyguards. Would the government impose curfews and issue shoot-at-sight orders? All my life, I'd never experienced anything hair-raising until then. I'd only read of the events that preceded and followed the Partition in 1947. Tossing and turning in bed, I was wondering whether anyone spotted past curfew would be gunned down. My thoughts were pierced through by a loud scream in the distance. Rushing out, I saw that the Trilokpuri Gurudwara on the other side of the road was obscured by a wall of smoke and fire. There were shadowy figures all around the place and I was unable to process what exactly was happening. Were they trying to burn down the gurudwara? I told Nalini to lock the doors from the inside and I went to the gurudwara to see for myself.

To my horror, I saw that four people had been set ablaze. They were still alive and running frenziedly while the mob pelted them with stones. Some were even hitting them with sticks. Suddenly, Rekhi crossed my mind and I ran to his house but it was locked. Thinking and hoping they'd escaped this hellish chaos, I returned home.

I couldn't sleep that night. When dawn came, I was still awake. At midnight, I watched the newly elected prime minister eulogize Indira Gandhi on television.

"The late prime minister was not just my mother; she was mother to the entire nation. In this difficult moment, let us remember the words of our mother who said, 'Don't kill other people. Kill the hate you feel towards other people,' and maintain peace and observe patience. Let us show the world what Bharat's culture is."

This he said calmly and clearly. (However, the very same man, when asked about the riots at a later date, said, "When a big tree falls, the earth shakes.")

At daybreak, I got out of bed and made my way to

Block 27. Charred bodies lay in front of the gurudwara while hundreds of people shivered inside it in the bitter cold, huddled together like refugees. Almost everyone was armed with *kirpans* or sticks. I walked up to a middle-aged man and asked if he was from Trilokpuri.

"This place is not safe," he said. "Aren't you aware of the things that happened here yesterday?"

He told me that the crowd in the gurudwara was from Kalyanpuri. They'd come to Trilokpuri thinking they'd be safe there as Trilokpuri had a considerable Sikh population. However, upon their arrival, they realized that Trilokpuri had suffered much more than other Sikh-populated areas.

A deathly silence hung over all the houses in Block 27, most of which were locked. I returned to the gurudwara and to the man I'd spoken to.

"Where are all the people in Block 27?" I asked him. "All the houses are locked."

I was told that half of the residents were hiding in their houses. They'd locked the front door from the outside and entered through the back door. The other half had fled to Block 28. I was confused.

"Wait, Block 28 is full of Hindus," I said. "How could and why would they go there?"

"You don't understand, brother," the Sikh said. "It is the Hindus who have been protecting us. Many Sikh families from Block 27 are being sheltered by Hindu families in Block 28. Do you really think that the people who are trying to kill us are Hindus? No. The people who are trying to kill us are godless beasts, not Hindus. They just appeared out of nowhere in ten, maybe fifteen, jeeps. They went to each house and if there were Sikhs in it, they dragged them out and set them ablaze. I recognized those thugs. They came to me asking for votes. They've ensured I'll always remember them."

The radio news said that army units had been dispatched to places where riots were expected to break out. A curfew had been imposed and the situation was said to have been under control. But I saw neither cop nor soldier even after two hours. The night news said that shoot-at-sight orders had been issued to deal with rioters. But who was to implement these orders? The entire political troupe was holed up in Teen Murti Bhavan.

The day before, when the prime minister had been shot, the President was abroad. When the news reached him, he rushed back to Delhi that same evening. BBC news reporters said that his car had been stoned as it was being driven to AIIMS. If this was the plight of the Sikh President, then what would the plight of ordinary Sikhs be? And then I remembered that I saw their terrible plights with my own eyes.

Some extraordinary slogans were heard by the mob that had come to pay their last respects to the prime minister in Teen Murti Bhavan. Nobody had thought it necessary to censor these slogans.

"Bharat ki badi beti ko jisne khun kiya, us vams ko mitayenge! Who murdered India's daughter? We shall wipe out that race!"

I was exhausted after not having slept the previous night. Half-asleep and half-awake, I sat before the television. Suddenly, a foul smell assailed my nostrils. It was the terrible smell of burning flesh accompanied by the smells of petrol, kerosene and diesel. I wanted to throw up. The road was littered with corpses and a man was counting them.

"Who are you?" I asked.

"A journalist," he replied. "I've counted 639 bodies so far. Will you help me count the rest? Then we can tell the world how many lives have been lost."

Just then, one of the burnt bodies rose up from the heap and started to walk towards us. The stomach had been bound with a turban. When the turban loosened and fell off, the person's entrails spilled out of his stomach.

I heard a sound then. It was almost like somebody was clapping. Was this some sick play that some heartless non-human found amusing? Or was it the sound of a battle drum? One? Several?

The sound grew deafening. I felt the earth tremor and blood trickle down my ears.

I woke up screaming. Nalini was shaking me violently.

"I've been trying to wake you up for so long," she said. "Someone's at the door. Let's go see who it is."

It was Rekhi and his mother. As soon as I'd let them in, I closed the door and locked it.

"What happened? I came to your house to find it locked. Where *were* you?" I asked agitatedly.

Neither of them was able to speak. I brought them some water. After a while, the mother rallied and narrated her harrowing tale.

When the violence had begun, all the Sikhs fled to the houses of the Hindus on Block 28. The goons also went to Block 28 where they'd begun to search for them. Initially, mother and son had concealed themselves in a quilt box, but they fled the house when they realized there was a high chance of being discovered.

I immediately took a pair of scissors and cut Rekhi's hair short. His mother didn't protest. I told her that they should call themselves Bindiya and Rakesh for a while and that Rekhi's mother should give up her *salwars* and wear *sarees*. Nalini gave her one.

The army and the police showed up the next morning but they were no match for the rampaging mobs that kept arriving in jeeps. This time, the mobs didn't go banging on people's doors. They went to the ration shop and summoned the owner. They got him to open the shop and take out the register which contained the names of the ration-card holders. They identified all the Sikhs from the register and took down their details. I was standing in the crowd and watching this unfold. Then I realized with a shock what they were planning to do and what was going to happen. The mob then made its way to another shop that sold kerosene. They loaded drums and tins onto the jeeps.

I rushed to the gurudwara where the army had pitched

its camp and told the soldiers what was happening. They gave me a deaf ear.

"There is nothing we can do," they said.

"But I heard it in the news that people indulging in violence would be shot at sight!" I protested.

"Why don't you ask whoever said that on TV to actually come and carry it out?" a soldier rebuffed.

An older policeman who had witnessed what had passed between me and the soldiers said, "Brother, as the two people who shot the prime minister were policemen, the entire police force is running scared. Our senior officers are frightened as they don't know whose heads are going to roll once the last rites are over. In this situation, what *can* we do? If we spray bullets at this mob, what will happen to us? Who do you think the mobsters are? They are the same people who give orders to our superiors. Just keep your TV on and remain in your house."

Instead of going home, I went to the gurudwara. As the Sikhs from Kalyanpuri had *kirpans* and sticks, I thought of informing them about the mob so that they could mobilize. But there was no one there. Had they all been killed? If they had escaped by some stroke of luck, where had they gone? While I was wondering what to do, I saw the jeeps. On it were several Sikh men. There were a few youths and even children who couldn't have been any more than five years old. The mobsters upended tins of petrol and kerosene on their heads and set them on fire. Those who attempted to flee were cut down with swords.

Trilokpuri will not have even a single male Sikh left, I thought despairingly as the jeeps sped to Kalyanpuri.

In the afternoon, the army conducted a march past. Thirty minutes after it was over, the jeep-mob returned to Mayur Vihar. Addresses in hand, they went from house to house, dragging more Sikhs out and setting them ablaze. When the people who lived next door to us declared they were Punjabi Hindus, the mobsters refused to believe them. The madmen were still not convinced of their religion even after they were shown the *puja* room.

The man with the addresses asked haughtily, "Who is Darbara Singh?"

Immediately, the husband said, "He is the owner of this house and lives in Tilakpuri."

"You should have mentioned that first, my friend," he said.

They came to our house next.

Before they had the chance to say anything, I summoned Rekhi and Harpreet and said, "This is my *bhabhi*. Her name is Bindiya. My brother is in the army; he had a love-marriage. This is their son Rakesh. As my brother is in Agra on special duty, they are staying with me and my wife, Nalini and our daughter."

The leader of the mob turned to Kalpana.

"What's your name, girl?" he asked.

Kalpana looked at me with terror in her eyes.

"Kalpana," I answered for her.

The leader stroked her head.

"Why are you afraid, *beti*? You're not a Sikh. We won't harm you."

Then he turned to me and said, "*Madrasi babu*, a girl from our village has come to your house. I hope you haven't lied to me. If I find out you have, you won't be spared."

With this warning, they left.

That night on TV, the commissioner of police announced, "Today, around fifteen people have lost their lives, but the situation is under control."

The next day, the governor told the same sick lie, "The situation is under control. We have received news that nothing untoward has happened today."

The BBC reporters told on that very day, the worst of the killings had happened. 200 bodies were lying in the Tees Hazari police morgue; a thousand Sikhs had been killed in Shakkarpur, Kalyanpuri, Shahdara, Krishna Nagar, Parpar Ganj, Shivpuri, Chandar Nagar, Gandhi Nagar, Geetha Colony, Durgapur, Bhajanpura and Seemapuri, all in East Delhi; another thousand had been massacred in Nathu Colony and Trilokpuri alone; in Mongolpuri, Sultanpuri and Budh Vihar in West Delhi and in many colonies in Narela and Jehangirpuri, almost the entire male Sikh population had been wiped out. Even the trains were full of corpses. Except for New Delhi, there seemed to be no police or army presence anywhere.

In the morning, I went to Trilokpuri. The roads were littered with bodies of Sikhs who had been burnt or beaten to death. The remains told me that there were also those who had been hacked to pieces. The houses in Block 27 – Rekhi's included – had all been burnt black.

When I reached Block 28, I saw army trucks driving away with more bodies. It was then that I saw a curious structure that resembled a shed – or did it resemble a tent? I really didn't know how to describe it to myself or to anyone. It had obviously been constructed with scant resources – wooden boards covered with tarpaulin. Where there were no wooden boards, there were sheets of tin. There was also a barbed wire fence. The thing must have been torched the previous day. The army personnel, who I'd assumed were accustomed to pathetic sights, were themselves staring in shock and disbelief at the fully gutted tent. I walked towards it as I needed a closer look. The tarpaulin had been burnt and the roof was open.

Two small children were sitting on a set of planks that was precariously held up by sticks. Their heads were on their knees and they were hugging their legs to their chests. One of the children was around four and the other was probably a little older, six or seven maybe. They were dead, burnt. I was looking at their charred bodies; I was looking at how they died. A young solider covered his face and began to weep while another soldier kicked open the burnt door. Inside stood the charred corpse of a sixty-year-old man looking up at the children with one arm raised.

Everyone from Block 28 was there to take in the grisly sight. We were told that the previous evening, an elderly Sikh and his two grandchildren who were being sheltered in a Hindu house got discovered by the mob. They managed to escape and hid themselves in the ramshackle structure, whatever it used to be, but the mob hunted them down and set fire to the shack saying, "*Achcha hua!* Let's burn them and celebrate Lohri here itself!"

The Sikh women and children who had been hiding began to come out when they spied the army trucks. Their women were now widows, their girls were now fatherless. Keening and wailing, they were also taken away by the soldiers.

I returned home, numbed by all that I'd seen. I didn't tell Rekhi or his mother that there was nothing left of Block 27.

"The leaders in Teen Murti Bhavan must have dispersed. I think things will be better tomorrow," I was telling Nalini when we heard a light knock on the door.

Wondering who could be knocking so gently, I went to the door and opened it to find the mobsters standing there, the same beasts who were responsible for the carnage the day before yesterday.

"So, *Madrasi*, you thought you'd take us for a ride, huh?" one of them barked, slapping me hard across the face.

"*Arrey bhaiya, Madrasi ko chod do,*" said another one. "*Sardar kidhar hai?*"

On hearing this commotion, Rekhi and his mother came out of the room. A mobster caught Rekhi by the neck and threw him with such force that he landed against the wall and broke his nose.

"Idhar hi Lohri banayenge!" said one fellow with a tin in his hand.

"Bhaiya, nahi, we don't have enough petrol. There are four other people in the street. We don't want to burn them off one by one and waste the petrol, do we?"

Saying this, he picked up Rekhi, who was stuporous, and threw him into the jeep. The rest of the mob hopped onto it.

Rekhi's mother and Nalini tried chasing the jeep. I ran after Kalpana who had run out to follow them. I picked her up and we stood there, frozen.

Shortly after this painful incident, Nalini wanted to move to Chennai and I got transferred there. A couple of years later, she divorced me. For four or five years after the divorce, I kept my distance with women. I had nothing whatsoever to do with their kind. Being a man, I needed sex, but I was not willing to put my hand into a pit of snakes for it. Then, I met Peundevi and married her.

Note: The following stories were told to me by Perundevi. I had written them out as she'd told them to me and I titled the collection *Perundevi's Snake Stories.*

"Those who have committed at least one murder in their lives,

Those who have raped at least one woman,

Those who feed drugged biscuits to passengers on trains and loot them,

Those who hire hitmen to kill their husbands for the sake of their lovers,

Actors, army brats and activists,

Drivers, drug-addicts and drunks,

Eunuchs, eccentrics and eggheads,

Journalists, junkies and jacks of all trades,

Ministers, mistresses and mistresses of ministers,

Pickpockets, psychos, pimps and policemen

Prostitutes, priests, petty politicians and presidents,

Street-singers, strippers and sex-offenders,

Teachers, tramps and terrorists,

Widows, witches and wenches…

If all these people can write 'literature,' why the fuck can't commercial writers*?" I asked Cockaphonix.

He told me that it was beyond me.

I rose to the challenge and insisted I'd produce class literature and moreover, he would be my stenographer.

When Cock readily agreed to be my stenographer, I knew that he was all out to humiliate me. He said that if someone like me could write literature, then he had no problem being the scribe. Every word of his was dripping with scorn.

(*After resigning from the postal service, I began to write gossips on actors and actresses for a livelihood. I did this for three years and my fellow litterateurs began to club me with writers of pulp fiction. So, a few years later, I gave up the gossip articles and became a pickpocket. This helped me recover my literary status. I am deeply indebted to Monsieur Jean Genet for this.)

Cock has his own understanding of what literature is. When language is twisted, wrung and strangled until its eyes bulge out, it becomes literature. Otherwise, it is mere newspaper reportage.

I feel that reportage can also qualify as literature sometimes. Don't you think so too? Only this morning, a newspaper article I read wrung my heart because it was, in its own way, a tragic poem.

A lorry coming from Pallavaram crashed into the E. S. I. compound in K. K. Nagar and ran over some people who were sleeping on the pavement. The newspaper carried the names and ages of those who were crushed to death, those who survived with grave injuries, those who died on their way to the hospital.

In the *Ramayana*, Dasharatha, Rama's father, promised Kaikeyi, his second wife, that he would grant one request of hers. She asks him to exile Rama for fourteen years. Rama goes into exile, telling his father that he should not go back on his word, and the people of Ayodhya follow him. When they come to a river, Rama looks back and says, "If you accompany me, my exile will be fruitless, for the wilderness will not be the wilderness but Ayodhya if you come along. So, children, women, men, please return to your homes."

After completing his fourteen years of exile, when he returns to the river, he sees a small band of skeletal figures.

"Who are you?" he asked them, a sense of unease settling over him.

"We are eunuchs, Rama," they said. "You forgot to mention us when you asked the people of Ayodhya to return home. So we stayed here."

How many kinds of human beings have we tried to write out of history? We have banished so many people from society just because they're slightly different from the rest of us and we relegate them to the margins. This is not something new. It's been in practice for eons. When I think of the plight of the outcasts, I feel that the chance to create literature is a discriminatory privilege that is unreserved for the castaway. It is only available to promiscuous women and royal men who fuck around in harems as all these people have much to say – things that polite society is interested in.

I don't know how kings in days of yore had the stamina and the virility to fuck women from sun-up to sundown. For the common man today, the mere thought of fucking *one* woman is frightful.

There have been several nights when I sat trembling because my dick refused to behave the way a dick should. When Nalini approached me, it would curl up like a centipede that had been kicked and disappear. How the fuck could you expect me to fuck with a trembling dick the size of an areca nut?

YOU ARE
A BLOODY
EUNUCH, MAN

This was why she divorced me, but she chose the sophisticated euphemism of "irreconcilable differences" for the court papers. She was kind to not bring up my unmanliness and my many perversions. She concealed her reasons for divorcing me between lines, underneath words and between spaces. (Oh looky here, Cock! Who said I can't write "literature"? Let me give myself a pat on the back.)

After I married Perundevi, a friend called Vasanthan asked me, "How's life? What are you doing now?"

"Fucking, fucking, fucking and fucking a little more."

"Really?"

"Why do you doubt?"

"Well… People are saying you're a eunuch."

"For some time, I thought I was a eunuch too. Maybe I was. But not any longer. Hear this: my areca nut grew to the size of a giant fucking king cobra, man. Sex is in the brain, my friend. Sex is in the brain."

Nalini used to often tell me that my mouth smelled like a sewer. It baffled me as to how she knew what my mouth smelled like as we'd never kissed in spite of being married for ten years. Whenever I'd try to kiss her, she'd move away, saying that she didn't like kissing. Instead of admitting that she was an arrogant bitch with a stick up her ass with a limp and lifeless tongue, she started complaining that my mouth smelled.

After kissing Perundevi for the first time, I asked her, "Does my mouth smell?"

"No, sweetheart, but if you suffer from halitosis, we can go see a doctor. Don't worry. Even I'm conscious of the way my breath smells sometimes. It might have something to do with the stomach."

She took me to the doctor like a mother would a nursery-schooler. After my visit to the doctor, all my fears of odor were dismissed.

Your breath stinks.
Your sweat stinks.
Your shit stinks.
Your piss stinks.
Your flatulence stinks.
Your armpit stinks.
Your groin stinks.
Your clothes stink.
Your side of the bed stinks.

After Perundevi entered my life, Nalini's opinions of me ceased to ring as loudly as they used to.

You are a filthy gutter rat.
You are an obscene reptile.
You are a deviant.
You are a pervert.

And all her bitter anathemas lost their sting.

YOU SHOULD DIE THE DEATH OF A STREET DOG.
YOU SHOULD ROT LIKE A WORM.
YOU SHOULD BE GUTTED.
YOU SHOULD HAVE YOUR EYES GOUGED OUT.
YOU SHOULD HAVE AN ELECTRIC CABLE SHOVED UP YOUR ANUS.

I HATE YOU, EMASCULATED BASTARD!

I first met Nalini when I went to watch a play at Shri Ram Center in Mandi House. She was the roommate of my friend's lover. They stayed in a hostel on Bhagwan Dass Road which intersects Mandi House. I was so badly starved of sex then that you could say I was going through a sexual drought. Even masturbation had become unamusing. When I saw Nalini, it was lust at first sight, not love. Within a week of knowing each other, we began a live-in relationship. During our relationship, we lived in a number of places – Kalyanvas, Kalyanpuri, Mayur Vihar and Possangipur. Possangipur was a tiny village in Janakpuri. The villages and forests that thrive alongside the urban centers are Delhi's real wonders. There were many buffaloes in Possangipur, so the air smelled of dung at all times.

Of all the houses I'd rented in Delhi, the house in Possangipur was the worst by far. The owner, a seventy-year-old man called Choudhary, carried himself with the air of a dictator. There were ten families staying in the houses he'd let, spread over three floors, all Tamils. Wait, did I just say Tamils? Correction – all Tamil Brahmins, except us. Wait, did I just say "us"? Correction again – Nalini was a Brahmin. All these Brahmin families had moved from Chennai after the advent of Periyar and their speech was a curious mix of Tamil and Hindi. Nalini and I lived on the second floor in a ten by eight rat-hole of a room where there was just enough space to accommodate a bed. As for our clothes, we had to keep them in a trunk under the bed. The kitchen had standing space for one person only. There were two other rooms adjacent to ours in which a family of four – a husband, his wife, and two teenagers – lived. When they talked, you'd hear a peculiar mix of Palakkad Tamil mixed with Hindi, and their speech was so loud that the whole of Possangipur would hear them. I never once saw the woman of the house walk; she moved slowly and I'd assumed this was because she'd had a hysterectomy (as she was always grumbling about some surgery that had reduced her to a corpse). Our families shared a toilet and a bathroom.

In summer, the sun threatened to melt our skulls like wax and in winter, we had to brave the cold like people from the Stone Age. There was no outlet to plug in a heater and even if we had both an outlet and a heater, it would have been futile as there was no power on winter mornings anyway. We considered heating water for our baths on the Nutan stove but kerosene was in short supply. It would take the administration five damn years to give us a gas connection, so we had no choice but to bathe in ten-degree water. During summer we'd sleep on the terrace which had no walls. Sleepwalking would result in instant *moksha*. We had to climb to the terrace on a metal ladder in the kitchen. Also, there was no handrail on the staircase that led from the first floor to the second. The best thing a misstep could do was send you tumbling down with a few scrapes and bruises; the worst thing it could do was cost you a limb.

We died every day for two years in that hole. That the tenants who had been staying there happily for years were still alive was one of the many bizarre miracles one can witness only in India.

Nalini hated Delhi and wanted to return to Chennai. As I worked for the Delhi administration, I could ask for a transfer to a place of my choice. I asked to be posted in Chennai's income tax department but was refused.

"It's a wet department," they told me. Supposedly, the department's trade unions did not like outsiders and newbies infiltrating it as they felt it would upset their yield in terms of bribes. I refused to be inducted into central intelligence as I knew I didn't belong there. Finally, they fixed me up in the postal department.

Soon after we landed in Chennai, Nalini suggested we have a child but I refused. Once our phase of lust was over, there was no love or affection in our relationship which had stopped making sense to me.

I didn't think Nalini would be able to raise a child as she couldn't even take care of herself properly. Her body was her biggest foe. She always fell dramatically ill during her period and it was I who used to wash her menstrual pads. No one – not even my closest friends – believes me when I tell them that I'd been hand-washing her bloody menstrual rags for ten whole years. Though disposable sanitary napkins were available, Nalini refused to buy and use them.

Tamils have some extremely peculiar ways. Instead of spending reasonable amounts of money on immediate, everyday necessities, they squander unreasonable amounts on gold jewelry. They wear aged rubber slippers with broken straps fastened with pins while their hands and necks are decked with gold. The women wear two dirty nightdresses alternatively for an entire year, but they will own two houses. If a guest has to spend the night, there will not be an extra pillow and the ones they have will be greasy with oil and stink to high heaven because they never see the inside of a washing machine. Women's panties will be stiff with age and years of scrubbing while men's underwear will be riddled with holes. As Nalini adhered to this culture of miserliness, she used the same menstrual pads every month.

Now tell me, can a woman like Nalini take care of a child? Not at all, but this didn't stop her from giving birth to one. Three years after the child was born, she asked me for a divorce and refused to take the child with her. After she left me, I quit my job and started picking pockets and writing gossip columns about actresses. I was suffering a severe mental breakdown.

It was after this phase of my life that I met Perundevi and married her. Soon after the marriage, Nalini came to see me to ask for the child back. I returned the child in everyone's best interests.

I'd started to believe I was a eunuch after Nalini repeatedly called me one, but Perundevi called me the God of Lust. In a trancelike state, she'd say, "Let me plant a trail of kisses on your musk-scented skin that awakens my lust. Your smell makes my eyes roll back, it makes me drunk. Your gaze makes every cell in my body come alive. You fill your mouth with wine from my cellar and pour it into mine. When you enter me, my body forks like lightning and I become wet like rain-drenched earth."

We lose track of time when we make love. When we were done, the mattress would be soaked through with sweat. Sometimes, I'd go to the toilet to urinate, but then my dick would be so hard that urination was impossible.

"Are you a man or an animal?" Perundevi would ask as she drew me in.

Cock, who was taking down all that I was saying, commented, "What a tall story!"

I wondered what a fellow like him, who knew nothing about sex, would achieve in the literary world. I've spent more time on pedicure than he'll ever spend in literature. As I spent a lot of time on my feet, my heels cracked. Perundevi would give me a weekly pedicure. Before her, I didn't know what a pedicure was. Before her, I didn't know my body. I discovered my body through her.

She told me that if she ever became a writer, she would call her first book *My Sexual Experiments with Udhaya*.

WHAT A SWELL FUCKER YOU ARE, MAN!

Our sexual encounters would end with Perundevi saying this. Hearing her say it, my frigid nights with Nalini became a thing of the past. With Nalini I felt fear, shame, anger and rage, and towards the end of our relationship, insults always hung in the air like perpetual smoke. Humiliated as I was by Nalini, I never thought I'd be able to bed a woman again. In that desert of derision, how could I have hoped for a revivifying stream of fresh water?

Perundevi, in her stark naked glory, was thunder and lightning. The mirror-reflection of our entwined bodies looked like beautiful abstract art. She slithered across my sweaty torso and settled herself into a comfortable position to give me a blowjob.

In return, I pleasured her lady-parts with my tongue, exploring all her unexplored regions. She pushed me down with such force that the bed creaked in pain. Post-orgasm, she would pass out. When she did regain consciousness, I would mount her again.

Cockaphonix had been patiently scribing. When I'd finished my story, he remarked, "It's awful! You could have written a meaningful story but you chose not to. That newspaper article about the truck that rammed into the E. S. I. Hopsital wall could have inspired you to make an excellent novel. You began well, but you meandered. There were so many things you could have explored:

Poverty,

Uncertainty,

The pathetic condition of human existence,

The world from the perspective of a truck driver,

The problems of pavement-dwellers,

Loss of life and loss of limbs,

The negligence of doctors and nurses,

The tragedy of unclaimed bodies of accident-victims in morgues,

The life of a morgue-worker,

Chennai's high accident rate,

Corpses that lie unnoticed on the side of the road…

You ignored all of that and chose to go for a titillating porn tale. This is not literature, not by any yardstick!"

"Fuck off," I said.

(Yet Another Bloody Author's Note: When I was collecting my notes on Delhi for this novel, I came across another note I'd written later about a short trip I made to Delhi – after moving back to Chennai – to attend a film festival. This must have been written seven or eight years ago.)

After moving back to Chennai, I returned to Delhi only to attend film festivals in the Siri Fort Auditorium. After watching five films there each day, I'd rush back to Chennai.

This journey was one hell of an experience.

The second-class coaches in Tamil Nadu Express were like underground sewers on wheels. The questionably low ticket price made me suspect as much. While a deluxe bus ticket from Chennai to Nagercoil cost four hundred, a Tamil Nadu Express ticket from Chennai to Delhi cost five hundred.

I understood why after the journey.

At each station, huge crowds of beggars clambered in – eighty-year-old women, cripples, eunuchs, women with babies (who, I believe, were drugged) in their arms. If you didn't give them money, they shouted the worst kind of abuse at you.

Like the beggars weren't enough, a band of eunuchs entered, clapping their hands in their signature eunuch style. They approached the men seated in front of me. One fellow gave them a one rupee coin, but eunuchs are not satisfied with anything less than ten rupees as they have particularly lavish lifestyles. They cannot find employment easily, they have no security anywhere and they are ragged on public transport. They have to make themselves happy by buying flashy clothes, jewelry, fancy accessories and cosmetics. They spend a lot of time clapping their hands to earn money for their pains.

The child-beggars stood in hordes, like an army, at every station. Their eyes had the desperate cunning you see in those of hungry beasts of prey. I shuddered to think of what they must have endured in life to have acquired such an unsettling gaze.

As for the food I got on the train, even a street dog would walk away from it: two spoons of overcooked rice and a dal that tasted like brine. And the "meal" cost twenty-five rupees!

All the other passengers had brought homemade food. The Tamils sitting across from me were breakfasting on tamarind rice and lemon rice. To my left, some North Indians were chopping some onion and green chili which they mixed with puffed rice. This was their breakfast. For lunch, they ate dry *rotis* with pickle and onion. I threw away my plate of overcooked rice and brine and made do with some fruit.

Now for the toilets. There were two problems: one,

there was no water, and two, the stench was overpowering. Luckily, Perundevi had packed some tissue paper into my travel bag. It surprised me that none of the passengers thought it necessary to protest against their travel conditions.

The ordeal was compounded by the heat and humidity. The weather was no better at night as I was leaking like a faucet.

I endured this hellish journey for thirty whole hours!

Upon alighting at Delhi Railway Station, I was accosted by an auto driver. I'd planned to stay near Uphaar Cinema which was close to Siri Fort Auditorium.

"Take me to Uphaar Cinema," I told the driver.

As we wended our way through the streets of the capital, he casually asked me what the purpose of my visit was. (He probably figured from the looks of me that I was a Madrasi.)

"Uphaar is in Safdarjung Enclave," he said. "The rents there are unreasonable – two thousand to three thousand rupees. If you stay in Karol Bagh, you'll get excellent rooms for one thousand."

"One thousand?"

"Don't get agitated, *saab,*" he said. "How much are you willing to pay for a room?"

"Five hundred," I said hesitantly.

When we arrived at Karol Bagh, I was worried about how far it seemed from Siri Fort.

Entering the lodge, the auto driver had indicated,

I enquired about the room tariffs. It was thousand five hundred rupees a day. As it was way beyond my means, I began to leave, but the lodge manager came running after me and grabbed my hands.

"I can reduce it, sir," he said. "If you stay for a week, you need pay only eight hundred."

"Arrey, aat sau pachaas pucho!" the auto driver ordered him.

He must have thought I was ignorant of Hindi. When I realized that room rents could be bargained over, I left.

We went to another lodge and after some lengthy bargaining, we settled on six hundred rupees on condition that I stayed at least for a week. I agreed, handing over an advance of three thousand.

I later realized that the auto driver was actually a broker for the lodges in Karol Bagh.

Auto drivers in Delhi are generally honest and don't charge a paisa more than the meter-fare. I paid only sixty rupees for a forty-five-minute drive to Siri Fort.

I vacated the room after two days as I felt it wasn't economical for me to take an auto to Siri Fort every day. With one magic word, I managed to wriggle out of my agreement with the owner of the lodge. If I'd merely said, "It's not your fault. I'm going to catch that auto driver by the collar and drag him to the police," the owner would have laughed at me for being a *bewakoof Madrasi* and wouldn't have returned my advance. I just polished off my sentence with a *'behenchod'* and that word worked wonders.

CHAPTER SIXTEEN

1 – The Saint who was My Friend

Before Siva became a saint, I used to go and visit him in his room whenever I went to Nagore.

"Coming to the *silladi*?" I'd ask him.

Growing up, Siva and I spent a lot of time in each other's company. We used to hang around in Chettiar's house on "Shit Lane" during the day and in the *silladi* in the evening. When dusk fell, we'd make our way to the *dargah*'s *kulundha mandapam* or Vettar Bridge and start making our way home at nine. Siva's house was near the Perumal temple. My house was situated between the cremation ground and Rangayya Madam near Eluthiyarankulam. We took a detour to go home – we'd start from "Shit Lane" at nine, cross Sivan Kovil West Street, get onto Perumal Kovil Street, turn right onto Perumal Sannidhi Street where we would stop and talk for an hour or so. Then, we would resume our journey, taking another right onto Perumal Kovil South Street beyond which the haunted tamarind grove lay. (The stories I'd heard about the tamarind grove made me hesitant to go there even in broad daylight.) By the time I reached home, it would be eleven, and even at that late hour, Amma would get up from her sleep, light the firewood stove and make *dosas* for me.

After Siva became a saint – or as the townspeople say, a madman – I met him once and I asked him, "How do you stay shut up in your room for years on end? What do you do with all that time?"

He did not think of a response. He simply said, "Time has stopped, *da*."

I started to think that the real mad people were the ones who thought Siva had lost it. Siva is not mad. He is a seer.

"As for me," Siva said, "I'm not mad either, but everyone seems to think I am. How I'd love to stone those people to death!"

2 – Between Lovebirds

-i think i love you more than you love me, udhaya dear.

-that cannot be! i love you like a madman.

-*that* i will not deny. oh udhaya, i want you next to me. i don't like to have to hear your voice over the phone.

-i love the way my name sounds on your lips. you make it sound like music.

-i'm watching *shakespeare in love* as we speak. and i'm reminded of you because shakespeare's words in this movie sound so much like yours. love is so beautiful, don't you think so?

-ah, love! of course, it's one of the greatest miracles known to humankind, but when we fear losing it, it turns to pain.

-don't ever fear losing me, udhaya. i'll never be the cause of your pain. just know this: i'm not willing to lose you.

3 – *La petite mort*

-When I'm with Udhaya, my self-consciousness takes leave of me and I turn into an animal. He remembers nothing of what he says or does when he's three sheets to the wind. As for me, when I'm in bed with him, I forget the rest of the world. Nothing else exists, no one else exists. It's just me, Udhaya and the moment.

-This is what Roland Barthes refers to as *la petite mort*, Anjali. The little death. Sex is indeed a small death.

-So you're telling me I really bit the pillow? Oh god, I don't even remember! I just don't, Udhaya!

Eager to know what Anjali thought of my writing, I gave her one of my short stories to read. Twenty-four hours passed and she didn't bring it up. I usually don't like nagging people, but I couldn't help myself, so I asked Anjali about the story the next day.

"I didn't exactly have the time to read it yesterday, but I'll certainly read it today," she promised.

When I spoke to her over the phone in the evening, I was hoping she'd bring it up, but she didn't.

Finally, unable to control my curiosity, I asked her, "Did you read it?"

"Yes, I did."

Three words. That was all she had to say.

"You are insensitive," I railed and hung up.

This was her reply to my outburst:

"You said I'm insensitive. Well, I wasn't always insensitive, just so you know. I wasn't born that way. I'm not angry with you, but there are just things about me you won't find easy to understand. I feel castrated. I feel inexpressive. I feel scared to tell people what I feel. Please try to understand that. I don't feel qualified enough to comment on your work. If I appreciate it and tell you how much I loved and adored it, how much it made me respect you as a writer, I will only end up spouting clichés."

This was quickly followed by another message.

"You know what? I often wonder whether I'm the right woman for you. You are a mind-blowing writer. I feel so small beside you because I'm not as well-read as you are; my knowledge is far inferior to yours. I fell madly in love with you after I read your novel. Why else would I pounce on you a mere four days after we'd met?"

There were at least a dozen more messages like these, but I'll spare you the trouble of having to read them.

Udhaya said, "Any other woman with a libido like yours would have bedded a dozen men by now. You are divine."

I told him he was wrong. I immersed myself in my

work just to keep sexual thoughts at bay. While other women went to meditation and yoga classes, I trained in karate. I turned myself into a relentlessly spinning top.

I told Anjali about one of my female friends.

In seven years of marriage, she had two kids, and maybe ten sexual encounters with her husband. He was a workaholic and he returned home at midnight, eat dinner, and immediately crash. In spite of not being an alcoholic, a smoker or a womanizer, he was not a satisfactory husband to his wife who used to ask him openly, "Shall I take a lover?"

He would casually reply, "I know you won't stoop so low."

"Get a girlfriend or go whoring!" she told him. "You'll want me after that."

"You don't find me amusing, but still, I impregnated you twice," he'd boast.

The poor woman suffered for many nights. Every cell in her body burned and ached with desire. Some nights, she'd stand under the shower, naked, for hours.

"Did you sleep with her?" Anjali asked me quizzically.

"I couldn't even kiss her," I said. "She and I decided to meet privately. She was so stupid – she knew nothing about sex, and instead of cooperating, she just made a nuisance of herself. We ended up doing nothing and going home. Only men who stand in queues to sleep with whores can deal with women like her.

The next day, she sent me a message: 'Yesterday, you didn't use me properly.'

'You are not a commodity for me to *use*,' I replied. 'Maybe we could have had sex if I was like you, but I don't think my dick will ever be compatible with your hole.'"

What follows is the story of the woman you might have judged harshly from her appearance in this novel. This is her story in her own words.

"When I attained puberty, I had no idea what was happening to me. All I remember is being scared because I was bleeding. My mother just gave me a napkin and told me how to use it. She didn't sit me down to talk; she didn't call me aside to explain – nothing.

"She asked me out of the blue one day, 'Have you bled these past three months?'

"Surprised, I said, 'No, I haven't.'

"'What? Nothing? Nothing for three months?'

"'No, *Amma*.'"

"Diwakar, a family friend who'd been staying with us butted in. 'So young and she's spread her legs already. I keep telling you that she's running about and rolling around with all kinds of fellows. After you leave the house, she abuses me in such vile and obscene language.' He continued in this vein for a while.

"'I shall take you to a doctor,' my mother said grimly.

"Diwakar picked me up from school on the day my mother was supposed to take me to the doctor. He told me my mother was waiting in the hospital. However, when we arrived, she was nowhere in sight.

"'She will come. You go on inside,' he told me, pulling the doctor aside and speaking to him in hushed tones.

"There were three nurses inside the room. I still haven't forgotten their contemptuous stares. I don't think I ever will.

"'Take off your clothes,' one of them said.

"I began to cry. How could they ask me to remove my clothes in front of them? What were they planning to do to me?

"The second nurse said, 'We all know you've done much more than you seem capable of doing. Come on now, be quick!'

"Shivering uncontrollably, I removed my school uniform.

"The nurse forced me to lie down and inserted a gloved hand into my vagina. The pain was so unbearable that I screamed aloud and clutched the hand of the nurse standing beside me.

"'*Chee!* she spat, snatching her hand away like filth had touched her.

"I was a newly-matured thirteen-year-old girl being subjected to such an ordeal by a nurse. Would you like to imagine that, dear Reader? You who have been judging me until this page?

"It was not just my body they violated. They shattered my mind as well. After a few minutes that felt like an eternity of agony, the nurse, pursing her lips, removed her gloved hand. She went outside and spoke to Diwakar.

"'Oh, so she wasn't pregnant?' I heard him say.

"Only when I married did I begin to feel shame and humiliation when I thought back on this incident.

"Sometime after my marriage, I befriended a gynecologist who had a different story to tell. She told me that she was approached by a number of schoolgirls seeking abortions and when I expressed my disbelief, she took me to her clinic to prove her claim. The girls who came to her were really no more than fourteen or fifteen.

"'I scrape teenagers' wombs from morning to night,' she told me. 'I have to dirty my conscience just so these girls will not tie nooses around their necks or get disowned or stoned to death. Do you know how it makes me feel to see little bloody arms and legs?'

When I heard her story for the first time, I asked her, "Why didn't you tell your father anything?"

She'd never reply.

When I didn't drop the question, she told me, "Udhaya, my father was a short-tempered man. I didn't want to cause trouble in the family."

When I tried to get her to tell me more, she said, "I can't talk about it, Udhaya. I don't know why."

She put her head in my lap.

"Woman, don't cry now," I said, kissing her gently. "I'll be your father; I'll be your mother; I'll be anything you want me to be."

CHAPTER SEVENTEEN

1 – Mind over Matter

When I returned to Nagore to do some research for this novel, I heard people saying that Siva's madness had gotten worse. Apparently he was no longer Amba; he had taken to wearing saffron clothes, sported a beard and a moustache and wore a *rudraksha*. Physically, however, he remained undiminished. I started to wonder what he ate, and, like a telepathic connection had been forged between us, I got the answer.

"Udhaya, this body is just a shell. Once the *kooththan* which resides within it leaves, it is nothing but carrion; a scorned thing. Have you heard of Karuvoor Siddhan who sculpted the statue in Chidambaram in one hour? Lord Shiva himself used to tremble before him. Karuvooran would stand outside the temple and call out to Shiva and if there was no response from the inside, he'd leave at once, declaring that Shiva was not present in the temple.

"When Karuvooran went to Srirangam, he crossed paths with a *dasi* called Aparanji. Praising her knowledge, he gifted her a *navratna* necklace which he had received from Sreeranganathar* and said, 'Whenever you think of me, I will appear before you.' Aparanji went to the temple where everyone was looking for the necklace. When they saw it round her neck, they started interrogating her. She told them it was a gift from Karuvoorar and she called him to bear witness to this. Karuvoorar instantly appeared before her, but no one believed him either. Ultimately, the god Ranganathar himself came to his defense.

"As Karuvoorar's fame spread, certain people became jealous and plotted to kill him. When conspiracies didn't work, they decided to kill him openly and gave chase to him. Karuvoorar found safety in the Aanilayappar Temple where he embraced the deity. The moment he did, his body vanished into thin air. You see, Udhaya, Karuvoorar renounce his corporeal form and today he sits before you, having possessed the body of the person you are now speaking to. You have been good in your previous birth which is why I have chosen to speak to you and reveal the truth to you. Thus far, I have given my *darshan* to seven people and I am not bothered in the slightest about the fools in this town who call me a fool."

Wow! Siva is talking like Karuvoorar himself!

"Yes, Udhaya. How does it feel to know the truth?"

Damn! He knows what I'm thinking!

He laughed and continued.

"In my hut, you are transparent. You can conceal nothing from me. Your mind is like a mirror with its veil drawn aside. I can see your thoughts so clearly.

"*Ashta sithukkal* are the eight *siddhis* – supernatural powers – that lie within our root chakra.

The first *siddhi* is *anima* – the power to transform oneself into an infinitesimally small particle. Bhrungi, a sage, worshipped only Shiva. One day, when Shiva and his consort Uma were in Kailash, Vishnu, Brahma, Indra and his *devas*, the 41,000 sages, the *ashta vasus* and every other celestial being bowed before them. Bhrungi genuflected only before Shiva. An infuriated Uma took the *ardhanaari* form the next day. In response, the unruffled Bhrungi turned himself into a wasp, drilled a hole in the female half and flew around the male half alone. Furious, Uma demanded an explanation of the sage's behavior whereupon Shiva said, "Bhrungi seeks only *moksha*, not good fortune, which is why he only honors me and not you." So Uma says to Bhrungi, "I gave you my flesh and my blood. Return them to me!" Bhrungi returned the flesh and the blood and was left in a vegetative state. On seeing him thus, Shiva pitied him and gave him a third leg which is why you will find Bhrungi standing on three legs in Shiva temples.

Mahima is the power to enlarge a small object. The Lord used the *mahima siddhi* on his feet in order to measure the world.

Lahima is the power to become weightless like the air that blows. When Thirunavukkarasar was tied to a stone and immersed in the ocean due to a religious dispute, he saved himself from drowning by using the *lahima siddhi* to transform the stone into a float.

Harima is the converse of *lahima*. When the Lord went to Amarneethi Nayanar to obtain his loincloth, he was unable to balance the weight of the cloth even with the entirety of his possessions. He resorted to the *harima siddhi* that made him and his wife heavier. When they sat on the balance, the scales were balanced.

Prapthi is the ability to travel anywhere and everywhere without hindrance or restraint. The *Thiruvilayadal purana* contains a song explaining it. The song can be found under the section *Ellam Valla Sitharana Padalam*. Paranjothi says that throwing his stick into the air, he made it stand upright. He then places a needle atop the stick in the same upright fashion. He balances himself on the needle, standing still and on the tip of his toe. He inverts himself on the needle and whirls around.

Thayumanavar sings a song whose words in translation go thus: "One can master an elephant in musth, bind shut the jaws of a beast, mount a lion, or subdue a serpent; feed mercury to the flames and make gold and prosperity for oneself.

"One can travel the world unseen, make menservants of gods and handmaidens of goddesses; one can remain in perpetual youth, and jump bodies.

"One can walk on water and not drown and sit on fire and not burn.

"But more difficult than all of these put together is the power of mastery over the mind, the power to still oneself, the power to do nothing."

With the aid of *pirakamiyam*, you will be able to assume the physical form of another in addition to being able to appear before the person who thinks of you. This was how Avvaiyar assumed the form of an old woman in her youth and also how Karaikal Ammaiyar transformed her beautiful self into a ghoul.

Eesathwam is the ability to attain a form that is worshipped even by the gods. Using this *siddhi*, Gnanasampanthar at Mylapore restored Poompavai's ashes to life.

Vasitwam is the ability to take on the seven fold appearance of god: human, animal, avian and reptilian, arboreal, planetary and astral. It was through *vasitwam* that Thirunavukkarasar stopped the elephant that was on the verge of killing him and how Rama stopped the noisy twittering of the birds on the banyan tree.

Siddha is comprised of five disciplines: yoga, medicine, *vatham*, astrology and *mantra*. The *ashta sithukkal* pertain to the discipline of *mantra*. The *ashta sithukkal* are known by a number of names:

- *Vasiyam* (effects *mojo*)
- *Mohanam* (effects desire)
- *Sthambam* (stuns a foe)
- *Akrushanam* (effects *mojo* on angels)
- *Uchchaadanam* (chases away a foe)
- *Bhedanam* (brings about confusion)
- *Vidhweshanam* (sows misunderstanding among friends)
- *Maranam* (brings about death via black magic)

There are eight kinds of *vasiyam: jana vasiyam, raja vasiyam, purusha vasiyam, sthree vasiyam, miruga vasiyam, deva vasiyam, shatru vasiyam* and *loka vasiyam.* These are all practicable, but the effecting mantras were never revealed to humanity by Karuvoorar for its own good."

2 – G-string

Before I met Anjali, I never knew that there was such an accessory called a stole. As far as I was concerned, "stole" was the past tense of "steal." Anjali and I weren't able to have much of a conversation when we met for the first time in the Tamil bookshop in La Chappelle, so she asked me to meet her the next day at a café. It was an unforgettable meeting for both of us. I reached the café ahead of time and was waiting outside when a bus stopped and a woman got off. She smiled and waved. I turned around to look if there was someone behind me and when I saw no one, I realized she was smiling and waving at me. I managed a tentative smile as I couldn't believe that the glamorous creature in front of me was the same woman I'd seen the previous day. She was dressed in a pair of jeans, a white t-shirt and around her shoulders was a very curious *dupatta* that looked like an extra-long muffler. I just assumed that in France, *dupatta*-muffler hybrids were meant to be worn with casual clothes.

When I next met Anjali, I asked her about the *dupatta*-muffler.

"It's not a *dupatta* or a muffler or a *dupatta*-muffler," she told me. "It's called a stole."

She was wearing a skirt then and her hips swayed like a pendulum and the sight of them inflamed me.

Anjali contributed much to my meager knowledge of women's clothing.

We went to a clothing store to shop for her and she gave me a lesson there. She indicated a skintight stretchy piece of clothing that resembled a swimsuit and said "That's called a *leotard*. Gets its name from Jules Léotard, the French acrobat."

How Udhaya has fallen! It distresses me so greatly! (I say this with my hand on my heart.) He used to write about Umberto Eco's *Foucault's Pendulum* and now he's writing about another kind of pendulum. He used to write essays on Jean-François Lyotard that discussed his concept of "End of Grand Narratives" and now he's writing about Leotards that women wear. Empires have fallen because of women. Can Udhaya be any different?

My most fascinating lesson by far was the lesson on the g-string, a postmodern version of the Indian loincloth. Do you know why it's important? It was created so that women can wear sexy clothes without worrying about their panty-lines showing. The g-string is like a fig leaf with strings. Now, there was a g-string revolution which is comparable to all other revolutions in the world. This revolution took the g-string, chopped off its strings, and transformed it into the c-string. The c-string is the world's smallest panty and it's shaped like a crescent moon. It's like a fig leaf with a tail, that's all.

"Won't it fall off?" I asked Anjali.

"Not likely," she said.

So I asked her to show me how women wore c-strings and she shyly obliged.

After the c-string I don't think there can be anymore revolutions – at least where women's panties are concerned.

One day I went to Delhi's Khan Market. The entire place was full of women wearing tiny shorts. They say the real estate value of Khan Market is equal to that of USA's Manhattan. Perhaps the price of land had an inverse relationship with the length of women's pants.

I mentioned this to Anjali over the phone. She stunned me when she said that she loved shorts. I'd never seen her in shorts but I still imagined she'd look gorgeous in them.

"So, you're enjoying the sight of women's thighs, huh?" she asked me.

"I wouldn't be a man if I said no, would I?" I replied. "Which man wouldn't enjoy the sight of sexy thighs? But you know what? I think we're visually raping women. And I've been dying to ask: Do women wear skimpy clothes because they're exhibitionists? What's the psychology behind the wearing of revealing attire?"

She told me that most women dress to compete with other women and to keep up with the latest fashion trends. She also told me another very interesting thing. Women fear women when it comes to clothes and body shape. A woman will feel reluctant to take off her clothes in front of another woman because she fears her body will be judged. There is no such reluctance with a man because a man will tell a woman she is beautiful like no other even if she has a lousy figure.

3 – Sitting on a Throne of Lies

When I visited Paris in 2001, I saw a most intriguing sight. A young woman – she wouldn't have been more than twenty-five – was urinating near a platform in the Montparnasse Metro, her pants around her ankles. This she was unabashedly doing in broad daylight. When I pointed this out to my friend, he told me, "She's doing it here to avoid going to the fifth level, searching for the toilet and fishing out change from her purse. Nobody bats an eyelash at the sight of pubes or an ass here."

"I want to kiss her piss," I told him.

Only people who live in a master-slave country like India will understand why I wanted to do something so extreme. For me, that girl's urine was a symbol of pure freedom. In India, if you are found loitering on the roads at night, the cops will haul you off to the station for suspicious behavior.

After I wrote about the Montparnasse incident, one of my friends, a frequent flyer to Paris, asked me, "Is there no end to the lies you tell?" Well, here's the thing. Even if he'd visited Paris a hundred times, he would never have seen what I saw because affluent chaps like him take the number one route while ordinary folks like me take the number nine. When I told him this, his sarcastic response was, "Whatever you say." As far as he was concerned, what I had written was nothing but a fib.

Before I met Anjali, I'd been to Paris only twice, but for forty years, my life has been revolving round French literature and cinema. This is how I know the story of every stone in Paris. I could fill a thousand pages with stories about the Notre Dame Cathedral. When I stood before the cathedral, Quasimodo's story played like a motion picture before my eyes.

When I visited Notre Dame in 2006, I saw a statue of a saint with his head in his hands – Saint Denis. This saint was a Catholic bishop who was beheaded by the Romans who were angered by the number of conversions he was effecting. Denis is believed to have picked up his severed head and walked a great distance before giving up his ghost. The head kept speaking as he walked.

It is odd to note that the commune of Saint-Denis is both a religious and a red-light zone. Hookers between the ages of 18 and 80 with bright red lips get their clients from the streets. I was not surprised to see such old hookers as in India, the newspapers feature an article at least once a week about the brutal rape of some infant or toddler who is killed and casually thrown in the nearest well. So, nothing about sex surprises me anymore, not even the fact that some men like to fuck 80-year-old women.

I have written extensively about contemporary Moroccan literature which has a deep connection with the politics that underpins my writing and its background philosophy. If you have read my previous novels, you will easily perceive that my writing has blood ties with the American Beat Movement. William Burroughs, Allen Ginsberg and Jack Kerouac chose their own paths and left America. Burroughs immersed himself in Arabian culture, Ginsberg went the Indian way and Kerouac became a follower of Tibetan Buddhism.

My writing is similar to Burroughs' and I think it stems from the fact that I was raised in a place with Islamic connections. One of the cities Burroughs lived in was Tangiers, Morocco. I know that town's every street and I can very well claim to more about it than someone who's been born and raised there. Tangiers was a shelter of sorts for a number of American and European writers. This was because of the casual manner in which they looked upon homosexuality which was banned in America. When having sexual relations with fifteen-year-olds was a grave crime in a number of other countries, it was something quite casual in Morocco. Tangiers was also a popular destination as drugs like hashish were easily available.

There is a café in Tangiers called Hafa which is known for its mint tea and *kief*. *Kief* is a hookah containing tobacco, ganja and a variety of recreational drugs. The likes of Paul Bowles, Tennessee Williams, William Burroughs, Jean Genet, Jack Kerouac, Allen Ginsberg and Truman Capote had frequented this particular café which has been standing on the shores of the Atlantic Ocean since 1921.

Are you wondering why I'm writing all of this? Let's suppose there's a Tamil writer who's been living in Tangiers for twenty years. Do you know what he will say? "There is no limit to Udhaya's fibs. I have been living in Tangiers for twenty years and trust me, searching for a café called Hafa will be a futile exercise simply because such a café does not exist."

Another Tamil writer will immediately jump into the picture and say, "What that clown Udhaya writes is not to be taken seriously. He writes jokes for us to laugh at."

These are the absurd circumstances under which I write. There is just one teeny-tiny consolation. Whenever I feel suffocated by the situation in the Tamil literary world, I find some relief by showing my face in the English literary world. Recently, there was an international literary conference in Delhi during which I met several writers. When someone there mentioned that I'd translated Juan Rolfo into Tamil, a South American writer came over and embraced me.

4 – A Letter Written in the Sky

Dearest Udhaya,

I went to Arizona recently and had one hell of a psychedelic experience. I feel we should go there together someday. There was a sandstorm that blurred the entire city. This is a once-in-ten-years occurrence. Can you believe that? Because nothing was visible, traffic was at a standstill and even the airport shut down for a few hours. It was then that I began reading the soft copy of the *Marginal Man*. When the storm subsided, I hopped my plane to Paris and raced through the pages till I reached the end. You've mentioned that the book isn't done yet. When will it be finished? I'm desperate to read it in its entirety and from the beginning.

I was looking at the sky through the airplane window every now and then while I was reading. The novel evoked such conflicting feelings at the same time – I felt calm and restless, clear and hazy.

Only a few things in my life have impacted me deeply. *Marginal Man* is one of them.

Ciao,

Anjali

P. S.: Thank you for encouraging me to write poetry. I've written two so far.

5 – Honey and Butter Never Sounded This Spicy!

One fine day, a four-page article accusing me of being a sex-psycho appeared in a leading magazine. The day this happened, other magazines refused to publish my articles.

Perundevi, who was closely associated with Jymka Saamiyar, declared one day, "I'm never more going to his *ashram*. He's not a righteous man and he's going to be destroyed."

Three days after she said this, videos of Jymka's sexual romps with an actress got leaked. When this happened, the public torched his *ashram*.

I wrote a series of articles about this charlatan, who had ruined families and brought disrepute to his saffron robes which symbolized the purest form of renunciation. Besides, I had bad blood with him because he tried to brainwash Perundevi and turn her into an *ashram*-worker.

Perundevi fell at my feet and begged me to desist.

"The *saamiyar* does black magic, Udhaya," Perundevi said, trembling. "He will destroy you! Please stop writing about him."

"One values one's life above everything else, but I value my writing more than my life. Do you think I'm afraid of a scoundrel like Jymka?" I said, full of bravado.

The sound of the telephone ringing made my stomach churn. Every day, various newspapers kept calling me because they were going agog over one of my sex chats that had gone public.

Anjali and I have had several hundred spicy chats. So tell me, how the fuck can anyone publish it in a newspaper and accuse me of being a pervert and a psycho?

I was receiving legal notices from Jymka and his actress-girlfriend almost daily. That actress even gave an interview in which she lashed out at Perundevi and me. Jymka even went so far as to release a forged letter to the press which was supposed to have been from Perundevi about me, but neither of us took it up because Perundevi hated the limelight and she was acting like a child who'd just been raped. And Perundevi was the kind of woman who believed that if a wife complained about her husband to other people, she couldn't be a good woman.

Oye, Udhaya! Did Anjali read that last line?

Keeping Perundevi's mentality and convictions in mind, do you think she'd write a letter to a fucked up *saamiyar* saying...

My husband Udhaya is a womanizer. He lusts after the cow and the calf. He is an abusive alcoholic who beats me and my son.

Those publishers who tried to shame me didn't realize that their publications were in fact shaming a woman. Did they think they were helping Perundevi by exposing her supposedly psychotic husband? They only caused her a great deal of mental trauma. I feared that Perundevi would lose her wits as her mother suffered from mental illness. The woman's head conked when she was twenty-five and she suffered till she died in her eighties.

I was not at all bothered about them having stripped me naked and paraded me on a donkey in public for I am a shameless bastard who will just take all of this shit and use it as raw material for my writing. But this is not the case with Perundevi. She was a woman with a frail mind whose only mistake was marrying me, a writer. Perundevi was so shaken up by the entire affair that she would faint if anyone brought up the matter.

"I told you not to write about that scoundrel, Udhaya," she said, sobbing.

I was reminded of what Hattori Hanzo said about revenge in *Kill Bill*: "Revenge is never a straight line. It's a forest, and like a forest, it's easy to lose your way, to get lost, to forget where you came from." So, did I take revenge on Jymka or did he take revenge on me? But is the answer to that question important when you consider how an innocent woman suffered? And to think of how I stubbornly insisted that I wouldn't cow in the face of Jymka's threats!

It was because of Perundevi that I'd stopped going to the police about Jymka. If I'd persisted a little longer, I would have had the satisfaction of seeing him in cuffs and in jail for obscene forgery, for virtual rape. When I saw Perundevi suffering, I decided to let the matter go and I began to wonder if writing about Jymka was something worth doing at all.

The whole scenario reminded me of clichéd Tamil films where the villain, when he is unable to take revenge on the hero, kidnaps his daughter or his wife and threatens him.

If Perundevi had been like her mother, she would have lost her mind, but her spirituality had endowed her with the endurance to carry on.

A new birth is a miracle, but with Nalini, the house was like a place where someone had died. After the child was born, my mother did not come to help us. "How could you marry a Brahmin woman?" she asked me. I never spoke to her after that. Nalini's parents, although they lived nearby, didn't come forward either. They had a well whereas we had only a hand-pump. I had to take the baby's soiled nappies to Nalini's parents' house to wash them at the well. I had to do a thorough cleaning job because we didn't want the baby to suffer from rashes. My hands would ache from all the hauling I had to do unassisted under the blazing sun. By the time I finished, I'd be close to fainting from sheer exhaustion. We could have used diapers, but we didn't have the money to afford them. After the washing of the nappies, I'd return home to find a hungry Nalini for whom I'd have to cook special food.

Nalini was in great pain as her breasts were producing excessive milk. She even told me that the pain in her breasts was worse than labor pain. When we went to the doctor, she was told she had two options: either use a manual breast pump or have the breasts removed. Nalini was all for removing her breasts as they felt very tender and she would writhe and scream at a mere touch. But when I refused to hear of a mastectomy, the doctor suggested that I suck the milk out myself. He said it wouldn't cause much pain and he warned me not to ingest the milk as it had gone bad. I had to suck Nalini's breasts at hourly intervals. It tasted rotten – like sewage water. I had to spit this sewage water into a vessel kept at hand. If I sucked too hard, Nalini would scream in pain.

In retrospect, I think the poisonous milk I was forced to suck was a product of Nalini's then unexpressed hatred of me. This milk-sucking business carried on in the night as well, and as a result, I was unable to get proper sleep. Once I'd sucked out the milk, Nalini would temporarily feel better, but then, an hour later, she'd become hysterical again. One night, I was exhausted and fell asleep at her breast. Unable to bear the pain, she jumped up and screamed that she was going to take her life. At that moment, all I wanted was to chop her to pieces with an *arivaal.*

"This is why I said we shouldn't have children!" I furiously yelled at her once, in the middle of the night. "You're a lazy bitch who needs nine people to clean your ass. When you can't take care of yourself, what makes you think you can take care of a child, you whore?"

Did Jymka and the progressive cunts who had fun releasing forged letters which described me as an abusive drunkard know that I'd washed a woman's soiled menstrual cloths for several years?

Oftentimes I think of the curious case of a certain pair of Indian cricketers. One was a gentleman while the other was like me – he was into drinking, women and parties. And like me, he too had married and divorced. He was a better player than the gentleman, but because of his lifestyle and his bluntness, he attracted a lot of controversy that led to his premature exit from the cricket world. Even my frankness has cost me much in life.

This brutal honesty is something I've inherited from my ancestors. It has taken me sixty years to transcend the genetic memory of a people who had languished at the bottom of the social ladder. The cricketer I spoke of, like my family, belonged to a low caste. We can presume it was the elitist mentality in the cricket world that drove him to its margins and finally out. But if we wish to make progress in life and reach our goals, we must be mentally fortified so as to not be knocked out of the game by the elites.

Again I tell you, if you are a Tamil writer, you are an unfortunate wretch. Once, a writer from France visited Chennai's Alliance Française and I went to meet him. The man had participated in a few literary meets and was received at the Alliance Française centers in the metros and in every university that offered a study program in French. After his visits, pictures of him were splashed in the papers. Several copies of his book – the only book he'd written – were distributed to the students who were asked to read it and come prepared for his lecture. And then there's me, author of forty books, still waiting for that glorious day when a college will invite me as a guest speaker.

When I applied for a visa to Canada, I was refused as I didn't have sufficient funds in my bank account. And since this reason was mentioned in my passport, it became an excuse for the embassies of other countries to deny me visas as well.

A sculptor, while breaking stones, came across a toad living in a cavity within a stone. When he saw that the cavity had water for the toad to survive in, he thought, "If Arangan* can sustain this toad, surely he will take care of me." Infused with hyper-ecstasy and faith, he went into a trance and spent the rest of his life sans speaking or moving. During this time, Arangan, saying that Sri Ramanuja had sent him, visited his family every day with *prasad* from the temple. After the sculptor died, his wife went to Sri Ramanuja with a request to continue sending the *prasad* home. When Sri Ramanuja realized who had been taking the *prasad* to the sculptor's family, he said, "You shall have your *prasad* and Arangan will not have to carry it to you."

You could say that something similar had happened to me. At the age of twenty-three, I left my lover Mekhala behind in Thanjavur and went to Delhi to earn a livelihood. Once I landed in Delhi, I renounced the world. My life revolved around literature and cinema and Arangan ensured that I did not starve to death. But although he took care of my stomach, he did not take care of my bank account or help with the officials in the embassy.

I have extensively written about and translated the

*Resting form of Lord Vishnu)

works of a number of French authors – Apollinaire, Rimbaud, Mallarmé, Sartre, Camus, Céline, Genet and Perec to name a few. I spearheaded an entire movement on Marquis de Sade and Georges Bataille in Tamil Nadu and I did all of this in a time when computers were not in widespread use.

Perec wrote a lipogrammatic novel – *La Disparition.* He wrote the entire novel omitting the letter 'e,' the most frequently used letter in French. Do you know why? Perec's life was a lonely life. His father died during the Second World War when he was four and his mother died in a Nazi concentration camp when he was seven. Perec felt that his sense of self and identity had vanished. In French, it would be said that Perec wrote the novel "*sans e*" (pronounced "saanz uh"). "*Sans e*" is a homophone of "*sans eux*" ("without them"). This "without-ness" is the essence of *La Disparition.* The English translation of this novel is titled *A Void* and it also follows the lipogrammatic style. The most commonly used word in English is "the," but this word does not occur in *A Void.* Similarly, when the novel was translated into Spanish, the letter 'a,' the most commonly used letter in the language was eschewed.

"How can one write in French without using the letter 'e,' and 311 pages at that?"

When I asked Anjali this question, she read out a few portions of the novel to me. Perec had mostly stuck with the past tenses. There are five forms of the past tense in French: the *passé composé*, the *passé récent*, the *imparfait*, the *passé simple* and the *plus-que parfait*. Of these, it is the *passé composé* which often uses the 'e,' so Perec avoided this form of the past tense and chose the *imparfait* and the *passé simple* in its stead. He also deftly sidestepped the 'e' with other strategies. For example, he wanted to convey that a man looked at his watch. The French word for "watch" is "*l'horloge.*" As it contains an 'e,' he writes something like this: *Son Jaz marquait minuit vingt.* "Jaz" does not mean watch, but it is the name of a brand. It would be like saying, "His Titan showed twenty minutes past midnight." In other places, he uses abbreviations such as "*PDG*" instead of "*Président Directeur Générale.*" He also had to get around the conjunction "*et*" ("and") with commas.

Even before I heard of Perec's *La Disparition*, I'd written a lipogrammatic novel without the Tamil word "*oru*" ("a," "an" or "one"). It is quite possible that mine is the only Indian-language lipogrammatic novel. But unfortunately, because the English and the Malayalam translations have not followed this style, hardly anyone is aware of this fact.

I have served the French for forty years from my humble abode; but to visit Paris, I had to undergo a grueling ordeal. Appar Peruman, unable to walk, crawled all the way to the mountain Kailash, and at one point, he was unable to proceed any further. In that bleak and helpless moment, god appeared to him and said, "You cannot go any further, but if you immerse yourself in the lake at Maansarovar, you will rise up in Thiruvaiyaru where I will grant you a vision of Kailash." Methinks my Kailash is Chennai's Alliance Française.

How I managed to get to Paris is a pitiful story. I had to

tell lies of every sort to get my visa. At the French embassy, they looked at me like I was a refugee who was likely to apply for asylum the moment I landed in France. When I told them I was a writer, they looked at me skeptically. In Paris, all I did was wander around Sorbonne University like an orphan and stare goggle-eyed at the classroom where Foucault taught.

The Tamils know of French writers, but do the French know of Tamil writers? For how much longer are the Tamils going to keep translating and reading western literature? When are the westerners going to read us? The world is ignorant of Tamil literature because the Tamils are ignorant of Tamil writers. The only people they care to know about are Tamil actors and writers of dime novels. Under such circumstances, can I expect any recognition?

Lacan said that *"la femme n'existe pas."* In Tamil Nadu, I must say that *"l'écrivain n'existe pas."*

Anjali loves to speed on her bike early in the morning. Whenever I rode pillion with her, I'd get a boner. One day, during one such excursion, my erection became very obvious as I was wearing linen trousers. Suddenly, Anjali stopped the bike and said, "Udhaya, time for you to get off. We've reached your destination." I felt very exposed and humiliated.

6 – Eighteen Steps to Salvation

I think it's good to observe a fast for one *mandala* – a period of forty-eight days. Forty-eight days is a long time for a man to forego meat, mead and women. If the fast is broken midway, the devotee should brace himself for Lord Ayyappa's wrath.

From the age of twelve, I have satisfied my sexual cravings through masturbation. My masturbation days were over once I met Anjali, but how was I going to be able to resist Anjali who was temptation embodied?

I decided to fast for eighteen days and during that period, I was to see a mother in every woman which was going to be one hell of a task for me.

Before I began my fast, I tried to lift Anjali and ended up spraining my hip. Bending or rising sent waves of intense pain through my body. But I was determined to see my fast through even I'd have to crawl up the hill to his abode. Also, I'd received Ayyappa's call, so ignoring it was out of the question.

I met my *gurusamy* and wore the garland. He advised me to not submit to the desires of the flesh.

But samy, that's my life in a nutshell, I thought to myself.

A week before I began my fast, I'd gained some mastery over my body, avoiding all that had to be avoided. Thoughts of meat occasionally tempted me, but once the garland was round my neck, they flew my mind.

Gurusamy had composed a song in honor of Ayyappa. He was illiterate and I wondered how he did it. He told me how.

Ten years ago, he had taken a pledge to observe a fast for one *mandala.* He was hell bent on writing a song to Ayyappa and wanted the help of the god himself to accomplish this feat. To incur the god's grace, he went without food for forty-eight days, subsisting on water, milk and fruits and that too only when he was unable to bear the pangs of hunger. He would go to Ayyappa's temple every day in Mahalingapuram. After placing his pen and paper before the *sannidhi,* he would circumambulate the temple until he was close to collapsing from exhaustion. When the priest enquired after his curious ritual, he told him that he was keeping the fast.

The priest said, "Do you think this is the *krita yug*? Don't you know that we're living in the *kali yug* presently? Ayyappa will not reveal himself to you and loose your tongue."

In spite of the priest's discouragement, *Gurusamy* was not disheartened. He continued his fasts and his visits to the temple. After forty days, a Malayali couple came to the temple with their two-year-old child. The child looked at *Gurusamy* and said, "Ilango, come here!"

The parents were astounded and confused for the voice that came out of the child was that of an adult. A stunned *Gurusamy* slightly wet his *mundu*.

The child spoke again: "*Dei* Ilango, it's you I'm calling. Bring that paper hither and write down what I say."

Then, the child, who was yet to say *amma* and *appa*, uttered his first word – *ulagamellam* – and fainted. Ilango, my *gurusamy*, then proceeded to write his hymn to Ayyappa which begins thus: *Ulagamellam unnarule onkiye thazhaikka vendum.*

When the garland was round my neck, people started falling at my feet and exclaiming, "*Samy, samy!*" Trembling, I thought, "I am not a man, but *god*."

During the fast, I had to walk barefoot and sleep on the floor; wake up at dawn, have a cold bath and do *puja*. I was worried about my health and more before I began the fast, but the garland eliminated all my anxieties and turned me into a god. I felt lighter, unburdened. My temptations no longer assailed me. Without them, I felt like a stranger to myself.

Climbing the hill with the *irumudi* on my head was an experience like no other. At certain moments I felt emotional and wept for never having allowed myself to experience this bliss earlier.

There were eighteen steps that led to the summit of the hill, each with its own special significance. The first represented lust, the second anger, the third greed, the fourth religion, the fifth competition, the sixth dandyism, the seventh arrogance, the eighth *ahimsa*, the ninth *rajasam*, the tenth *tamasam*, the eleventh knowledge, the twelfth mind, the thirteenth body, the fourteenth the mouth, the fifteenth the eye, the sixteenth the ear, the seventeenth the nose and the eighteenth the skin.

I understood how the things we smelled influenced our mind, temperament and thought in these eighteen days.

"All that which gives off a rotten odor should not be smelled," *Gurusamy* explained. "Menstrual fluid, feces, urine, corpses, meat. Enjoy instead the fragrance of all that's aromatic and dear to god – flowers, camphor, incense, *kumkum*, sacred ash and the like."

I remembered how, in western countries, people lit scented candles – a different fragrance depending on the mood, the time of day and the activity being performed.

I felt my mind being washed clean as the fragrance of the *ghee* lamps and camphor enveloped me. I realized that faith and devotion had nothing to do with standing before a temple and making demands. Faith was a profound experience, like the experience I was having at that moment.

In Indian philosophy, the number eighteen assumes a special significance. There are eighteen *Maha Puranas*, eighteen *parvas* in Bharat, and eighteen mountains surrounding Sabarimala. The *Gita* has eighteen chapters and the significance of each step on the mountain can be explained using the *Gita*.

While returning from the *darshan*, the *gurusamy* told me this story. This was not the *gurusamy* who had put the garland on me but one who had tied me the irumudi and his six year old grandson had also accompanied him. They had been present in Sabarimala in January 2011 when hundreds of people lost their lives and thousands were injured in the stampede that happened at Pullumedu in the Uppuparai area. Whenever I think of Ayyappan, I hear the pitiful cries of the injured and the screams of the dying which rent the air that day, he reminisced. As he searched for his grandson he had to keep dragging aside the dead bodies he stumbled on. He could not understand why such a gruesome tragedy had befallen people in a sacred place though he felt that human greed was to some extent responsible. When people tried to take shelter in some of the shops in the vicinity, to escape the stampede, the shopkeepers had chased them away with sticks. The sound of the *chenda* which I had heard during the *padipuja* rang once again in my ears.

CHAPTER EIGHTEEN

(Not So) Love(ly) Letters

Dear Udhaya,

Learn to expect the occasional tomato, egg, slipper and letter from Kokkarakko just like you do the bouquets, the heart-shaped candies and your other mushy, lipstick-sealed, tear-stained letters from your Lady Readers.

Allow me to explain something to you: I am not someone whose existence is confined to the innards of the *Marginal Man*; I am a presence outside the novel, an onlooker, seeing all as it unfolds. But Anjali is a round character in the novel.

Apart from being the writer, Udhaya, you double as a character. Your task is doubly burdensome.

Now let's talk about the credibility of your source. You have thus far written of events that featured your presence – at the center, in the sidelines, in the shadows. And here in this novel, for the very first time, you leave the witness stand, choosing instead to record the testimony of a woman as she would have you believe it. As a character in the novel, you are free to believe what you will of what she tells you, but as a writer, did you ever ponder the reliability of her claims before you reproduced them?

All women seem to be wired the same absurd way. Their whole lives are squandered in the endless and fruitless search for a hero, and in this respect, their hearts are like compasses with a lousy sense of direction. In my opinion, the things women do in the name of love boil down to some strain of mental illness.

Moving on…

I've been dying to ask, Udhaya. Why does every woman who loved you have only tales of woe to tell? I invite you to bare the truth to your readers. Is it your peculiar misfortune that such woeful women always fall to your lot?

I have read of how, after you married Perundevi, and before she became celibate, your boisterous writer-friends would come to the house at unearthly hours, all boozed up, to drink a little more with you. Simpering, you would bid them welcome. Like a saint suffering in silence, Perundevi would drag her weary feet to the kitchen and cook for them with burning, sleep-wanting eyes. Had Perundevi written this story, the fame you are now basking in would be swallowed by hers. Because you wrote the story, it didn't find many takers. Can readers like myself, familiar with that story, participate in Anjali's tale of sorrow?

A writer is the foremost of all things in this world that are not understood or deliberately misunderstood. To understand Dostoevsky, one has to be like Dostoevsky, or try to at least. Take the case of those who call you a psychotic sleazebag. It is the likes of them who would accuse Dostoevsky of pimping in *White Nights*.

Look, I go by an alias, but in your novel, you have aliased my alias, twice removing me from reality. Forgive me then if I fail to recognize myself on your pages. In your novel, Anjali's story falls flat. You have homogenized everyone who is part of her story – they are all evil, and they are all her enemies. You threw her smack-dab in the center of a miserable world. You could have cut the poor woman some slack for Christ's sake!

It's not as easy to be your friend as it is for me to be your reader. Now read me carefully: what I am saying now does not count as criticism, but advice, as it is coming from me before the publication of your novel. Should it have come after, it would rightly be criticism.

As I have already mentioned, I remain a character outside the novel while Anjali is a character within it. I strongly condemn your discussions of the novel with Anjali during which she convinced you to modify hither and reword thither. I call this unethical. You are defacing postmodernism. You ended your Ayyappan story with the lamenting and mourning of the dying. So, why this rose-tinted Mills and Boon affair to rescue a damsel in distress? Bluntly speaking, you have become compassionate despite being the one who insisted that a writer should be as merciful as the Black Death. Now you are losing your senses. Let me remind you that a woman brought sin into the world, that the most beautiful Greek woman left chaos in her wake, that France was lost by a woman, etc. But for some reason, I half-expected you to flip because of a woman, you who have been alone all your life.

I take it that the climax of this novel will take place after its publication and will serve as the opening of your next novel.

Yours truly,

Kokkarakko

October 9, 2011

Kokkarakko,

I am writing to make two things clear to you:

1. Since you often remark that you exist "outside the novel," I have fleshed you out in it. Now, you will find yourself inside it, not a mere name tucked away in a bottom-right corner, but a central character.

2. Though our views be in diametrical opposition, you should have noticed that, on occasion, our thoughts flow in the same direction.

Udhaya

CHAPTER NINETEEN

Ask for an *Idli,* Get a Spiritual Discourse

There was this one time I was traveling by train.

I don't enjoy train-travel at all. In the first class coaches, no one talks to anyone. Do you know what it's like if someone starts talking to you? It's like having your bag-covered face repeatedly punched. What I mean to say is: you'll be assaulted by the common man's stupidity.

The second class coaches are like slave ships bound for America which is why I never travel second class.

Humans are not packed like sardines in the first class compartments, but to make up for the lack of humans, you have cockroaches that scurry about as you eat, waterless toilets and retards who loudly murdered English. As the coaches are air-conditioned, all the windows are closed and nuisances who bawl into their phones will mercilessly murder your eardrums.

I felt I wouldn't be able to write this novel at home. In the mornings, I had to walk, meditate and perform *puja*; then, I had to eat breakfast at some restaurant and I had to wander around looking for a suitable one. Rayar Café was perpetually crowded and Saravana Bhavan's *idlis* were like soggy leaves. Worse, the *sambar* and the chutney were insipid. And there were spoons to eat idlies! Can anyone eat *idli* with spoon? What a shame! It's a pity to taste such pathetic *idlis*. Only in Vellore, Tirunelveli and Madurai will you taste the true Tamil *idli*.

Three identifiers of the Tamil *idli*:

1. When you press it with your finger, it shouldn't get dimpled.

2. It should be as soft as a baby's bottom and it shouldn't stick to the fingers.

3. It should be round, not flat.

As the perfect *idli* cannot be found in Chennai, I resigned myself to eating soggy Saravana Bhavan *idlis*. If I went to another restaurant hoping for better *idlis*, I was served with disappointment. Their *idlis* disintegrate if you press them too hard.

Idlis never fail to remind me of my mother. For forty years – from the time she was twenty to the time she was sixty – she made *idlis* every single day for her six children, her husband and herself. She had to grind the batter in a huge mortar called the *kodakkal*. Women these days will have to go to the gym just to be able to lift that grinding stone. When I think of my mother, I see her grinding rice in the *kodakkal* with the heavy grinding stone. When grinding the *urad dal*, she used her left hand to push the mushy batter to the sides of the *kodakkal* so that it would be ground smooth.

I also remember her grinding the ingredients for chutneys and gravies on a flat stone with a cylindrical pestle that had to be rolled back and forth. She saw wet grinders and mixers only when she was sixty.

Perundevi hated the wet grinder as she felt it was a waste of time to wash and clean it. Besides, she didn't have the time or the physical strength to take on more work than she'd already burdened herself with. She could have ground *idli* batter for us in the mixer, but she preferred to buy it readymade from a shop.

"One should control one's cravings. One should not become a slave of food. There are so many higher things in life. Think, Udhaya! How did we come into existence? What is the purpose of our birth? What form will we take when we are reborn? If you ask me, I don't want any more births. If one's soul can merge with the *paramatma* which is both light and sound, then why do we need rebirth? Why do we even need *this* birth? Are we here just to eat and reproduce like animals? Are we mere *sothupindams*? We can find God everywhere every day. God isn't somewhere in a palace on a cloud. He's within you, Udhaya. Why do you refuse to acknowledge the presence of the divine within yourself? You'd rather just waste your life with drinking and merrymaking. Worldly pleasures have enslaved you, but they are not immortal. *You* are, because your soul is indestructible which is why you are free. Are you not aware of this freedom? Do you not see the light of God? Do you not hear its music which has traveled across worlds just to seek *you* out? Why do you act blind and deaf when you have eyes to see and ears to hear, Udhaya? Allow that light to penetrate you and cleanse you of your impurities. I tell you this in your best interest and with firm conviction.

"I was telling you about the indestructibility of the soul, wasn't I? The soul is beyond time. This brings us to the question: what is time?

"1,728,000 years made up the *Kritayug*; 1,296,000 years made up the *Tretayug*, 864,000 years made up the *Dwaparayug* and 432,000 years make up the *Kaliyug*.

"If you will notice, there are interesting facts in these figures.

"Two *kaliyugs* make a *dwaparayug*, three *kaliyugs* make a *tretayug*, a *kaliyug* and a *dwaparayug* together make a *tretayug*, four *kaliyugs* make a *kritayug*, a *kaliyug* and a *tretayug* make a *kritayug*.

"When these four *yugas* are combined, they make a *mahayug* or a *chaturyug*. A *manvanthiram* is made up of twelve *mahayugs*. A *kalpam* is made up of fourteen *manvanthirams*. There are thirty *kalpas*: *Vamadeva, Sveta-Varaha, Neelalohita, Rathantara, Raurava, Deva, Vrhat, Kandarpa, Sadya, Ishana, Tamah, Sarasvata, Udana, Garuda, Kaurma, Narasimha, Samana, Agneya, Soma, Manava, Tatpuman, Vaikuntha, Lakshmi, Savitri, Aghora, Varaha, Vairaja, Gauri, Maheshvara* and *Pitr*.

"This is not some concocted story, Udhaya. Sages calculated all of this thousands of years ago. Even Aryabhatta corroborates it. Their calculations are so accurate that we know exactly when *kaliyug* began and what will follow it.

Look at where you stand in this limitless expanse of time, Udhaya. Again I tell you with complete certainty: your soul is indestructible. Don't trap yourself within the impurities of this *kaliyug* and worsen your karmic consequences. The soul takes eight hundred and forty thousand births in total, but this is just an approximate figure. The Buddha attained enlightenment only during his last birth. Our souls have more power than a million suns. If you use this power to burn away your karmic consequences, you will never have to be born again. You can liberate yourself from the cycle of birth and death. Then, you will come face to face with the divine light, you will hear the music of this universe."

Dear Reader, this was the discourse Perundevi had subjected me to when, one day, after my morning walk to burn my body fat, I made the mistake of telling her, "Perundevi, I'm hungry. Give me some *idlis*." She'd been sweeping the garden and she didn't even pause to put the broom aside. On hearing her discourse, I almost fell unconscious. In my dazed state, I thought I saw a great light before my eyes. I still wonder whether it was the result of her philosophical and numerical sermon or my hunger pangs. That day, I firmly resolved to never speak of *idlis* to Perundevi again.

Back when I was a child, I used to eat fifteen *idlis* and now, at the age of sixty, I eat only ten. I am a maniac for only two things – food and sex. How did I expect to survive on a mere ten *idlis*?

One night, I had sex for two hours continuously. The following morning, I went for a walk on Rue St. Denis in La Chapelle. Whenever I go to Paris I stayed in one of the lodges at La Chapelle so that I could be near to Anjali whose house too was perched there. My body was aching above the waist, but there was something enjoyable about that pain. My gastric muscles were hurting and I wanted them to hurt even more. Surprisingly, Anjali too was experiencing the same pains.

I was walking on the Rue St. Denis, when I was contemplating how that street that was built by Romans in first century pacified the libido of men these days, my friend Vikram accosted me and asked, "Were you binge-drinking yesterday, Udhaya?"

"No, why?"

"Your eyes look peculiar, that's why."

"Oh, I had sex for two hours on the run."

Vikram couldn't give me a coherent reply. He blabbered and smiled sheepishly. Finally, he closed his mouth with one hand and hurried off.

I could have lied to Vikram, but I don't know how to tell lies. If I had to tell a lie, I'd have needed an hour to make one up. Speaking the truth was the most convenient thing for me to do. The truth is like fast food – it can be delivered at once. But just like fast food is bad for health, telling the truth is also bad for one's life and reputation. Now, Vikram will find someone else to tell my story to and that someone else would find someone else again and eventually, the whole place will be ringing with the story of my sex-marathon and all the common men will conclude that I am a sex-psycho or a Tamil Don Quixote. But hey, your sex-life shouldn't deteriorate with age. Back home, I know of seventy five year old men who could father children. Dear Reader, don't rap out that it might not be the old man's kid. I know a sixty-five-year-old writer who has four wives and three dozen lovers. I've met some of his women who have told me he's still a livewire in bed. I came to know from a source that he'd slept with more than three thousand women. But you know what? I don't think this is anything unusual.

If these stories are inspiring, remember that I've given you a lot of virility-enhancing tips in this novel.

During that marvelous time in bed with Anjali, I laughed and said, "And that Maravarman Sundarapandian wrote me off as an old man."

"Who's Maravaram Sundarapandian?"

"Who do you think? A Tamil writer. As a Tamil writer, even if I make it to heaven, I'll still be thinking about hell. That's why I remembered that fellow now."

"Oh, forget him Udhaya! *He's* the old man, not you," Anjali said, hugging me to her bosom.

Do you know that Michael Phelps consumes 12,000 calories daily? A young man, to be fit and healthy, needs only two thousand calories. Like Phelps, my food habits and my sex habits are extraordinary.

When I think of calories, I am reminded of an amusing incident. Balu and I had gone to Coimbatore where we stayed with Rajesh. Rajesh is someone who is obsessed with health to a fault and he tries to extend his interest to other people as well.

In the morning, the three of us had omelets with bread. In the afternoon, Balu and I had two pegs of whiskey and ate *biryani*. For dinner, we thought of ordering chicken kebabs, but Rajesh was not for it.

"You've already consumed enough calories for the day," he said. "Five hundred calories for breakfast and more than two thousand calories for lunch."

When we returned to Chennai, Venkatesh, Rajesh's brother asked us, "How was your trip to Coimbatore?"

"Fantastic," I replied.

Balu looked less than enthusiastic.

"What's the matter?" Venkatesh asked.

"It was okay, but your brother goes slightly nuts when it comes to food."

"Ah, yes! He counts calories."

"Yes, he does. In the morning we had bread with omelets and for lunch we had whiskey and *biryani* and the bugger kept saying we ate calories. Neither of us ate calories!"

Venkatesh and I had to drink two extra pegs that day to explain to Balu what calories were.

There was a teacher in Chennai's Alliance Française called Indu who told us about a French candy manufactured by Carambar. It was a chewy candy that was made of caramel.

"There is a similar Indian sweet," she said, "but I can't remember what it's called. The word ends with 'kattu.'"

Immediately, a North Indian girl shouted, "*Jallikattu!*"

Thereafter, everybody called her Jallikattu. (She meant to say '*kamarkattu.*')

Indu told us that the Carambar candies had word jokes printed on the inside of their wrappers like: *If a vampire goes to America, where would it stay? In the Vampire State Building.*

Our first day at AF actually began with a Carambar joke. In AF, French is taught in French (which was the reason for my repeated failures). When Indu entered the class, she greeted everyone in French.

"*Bonjour!*"

Everyone knew what that meant, so we happily returned the greeting.

She approached a girl sitting in the front row and said, *"Je m'appelle Indu. Comment vous vous appelez?"*

Nobody understood anything. Indu tried actions.

Pointing her index finger to her chest, she repeated, *"Je m'appelle Indu."* Then, she pointed at the girl and said, *"Comment vous vous appelez?"*

"Muslim," the girl replied.

Indu burst into peals of laughter and nobody understood why.

Let's return to my problem of completing this novel. How the fuck was I supposed to do it if I'm spending most of my time foraging for food and listening to lengthy spiritual discourses? Thinking I'd need another year, I left for Ooty.

It was so cold in Ooty that I ended up spending most of my time trying to keep warm instead of writing. As it was raining, I couldn't go out. I wasted one week in the company of friends, drinking and chatting. When I returned home, I had to deal with the double-burden of hunger and work...

During this time, I was plagued by the people who came calling and tapping at the gate – the men who deliver cooking gas, the water boys, the vegetable vendor, the people from the Board of Electricity, the maid, the maid's daughter, people seeking directions to people's houses, North Indian carpet sellers, beggars, the milkman, the fellow who came around collecting the monthly cable TV fee, the ironer, the flower seller, the newspaper man, sales representatives, the postman, couriers... Okay, I could even deal with all those folks, but not the garbage collectors. Every morning, I'd wake up at four and start working on my novel without even having a cup of coffee. The garbage collectors would knock at the gate at six and demand money. Perundevi had spoiled them. The neighbors wouldn't even part with a paisa. They felt that the garbage collectors were being paid salaries and hence didn't need to ask for money like beggars. And these neighbours were wealthy as fuck, mind you.

Garbage is collected twice a day on this street. After visiting at six for money, the garbage collectors would return again at eleven asking for water. One day I asked them why they never bothered the neighbors. They told me that the neighbors would only give them tap water which was infested with worms.

With all these botherations, I was only able to write a few pages over a period of one month. Wanting to get the novel done with, I decided to go write in Bangalore. The weather there was clement – ideal for writing. As always, I stayed in Brindavan Hotel. There were at least fifty pubs within a one kilometer radius and Brigade Road – the most happening place in Bangalore – was just a stone's throw away. Again, with so many tempting distractions, how was I supposed to write? On the first day of my stay there, I went to a discotheque called Hind on the terrace of Central Mall with Kokkarakko. It was a space for two hundred people, but there were close to five hundred people packed into that room – 450 women and 50 men. Drinks were flowing everywhere and rock music was blaring. That music was infectious, but in spite of that, nobody was dancing. Everyone was just standing around, tapping their feet and bobbing their heads. When I enquired about this state of affairs, I was told, "The police commissioner has strictly forbidden dancing."

All the women in Hind were skimpily dressed. How beautiful their thighs looked in their little mini-skirts and shorts!

Wait, hang on! What the fuck am I talking? How could a one-woman-man like me feel so tempted? A little while ago, I was sure I could have sex and friendship with no other woman but Anjali. How did a few pairs of sexy thighs change my mind?

"Right now, I feel like a male chauvinist pig," I told Kokkarakko, "and I'm ashamed of it."

Anjali and I have had countless petty fights over petty affairs because of my possessiveness.

She had a guitarist cum globetrotter friend called Arvind who shared all his love affairs with her. He was committed to a female named Shilpa. One day, when he was leaving her apartment, a group of loitering youths asked him, "How much for one night?"

He, noble heroic defender that he was, started barking at them, but they calmed him down and gave him some valuable information.

"After you drop her off, a fellow on a bike comes here. She leaves with him and returns only the next day."

On hearing this, Arvind parked his car out of sight and hung around near her apartment to verify if this was true. Half an hour later, a fellow on a bike arrived and Shilpa came out, hopped on and rode off. Arvind followed them, keeping a safe trailing distance. When the dude dropped Shilpa home, it was midnight. He figured Shilpa was up when the light came on in her bedroom (but the mystery man didn't come down) and shortly after, the light went out. He waited there till seven in the morning. Shilpa was still in bed. He went upstairs and knocked on her door. A middle-aged man answered.

"Who do you want?" he asked Arvind.

Arvind pushed him aside and barged in. He banged on the bedroom door. It was opened by a groggy, surprised young man who clearly hadn't been expecting an angry male visitor so early in the morning.

"Who are you?" he asked sleepily. "What do you want?"

"That bitch in the bed you've been fucking? I'm her boyfriend. I mean I *was*."

Though Arvind said he broke up with her after that fiasco, the lovers have patched up now. I don't give a shit about all these but what bothers me is he calls Anjali as "princess."

When I told Anjali I didn't like the idea, she told me, "You have female friends too, Udhaya. What's your problem with me having a male friend?"

"He calls you 'princess.' *That's* my problem. Shouldn't it only be *me* calling you that?"

Udhaya, you call yourself broadminded and now you're telling me a "princess-matter" has ruffled your feathers? Do you think a "princess-matter" would have made Suresh toss and turn in his sleep?

If Suresh had been the kind to be affected by such things, I wouldn't have pursued things with you, Udhaya. I don't matter to him, so do you think a "princess-matter" matters to him? Your friend Kokkarakko doesn't know anything about women. Anjali.

"Look Udhaya, Arvind is a longtime friend. He grew up in France which is why he talks that way and thinks nothing of it. If you could meet him just once, it will put your mind at ease."

"Why the hell should I meet him? Does he know about me?"

"No."

"If he knew, he wouldn't dare call you 'princess.' Besides, what does *he* know about your life?"

"Even after the two of you meet, he'll continue to call me 'princess.'"

"No, he will *not*! Don't ever talk about him to me again."

Anjali never did talk about him again. But still, I kept thinking of him.

Now let me tell you about another incident.

Anjali was going gaga over a Hindi film and I went to see it on her recommendation. She told me that the lead actor's eyes were "divine." When she said that, I wasn't able to watch the movie any further. True, he had green eyes – a rarity in India. But why the fuck did she have to call them 'divine?' And, truth be told, I don't think she was swooning over his eyes. I think it was his bare torso and his low trousers that had her drooling. And in one scene, the camera gave us a generous shot of his navel. That camera was like a woman, its lascivious glass eye roaming over the actor's body.

Alright, Anjali. If you want to ogle at that actor's eyes, don't mind if I drool over Priyanka Chopra's lips. Nobody in this world has her luscious lips. I'm going to write her a sexy love letter, okay?

I left the theater after sending Anjali a message telling her that I hated the film and why. She replied to me the same day.

I don't need a hero when I have you. If you don't like something, fine. I don't like it either. Don't ever doubt my feelings for a split second. I love you, I can't wait to see you and have you hold me in your arms. It's been long, so long...

When I met her in my next visit, she told me, "Nobody's ever been so possessive about me, Udhaya."

Uh-oh.

"You know; your possessiveness doesn't annoy me. I rather like it."

Phew!

There was this other time I was traveling by train when Anjali sent me a text.

Are there any young women near you?

I've never been blessed with such good fortune.

Oh, you poor thing!

How would you feel if there was a young woman sitting next to me?

What kind of question is that? I'd be irritated!

Why? You don't trust me?

I do trust you. And you want to know something? Just as you are possessive of me, I am possessive of you. I've never been this way with anyone, never felt this way about anyone, never cared this way about anyone. Get that straight, Udhaya. I love you.

CHAPTER TWENTY

Ladies and Gentlemen, The *Harami!*

If there is one word to describe Kokkarakko, it's *harami.* Hearing the kinds of things he did would turn anyone's hair grey. Once, while driving down to Chennai from Bangalore, he stopped his car and took a picture of his three-year-old daughter standing in the middle of the highway! I nearly had a fit when I saw the picture. The child was standing bang in the middle of the highway with vehicles zipping past at more than 100 kmph. "It's just a matter of timing, Udhaya. How far away are the vehicles? When will they approach the child? How much time will clicking the picture take? You just calculate all this and voila, you have a snap!" he said nonchalantly.

The *harami* wept once when he recounted a harrowing experience he had with a *harami* family. That was the only time he seemed less like a *harami* and more like a saint. When he was driving from Bangalore to Chennai, he spotted a family of four – a husband, a wife and two children – traveling on a bike. Since it was raining, he offered them a lift. He didn't expect that they would also be traveling all the way to Tamil Nadu. The husband immediately abandoned his vehicle at the shop of an acquaintance. The wife wanted to ride shotgun but the husband didn't approve. He made her get in the back with the kids while he got in the front. The children stood on the seats while the mother removed their soaking wet clothes and wrung them out right there inside the car! Like this wasn't enough, the father too removed his shirt, squeezed it out and put his legs up on the car seat. Imagine Kokkarakko's horror when he realized the family was going to Krishnagiri. When they got off, his seats were wet, filthy and torn. But what rendered Kokkarakko speechless was the question the man asked him, "Were you returning after dropping off a passenger?" He thought Kokkarakko was a driver! It cost him eighteen grand to replace the damaged seat covers.

Kokkarakko was eight years old when he was in the third grade. At that age, most kids played house, but Kokkarakko played doctor, and his patients were always little girls. After the girls were made to lie down, he would lift their skirts and give them an "injection" in the vagina with a bristle from a broomstick. But this is easier said than done. First, and most importantly, the patient had to be taken to a secluded place. The girls always dithered when he told them to lift their skirts and even when they agreed, they would only lift them inch by inch. But there was one girl who gave *him* the shivers. She once went missing when he was playing hide and seek with a group of girls and when he finally found her, she was in a scrub forest. When she saw him, she immediately lay on the ground, lifted her skirt and opened her legs. Spreading her vagina open with her fingers, she said enthusiastically, "Come, come." She was in the third grade and heaven only knows where and how she learned to do such things. Once she grew up, she would lower her head and walk away whenever she saw him.

"Nice looking chick. Wish she would play with me now. They never want to when the time is right," he sighed.

Until he was about eight, he used to bathe naked in the pond. One day a girl called out, "*Dey* Kokkarakko! Why are you bathing in the nude? The fish will bite it off."

He shot back, "My dick looks like a fish so it won't get bitten. But your pussy might get bitten because it looks like a *vadai*."

One of the things that caused great distress to students was the report card that was sent to their homes by post. The postbox was near the school entrance. When Kokkarakko made the breakthrough discovery that a stick of ice dropped into the postbox could deliver one from the nightmare of the report card, he was less than ten years old.

There was a girl of twenty-one with a stunning figure who lived just across Kokkarakko's house. He was ten at the time and looked handsome with his caste-mark. The girl would often call him over to her house and make him sit on her lap. One day, the little *harami* squeezed her tits but she did not complain. Since that incident, she would call him and talk to him whenever she was alone at home. Sometimes, she took him to the shop, saying there was no one to accompany her. Another day, Kokkarakko the *Harami* lifted her skirt. The girl began laughing uncontrollably. Yet another day, the *harami* kissed her full on the lips. "Dirty fellow!" she scolded, pushing him away. She spat into the sink and rinsed her mouth thoroughly. (In those parts, kissing on the lips is a dirty thing.)

Though he was involved in several *harami* activities, Kokkarakko was a good student. He took part in debates, essay competitions, *Thirukkural* competitions and elocutions, winning medals and certificates that brought glory and fame to his school. He was the principal's pet and there was hardly a day his name was not mentioned after the morning prayer for all to hear.

In those days, there were close ties between students and Tamil teachers. Kokkarakko had a Tamil teacher in the sixth grade who, according to him, was one hell of a beauty. The teacher was young and her son was in the same class. As Kokkarakko used to win many prizes, the teacher was very fond of him. Once, he took part in an interstate elocution competition and won the first place for the topic, "Bharatidasan: The Greatest Poet in the World." Kamban, Thiruvalluvar, Ilango Adigal and all the others failed to impress. The Tamil teacher summoned Kokkarakko to her side and kissed him on the cheek. Kokkarakko was unable to sleep that night. The next day, he went to the teacher's son and told him, "I am in love with your mother and I'm going to marry her." The news spread like wildfire and the librarian came to know of it. Kokkarakko was summoned to the library as that was where inquisitions were held.

"Stand on the bench," said the librarian.

A teacher interrupted him saying, "Wait, let's find out what happened." Turning to Kokkarakko, he asked him, "What did you say about the Tamil teacher?"

"Nothing *saar*. Only that I love her and that I am going to marry her."

All the teachers laughed and the *harami* was not punished.

He also had a Tamil teacher called Muthiah in the higher classes. The man would force the boys to speak chaste Tamil while liberally using English himself. He had a penchant for using the invented word "*soiing*" to describe the movement of vehicles. The boys therefore nicknamed him "*soiing*." When he came to know that he was being mocked, he stopped using the word. Still, whenever he came close to using it, the boys would stare at him expectantly and this made him nervous.

One day Muthiah had to talk about planes.

The blame for the incident I am about to narrate lies squarely on the shoulders of Ilango Adigal who wrote *Silappatikaram* and not on Kokkarakko's, though he was a *harami*. Adigal speaks of Kannagi traveling by air with her husband Kovalan who had died a fortnight ago. When the teacher was reciting the lines of the text, Kokkarakko uttered the word "*soiing*" thrice.

Muthiah said, "There is the *vaanavoorthi* that is mentioned in *Seevaka Chinthamani*. Sachanthan, who creates a peacock-shaped flying machine, teaches his wife,

Visayai, to fly it. But she is unable to operate it properly and it lands in the cemetery."

"Soiing, soiing, soiing."

"The westerners invented the airplane only recently–"

"Soiing, soiing, soiing."

"– but our ancestors had already invented aircraft centuries ago."

"Soiing, soiing, soiing."

"Similarly, the *Ramayana* also features an airplane –"

Muthiah didn't even finish his sentence, but Kokkarakko continued to repeat his *soiing*-mantra imitating the sound of the airplane. All the students laughed and the teacher turned to glare at him, trembling with anger.

The classroom had a dais where the teacher stood and taught. It had two steps too. Muthaiah was drenched in sweat and his face insipid. Breathing hard, he bent down to remove his slipper to beat Kokkarakko, but when he tried to stand upright, he found that he couldn't move at all. He stood there, half-bent, the slipper dangling precariously in his hand. He made another effort to rise but he suddenly collapsed. The students ran to the teacher and revived him by sprinkling water on his face. They gave him a soda to drink. Kokkarakko sat unfazed, while all this chaos was unfolding.

He was taken to the headmaster who said, "You fool! What have you been up to? I'm hearing people complain a lot about you these days. What were you doing in class?"

"I didn't do anything, *saar*. Muthiah *saar* was teaching

us about airplanes in a very interesting manner and I only said *'soiing'* to make it even more interesting."

Muthiah, who was quite alright then, butted in saying, "Don't believe him, *saar*. He used the word mockingly and repeated it several times."

"*Saar*, airplane goes *soiing* only, no? That's why I said it."

"*Saar, Saar*, Look! How many times he says '*soiing*' in front of you!"

The headmaster was amused.

"Get lost, you useless fellow!" he said, sending him off with an indulgent smile. If he called anyone a useless fellow, it meant he was in a jolly mood.

That was the last and after that Muthaiah never set his foot in that class.

When he was still in school, Kokkarakko used to scalp tickets to earn money for cigarettes and drinks. It was a risky endeavor as there were rowdies who did this as a full-time job. To escape them, he developed some strategies. As he wore a school uniform, the rowdies did not suspect him. Sometimes he would ask the customer to meet him at a building near the theatre and sell the tickets secretly. Or he would approach the rowdies themselves and say, "*Anney*, my friends and I bought these tickets so that we could see the movie, but they didn't turn up. Can you buy them?" They'd buy the tickets from him for twenty-five and sell it for fifty. He was a smart and a crooked *harami* who knew many tricks of the trade. He knew that tickets for movies starring Kamal or Rajini had to be sold for higher prices than tickets for Vijaykanth and Satyaraj starrers. The story of how Kokkarakko bought tickets for movies like *Iruvar, Kuruthi Punal, Indian* and *Muthu* and later resold them at a profit should be etched in stone like the Kalinga edicts. There is no place here for all that; besides, this is not Kokkarakko's novel.

As far as he was concerned, ticket scalping was a good solution for his money problems. The main reason why this illegal business thrives in Tamil Nadu is the attitude of the Tamils. It works like this: The day before a holiday, they decide to sit and sleep at home. On the day of the holiday, at around four in the evening, they are hell bent on going to the cinema. If they plan in advance, they can buy the tickets legally and cheap, but the Tamils just don't care. Hence, one can do roaring business as a ticket reseller.

Another solution to solve his fiscal problems was stealing from his mother's purse. He followed a new technique. He would take money and hide it in the different section of the same purse itself. If there was no talk about the missing money for a whole week, he would take it.

He had his first drink when he was in the ninth grade. There were several boys willing to give him company and they formed a gang. People who gave him bland and unsatisfactory reasons for not wanting to join were punished by Kokkarakko.

Nowadays, herbal remedies for impotence – *siddha, ayurveda* and *unani* – are available everywhere and are heavily and openly advertised in the media. In Kokkarakko's salad days, these medicines were not only used by men but also by men who had become debilitated and weak due to frequent masturbation. Amulets were also popular. All of this could be ordered through a letter to the company and your package would be sent by VPP and the money would be paid on delivery.

Kokkarakko meted out innovative punishments to boys he had bad blood with. He would send a letter to the company that sold medicines for impotency using the name and the address of the offender. The aphrodisiacs would arrive by VPP. As the boy would be in school, the parcel would be received by his confused father who would have to shell out two hundred rupees. When the father opened the box and realized what its contents were, he would scream at his wife, "Woman! Look at what your scoundrel of a son is up to!" The couple would then shout recriminations at each other and eventually settle down to wait in grim silence for their wayward son who, like a meek lamb, would amble in after a tiring day at school only to realize he'd stepped into a warzone. Around a dozen members of Kokkarakko's gang had endured this punishment.

This incident happened when he was sixteen years old. Those were the days when people could smoke cigarettes in movie theaters. Though there was a law that forbade people from lighting up there, it was ignored by most people. At that time, a young police officer was posted in Chidambaram. The young ones are always idealistic and patriotic. They believe that all it takes to make the country super power is to nab 'criminals' who ride doubles on a bicycle, and who demand a bribe of fifty bucks and throw their asses in prison. This particular police officer had gone to Singapore to see his family and returned with the lofty dream of turning India into another Singapore. One day, he saw some men lighting cigarettes in the movie theater in Chidambaram. He stormed the theater with his men and hauled the offenders in lock-up – one of them was Kokkarakko. He argued that the police made it difficult to have a smoke anywhere in town. The cigarette vendor himself would curse him: "Hardly out of his nappies and he wants to smoke!" And when he sought a secluded place, there was the probability of him running into one of his father's friends. Under such circumstances, the best place to smoke was obviously the movie theater. Even in lock-up, Kokkarakko managed to smoke.

The lone policeman in the station was fast asleep. Kokkarakko's parents had not been informed and they'd worry if he didn't return home at night. Silently, he inched his way closer to the phone on the table and called his friend. "Go home and tell my folks that I'm studying at a friend's place and won't be going home tonight."

The next morning, when the senior officer arrived at the station, Kokkarakko begged him with narrowed eyes and folded hands, "*Saar*, today we have our practical exam. Please let us go. We won't do it again." Not wanting to spoil their education, the officer let the *harami* and his squad go.

Kokkarakko was in the eleventh grade when a new teacher came to his school. He called Kokkarakko and asked him to get him some water. Our boy went straight to the toilet; it was a village school, so I'll leave it to you to imagine the facilities there. Kokkarakko found an old, dirty plastic mug with a broken handle, filled it with water from the toilet tap and gave it to the teacher whose eyes reddened with fury. Through gritted teeth, the teacher said, "I too was like you once!" Unable to speak any further, he left the classroom and never set foot into the school again.

Research has claimed that Tamil Nadu has the highest proportion of suicide in all of India. Here, people commit suicide because they are forbidden from watching their favorite TV show or because of a failed love affair; students commit suicide because of bad grades; fans commit suicide because their favorite actor's hero was a box-office failure; followers immolate themselves when their political leader is arrested (and he or she will be released the very next day which is another story). There are also those who commit suicide when their leader receives a garland of slippers from his enemies or when their parties lose elections; wives commit suicide when their husbands say mean things about their families, criticize their cooking or refuse to buy them jewels. Some others commit suicide due to failed demands for a separate state. Women commit suicide when their husbands torment them after they casually talk with male friends. There are still more who commit suicide due to headaches, backaches, and stomachaches. As the number of suicides in Tamil Nadu is very high, there are suicide prevention centers in every district. People contemplating suicide make missed calls to these centers and a representative calls back and counsels the person in an attempt to dissuade him from committing suicide. To punish an offender, Kokkarakko would simply make a missed call from the person's number. Imagine trying to convince some stranger that you have no intention of taking your life and that you are, in fact, having the time of your life doing illegal things.

When Kokkarakko was studying in a Chennai college, he and his friends would often go to Devi Theater to watch late-night movies. The theater was quite a distance from Pazhavanthagal where he stayed. By the time the movie got over at midnight, no public transport would be available, so they would hitch a ride on some truck that was loaded with freight. But it was a terrible ordeal. They would have to sit on the load which was very uncomfortable for their bottoms. But the trucks sometimes helped them make money on the sly. If there was a hole in the packing material, they would enlarge it with their fingers and steal iron nuggets. On reaching Pazhavanthagal, they would pay the truck driver five rupees and make off with the iron which would fetch them twenty-five rupees the next day in the market.

During this time, Kokkarakko used to cook his own food. His friends were always broke, so while Kokkarakko sponsored the drinks, they would steal rice, *dal*, tamarind, coriander and vegetables from their homes and give it to him. This was how he subsisted.

Kokkarakko's English was not flawless, but he knew how to speak suavely and sophisticatedly in order to get whatever it was he wanted. Whenever he wanted to have expensive drinks he couldn't afford, he would consult the Yellow Pages directory, find the number of a star hotel and ring the bartender. "I'm a regular customer at your bar, but now I'm out of town. I've tried a lot of places, but none of them make cocktails the way you do. Could you tell me how to mix myself a cocktail?" Flattered, the bartenders would blurt out their recipes to him. He would buy some cheap Old Cask rum, mix it with pomegranate juice and orange juice and hey presto! The five star cocktail would be ready.

Kokkarakko used to travel by bike in those days. If he didn't have the necessary papers on him and sufficient cash for a hefty bribe, the cops would seize his license and ask him to collect it from the station the next day. But no matter how many times he got caught, he didn't have to go down to the station for what he gave the cops was only a photocopy of the original license and he always had four or five at the ready.

Later, he began to tackle the problem differently. He wouldn't beg the cops to let him go, but he would park his bike in a corner and act like he was the cop's assistant. He would stop motorists and ask them to get off their bikes. When the cop asked for their papers, he'd say, "*Saar* is asking, no? You'd better hand them over." He ended up befriending the cop and he started presenting himself at the station, enquiring about his well-being. "There used to be nothing for me to do when I returned home. That way, I was able to pass my time without getting bored," he explained. In this manner, he made several friends in the police department, including an assistant commissioner.

Kokkarakko liked to change his hairstyle often. The shaved head, the *kudumi*, a French beard, a luxuriant moustache, or no moustache – the experiments were many. You could even say he started a mini-revolution with his hair. He even sported a police crop once. This hairstyle accessorized with a beer belly gave him the appearance of a cop. One day, while driving on the highway, he stopped for toddy in a small village. Having mistaken him for a cop, the shop owner tried to flee. Sensing an opportunity, Kokkarakko's friends told the shop owner that the cop had come to drink toddy and not to conduct a raid. Relieved, the fellow served them fresh and unadulterated toddy. He not only refused to take money from them, but also offered a bribe of fifty rupees. To his credit, Kokkarakko refused it.

If I write about Kokkarakko's whoring, this novel will never end, so I will restrict myself to a couple of incidents.

On the way to Mahabalipuram, there are many cottages suitable for clandestine trysts. Even though there were boards on the beach saying that the cottages were private property, who could prevent people from hanging around there? The loiterers just found it convenient as they were spared from paying two thousand by way of rent. It was Kokkarakko's habit to have drinks with his friends in such places. On his birthday, he went to the beach with his gang. He'd also invited a woman who arrived an hour before midnight. Telling his friends he wanted to buy her some food, he took her to a nearby casuarina grove and returned two hours later. If it wasn't obvious, he went and had sex at midnight on his birthday.

In a village that shares borderlines with three states – Tamil Nadu, Kerala and Karnataka – can be found some of the most beautiful Indian women and they will give you sex for just three hundred rupees. The reason? Poverty. Kokkarakko's American buddy, Robert, wanted to sleep with some Indian whores as he was tired of the homegrown variety. He had a thing for oral sex.

"Don't worry," Kokkarakko told him. "I know a place. I'll take you there."

But Robert was bitterly disappointed when the girl ran out of the room screaming blue murder when he tried to have oral sex with her.

Kokkarakko was furious. He yelled at the woman in Tamil and she yelled back in Telugu. A huge fracas ensued after which the woman returned the money.

While on a trip to Hyderabad, Kokkarakko and a couple of his friends decided to engage a modern and sophisticated whore. They rented a room in a luxury hotel and were subtle when it came to the women. Instead of just having a romp under the sheets, they were told that they were to accompany the men to a party where they would be their dance partners. The girl who was supposed to entertain Kokkarakko and his friends was from a village near Nellore. She would visit Hyderabad monthly, make some money there over a period of two days and return home. Each man had to pay her one thousand rupees. As Kokkarakko wasn't interested in her, the other fellows agreed to pay her two thousand. While she was having sex with one of the friends in the room, Kokkarakko was sitting outside and drinking with the other friend. After the first customer walked out, the second customer walked in.

His friends told him many things about Nellore girls. They were fiery creatures who couldn't be approached without first having handed over the money and they were very particular about who slept with them – they wouldn't just do it with anyone. On hearing this talk, Kokkarakko challenged his friends, saying he'd screw her without paying her a paisa. When the second friend finished, our *harami* went in. The woman had been drinking. He discovered that she knew only Telugu but could understand a handful of Tamil and English words. Kokkarakko tried to make his intention known by speaking an odd-sounding mixture of English, Tamil, Telugu, Hindi and unofficial sign language.

"Look, see, *ikkada* fuck *nahi* – no fucking, only drinking, only eating. You, me friends. *Dosth, teek hai? Dosth, dosth,* we all *dosth.* Life enjoy. *Biryani*, drinking enjoy *karo.* Fuck *nahi. Ikkada* no touching. Me your friend. Me your *dosth. Dosth, dosth, jolly, jolly, enjoy, enjoy.*"

He kept talking like this and touched her shoulder lightly. She had finished three rounds and did not object, so he shifted his hand to her thigh. Still she didn't protest. He didn't stop talking. ("Jolly, jolly. No fuck, fuck *nahi.* Only touching.")

She suddenly interrupted him saying, "*Kannamittu, kannamittu.*"

He didn't understand. For a moment, he was wondering whether she'd fallen in love with him because of the way he'd stroked her. She kept repeating the word. What did she mean? Did she want him to kiss her on the cheek? When he brought his face close to hers, she pointed at a spot below his waist and said the word again, articulating every syllable. Then it dawned on him. She wanted him to wear a condom. He immediately slipped one on, and, rubbing his dick against her thigh, he said, "Only here, no fuck. Only here."

She didn't say anything.

"*Akkada* no, *ikkada* only," he said, pointing to her thighs.

Suddenly, he penetrated her and finished his job. She did nothing to prevent him.

Before she left, she said something to him in Telugu laughingly. He didn't understand what she said, but the words "*ikkada*" and "*akkada*" occurred. What could she have meant? Probably: "You scoundrel! You tricked me with your *ikkada, akkada.*"

Kokkarakko and a friend went to a luxury hotel which specialized in high-class prostitution. Three thousand bucks for two hours. The friend who went in first walked out in twenty minutes. When asked why he came out so quickly, he said, "According to the woman, we are only allowed one shot even though we're paying for two hours."

It is precisely this kind of challenge that stimulates Kokkarakko. He went inside and began talking to the woman and stroking her. "This is what I've been wanting to do for a long time," he said as he masturbated. He went and took a shower and returned for an extended session of foreplay. After an hour and a half, he began to have sex with the woman. As he had masturbated earlier, it took him longer than usual to climax. In this manner, our *harami* managed to make his two hours with the prostitute worth his while. The whore was furious when he finished. "I've never seen anyone like you, you fucker!"

Kokkarakko had a rubber snake that could easily pass for the real thing.

One of his friends from his hometown would make a beeline to the toilet whenever he visited him. Kokkarakko was thoroughly fed up of this and wanted to put a stop to it. When he heard his friend would be arriving at five in the morning, he left the snake in the toilet. His friend, as usual, rushed to the toilet as soon as he arrived but came running out immediately like he'd seen a ghost. He called the police station and shouted nothing but, "Police! Police!"

"He forgot he had to call the *fire* station and he called the cops!" Kokkarakko said, laughing like a hyena.

He was once stopped on the highway by the cops who were inspecting vehicles for bombs. The cop asked him to get out of the car and when he put his head inside the window to check for bombs, he saw the snake. Scared out of his wits, he withdrew his head immediately, hitting it against the frame of the window. When he realized it was only a rubber snake, he sternly admonished Kokkarakko for endangering public peace.

Kokkarakko calls cars coffins.

"I've taken the coffin out. It's ready. Shall we go?"

"Why take an auto? We can just go in the coffin."

Even his wife, a simpleminded woman, was not spared from his eccentricities. One day, Kokkarakko and I were in Coorg, playing golf. It was the first time he was playing the game. Golf, I must say, is the most difficult sport I've ever played. Swinging the club five times is more exhausting than running a 1000 m race. The club doesn't hit the ball – it only mows the grass.

People were sniggering at Kokkarakko who was mowing grass for about an hour. As he was thus engaged, he had a call from his wife. He tells her that he is playing golf, whereupon the woman asks him, "Are you playing well?" This was how naïve she was.

Anjali asked me about Kokkarakko's wife one day.

"She's a dumb one, isn't she?"

"How would you know?"

"*Haramis* like Kokkarakko tend to choose such women."

When I told this to Kokkarakko, he said, "Even if they are clever, *haramis* take them and turn them into dummies. When they are dumb, they don't have problems with our *harami* lifestyles and everyone is happy."

Imagine how a woman like that would have been frightened by his talk about coffins!

"Look at it this way," he told her. "If we travel by car, there could be an accident and we could die. But if we travel in a coffin, will there be an accident? Have you ever heard of a coffin that has been in an accident?"

One day, he called her from the airport.

She asked him, "Has that thing – whatever you call it – left?"

"You mean the flying coffin? Not yet."

Need I say more?

Once, Kokkarakko wrote something nice about me on Facebook. This is what he wrote about my death at the end of the post:

When Udhaya dies, he will have no bank balance. Provided that he has no quarrel with any of his longtime readers, they will dispose of the body. If not, some new readers will come together and dispose of the corpse. If Udhaya knew he were to die tomorrow, he would post something like this on his blog:

> *I bid goodbye.*

> *As I am going to die at four p.m. tomorrow, I request my friends who wish to meet me for the last time to come at three thirty. It's been my long-term wish to go on my last journey in a luxury coffin and I request one of my readers to incur the costs and build me a grandiose coffin. There's no time for me to order and customize it and I'm not giving anyone my account number for the cash transfer.*

> *Readers who come for the funeral may pool money to buy Rémy Martin.*

> *One person can buy some real good chicken, fry it and bring it along for the celebration.*

Usually, nobody takes good pictures – any pictures – of me when I attend festivals and events. Readers with good cameras who are planning to attend this grand celebration may take lots of pictures of ME alone. Take a nice picture of my smiling corpse, because, even after I die, I wish to live in the hearts of women.

When I read these paragraphs of *my* last message, my eyes misted and I let people know I was moved in the comments.

Immediately, a friend asked me, "Udhaya, did you read the post from bottom to top? Is that why you're crying?"

This was my reply to him: "Dear brother, I would like to inform you that I know the *Mrutyanjaya mantra.* Here it is: 'O fragrant and three-eyed god who protects this world, I bow before you; just as the ripened cucumber parts from its stem, I attain completion from death.'"

One who knows the *Mrutyanjaya mantra* will not fear death. And only in sex do I go from bottom to top, not in other matters.

Methinks there is a connection between sex-heavy writing and Thanjavur. This kind of writing, like a tree, fruit or soil type, is particular to the region. Are you aware that the dozen writers who brazenly write about sex all hail from Thanjavur? *Pasitha Maanidam,* the only Tamil novel featuring homosexuality, was written by Karicharan Kunju from Kumbakonam. T. Janakiraman, all of whose novels revolve around sex, is also from the same place. So are K. P. Rajagopalan and Thanjai Prakash.

In sex, people usually proceed from top to bottom.

Okay, that sounded vague and boring and meaningless. Consider this sequence instead:

Top meets bottom

Top meets top

Bottom meets bottom

Bottom meets top.

Understood? No? Fine, I'll explain.

Top = mouth

Bottom = genitals

Do you get it now? No? Ugh!

Listen carefully now.

When Anjali and I begin to have sex, my mouth and her vagina meet – top meets bottom. After a lot of foreplay, my mouth will suddenly seek hers – top meets top. Then, bottom meets bottom. (I'm sure you understand what *that* means.) When I'm about to climax, I withdraw my penis and shove it into her mouth – bottom meets top. All this is possible only when the two lovers are of the same mind and when they have the same degree of passion. Try doing this with a woman who comes home tired after work. All you'll end up getting is a couple of blows and a couple of kicks.

CHAPTER TWENTY ONE

Lesbian Mothers and Whorish Wives

As I neared the end of my novel, I decided to pay Siva one more visit. On reaching my home town, I met Kamal, Siva's brother and enquired about him. He said, "Siva looks like and talks like a wise man, but you have no idea how we suffer because, in truth, he is a madman. Our neighbors complain that he throws stones at their houses. When I asked him why, he said, 'They are all whores. They are spying on me. Those bitches are trying to seduce me.' He says all kinds of nasty things. I think he went crazy because some woman jilted him. He has scribbled all over the walls of his room that this woman is a whore and that woman is a whore and so on. When I requested him to seek treatment, he beat me. He even beat our mother once. I can take you to his place, but you'll have to enter yourself and at your own risk. He will fly into a rage if he sees me. The best thing would be for you to just look at him without his knowledge. Come and meet me at three in the afternoon."

Siva lived in an outhouse that adjoined the main

house. The entrance that opened into the street had been permanently locked. Kamal took me to the back door and told me to peek through the hole in it.

What he'd told me was true. Siva had scrawled all sorts of obscenities on the wall abusing women. The word "whore" occurred often. I no longer doubted that Siva was a psycho. He lay asleep on an easy chair. It was while I was reading the rantings of his diseased mind that I experienced one of the biggest shocks of my life.

Siva and I had had a misunderstanding once due to which we'd fallen out with each other and lost touch for a long time. I was working in Delhi and had gone home during the holidays. Siva was jobless and in dire straits. He kept saying he'd be leaving for the Gulf shortly.

Out of the blue, he said, "Udhaya, you won't get angry if I ask you something, will you?"

"No," I assured him.

"People here are saying your mother is a lesbian," he said. "Have you confronted her about this?"

We did not contact each other after this incident.

Another time, when Nalini and I were living in Pondicherry, he came to visit and started telling me about his privation in Qatar. After he left, Nalini said, "Your friend must never come near our house again." When I asked her why, she said, "When I gave him a mug of coffee, he squeezed my hand deliberately."

Then I remembered the question he'd asked me before he left: "Your wife is a nice sort, isn't she?" There was a hint of wickedness in his tone. I didn't reply. After that, I decided to have nothing more to do with him.

My eyes lingered on the words scribbled on the walls in a clear hand:

Udhaya's mother is a lesbian.

Udhaya's wife is a whore.

CHAPTER TWENTY TWO

A Climax

"What is it, dearest Anjali? Did my writing sound false? Did it make you sound like a liar? Hear me, not even God would be able to find a grain of dishonesty in you! My only concern is that your talk only revolves around your friends and acquaintances."

The day I left Paris for Chennai, Anjali was unable to see me off at the airport as it would have interfered with her plans with Suresh. We did, however, have a little rendezvous at a park. That was when and where I made known and clear my concern for her.

"Let me not argue with you, Anjali. I am a changed person."

"I've lost count of how many times you've said that to me, Udhaya, but I have done well to remember that you never deliver what you promise."

"No, Anjali! I do want to change. I had a friend once who smoked like a chimney. The day he decided he wanted to quit, he reiterated his decision like a mantra one-hundred times daily. He vehemently announced his decision to kick the habit and ended up making good his resolution. So, maybe if I keep telling you with confidence that I am a changed person, I will be a changed person someday."

"Let's see," she said dryly. "In your novel, you did not spare even Lord Ayyappan, but you let Kokkarakko go scot-free. Why? Because he's your friend?"

"His existence is punishment enough to him. Anjali's voice was a billion in unison. Anjali is every Indian woman. Didn't I tell you that, after Nalini and I had separated, I raised my daughter single-handedly for two years? I met her recently. It had been fifteen long years. She narrated to me, at length, all the circumstances that befell her and inspired the plot of my next novel."

"You never once told me what she said."

I sighed.

"What she told me sounded exactly like your story, only it unfolded in a different place. Like you, she recited a familiar litany of names – the names of my friends, writers and readers of world literature – and with a shadow of hate darkening her face, said she wanted nothing but to bash them unconscious. I was shocked to hear this, but even more so when she confided to me that most of them had taken sexual advantage of her. When I asked her why she hadn't told me this earlier, she said, 'I neither knew nor understood what was happening to me then. I do now.'

"Now Anjali, what will wordy Kokkarakko have to say? Would he call my next novel, my daughter's story of sexual abuse, pulp fiction? Pray tell, is there another way to tell stories like hers and yours?"

Indeed, I feel I share points of similarity with Dostoevsky's nameless narrator in *White Nights*. We both live solitary, womanless lives. He meets Nostenga, a woman pining for her lover. Their feelings for each other intensify as the former writes and the latter narrates her story. He falls for her, but her lover returns and she leaves with him.

"Doesn't Kokkarakko know that Anjali has no other lover? When I read his letter, I remembered a proverb that was taken quite seriously in the village: *Ozhathavan veedu paazh.* – That house shall fall apart whither lovers do not fuck.

"Oh Udhaya, let's save the literary discussions for phone conversation, but tell me," she said, "what punishment does the character Udhaya deserve?"

I was sitting on the bench and she was standing with her arms crossed over her chest. An impish smile spread across her face. When I leaned in (expecting a kiss), she yanked down her blouse, baring her breasts to me.

I teased her from the airport.

'I never expected you to do something like that in public. Rascal. Are you a Tamil woman? Shame on you...'

'You are the one who spoilt me. Shame on YOU...

'By the way, I've been meaning to ask. Did you read Kokkarakko's letter? I'm assuming he had a lot of niceties to convey. Are you going to reply to him?"

"I did read his letter and can very well reply to his every sentence in paragraphs, but I am not going to. Why should

I waste ink over that male chauvinist pig? You needn't worry about him either. And do just one more thing for me."

"What?"

"Come and kiss me!"

CHAPTER TWENTY THREE

Another Climax

From Kokkarakko to the Reader.

Anjali calls me a male chauvinist pig, but there is no such thing as a male chauvinist or a female victim any longer. Power-play is ancient history.

Today, when a woman demands her rights, the whole world hears. But why, oh why, must her tales of woe, theatrics and tears come to her assistance when she does? Why is she so attached to her past like a child to the umbilical cord? Why does she drag the weight of it around like a ball chained to her ankle? Why does she use her misfortunes as tokens of sympathy?

I have nothing personal against Anjali and I don't think she is a bad person. However, I do know that she is a very stupid person, and her stupidity is often mistranslated as innocence. It is not. If you consider Anjali's life and her account of it, your estimate of her stupidity will commensurate with mine. According to her, there is no one in her life with a grain of goodness – her mother is a bad woman; her father is a bad man; the other guy, what's

his name, is a scoundrel – a bad man; the nurses are cruel
– bad people; Suresh is indifferent – hence he is bad! Even
the nature is cruel to her. Think of the desert storm in
Arizona! Thank God! She wasn't assigned many pages in
this novel; she would scorn everything under the sun!

For Anjali, Udhaya's badness – yes, Dear Reader, she
spares no one – pales in comparison with all and everything
else that is bad in the world. It wasn't long before her good
graces for him became scarce. After all, Udhaya did become
a bad person in the climax of the novel, prompting Anjali
to say that *he never delivered what he promised!* But by what
whimsical standards does Anjali judge? The incapability to
deal with people and a jaundiced view of the world are the
telling signs of mental instability. "Every person in my life
has been bad, every circumstance in my life has been sad!"
Boo-hoo! Anjali, take a look around you where so many
men are starving. Your Udhaya is among them – lying
with hunger-pangs gnawing at the walls of his stomach in
the park, feeding on grass like a cow, while next to him, a
mangy dog is eating sun-dried human feces. Do you know
of any woman who has starved in like manner?

Did you ever stop to think of all the men who are dying
of loneliness? Men who are dying without ever having
known a woman's companionship, the feel of her skin,
the pleasure of her body? I suggest you visit the lodges in
Triplicane where you might get a better idea of what I'm
talking about, but on second thought, don't, because you
will only come back with reports of how bad they are. Can
you show me one woman in the selfsame situation as these

men? If you ask me, I think the man is the slave of the woman. Don't believe me? Go to a booze party and observe how the men tremble at the mere thought of their wives who might be waiting for them on the porch swing with divorce papers.

I am of the unshakeable opinion that women, the world over, are the same. They always want or need something, and men are their favorite human vending machines.

There was once a woman who was transferred to my office from elsewhere. I was her boss and she was fearless in her advances. She would wedge herself between me and any other woman who stood beside me, between my chair and my desk. For two days, I held off. On the third day, I pulled her onto my lap and we smooched around for a bit.

The next day, the brazen thing plopped down on my lap herself and asked me whether I was married.

"Yes," I replied.

"Then why did you kiss me?" she asked. "The man who marries me would want to be my first kiss, wouldn't he?"

That morning, I made some things clear.

"Listen, come tomorrow, and we will conduct our business *outside* the office," I said. "Am I making myself clear?"

She did come to me during the evening sometime later that week when I was busy working. She kissed me on the cheek, said bye and she was gone.

The next day, I called her company with instructions to never send her to our firm again.

The bitch really had some brazen guts to play me dirty the way she did.

How about my encounter with Caroline, the Frenchwoman?

I belong to a certain club whose members are not supposed to stay in hotels when they go abroad. Instead, they should stay at the house of another club member. Similarly, if a member from abroad visits our city, he should stay at local club member's house. The club members also organize get-togethers for their amusement. Recently, we all met at a resort in Mahabalipuram. Among those in attendance, there was a woman called Caroline, a French native based in Chennai, a real mantrap, around twenty-six. Midnight found the pair of us sitting in the beach-sand, an empty bottle of Rémy Martin between us. She picked up her guitar and launched into a French song, not that the situation demanded it. Once she was done, she said, her words slightly slurred "I want another drink!" God knows where and how she expected me to find her a drink. I ended up having to surf the streets with her. In the end, we found a shop that had only Old Monk and some lousy varieties of brandy in stock. After much deliberation, she settled for an Old Monk. It didn't take as much deliberation to solve the problem of having no glass. Caroline just picked up a discarded plastic mug that was rejected to the side of the road, poured the rum into it and drank the rum raw, like it was the sophisticated thing to do. What she did next eclipsed what she had just done. She hitched up her skirt and squatted by the roadside like a child about to defecate and gulped the rum down like it was water in a desert. The woman who, not long ago, had the aura of a goddess now looked plain disgusting and obscene. However, these significantly alarming instances of her shameless public behavior hardly aggravated me as much as what had happened the following morning.

We had to return to Chennai. I had a car. She didn't. I was wondering how she'd manage to get by with no working knowledge of the local language and a hangover. What could she do now?

"Kokkarakko, could you drop me off in Chennai?"

She asked me to take her all the way to Kodambakkam. Shit! I was stuck with her for longer than I would have liked.

Oh, a woman would expect a man to pick the stars out of the sky or pick whatever it is she drops out of a toilet just because she has two tits and a cunt. If they profess themselves to be staunch believers in equality, why do they exercise their cunning charm to render a man servile? I agreed to drop her off. We agreed to leave at nine. When she hadn't appeared at ten, I went to her room where she casually told me that she needed an hour for her toilet. Once she was done, she would have to find her own ride into town as I had left. I am a man of principle. Unlike Udhaya, I am not wrapped around the finger of a "stunningly beautiful Frenchwoman."

The world has women of Caroline's breed in full supply. Last year, Udhaya and I were at Kaladi, a town in Kerala, to undergo *panchakarma* treatment. During our fortnight stay, we met a couple of women from the room that faced ours – Julie, a Frenchwoman, and Asya, a Russian. As Julie was rather unattractive, Udhaya ignored her. Had she been a ravisher, he would have launched into a diatribe on Georges Perec, Georges Bataille and Michel Foucault, and when he finished, he would leave one wondering whether he had been personally acquainted with all three. But since Asya was the better looking of the two, Udhaya approached her and started expounding on Tchaikovsky, Tarkovsky Dostoevsky and other 'esky's.

I disliked both women. Julie, especially, was an eccentric number. She stank worse than a roadside bum, making me wonder if the French had an aversion to cleanliness. Udhaya, in his books, word-painted France like paradise, but Julie and Caroline made me think otherwise.

Julie behaved like a lunatic. *Panchakarma* incorporates *vasthi* – an enema – to purge the body of toxins. Julie asked me if I'd had mine. I answered in the positive. The little imbecile doubled over, sticking her ass in the air and exposing her anus to me.

"I had a *vasthi* too," she said.

Now what if I tell you she never did this in private? How about I throw in the fact that the ill-behaved stinkball was a schoolteacher in Paris?

One day, she put in a request for a favor. She had close to four thousand songs on her laptop which she wanted me to categorize by genre and put in separate folders. The job would have surely taken me five hours to finish and Julie had no remorse whatsoever about asking a man do her bidding. Just because she was a woman she expected a man to do her that favor.

Asya was none the better. She intended to go to the city to buy some clothes. For this, she requested Udhaya's company, but he passed, saying he had much to write. I ended up going with her only to realize that I was a fool again. She bargained for close to an hour to save on ten bucks, sipping dishwater tea like it was vodka. It took her another two hours to buy a nightgown.

Castigating myself for my foolishness, I went to my room.

The next day, Asya announced that the nightgown was two sizes too small. "Let's go back to the shop!" she said, like it was going to be a joyride.

No man with his senses about him would indulge her.

I call this unacknowledged slavery. If you, woman, could stop treating your male counterpart like a dog on a leash, I would receive your kind more warmly than I do.

Kokkarakko

P.S.: Udhaya, deceiver that he is, lied to me that the novel was over. Sometime later, he called me to say that he had written another thirty pages which, quite unsurprisingly, featured him doing something that was equal parts crooked and heroic to rescue Anjali. He asked me to read it and call him upon finishing so that we could have a discussion. And this time, unlike before, he sent me a read-only file. But cunning has to be met with cunning, so I took him unawares and shot those thirty pages to the publisher with a note to make allowance for them in the novel. And that, Dear Reader, is what you are now reading.

PART – II

"Gaunt, wasted, lame, deaf, sunken-eyed, tail-less, worm-affected wounds, body wet with pus and insects, starving, feeble voice. A dog suffering from all this wretchedness will still chase a bitch."

--- *Bhartrhari, Sringara atakam, 78*

One day, Anjali was pottering about in the room, her breasts sheathed from view by the scarlet satin of her nightgown. I gathered the little temptress in my arms and laid her on the bed. With my middle finger, I sensuously caressed the hardened bumps of her nipples under the satin. My finger smoothly traveled the contours of her bosom, like it was being guided across an Ouija board by a spirit.

"What is your finger doing?" Anjali asked, derailing my train of thought. "Don't you *ever* get tired of sex, Udhaya? This is the third time we're doing it today."

"Unlike other women, every inch of your skin is erogenous. That's why I never tire of having sex with you."

"How many women have you known?"

"A couple, but you are the last," I said glibly. That silenced her, thankfully. Once Anjali showed me a French film in which she had acted as a Srilankan Tamil. The film was good and Anjali too had acted well. She got lot of offers to act after that movie but I didn't want her to act. What if she had to do a prostitute character in one of the films? So I just told her that modelling and acting would not suit her. She obliged and quit acting out of deference to my wishes.

Now suspend your moral judgments right there! It would please you to know that this seemingly old-fashioned fart does not interfere in Anjali's choice of clothing. I let the woman wear her beloved skimpy daisy-dukes and mini-skirts that leave little to the imagination. However, I did lay down but one condition: she is free to wear as little as she pleases only when she is with me.

"When do I ever get to wear any clothes when I'm with you?" she teased.

"The condition stands only when you go out with me," I clarified.

"All I ever do when I go out with you is lie on my back staring at the ceiling."

There is truth in what she says. She is indeed compelled to stare at the ceiling for a good chunk of time as we are always in bed, I on top of her. Even when we went out, our sexual appetites would urge us to return to the room as soon as possible.

"Alright, if you want a different view, we could always try different positions. Malayali women are reckoned to be experts in what they call 'peeling coconuts.' Want to experiment?"

"I'd rather you mount me while I gaze at the ceiling."

I told Anjali one day, "Sweet thing, should the day you despise me come, please don't go to the media and tell them that I forced you to perform unnatural sex acts." Women resort to this when they want to take revenge on horny godmen. "I just assumed you were tired of me fucking you missionary-style. Shouldn't we try something new, something unconventional, for a change?"

"Of course."

"If you want to have mindblowing sex like you've never had before, promise me one thing – that you'll do whatever I tell you to."

"Oh, you know I'm your slave in bed, Udhaya."

"Good. Come here. Have you watched Catherine Breillat's *Romance*?"

"Have not."

"Are you familiar with the Marquis de Sade?"

"Only with the name."

I gagged her, blindfolded her and bound her hands. After some intense foreplay, I fucked her hard, doggy style. I felt the lust rise like furious waves from within my body and crash within her softness. Her body tossed like a catamaran in a storm as she neared her climax. I untied her. She screamed in ecstasy when she came, clawing my chest and biting my shoulders.

Her attempt at pleasuring me in the same manner failed miserably. There was bondage – she tied me to a chair – but no sadism. Sex without the violent obscenities and the bestial frenzy with which I took her did not thrill me. I repeatedly called her a whore and a variety of smutty names in Tamil, English and Hindi: *kuchchukkari, kandaraoli, koodhikaari, pundakkari,* slut, cunt, bitch, and so on.

We began to film our frolic in bed with a video camera and when we watched our sessions, we understood why couples filmed their coitus. Watching our sexual union was by far one of the most exhilarating experiences we'd ever had. Anjali and I filmed our romps with abandon and resolved to destroy our cameras if ever they stood in need of servicing or repair.

"Our videos would make the best porn films in the world, wouldn't they?" I asked her once, after two hours of watching. "No doubt people will spit shame at us, and our families will be ruined, but a connoisseur of porn films might tell us to sign on the dotted line."

Anjali and I were having casual sex, my organ smoothly executing its task. In the middle of our sex, I picked up a book – Mario Vargas Llosa's The Bad Girl – and began reading from where I had left off. Reading a book during sex is definitely something you could try if you know how to multitask, but reading a book is even better when someone is giving you a blowjob. If you don't read books, you can always turn on the TV and make love to the sound of a news anchor's voice or a volley of bullets, or to the sight of a peasant milking a goat or a tennis player whacking balls. You can write a story or an article if you're a writer with a steady hand. You can have conference calls over the phone if you're a businessman (just don't forget that some questionable sounds might escape you when you climax).

In a Hollywood film, I saw a woman giving this thickset dude a blowjob while he was casually talking to a group of people like it was the most natural thing to do. An actor I know told me of a similar incident. He was looking to make his big break in the industry when a celebrated screenwriter asked to meet him in his Kodambakkam office. When he entered the screenwriter's room, he saw a young woman on her haunches under his table giving him a blowjob. The man continued writing like it wasn't that big a deal for a small-time actor to stand gaping in the doorway at a woman with her face between his legs. Bewildered, the actor turned around to leave when the scriptwriter called him back and adjusted his *veshti*. The woman catwalked out of the room like nothing had ever happened. When I heard this, I thought to myself, *I should have been a screenwriter instead of a litterateur.*

Anjali asked me one day, "How many times have we had sex in these two-and-a-half years? You come here and stay fifteen days in three months; we had it twice a day so that means…"

"Add one to your final answer," I said, carrying her to the bed before she could finish her calculation.

Her body felt like desert sand, burning with the heat of desire, and yet so cool, as if springs of mountain water flowed beneath her skin. *Can both fire and water coexist within the same body?* I ask myself every time I make love to her.

The moment I enter the house, she would open both her arms like a bird spreading its wings before it takes flight. I would gather her into a tight, sensual embrace, my hands squeezing her ass, and my fingers slipping under her panty-line. More often than not, she would be dressed like she was on vacation in a tropical beach. I would slip my hand under her panties and caress her backside as we kissed passionately, our tongues like excited snakes.

The game of lust was a game with no end. The moment I set eyes on her, my whole body would metamorphose into one giant phallus. Lord Indra, the eternal philanderer of the Hindu pantheon, was once cursed and his whole body became covered with vaginas. In a similar way, Anjali's body also turned into one giant vagina, sucking me into its aperture like a black hole. It was our good fortune that the pair of us possessed good sexual appetites and bodies that were capable of prolonged sex. On occasion, Anjali's cave would become dry, so we stocked up on castor oil.

Though both of us were addicted to sex, the intoxication I felt was arguably different than hers. Everything signified sex to me – rockets, skyscrapers, keyholes, guns, ice-creams, fingers, trees, hot dogs, mechanical pencils, mobile phones, windows, doors, lifts, candles, brinjals, pillars, trains, buses, cars – any vehicle for that matter –, knives, pendulums, books – they were all sexual symbols to me. It was the same with language. Give me a word and I would turn it into smut.

Once, when Anjali went out, she warned me, saying, "There's a hole in the ground, Udhaya. Careful now!" I cast her a smug look. She got my meaning.

There used to be a time when she would never have

understood; it was I who transformed her. And sometimes, the disciple does become better than the guru.

When I bought her a chiffon *saree*, she asked me, one eyebrow arched, "When is the inauguration ceremony?"

I never caught on, so I said, "Wear it tomorrow."

"That's not what I meant!" she said, a smirk playing on her face. "What I meant was, when are you going to unwrap me from this *saree*?"

My arousal skyrocketed and I suggested we do it as soon as we returned home. I made her wear the *saree* with no blouse or bra and inaugurated it.

Anjali told me that she used to avoid her sexual urges by overbooking herself with lot of work till she got exhausted at the end of the day, before she met me. That was out of the question once I entered her life, but I was still curious to know what she did for the two and half months in a quarter when I was India. When I asked her, she told me, "The thought of you envelopes me in peace. No, wait, I'm not exactly peaceful because the wait thrills me, fills me with excitement. When your thoughts surround me, my body becomes irrelevant. It does not torture me in your absence, but the moment I see you, the feelings I have bottled up overflow like a forest spring."

Like an infant dependent on the lactating breast of its mother for nourishment, I was dependent on Anjali's body for sex. It was difficult for me to suppress my sexual urges at first, but controlled myself thinking of that fifteen days. Desire would start burning me from the inside those two months. Once Anjali's sex extinguishes that fire, all is normal again. To feed the fire in Anjali's absence, I could easily go to a prostitute, but I couldn't, not even in Thailand. My hand came to my sex-starved organ's rescue when Anjali was not around.

We indulged in sex during her period although we did contemplate avoiding it. But how long would kissing and embracing satisfy us? When intercourse itself crossed one hour and finished in the middle of the next, where was the time for foreplay? Most of the time, we would fall upon each other like famished beasts. A few cuddles and caresses would end in intercourse. When I withdrew my organ from her slot, it looked like a blood-soaked knife that had been thrust into a body.

Whenever I masturbate, I am grateful for the advancement of technology. During my boyhood, the only risqué books I got to read were soft porn magazines with erotic names such as "Youthful Escapades" and "Honeyed Moments" among others. The stories in these magazines were pathetic, except for the hardcore porn "*Sarojadevi* stories" written by hundreds of porn writers plying their craft anonymously. The stories were replete with spelling errors, courtesy of the printers' devils, and they were printed on substandard paper owing to which the pictures appeared as black squares. You could barely make out the breasts, but between the stomach and the thighs, all that could be seen was pitch blackness. Despite these printing defects, the boys derived great entertainment from the books. One boy would say, "This is the thigh," and another would argue, "No, it's the tit," and other boys would mock them for being unable to tell thighs from tits. These books ended up following us into college as well.

When my friends squinted and fought over body parts in those magazines, I would theatrically exclaim, "How wonderful would it be if scientists could gift us a device that would play out our fantasies!" It was a sheer nuisance to thumb through those *Sarojadevi* magazines with their fuzzy pictures. When we were youth, the Internet hadn't been conceived yet. My only consolation is that it was discovered during my lifetime rather than a century later.

In my youth, actresses did not expose themselves as much as they do now. A woman's body was like the gods – mysterious. I was a schoolboy with ten girls in my class when puberty hit. When it came to girls, I never spoke a single word during my whole 11 years of schooling and got no closer than five feet. If a word passed between me and a girl, the other boys would advertise our love – which was unknown even to us – with much fanfare, news headlines on the walls accompanied by hearts pierced with Cupid-arrows. The toilet walls were already canvases for *Sarojadevi*'s budding writers and illustrators. The watchman took it upon himself to erase the nude studies of the teachers that popped up every now and then, but probably not before jerking off himself.

If little birds carried the news of a "love affair" beyond the walls, the girl's education came to an abrupt end. The sequestered life of a cloistered nun was imposed on her until her parents married her off.

It would be an understatement to say that the Internet changed the face of the world and the way of things in general. Mention must be made of the countless porn films that are generated with a few taps and clicks. It is also interesting to note that the popularity of incest, in all its permutations and combinations, has not waned. It was a fad among porn aficionados of the *Sarojadevi* era and remains so in the present era of XXXVideos and PornTube. Indians really score like Nadia Comaneci at the Olympics with their radical incest stories featuring mothers and sons, brothers and sisters, mothers and daughters, fathers and sons, and even family orgies. Strangely, stories of father-daughter incest were rare. Being a writer, I could infer that the contributors to the websites were men, by taking into consideration their style, tone and staple characters (they had no inhibitions when it came to writing about the mother, but they were dithery when it came to the daughter).

The Tamil stories alone amounted to a whopping one hundred thousand. I would select anything between ten and fifty of these stories to turn me on when I wanted to masturbate.

Sunny Leone and Belladona, in my opinion, were the two porn actresses whose performances outstripped those of their counterparts in the industry. It is also my personal opinion that I have much in common with Ron Jeremy – except the paunch. Despite that enormous beach-ball of a stomach and the fact that he's almost pushing sixty, how well he fucks!

I know this sounds like a pipe dream, but if I manage to drag myself through another couple of decades, how I would love to become another Ron Jeremy! Vladimir Nabokov was both a writer and a lepidopterist so why shouldn't I be a writer as well as an adult-film actor? What hinders me when Tamil films feature oldsters, with a legacy of two generations at least, running around trees with sixteen-year-old girls? But that's all an act. What you see in porn is the real deal. Your dick has to do the fucking for real. It's not all mock eye-rolling, toe curling, name screaming and lip-locking. In a movie, if you need to jump from the Burj Khalifa because it's cleverer than using an elevator, if you have to punch a hole in a glass door because knocking is too conventional, or if you have to lift a car off the ground because that's the kind of pointless shit your character enjoy doing, you can always hire a stuntman, whereas in porn, you have to fuck a woman who is lying before you with her thighs open – for real. You can't just rock back and forth with your ass to the camera and pretend the job is done. I think I'd make a pretty good porn actor, maybe even a better one than Ron Jeremy.

In the West, I would be known as an adult-film actor, but in India, I would be described as a sex-crazed old psycho. My picture would be splashed all over the place and my reputation would be torn to shreds.

I also admit to having a fetish for watching films of groping in public. Something else that impresses me on a whole other level is Japan's free-fucking competition that draws thousands of participants. And what about

India? Duh, don't even ask. Just like Indian roads, Indian politicians and Indian life, the Indian porn industry too is very substandard.

Sometimes I wonder: what if Salman Rushdie had become a porn actor?

Good heavens! I forgot all about Anjali! The girl is going to chop off my dick.

But Anjali can bear with my absence just a little longer. I fancy a picture with my erect little soldier.

* * *

Our domestic help Kaveri's husband, an auto driver, would come home drunk daily and beat her up. One day he came to my house and hammered on the gate. "Send that wretch out!" he shouted. It was only eight in the morning and he was liquored up. Perundevi cajoled him somehow and sent him on his way – and what cajoling! "I'll fall at your feet, *thambi*. Don't hurt Kaveri now." Her words sobered him up slightly and he went along. He never came knocking again at our house but we could see from Kaveri's swollen and bruised face that the abuse hadn't stopped. Kaveri was only one among the dozen maids who had worked with us. The astonishing thing is that every maid who worked with us suffered domestic abuse. Their husband would beat them up so severely that they'd come to work all bruised and bloody. Poor women endure brutality from their husbands silently without lifting a finger in protest, let alone complaining to the police. "Shall I make a complaint to the police?" I asked Kaveri once. "Please don't do that, *saar*!" she said and began to weep.

She often used to say, "I want him to die soon. Only then can I live in peace with my children." The gods half-heard her prayers as one day, her husband began to vomit blood, but even then, he didn't stop drinking. Kaveri would often wonder how he managed to stay alive after losing so much blood.

Eventually, he stopped drinking, overcome by the fear of death. Six months later, he ran into Perundevi and told her about his having turned over a new leaf and she repeated this to me with great amazement. She could have stopped at that, but she went on to say, "For a moment, I thought of how nice it would be if, like Kaveri's husband, you too could stop drinking."

"What? How can you compare me to that wife-battering auto driver? He drinks cheap hooch whereas I drink Rémy Martin. We can*not* be the same!"

"Hooch or Rémy Martin, liquor is liquor," she said. "And your drinking disturbs me."

I quoted Thirumoolar to her. "In nurturing my body, I nurtured my life. If the doctor autopsies my body, Perundevi, he will see that I am not sixty, but twenty-five."

One day, I was lying spread-eagled on the bed after a very satisfying sexual joust with Anjali. She'd gone to have a drink of water. When she came back, she sat on the floor and took my foot in her mouth. She bit my toes one by one and this sensation reminded me of the nibbling of the fish in the pond where I used to bathe as a boy. My fish-eyed beauty continued to nibble at my body, progressing upwards from my toes. My feet are as soft as rose petals or the lips of a child. How I wished for a woman who would caress them and delight in the way they feel! After Anjali's delightful nibbling, I didn't have to worry about dying without my wish being fulfilled.

I have lamented enough about *idlis* already, but bear with me a little longer.

In all parts of India (except Vellore), the *idlis* you get are very flaky and it saddens me to see them. These flaky things are being eaten by the poor folks of Karnataka, Kerala and Delhi. In the good old days, *idli* batter was ground manually with a grinding stone, but with the advent of the grinder and the clarion call for women's freedom, the grinding stone vanished into the mists of time. A few years later, when women's freedom expanded, even the grinders disappeared and readymade batter became available in shops. If you make *idlis* with this batter, you will either get a mound of mush or a white rock.

My mother gave birth to six children and not once did she go to a hospital for her delivery. Only my grandmother was with her to assist her in labor and there was no doctor, nurse or midwife in attendance. Also, my mother didn't have the luxury of taking even a quarter-year of rest after each of her births. In those days, six children wasn't much as there were women who'd had as many as twelve, and they were surprisingly healthy and fit even after so many pregnancies and deliveries. The *uluthankali* was what gave them their strength. This was a porridge made with *urad dal*, sesame oil and raw rice.

These days, thirty-year-old women are weak or

overweight. Their lifestyles don't allow them to breathe outdoor air or slip in a half-hour of exercise. Most women cannot deliver normally and have to have C-sections.

When I visited a brothel in Pattaya, I was amazed to see that it looked like a corporate office. (In fact, all brothels are like this.) A bus stopped at the brothel and around fifty men, all of them Tamils – middle-aged, paunchy and attired in checked shirts – alighted and entered the building.

The sex worker who was talking to me knew only fifty words of English, but she managed to communicate with them aided by some facial expressions and hand gestures.

"Do you know why your men come here in busloads? It's because Indian women are so fat. Why are they so fat? How do you do 'boom-boom' to them?"

"How do you know that they're fat?"

"I see them on TV."

She made a barrel-wide circle with her arms.

Most Indian women are like Thanjavur nodding dolls. I too wonder how the Indian man can have sex with a nodding doll. He cannot. Not for long. That's why, every weekend, the Chennai-Bangkok flights are all booked. You only need 20K for a five-day Bangkok-Pattaya tour. Accommodation and food are free. You only need to pay for "boom-boom." But of course, they won't tell you that in any advertisement.

Well, let's leave women's lib for now and get back to *idli*. Coming back to the *idli*, I would say that it is the most wonderful delicacy in the entire world though Tamils don't seem to think so. Their food preferences have changed drastically – they prefer pizza. Every urban youngster craves pizza. You will find pizza shops on every third street in India, you will find pizzas being made in Indian homes, but will you find *idlis* in Italy? I am not talking about South Indian restaurants owned and operated by Tamils in Italy. Does the Italian make *idlis*? Does he eat them? Here in Chennai, pizza shops are a dime a dozen and they are run by Tamils, not Italians. *Idlis* are being replaced with pizza due to the foreign-culture-worshipping mentality of the Tamils. (If you start associating the Italian pizza with politics, I am not responsible for it.)

Today, the *idli* has lost its original nature and has assumed a phony avatar. In another ten years, the true *idli* will be long forgotten and nobody will complain. Everybody will forget the *idli* and move on. For now, they will be content to spoon mush into their mouths in blissful ignorance.

* * *

Anjali and I made love in every room in the house. One day, we made love on the couch in the living room; the next day, we were on the dining table; we did it once on an armless chair and a few times in the kitchen.

Nowadays I don't wear jeans; I've switched to linen trousers. This is because jeans are unsuitable for quick and illicit sex. If you have sex without removing your jeans, the metal zipper will poke and the hard metal buttons will irritate your sensitive stuff. Sometimes, Anjali and I would be having a quickie, and if someone turned up suddenly, it would be difficult to zip up quickly, whereas, when you're in linen trousers, you can zip up in the blink of an eye. Linen trousers are easier to pull down to your knees. Linen trousers are the greatest things in the world if you have a thing for groping.

I witnessed groping for the first time on the buses – 220 and 240 – that took me from the Central Secretariat to my office at Civil Lines in Delhi. Gropers used to have a field day on the bus with the hordes of female students traveling to Delhi University and Indraprastha College. However much I wanted to join these gropers, I didn't have the guts. In Tamil Nadu, where two hundred people squeeze themselves into a bus for fifty, I couldn't even think of moving my foot an inch or getting my nose out of someone's armpit, let alone grope. But astonishingly, even in that ridiculous crowd, there are fellows who manage to rub their dicks against women's bottoms.

The higher the price of liquor, the finer it is. Similarly, the more expensive your jocks, the finer they are. Calvin Klein jocks are soft and gentle on the dick and the balls. When Anjali was busy cooking, I'd stand behind her and rub myself against her sexy hips. I cannot describe the ecstasy those moments gave me. I'd trap her, placing both my hands on either side of her on the kitchen counter, and I'd make sure she turned off the stove first to avoid any mishaps. Anjali is the perfect example of a *samudrika lakshanam*. She is wasp-waisted with hips to make men swoon; when she walks, those graceful hips sway from side to side. I would rub my dick against her hips for a while before turning her around and going down on my haunches to lick her cunt.

A nightgown is *the* garment for sex. The *saree* is good too, but *churidars* and *salwars* are not suitable. Once, we went to Chennai's Alliance Française to watch a movie. We slipped away in the middle and went into a room on the same floor as the hall that not many people are aware of. The door was ajar. I surmised it was a small powder room. I pulled Anjali in and covered her tits with my mouth. What followed was some unforgettable sex during which I lost all sense of place and time. Truly, there is nothing that beats the thrill of illicit sex, that too in a public place.

After reading the novel to this point, Anjali said, "No more sex, please!" So I told her of a news article that appeared in a Tamil daily. There was a government officer in Tirunelveli who had a wife and a son. A young woman approached him for a certificate and the officer ended up getting into an affair with her, but was unable to keep it a secret. When his wife came to know of it, she rebuked him, but he told her that it was nothing but a nasty rumor being circulated by his enemies. One day, he took his son to his mistress' house. The woman gave him some sweets and when the boy returned home, he told his mother what had happened. The officer left for the woman's house the next morning, telling his wife he was heading off to work. His wife waited for him to leave and then told her son to take her to the mistress' house. The wife took two locks with her – one for the front door and another for the back door and locked the pair inside. When the officer realized that he'd been locked inside the house, he called the police and a *panchayat* was held.

"As this matter came to light, the newspapers published it. If a journalist picks up a story like this – where an officer goes and sleeps around with a woman who is not his wife – and writes about it, should he be branded as porn writer? I'll let you ponder that."

Once, after reading Mario Vargas Llosa's *The Feast of the Goat*, I visited the Dominican Republic and Puerto Rico. While in the Dominican Republic, I met a Tamil salsa dancer called Prakash in a salsa club. I was also delighted to hear that he'd read my books.

Prakash told me he'd learned salsa in the US, Venezuela and Italy. When I met him, he was teaching salsa in Zurich. He had come to the Dominican Republic for a holiday.

He'd learned the dance with great difficulty. He did not learn from a teacher, but from the troupe of dancers he lived with.

Though Latin music has been around for many years, it reached its height of popularity during the '30s. Salsa achieved prominence in the '60s.

Prakash told me two important things. The first was about the parallels between salsa and male-female relationships within the Latin American community. The second was about the difference between salsa and the Argentinean tango.

Latin America has a rigidly patriarchal society. Latin

dance reflects this attitude for it is the male dancer who leads throughout. A woman must wait for a man to invite her to dance, but the woman has the right to refuse the man who invites her, but this hurts his ego which is why he becomes insistent and tries to persuade her. Sometimes, this leads to scraps.

Latin American life is pretty much the same. A man tries to sweet talk a woman into submission. He has but one aim in life – to possess her completely – and he will stop at nothing until he gets what he wants. Once the conquest is made, he finds another target and the first woman has the arduous task of keeping him from straying. These kinds of relationships are short-lived and if they last, they are rarely ever happy. Salsa conveys this reality beautifully.

Prakash opined that there was no better place than a salsa club to observe people and recommended a wonderful Cuban film on this theme – *Hasta Certo Punto* (*Upto a Certain Point.*) A writer doing research on Havana's patriarchal society falls in love with a Cuban woman and gets married to her. But he is not able to lead a happy life with her as he finds it difficult to free himself from the patriarchal attitudes and mindset that he had inherited. Finally, they separate.

When a male salsa dancer foregrounds himself he is, in effect, asking his female partner to follow him and the woman also submits to it- this is the tradition of salsa.

In the tango, unlike in salsa, the woman can take the lead. A tidbit of Argentinean history is necessary to understand how this came to be so.

Argentinean tango originated in the port city of Buenos Aires with the port workers and whores who danced to the music of the bandoneon. The music that emerges from bandoneon is very electric and punchy. The port workers who slogged all day found themselves lonely in the evenings after work, so they sought the company of whores. The whores came to the port for want and need of money, but they had the freedom to choose their clients and were under no compulsion to accept the offer of a man to dance.

After that meeting, I lost touch with Prakash. I e-mailed him, but my communications went unanswered. Now when I think back on our meeting, it seems like a dream to me.

I've had several discussions with Anjali about all that Prakash told me. Both of us spoke of and argued over the salsa and tango artistes he'd spoken about. Ten years ago, I took down all these notes about salsa and tango music and artistes in a drunken stupor. Never did I think that I'd be able to enjoy discussing all of it with the woman I loved.

Our first conversation on the subject was something like this:

"Do you know about the salsa dog and tango cat, Anjali?"

"Huh?"

"If you feed a dog, it will treat you like a master, but if you feed a cat, it will treat you like a slave. In salsa, the woman is the slave; in tango, she is the master. By the way, you like Salsa or Tango?"

"If I learn dance, surely my choice would be salsa. You can dance the salsa with any man, but the tango is more intimate."

"Do you want to know what I think?"

She raised an enquiring eyebrow. Kissing it, I said, "I think salsa is the dance that's more in tune with your nature."

"You rascal! I am not a dog, I am a cat!" she said. After a moment of silence, she added, I love the melancholy of the tango."

She put on the records of Ástor Piazzolla. Anjali turned the man's music into an experience for me. She told me this when we were talking over the phone one day: "If I hadn't listened to his bandoneon, I'd have gone mad. Maybe I'd have jumped off a cliff and we'd never have met." I was stunned. I knew that she was a slave to Piazzolla's music, but I never knew that it had such an important place in her life. Our relationship was three years old then.

"I've been wanting to tell you this for a long time. I finally got around to it today. Do you know I have a recurring deadly nightmare? In it, I'm caught in a whirlpool, unable to breathe. I'm stuck in a torrent. It almost feels like I'm being tossed and thrown about in a sea or an ocean and my breath is becoming water, and then I hear it – Ástor Piazzolla's bandoneon. On one occasion, it was *Adiós Nonino;* on another, it was *Libertango;* then, it was *Milonga del angel.* The song was different every time. Just when I think I'm going to suffocate and die, I hear the music of his bandoneon and at that exact moment, someone yanks me up by my hair. My mind is trembling as I'm saying this. I'm getting goosebumps. When I'm awake, I lie on the ground and listen to his music, the delicate notes growing intense and swelling to a crescendo. Anguish assaults my nerves like bolts of lightning and my mind spins like a hurricane. I drown in Piazzolla's music, like a little boat in a huge tempest. Somewhere, a thought germinates: Death would be such a mercy. How beautiful it would be to die like this. Even if I want to scream aloud, I can't, because my voice is stolen. I feel like screaming for someone to please stop the bandoneon."

"Do you still have these nightmares?" I asked her.

"Yes, Udhaya. I still have them. It's not just the dream. When I'm alone, peace seems to elude me. I feel a great turmoil seething within. Though I appear calm on the outside, I feel like a bubbling volcano on the verge of erupting on the inside. It's something like that French proverb: *Soyez comme les canards – en surface, ayez l'air calme et pose; sous la surface, pédalez comme un fou.* I can keep my demons at bay as long as I'm engrossed in some physical labor or out and about. If I'm alone at home, or engaged in mental work, anxiety overwhelms me.

"There is only one way to solve your problem."

"Uh huh?"

"Sex therapy!"

"Oh, I'm waiting!"

Over and over, Anjali and I listened to not just Piazzolla, but also all the other artistes Prakash had spoken about, until their music became part of the blood that flowed in our veins and mingled with our breath. Pierre Dulaine was another artiste who had affected her tremendously. I read up on Dulaine and his life. I learned about his partner, Yvonne Morceau, and the valuable contribution their partnership had made to the world of dance for the past thirty years. When Pierre lifted Yvonne, it was with the grace of the wind lifting a peacock feather. When he dances, even gravity yields to him. He turns into the wind and turns everything he touches into wind itself.

"Since you are waxing eloquent about dance, can I join salsa classes?" she asked.

"No, you can join *bharatnatayam*. I have no problems with that," I offered. But in truth, I was not too keen on that either.

"No, thank you," she said. "I remember what you told me about *bharatnatayam* once."

I'd told her that I rarely went to watch *bharatnatayam* performances as I tended to visualize the dancers naked.

"If I tell you what goes through my mind when the female dancer lifts one leg up to her hips, you'd thrash me."

"You devil, I've never met anyone like you."

"Why don't you try swimming?"

"There might be male coaches. Is that okay with you?"

"I will kill you. Go someplace where they have female coaches."

"What will happen if you become a swimming coach for women, Udhaya?"

"What do you think? I'll make them float face down in the water and grab their pussies."

"Ugh! Fuck off! Dirty sod!"

"But women like you love dirty sods like me, don't you? Come here and show me your pussy, you whore!"

And that was how we started our day.

But I must say that the woman didn't seem to have a problem with my possessiveness; on the contrary, I daresay she reveled in it. She too was possessive about me and this helped because I could ensure that she remained mine and mine alone. Her orders: I was not to look at any woman, and if we went to a restaurant, I had to sit facing a pillar. I was not to give my phone number to any woman either. (Before I met Anjali, I used to give my phone number to women who approached me for autographs. Only to women, not to men.) She also took over my e-mail and my Facebook account. All the love letters that I received were deleted immediately. I was forbidden from using the word "dear" to address a woman – I was supposed to say "hello" instead.

As she had subjected me to a number of rules, I made one more for her.

"From now on, no man is to ride pillion on your bike."

"Not even Suresh?"

"He is the exception."

"You bloody devil!"

And thus, our world grew smaller and smaller until it held only the two of us.

* * *

I did not allow Anjali to add me as her friend on Facebook because her habit of frequently uploading pictures there annoyed me.

"What's wrong with that, Udhaya?" she'd ask me.

"What's *wrong*? Don't you see how many men like your pictures? All of them will think of you when they masturbate at night."

"Ugh, you bad, bad boy!"

Nevertheless, I kept her away from my circle as I didn't like the idea of other men praising her beauty.

"If a woman tells you that you look handsome, you feel happy, don't you? In the same way, if someone tells me I look beautiful, I feel happy. Why do you have a problem with that, Udhaya?"

"Woman, I have no problem if a woman praises your beauty. I have a problem with men admiring you because all men are scoundrels. There is a difference between a woman's appreciation of a man's beauty and a man's appreciation of a woman's beauty. Brothels all over the world employ women, don't they? I have never seen a brothel where men entertain women. The body of the woman is the capital for running a brothel. Why are women's bodies displayed in car advertisements? Isn't it because a woman's body offers voyeuristic pleasure? Even at weddings, only beautiful girls give out bouquets and welcome the attendees. When a man looks at a woman, he visually rapes her, and in a nation like India where there is no sex-ed class, if a woman smiles at a man he immediately assumes that she loves him."

"Were you a scoundrel too?"

"Before I met you."

I didn't say this to make her happy. It was true. When Anjali had everything I needed in a woman, why would I need to pursue other women? Besides, I was very possessive about her and expected her to be faithful to me, so wasn't I obliged to be faithful to her as well? My heart melted every time I thought of the sacrifice she'd made for me. Which woman would do something like that? She'd sacrificed so much for my happiness, so I resolved to never cause her even the slightest pain, to never be the reason behind a single tear.

Leaving such sentimental matters aside, the truth was that I never tired of having sex with Anjali. Sex was the most important aspect of our relationship. I did mention that we used to have sex even when she was menstruating, didn't I? On such days, her private parts would hurt terribly, but she never minded the pain.

The first time I tried to have sex with her during her period, I noticed a string of sorts hanging from her vagina. Later, she informed me that it was a tampon. I'd never heard of a tampon before. She told me it was very convenient. *Science has revolutionized everything,* I mused. Now that there was a vaginal plug to absorb menstrual blood, a woman was spared the hassle of disposing of sanitary pads. After a couple of months, however, the tampons had started to disagree with her. We realized that when, after her periods, the sex felt unnatural. Normally, having sex with her was like ploughing marshy land, but that day, it felt like I was grinding my penis against sandpaper. Even castor oil didn't help. It hurt both of us, but despite the pain, my desire was uncontrollable and I savaged her.

The pain worsened that night and she was unable to sleep. The next day, she rushed to the gynecologist who examined her and exclaimed in shock, "Oh my goodness! What have you done to your vagina?" Anjali mumbled something in response. (What did you say, Anjali dearest?)

Once, I'd gone to Coimbatore, and as my friends were with me, I didn't crave sex. After my friends had left, I was hungry for it. I wasn't even able to masturbate. All I wanted was to fuck Anjali. I woke up the next day feeling like my body was on fire.

I tried a trick I'd used many years ago. I placed three pillows on the bed, one on top of the other. Clutching the pillow on top with both hands, I stood naked, facing the mirror, and tried to masturbate. But pillows couldn't provide the warmth of Anjali's body. I tried for a long time, but when nothing happened, I left for the airport, consoling myself with thoughts of Paris. I sent Anjali steamy messages from the airport. As she had also been dying to have sex, her messages were just as horny as mine were. I found myself on the verge of climaxing when the police called the passengers for screening. I got up and stood in the queue, thinking that by the time my turn came, things would "settle down." I was wearing linen pants and my shirt was untucked to hide my boner. A policeman approached me and told me to shift to the adjacent queue as there were fewer people in it. To my shock, I saw a female police officer waiting for me.

Not even in my wildest dreams did I see something like this happening. The policewoman's rod hit my dick and the flustered North Indian woman exclaimed, "*Arrey, baapre!*"

Too ashamed to look her in the eye, I mumbled an apology shamefacedly.

Once the screening was over, I messaged Anjali and told her what had happened.

> Anjali! The policewoman's rod knocked my rod! What the fuck is that rod even called?

> I laughed so much I nearly cried! You dirty man! The rod that knocked yours is called a metal detector!

* * *

The ocean in this part of the country seems to reflect the aggressiveness of its people, with waves that rise to the half-length of a coconut tree, roaring like angry demons. On full moon and new moon nights, they rise even higher. On such days, one will see numerous warning signs posted in and around the Marina-Besant Nagar beach saying: *No bathing here. Death is certain!* But still, men and women brave the waves and venture far into the treacherous waters. Every week, we would learn that the ocean had swallowed a man, a woman, a group of teenagers, a child, but the people consider their right to bathe in the ocean more important than their own lives.

It was when I visited the Thai island of Yao Nai with Kokkarakko and Kumar that I realized how even the continuous mass of the ocean varied in hue and tranquility.

The Andaman Sea lay before our eyes, its water like clear green crystal and its surface was so placid that I could look into the water and see the ocean bed. Fish in all shapes, sized and colors flitted to and fro. The play of color and light created magic in the green waters, magic so marvelous that words would be insufficient to capture it. In that moment, I could not help but reflect on the wonders of creation and the existence of God.

As the water was saline, we could float on its surface like corks. This phenomenon astounded me. I was queasy at first, but when I saw Kokkarakko and Kumar snorkeling like professionals, I gathered some courage and put on my mask to explore the ocean. I caught sight of a young couple who, after fooling around in the water, had sex.

"Must we watch the fish or the lovers' live show?" Kokkarakko asked.

"The fish," I said uninterestedly. "We already saw enough of the latter in Bangkok and Pattaya."

And the live show we saw in Pattaya was something I'd had to suffer through. An old woman and a middle-aged man with a ruler-straight penis stood stark naked at the center of the stage. They assumed different poses like poorly trained gymnasts, fucked, and wrapped up the show by faking a climax. It was pathetic, but the tasteless audience – mostly comprised of couples – seemed to enjoy it. (The whole spectacle reminded me of Hassan whom I had met in Barcelona.) The event organizer gave me a balloon and asked me to release it. I knew they'd demand money for such pointlessness afterward, so I refused.

Kokkarakko took it, but when he was asked for fifty baht, he handed it back.

There was a petite island next to Yao Noi, a sandy little space nuzzled between a pair of hills. Our boatwoman had given us half the day to spend there. It was the sand on this island that captivated me just like the green water around Yao Noi did. It was of a milky white color and felt like talcum under my feet. The sand of the Marina is beige and large-grained. One could circumnavigate this island in under thirty minutes. It was also teeming with visitors – you could see bobbing heads, boobs and butt-cheeks wherever you looked. After one long sitting in the boat, I felt the urge to pee, but the place seemed to have no convenience. I did not know where to go. Kokkarakko told me that I could have finished my job in the boat itself, but I hadn't known that the boat came with a toilet. Peeing into the sea would be a little too obvious and embarrassing and cruel with the crystal-clear water and the fish and all. The island afforded no privacy as it was packed with folks who were sunning themselves. Traveling abroad has caused me to look upon Indians who urinate in public places with new eyes. In this vein, I must narrate a couple of incidents as they were told to me by my friend Bala when I was visiting Malaysia. Bala's father was taken to Malaysia from Tamil Nadu as an indentured laborer in the tea plantations. Bala was born and bred there. One night, at ten, he was having drinks in his garden with a European friend who was visiting. The friend suddenly rose, unzipped his pants and peed. Taken aback, Bala asked him, "You urinate in public despite being a European?"

The European, tucking his property back in and zipping up, casually replied, "Whenever I chanced to visit India, I saw people relieving themselves in public places. India is like an open toilet. And you're an Indian, so you shouldn't mind me pissing in your esteemed presence."

Bala went on to inform him that urinating in public places was a punishable offense in Malaysia.

In Thailand, Kokkarakko, Kumar and I visited a number of places, commuting in buses and vans that stopped only in specific spots with sign and shelter, not at some painted tree as in India. I am someone who has to pee a great deal during the night. So, to prevent my bladder from bursting and leaking through my pants on the journey from Keddah to Kuala Lumpur I abstained from liquids after dusk. Despite my precautions, I was overcome by the uncontrollable urge to pee at midnight. There seemed to be no stops ahead which made matters even worse. Finally, at three a.m., the bus halted. If only I'd had a Ziploc, or even a plastic bag or bottle with me, I would have peed into it. What do you want me to do? The Indian bladder is used to relieving itself wherever it pleases.

When I went to Sri Lanka, I learned that there is absolutely no connection between Indians and cleanliness. The length and breadth of the capital city was as clean as the surface of a well-polished mirror. There were no mountains of garbage anywhere. The place was so spick that I couldn't even guess what they did with their garbage and where they disposed of it. To my utter astonishment, the army personnel were cleaning the streets like they were corporation-employed sanitary workers. When I asked my friend in Colombo about this, he told me, "Now that the war is over, the soldiers have found something else to do. That's why they're cleaning the city."

"You're always taking a dig at Indians, Tamils especially," Kokkarakko would tell me.

I see. Well, if that is so, then answer my question, Kokkarakko. You are aware that there is an enclave called Little India in cities like Kuala Lumpur, Bangkok and Penang. Why do you think, that in all those cities, only the Little India enclave is like a vast garbage heap filled with noise and commotion, chaotic as a mental asylum? Let's talk about Singapore. If you so much as drop a cigarette butt or a bus ticket on the road, you are fined; if you spit, you are fined. Peeing on the road is out of the question. When the traffic lights turn red, pedestrians cannot dream of heroically dashing across the road or dodging oncoming vehicles. For Indians, public propriety is unthinkable. They throw garbage all over the place like confetti, the walls are their favorite urinals and the roads are their choicest spittoons. Unhygienic as they are, waste constantly issues from all nine apertures of their body and you'll see them digging every hole, be it their nostrils, their ears, their eyes, their mouths, or even their anuses. Singapore's Little India is nothing but Tamil Nadu in miniature. You will hear L. R. Easwari's devotional songs being played at earsplitting decibels and you will see discarded cigarette butts, boxes, matchsticks, bus tickets, and maybe even sanitary napkins and condoms, strewn everywhere. Damned ignorants think they're immortal and walk blithely across the road because traffic can't kill dead brains. A Singaporean Tamil told me that it would take the country's entire army and police force to bring Little India to heel, but the army and the police force evidently have better things to do, so they simply left it alone.

Recently, on a Saturday evening, an unfortunate mortal died in a road accident in Singapore's Little India because he tried playing immortal when the traffic light was green. He was a Tamil. In order to express their solidarity, and their hatred for the murderous traffic, the local Tamils drank to his memory and began to attack vehicles and shops in the area.

If you read the news that is published in Tamil Nadu about the Sri Lankan Tamils, you will be consumed by a raging frenzy to exterminate every last Sinhalese person on Planet Earth. Every alphabet, comma and period in those articles is fed by animosity. Who will dare deny that Tamils beat up the poor Sinhalese fisher-folk who came to visit the church at Velankanni? Tamils harass Sinhalas and hound them out of the state, but what if I tell them that there are two hundred and fifty thousand Tamils among the four hundred and fifty thousand inhabitants of Colombo? Their feathers don't get ruffled there, do they?

A friend called Ravi once invited me to travel in Colombo with him and his family and I accepted. During that trip, two incidents helped me understand the Tamil mentality better.

In Colombo, Ravi and I got into one auto while

Ravi's wife, Priya, and her ten-year-old son, Sundar, got into another. Our driver was a Sinhala, theirs, a Tamil. The Sinhala driver did not sound his horn even once. (The same was typical of Thai drivers. Kokkarakko and I never heard the faintest sound of a horn for five hundred kilometers, starting from Nong Khai to the Mekong river, and finishing at the villages.) The Tamil driver rode with the fury of a demon charging into battle, blaring his horn like a war trumpet the entire time. When we finally reached our destination, Priya and Sundar were already there. They had been waiting for us for ten minutes. According to Priya, he never stopped squeezing his horn.

After hearing this, I asked Ravi, "If this is the attitude of the Tamils after a fierce and bloody war in which they had to endure a most brutal ethnic cleansing, what would they have been like before it? I think they all have a serious problem on a subconscious level." How is it that the Prabhakarans of the Tamil media, who go to Sri Lanka to scream about the injustices the Sri Lankan army metes out to the Tamils, omit the other side of the story?

Now for the next incident. We were traveling from Colombo to Kandy in a rental car. Sundar suffered from motion sickness; long-distance trips in buses and cars did not agree with his system. On the way to Kandy, he asked the driver to pull up as he wanted to throw up. He did, and the driver immediately cleaned up the mess with a cloth which he folded and wrapped in a paper which he deposited in a plastic bag. The next time Sundar asked him to stop the car, he gave him a bag so as to avoid a mess.

It was a remote area where no one was likely to see, let alone pull up, the boy for throwing up on the side of the road, but still, the Sinhala thought it unethical to soil the place. With this in mind, let us consider the behavior of our homeboys on their own soil.

The Marina is one of the largest beaches in the world and what a horrifying, nauseating sight it is! Several folks squat at the place where the waves lick the shore. Talk about "public convenience!" Besides, the five-kilometer stretch of the beach is generously adorned with oil-stained squares and cones of paper, plastic covers that might hit you full in the face if the wind feels like you could do with a little harassment, empty beer and whiskey bottles left behind by people who want you to know they had a great time, cigarette butts to remind you that smoking the national pastime, and garbage in all its varieties to remind you of the amount of waste two hundred thousand folks can generate. And if, god forbid, you venture to walk barefoot on the beach, you will have to undergo the ordeal Gabbar Singh forced Basanti to endure in *Sholay* when he had her dance on broken glass.

Soon after I returned from my first visit to Europe, I put all my trash into bags which I responsibly dumped into a corporation bin and returned home. When I was taking a walk later that day, I saw the garbage strewn over a few miles. I decided that very day that in a land of lunatics, I should also behave like one. So I, in solidarity with my countrymen and women, began to dispose of my trash wherever it pleased me.

There are thousands of folks who pee and poo on the shores of the Marina, but even they follow certain rules: first, no indecent exposure in a hotspot; second, women are not allowed because the government has constructed free toilets for them. The communist concept of class difference is irrelevant here. Considering the amount of gold these people own, they cannot be called poor.

One evening, I was returning home from my walk at the Nageshwara Rao Park. There is a Sai Baba temple near Venkatesa Agraharam Street where three roads intersect. A few days ago, I had seen a huge banner on display at this very spot. It featured the picture of a saree-clad, heavily powdered and painted ten-year-old girl who had just hit puberty. Below her picture were those of several older men with Veerappan-moustaches, all of them her suitors, and coincidentally, her maternal uncles.

I could see that arrangements were being made to conduct a political meeting at the junction that day. The stage had been erected so that it obstructed the road. Rows of plastic chairs, all with ample hindquarters on their seats, were placed before the stage. In addition to those seated, there was a horde of others standing around and staring at the carry-on. As the political figures had not yet arrived, a man costumed like MGR was performing some pelvic thrusts with a buxom young girl to entertain the waiting crowd.

The Sai Vidhyalaya Matriculation School shared a boundary with the temple. The latter provided free food on leaf-plates thrice a day. A trash bin stood in front of the former and the leaf-plates always lie around it. This is another common Indian trait – if there is a toilet, an Indian will piss around it so that the next Indian cannot use it. There will be another buffoon who pisses at the entrance so that the next buffoon cannot enter and will have to piss around the first buffoon's piss. These pissers sometimes hold up traffic. A few potbellied, red-eyed and red-lipped traffic cops dutifully blow their whistles, but that just contributes to the noise.

On both sides of the street, different kinds of beggars were rattling their tins. It is believed that the Baba is especially receptive to the demands of his devotees on Thursdays. So, every Thursday, you would see hundreds of them, each with his backside permanently attached to a particular spot near the temple. You have to pay a good bit of money to be able to walk in or around the temple in peace. Now even beggars have a fairly good notion of ownership. A beggar owns the spot on which he sits and none of his counterparts can occupy that spot lest he wishes to be killed and tossed into the Cooum River that flows nearby. Free food, a tin-roofed straw hut to sleep in, no concerns about bodily hygiene, a strip of cloth to cover all that needs covering, and a bank passbook in a bag slung over the shoulder – who said a beggar's life is hard?

After the beggars come the vegetable-vendors with their litany of vegetables and prices. The vegetable market also relies on the Baba's blessings, so they operate on Thursdays. All these vegetable sellers display their produce on Mada Street. The policemen, who are supposed to get rid of these human roadblocks, merely collect their *maamool* and give these menaces a blind eye and a deaf ear. If you haven't been to Chennai before, I suggest you visit Mada Street's vegetable market in addition to the Marina, the Fort, the temples and the churches. On the one hand, you have traders screaming out the prices of vegetables, and on the other, you have the howl of the traffic, a howl like that of a cornered beast trying to escape. It is not something I can further describe in words.

Commotion of this sort is absent in Venkatesa Agraharam street, but here too, there are a number of roadside shops selling incense, camphor, *kumkum*, pictures of Sai Baba, spinning tops, small vanity mirrors, combs and whatnot. There were also vendors who had a spread of toys: rattles, pots, piggy-banks, god and goddess dolls and balloons. There were also dealers of plastic goods, tender-coconut sellers with their pushcarts, a man selling stone-studded metal rings, and of course, the ubiquitous fortune-teller with his parrot, a garlic vendor, a man selling slivers of jackfruit, a shop selling fancy gewgaws for women, a stationery shop, a plastic soapbox shop, a footwear shop, and in the midst of this hullaballoo would be a devotee of Jymka Saamiyar standing for hours, holding a placard announcing the details of the saamyar's next *satsang*. Just a few removes from him would be an old man on a wheelchair, circling a smoking pot of camphor before people's faces and dispersing blessings. He wore a turban on his head, a knee-length *kaili*, and a *jubba* of the same length. He is an everyday sight, because he has too many prayers to say and too many blessings to give. Thursdays cannot accommodate them all.

Two millennia ago, Thiruvalluvar wrote the *Thirukkural,* dividing it into three sections – ethics, politics and sexuality. And now, in the twenty-first century, all three heads come together in the form of the temple, the political meeting and the dance sequences in films.

Madurai is one place I visit very often, and whenever I do, the sad spectacle of the Vaigai River reduced to dryness never fails to move me. After one such visit, I was returning to Chennai in a first-class air-conditioned coach.

That was indeed an unforgettable journey because the faces of many of my fellow passengers were familiar to me – I had seen them all in the pages of investigative magazines. I am sure you remember Pakkirisamy's ghost. (You do, don't you?) These were also Pakkirisamys, but it was not yet their time to become ghosts, so here they were, moving around like human zombies in their massive bodies. One of them was missing his arm below his elbow (probably a rowdy-turned-politician). Villains in films paled in comparison to the next guy who had a scar on his chest, who wore thick, rope-like gold chains on his neck like a rapper and whose fingers sported rings bearing the image of a political leader. He and his crew sported *veshtis* that bore the party's colors, but the sight of their bellies – that looked like inflated balloons – was what had me staring.

They were talking so loudly that you'd think they'd had loudspeakers implanted in their throats. I was curled up like a baby rat in one corner and I was insignificant, besides, so they wouldn't have noticed me, let alone my staring. After the ticket-inspector came and went, they opened their pricey liquor bottles and began to drink, and I was shocked to discover that their "travel bags" were actually carrying packages of food. Boxes of chicken-65, fried liver, ginger chicken, fried seer fish, meatballs, fried brain, *sura puttu*, fried mutton and more were opened and consumed. They had whipped up a banquet. Oil was dribbling everywhere – down their fingers, down the corners of their mouths, down the oil-soaked chunks of meat. These pregnant-looking men, ten in number, were eating a meal meant for fifty. The feast continued till midnight. Their booming conversations would easily have provided me with fodder for several more stories – Pakkirasamy Two, Pakkirasamy Three, Pakkirasamy Four, and so on and so forth. I had believed that newspapers were exaggerators, but after hearing the ten potbellied Pakkirasamys prattle, I realized that what the newspaper reveals is only the tip of one titanic iceberg.

The next day, when I had reached Chennai, I met Santhanam and told him of the events that had unfolded on the train. He observed, "Fifty years ago, the fathers of the politicians you saw on the train must have been pushing handcarts, or selling vegetables, or laying bricks, probably even butchering cows and pigs. Now, their sons, by some stroke of luck, have entered politics and become prosperous."

"Be that as it may, but have they been able to lead the peaceful lives their fathers led? Their fathers must have lived to be ninety, but these fellows have undergone bypass surgeries at the age of thirty-five and are still wolfing down prodigious quantities of chicken and mutton. When the political tables turn, when the regime changes, they are thrown into prison under the *Goonda* Act. In politics, only the party leaders live to ripe old ages, hale and healthy with children and grandchildren, while their followers die at the age of fifty. All their ill-amassed wealth and power are cursed, don't you see?"

On hearing my words, Santhanam told me a story from the Ramayana.

Though Dasharatha had three wives, he did not have children with any of them. Filled with grief, he wandered into the forest one day. Suddenly, he heard the sound of an animal drinking water in a nearby stream. He had mastered the technique of *shabdavedi*, an archery skill that involved the striking of a target by relying on sound rather than sight. Dasharatha released an arrow in the direction of the sound. No sooner did the arrow fly than he heard a young boy cry out in pain. The sound was not from an elephant, as he has assumed, but from the boy, Shravana Kumaran, who had been fetching water for his parents in an earthen pot.

Shravana looked at Dasharatha and said, "I came hither to fetch water for my parents, both of whom are blind. They will be waiting for me. Slake their thirst by taking this water to them."

On hearing that their son had been killed by Dasharatha's arrow, the old blind couple cursed him, saying that he too would feel the pain of separation from his child.

Dasharatha conveyed this to Kaikeyi.

"That's not a curse," she replied, "but a boon."

It's one of life's riddles when sometimes, a curse turns out to be a boon and a boon turns out to be a curse.

In Malaysia, Muslims constitute fifty percent of the population, Chinese Buddhists twenty-five percent, and Tamil Hindus eight percent. The Tamil Hindus have erected temples on every street corner and this has had a deleterious effect on social harmony. Every alternate day, their community has some festival or the other and several cars would be parked at the entrance of the temple and all around it. This throws the traffic into pandemonium and disturbs the peace of the rest of the locals. If the Muslim population raises an objection, the Hindus start whining about being denied the right to practice their religion. Incidents fueled by such disagreements led to a communal conflict between the Malaysian Muslims and the Tamil Hindus in 2007. The Tamils felt that they were being treated as second-class citizens in the country. When I questioned a Malaysian friend on the subject, he said, "That is true to a certain extent. If we don't treat them that way, they will make fishermen of us all, no doubt fishing was what we'd been doing for several generations, but should we continue to do it even now?" However, the Malaysian Tamils, unlike the Lankan Tamils, have not recourse to arms and violence, so the government was able to make certain compromises and adjustments. For instance, the government in Malaysia celebrates Diwali. The political leaders in India wear skullcaps during Ramadan to please the Muslims. Similarly, when the elections come round, the prime minister makes the Tamils happy by speaking a few words in Tamil.

I was once traveling in an auto from Alwarpet to Nageshwara Rao Park. The auto driver, a stranger, struck up a conversation with me.

"My body hurts terribly. I was about to go and have a beer when you flagged me down. Thankfully you're going my way. My body took a bad beating awhile ago, but I'm feeling the pain acutely now."

"Why, were you involved in an accident?"

"No *saar*. I was beaten up by the cops."

"It wouldn't be appropriate for me to pry, so I won't ask you anything further."

"Oh, you can ask all you want, *saar*. It's no big deal, really. You get drunk, have a drunken argument, the cops haul you like a sack of potatoes to the station and you get beaten. Look here, *saar*," he said, showing me his hand. "I don't grow my nails. Do you know why? The first thing these bestial cops do is pull your nails with tongs." He acted it out, expressions and all. "But now, they keep their sticks to scratch their backs and their backsides. Instead of beating you to a pulp, they send you straight to the coolers because they, with all their brawn and brute force, shit their pants at the thought of human rights activists. So, you spend a fortnight eating free food and you're released."

I will narrate three more incidents to you, all of which occurred close to a decade ago. I have them recorded in my time-yellowed notebooks.

Scene – 1: I was traveling by bus and I had no coins. I handed the conductor a ten rupee note, apologizing for having forgotten to carry change in my pockets. "Do you have brains or shit?" he asked me hotly. "Would you forget to eat for one day? Get off this bus!"

Scene – 2: Another bus, another conductor. A passenger hands him a fifty. The conductor politely asks him to pay the exact amount. Hell broke loose. The passenger barked filth at the cowering conductor and, like that wasn't enough, he attempted to strangle him. It was only after the conductor had begged him with folded hands that the passenger relented and released his hold on the man. The passenger was around twenty-five and the conductor would have been his father's age. Despite the brouhaha, the bus continued on its way and the conductor carried on issuing tickets like nothing at all had happened.

Scene – 3: A friend, who worked as the general manager for the telephone department, was an IAS officer and a literature aficionado. His position was like a king's, but it did not thwart his simplicity. One day, he went to the post office (on foot, as he did not need the prestige of a government vehicle and did not like asking errand boys to run around for him) and asked for an inland letter.

"Not available," came a brutish voice.

"Alright, could you give me an envelope, then?"

"I told you it's not available! Are you deaf?"

"Um, sorry,… You told me that you had no inland letters. I never knew you meant the envelopes too."

"Shut the hell up and get out of here. Who wants to give ear to you and your damn explanations? Go get what you want from another post office."

Had he made a twenty-second call to the officer in the postal department, the face that owned the voice would have been slapped and handed a letter of dismissal immediately. But my friend was a *sattvik*.

"You can't say when and where the blow will come from," he told me sadly. I still remember the quiver in his voice as he spoke those words.

Kokkarakko tells me that the temperament of the Tamils is determined to some extent by the natural landscape and the climate of the state. The ocean rages and rants relentlessly, the sun scorches the earth and all it touches. We experience four seasons elsewhere, but only three in Tamil Nadu – the hot season, the hotter than hot season, and the hottest of all seasons. Here, a man is drenched in sweat even when he is having a bath.

In between the hot, hotter and hottest seasons comes October and November, bringing with them a spell of rain accompanied by cyclones. The rainy season always reminds me of Nagore where rain usually portends fierce and destructive thunderstorms. The storm that blew in 1952 was called the "Big Tempest." Just as time is chunked into B.C. and A.D., the births and deaths of people, and other significant events in Nagore, are dated with reference to the Big Tempest. I was born a year after its destruction. One of reasons why the storm had etched itself into the memories of Nagore is because it took down the huge *kalasam* of the dargah's minaret and swept it across the town.

When I read poems in praise of the rains, I get peeved. For the dwellers of Nagore, the rains brought memories of war. My mother used to talk about "war reels." In her salad days, the British government screened news clips of World War II in the theatres, just before the main feature. The war reel featured scenes of battlefields, tanks, fighter-planes and bombings. The audience regarded these clippings with the same awe and enthusiasm with which they watched M.K.T.'s films.

Even after the British had left India, the free Madras Government continued this practice of screening government-related clips before the films. They still called it a "war reel." When the Tamil Nadu Government introduced the red triangle logo of the family-planning program, my mother called that a "war reel" as well. Then, she tut-tutted in disapproval, saying, "They screen such dirty war reels nowadays. The end of the world is near."

Mother's preparations for the rainy season gave me the impression of an impending war. The monsoons lasted only three months, but she had to toil for the other nine to prepare for these three. Cooking fuel was the biggest issue. She would begin collecting cow-dung to make *raatis* which would be stored in the house. They resembled very large plates and every house in Nagore was equipped with them. To ensure that the fire would burn well, women would add some hay to the dung as it was being trampled upon to make patties. Some folks even sold the cakes. But the stove wouldn't burn with dung-cakes alone. Firewood was a prime requirement if food had to be cooked for eight people. Babul trees that abounded in the village supplied us with all the wood we needed. We would cut branches and halve them and quarter them. We would then dry them in the sun and store them at home. The biggest challenge was to collect the branches without getting our flesh torn as the trees were full of thorns. Slippers had to be worn, else the thorns would prick our soles. If an unbroken thorn was lodged in the flesh, it was easier to extract when compared to a splinter that got embedded in the flesh and could not be easily extracted. There lay the possibility of the wound becoming infected and pus would form. One would have to see a doctor, and even after treatment, one would be rendered unable to walk until the wound was completely healed. There were certain women who could expertly extricate thorns from under the flesh with safety pins, no matter how deep the thorn had traveled. Whenever such an "extraction surgery" is done to me, I have not been able to resisit a hard-on. If the thorn could not be removed with a safety pin, the women would smear some coconut oil over the area and cauterize it with a heated glass shard from a chimney lamp.

The firewood would be stored at the back of the house where it was proofed from the rain. Scorpions, centipedes and snakes would take refuge among the logs, so one had to be careful when handling them.

It rained cats and dogs in Nagore. It was a town on the seashore, and when it rained, one might have thought there was a pillar of water between the sky and the earth. It would rain for days on end. All the ponds and lakes, swollen and bursting, would join forces with the Vettar and transform the town into one surging mass of water. It was also a time for old people to die, so the stink of burning flesh in the neighboring cremation ground would assail our nostrils on most days.

Our house was tiled, and during the eighteen years I lived in it, I don't recall the tiles being replaced even once. Bottle gourd vines covered the tiles. The gourds were plenty and mother would distribute them to others free-of-charge. When she was short on money, she would gather the gourds and put them into a large sack and send them to market. Ramu, who had a fruit shop at the market (that sold only bananas), would choose a couple and send the rest back. Vegetarians were only a few in Nagore, so the demand for vegetables wasn't exactly high. At least there was Ramu to buy a couple of bottle gourds every once in a while. But the irony was that we found it harder to sell chickens. The owners of the biryani shops around the dargah would examine the chickens and return them saying that they were diseased, or they would give me chump change. I would go home and ask mother about the chickens and she would confirm that they were diseased. She would finish off with: "So what if they are? They'll still taste fantastic." She would then cook them for us. I would go red in the face if my schoolmates caught sight of me trying to sell the chickens. I was the only boy in the class who did not come from an affluent family and although I wasn't discriminated against, my social status stigmatized me.

If I failed to get a good price for the chickens, mother would tell me I wasn't clever enough. I knew she wasn't berating me as her tone suggested sadness. I would hear her mutter to herself, "It's a pity that I have to send a schoolboy on such errands." Come to think of it now, I feel that my mother is the one to be held responsible for my arrogance and overweening pride.

During the rains, water would leak from the old tiles on the roof. Vessels had to be placed at strategic coordinates to collect the rain water that dripped from the ceiling. Every room would have at least a dozen vessels collecting rainwater, and Mother would line the floor with gunny sacks to regulate the dampness.

We had stocked up on dung-cakes and firewood, but in that downpour, what were we to eat? Of course, leave it to mother to have everything planned and executed. She would buy a goat, feed it, kill it and pickle it before the rains set in. She would plant two sticks in the earth, tie a rope between them and on it she would hang pieces of goat-flesh marinated with turmeric, chili powder and salt. After the strips had dried in the sun for three days, she would transfer them to a plate, dry it again under the hot sun and to prevent it from becoming desiccated, she would store them in an airtight pot. These salted pieces of goat-meat, which would last a year, kept us going during the monsoon. Now, this food is but a relic of the past.

Though life could be difficult during the rains, there were two pastimes children significantly enjoyed – catching fish with a piece of cloth by holding the ends and passing it through the water, and the making and sailing of paper boats.

Since the Nagapattinam port was not very deep, I had never seen a ship though I had seen catamarans. I always found ships to be more fascinating than planes. Many centuries ago, the Tamils had braved the seas on sailboats. Perhaps this knowledge is the reason for my interest in seafaring vessels.

My love for ships had intensified after I had watched Sivaji Ganesan's *Kappalottiya Thamizhan.* I was inflamed with the desire to work on a ship and fish. Long, long ago, a Tamil, A. K. Chettiar, traveled across the globe on ships. Now that air travel is the preferred means of going places, I have no idea if and when my dream will be realized.

It so happened that a ship once ran aground on the beach in front of my house in Mylapore. It pulled a huge cellphone wielding crowd. As for me, I was stunned to see the ship. I felt like it had dropped anchor on my doorstep. When the ship began to flounder, the captain ordered everybody onto the lifeboats. An engineer had lost his life and five had gone missing. The corpses were recovered one by one. The survivors had been rescued by the local fishermen and the coast guard.

PART – III

There used to be a time when cows were accorded the respect due to the woman of the house. Every house in the village had a cow – a Meenakshi or a Kamakshi – and the household subsisted on its milk and dung. It was said that if a house had a cow and a drumstick tree, its members would never know starvation. So now, after appraising this outstanding creature to you, I bring you to the question: is it possible – or even thinkable – to kill a cow and eat its flesh? The pitiful sight of cows crammed into trucks bound for Kerala like sardines in a box can move even a stone-hearted man to tears. The butchers slaughter them with a pickax – one blow to the center of the forehead and the poor animal drops like a sack of potatoes.

Again the burning question: should we, or should we not, eat the meat of the cow?

Twenty years ago, a counter-culture movement that shared traits with the American Beat Movement, reared its head in Tamil Nadu. I was part of it. We had decided to eat beef to register our opposition to the Hindutva-Brahmin hegemony that was sinking its teeth into the state. At the end of our conference, beef curry was served, but when dinner was wrapped, we realized that no one had touched the beef curry. The people at the forefront of the movement belonged to the middle-class. In terms of caste too, they occupied the middle ground. Having never eaten beef before, they were unable to bring themselves to sample the curry, let alone eat it.

In retrospect, I realized how foolish and cruel we had been. Vallalar sang that it ailed his heart whensoever he beheld a plant wasting away. His words, though not strange to the Tamil man, were handled like hollow superstition and cast aside.

It was among Perundevi's tasks to water the plants, trees and vines in our house. A spiritual conference removed her to Bangalore for three days. On the first day, I was too busy to tend the plants. In the afternoon, I did have some time on my hands, but it was too hot. The next day, there was a downpour. When Perundevi returned home, she told me, "I prayed that the clouds would water the plants if you couldn't for some reason."

In the present day and age, you might, with a roll of the eyes and a flick of the hand, dismiss all this as some kind of lunacy. Ten years ago, I would have too, but some marvelous experiences transformed my manner of thought.

In Pollachi, I had a friend named Sridhar, a toddy-tapper. Now the toddy-tappers do not tap just any tree. If there are ten thousand trees, a certain number of trees is allotted to each tapper, and for the rest of his days, each man will tap toddy only from the trees that had been earmarked for him.

The toddy-tappers' world is a microcosm replete with its own rove of stories. The tappers start their climbing at two in the morning as the toddy has to be loaded into the dispatching lorries by four if it is to reach the shops in Kerala for distribution by six or seven.

I met an eighty-year-old man named Marimuthu. (These days, one might consider an eighty-year-old man a bald, toothless, woebegone shell of a human being.) Marimuthu – prepare your youthful pride for a blow – climbed forty trees a day. In his youth, it used to be a few hundreds. He had recently married an eighteen-year-old girl. Sridhar told me, in Marimuthu's presence, that toddy and pussy comprised his world. Intrigued, Kokkarakko had a long conversation with him. An excerpt follows:

> Kokkarakko: They tell me you don't sleep without a pussy. Is it the same pussy or a different one everyday?
>
> Marimuthu: So long as it's pussy, who the fuck cares?
>
> Kokkarakko: So, you do fuck women other than your wife, huh?
>
> Marimuthu: The hell I do if I'm lucky.
>
> Kokkarakko: How do you find pussy everyday?
>
> Marimuthu: I just approach some petticoat and ask her if she'd like to come with me.
>
> Kokkarakko: That's *all*? Unfortunate bastards like us have to make complicated plans and chase bitches like dogs for years!
>
> Marimuthu: What else must I ask them? If they say no, I just keep my eyes open for another one. Why waste time over pussy that doesn't want cock?
>
> Kokkarakko: Do they come readily when you ask?

Marimuthu: Some do. There are others I might have to ask four, maybe five, times.

Kokkarakko: Where do you screw them?

Marimuthu: In some grove or bush, where else?

Kokkarakko: No offense, but, do you give them anything for their, uh, services? Money, trinkets…

Marimuthu: I sometimes buy them a bit to eat.

Kokkarakko: Is there any chance you remember how many women you've had till date?

Marimuthu: I don't know! I don't keep account for such business.

Kokkarakko: Was there ever *one* woman you fancied and chose to keep with you?

Marimuthu: There is one. She has a boy and I pay for his education.

Kokkarakko: Has there been a woman who loved you but couldn't live with you?

Marimuthu: Yes, there was a hopeless, lovestruck woman who committed suicide.

Kokkarakko: What happened after?

Marimuthu: I felt terrible. Almost went crazy. Didn't touch pussy for a whole month!

Kokkarakko: Do you have anal sex?

Marimuthu: I told you already. I do it every which way possible.

Marimuthu had never seen the entrails of a hospital. There was this one time he fell from a tree. Instead of relying on medicines in labeled bottles and blister packs of tablets, he treated and healed his injuries with a self-prepared paste of herbs. He did not climb his trees for a week. Another tapper did in his place, but the toddy he had collected lacked its characteristic taste and even the shopkeeper complained about it. Marimuthu's machete simply couldn't be used by another. It was only after he had returned to work that the toddy's flavor was restored.

I told Marimuthu that I wanted to see his machete and he obliged me. I extended my right hand to take it, but he said that it should be received with both hands. "I do not let anyone touch my *vettukaththi*. I conceded only because you're a writer," he said.

I was reminded of the movie *Kill Bill* – the scene where The Bride meets Hattori Hanzo to buy a sword. When she extends her right hand to receive it, he tells her she is to receive it with both hands, adding that the sword would kill even God if he appeared before her.

When Ismail's affair became known to his masters, they decided to build him a separate room in the garden, and for this purpose, they drained the fish pond. Ismail gave the koi hatchlings to Perundevi which meant we had to rear them in the house. There were other varieties too, and they were housed in three separate tanks on the first floor. There was a pair of flowerhorn fishes, and also some blood parrot cichlids, goldfish and sardines. Cory catfish were customarily kept in fish tanks as they were cleaners, stationed at the bottom of the tank for the most part, motionless. Despite the catfish, the water had to be replaced once every half-month. It was no easy task – one had to remove the fish using a net and temporarily hold them in a bucket of water while the water in the tank was being replaced and the oxygen tube checked. Warm water was introduced to kill the flatworms among the pebbles at the bottom of the tank. They came from food scraps and posed a threat to the fish.

There is another fish culturing method called the "sea aquarium" in which a mini-sea was created, plants and corals and all, and the water needed replacement only after two years.

My friends who kept fish told me that the two-hour load-shedding in Chennai made it impossible to rear fish as a continuous supply of power was required for the oxygen tube.

"In that case, how do the fishes in lakes, ponds and seas survive?" I asked.

"Plants," said Madan. He also told me that there were oxygen tubes that could feed oxygen into the bucket by artificial means in the absence of power.

"That won't work," I told Madan. "We're already struggling to raise two dogs. Who needs all that?"

So he suggested something else.

Four koi fish were placed in the second tank. I firmly objected as I had seen gigantic koi fish in the Buddhist monasteries in Thailand. Koi can grow to three feet, so it's impossible to raise them in glass tanks. They require a small pond, and they have a lifespan of fifty to two hundred years. In the third tank, which was smaller, there was only one fighter fish. Fighter fish has to be raised alone. Pardon me for going on a diatribe about fish, but it is necessary for you to understand what is to follow.

If you put two flowerhorns in the same bucket, they will attack and kill each other – there is no exception to this. If you put a male and a female flowerhorn together, the male will kill the female unless the female has a lot of places to hide. Perundevi, however, put them both together in the same tank, skeptical of all this hand-me-down wisdom. You should have seen the battle that ensued! It put India's and Pakistan's cricket team arguments to shame. Such commotion, such bloodshed! The bigger flowerhorn's kok was injured, so we placed a barrier in the middle of the tank. The flowerhorn doesn't fight with other fish in the same tank. Like human beings, it fights only with its own kind.

I once returned from Erode at around five in the morning, and in my house, five in the morning was no waking hour, so I stood at the gate, trying to reach Perundevi on the phone. Like V.O. Chidambaram who had to do toilsome physical labor in the British-run prisons, Perundevi toiled in the house. She would start by washing clothes in the backyard at ten and you could hear the scrape of her brush on the clothes till noon. Clothes are washed differently in every country. In my hometown, I had seen people washing clothes on stone slabs, slapping the cloths against the stone to dislodge the dirt. In our Mylapore house too, there was a stone platform on which Perundevi washed the larger laundry items like bed-linen. She would hand-wash and scrub my *veshti*, my shirts, my pants, my underwear, my handkerchiefs, my yoga mat, Madan's drawers, his shirts, his jeans, his underwear, her sarees, her underskirts, her panties, her bras, her *churidhars*, her nighties, our towels, curtains, bed-sheets, blankets, pillow covers, kitchen towels and rugs. She gave my linen shirts gentler treatment. The backyard received an abundance of sunshine that accelerated the drying of the clothes. If ever I asked her why she chose to wash the bedclothes by hand when there was a washing machine, she would sternly tell me, "Mind your own business, Udhaya."

I never quite understood if her obsession with washing clothes was some kind of disorder. When I heard the sound of her whacking the hidden dirt out of the clothes, I would feel centipedes and scorpions crawl in my head. Because of this obsession of hers, things were going haywire at home. To make it clearer, I would have to be at the mercy of a restaurant for breakfast. Perundevi would wash clothes all morning and open the kitchen counter for breakfast only at eleven-thirty.

I had failed to reach her on the phone, so I knocked at the gate.

The dogs came running long before Madan did on hearing the knocks.

The sanitary worker arrived shortly after. Noticing some dead fish in the trash, my heart lurched. There was a koi among them.

Grief and boundless rage took hold of me. The koi fish

were dying at the rate of one per month. And why were they dying, you ask? Due to the lack of space! Only one koi had remained and now, it too was dead. Now spiritualists ascribe all sorrow and misfortune to fate and expect us to reconcile ourselves to it. Remember the girl who died after being brutally gang-raped in a moving bus in Delhi? It was her fate to be brutalized the way she was. Similarly, it was the koi's fate to die and now all the kois had succumbed to the same fate.

"Couldn't you have taken a train that reached later? Was this the only train from Erode?" Perundevi asked. I didn't understand. She went on to explain that my arrival had excited the dogs who started jumping about frantically. In the melee, they'd ruptured the oxygen tube of the tank and the fish had died due to deoxygenation.

This had happened four years ago when Perundevi's workload was bigger on account of having no maids. She used to complain that the dogs were taking up most of her time and would ask me if she was born with the sole purpose of cleaning up after them. To complicate matters, she had sprained her ankle and was finding it difficult to walk. As she opened the gate to draw the *kolam*, Baba darted. I had gone to the park and Madan was out of town. With her injured ankle, she walked through the streets, found the dog and dragged it back home. When I returned home, she said, "Please give the dogs away, or I'll die young." The ordeal had traumatized her. I tried to coax her into changing her mind by telling her that the dogs were like our children. Finally, my friend in Pondicherry –

a billionaire with more than fifty dogs – agreed to take in Baba and Blackie. They were soon gone.

Two days had passed. On the third day, I did not know what happened, I banged my laptop on the floor and it cracked. That laptop contained years' worth of research. Like a madman, I began to rip my books and shouted that I'd kill anyone who dared to approach me. I shouted that I'd burn the house down if Baba and Blackie didn't come back home within a few hours. (Perundevi told me all of this when I had cooled down. I had no memory of anything I'd said.) Baba and Blackie returned home that very day. They were starved of water and drank by the gallon as soon as they'd arrived. They neither barked nor growled as they were exhausted. It took them a couple of days to get accustomed to us again. Dogs were possessed with a superior sense of understanding than human beings. They understood that I would return for them when, on occasion, I left them at Varun's clinic; they also understood that they were being sent away forever when we loaded them into my friend's car.

Old Baba would come and sit on my lap when I sat cross-legged on the floor. He would also climb into my lap when I was meditating. Baba was the size of a lion. I wondered how my lap held him. He did feel uncomfortable after a few minutes and would run off. Once he was gone, Blackie would appear and rest his head on my lap. I would rub my hands after I had finished my meditation. When Baba heard the sound of hands rubbing against each other, he would come running back to me, bully Blackie out of my lap and out of sight, and reclaim his throne.

When it came to food, Baba and I had similar palates. In the morning, I would eat tender neem leaves on an empty stomach and Baba would chomp through them as though they were *halwa*. We also shared an affinity for chapatti, idly, dosa, jaangiri, halwa, paalkova, murukku, jamuns (Baba once bit into the huge seed and, despising the taste, spat it out. Thereafter, I saw to it that I'd scooped out the seeds before giving him his share), apples, pomegranates, oranges, grapes, guavas, potatoes, ice cream (the doctor had warned me not to eat ice cream and the vet had warned me not to give Baba ice cream), curd rice, coconut water, apple, beetroot and carrot juice, bread and almonds.

One day, Perundevi was taking out some ingredients from the kitchen containers. Baba would usually sprawl in the kitchen when she was cooking. Labradors are generally lazy dogs and Baba was no exception. Even the apocalypse wouldn't make him budge, but when the almond tin opened, he would bark, bite Perundevi's dress and wag his tail, looking at her expectantly.

Blackie had a keen sense of time. He knew when I would return from my morning walk. At exactly seven-thirty, he would head to soundly sleeping Perundevi's bed and nudge her face with his ice-cold nose.

I was daily witness to a most amusing sight. When Perundevi approached the fish tank, the two flowerhorns would become frisky. They would talk to her with their mouths pressed against the glass and somersault in the water. All the trouble of rearing fish was worth it for this sight, I felt. Perundevi would coo to them like they were her babies. "Are you hungry sweetie-pie? There you go! Eat up, now!" She would feed them "Humpy Head" which was supposed to make their koks grow bigger.

When Perundevi was not around, I would try every trick I knew to get the fish to pay me some attention. I was completely ignored. When I had gone to the aquarium to buy them processed fry and worms, the owner of the aquarium told me that even the fish he sold would ignore him completely, but would get all excited at the sight of the shop assistants who fed them. How discerning fishes are!

One of the fish that died in our tanks was a blood parrot cichlid. It was a timid fish – the color would literally drain from it if I approached.

The flowerhorns, like stubborn children, refused to eat in Perundevi's absence. I would feed them twice a day, but the food remained uneaten. For three days they starved, like they had gone on a fast in protest, and I feared they'd die. When Perundevi returned, oh what joy! I thought they'd fall out of the tank, what with all the jumping they did. They would have even jumped into her lap if they could.

A few days later, we found the bigger flowerhorn, the more active of the two, floating upside down. It didn't eat; it hardly moved. We called the fish vet from the aquarium over. This was what he had to say: "It's old. Its lifespan is over. There's nothing you or I could do for it now. It might carry on this way for another couple of months and then die." Perundevi never gave up on the creature. She talked to it every day, hoping against hope that it would survive. It didn't. I had indirectly killed and eaten so many chickens, goats and fish, but the death of that flowerhorn affected me deeply. Fifteen days was what it took for its life to depart from its body.

In the twinkling of the stars, in the touch of the wind, in the smell of the earth, in the rustling of the trees, in the golden pollen of the hibiscus, in the swell of the ocean, in the blueness of the sky, in the fire of the volcano, in the softness of the clouds, in the loneliness of the mountains, in the music of the flute, in the first cry of an infant, in a tongue of fire, in the rays of the sun, in the sound of a gurgling stream, in the gentle rain, in the brightness of the full moon, in the mooing of a cow, in the croaking of the frogs, in the roots of the banyan, in the swaying of the leaves, in glittering ice crystals, flickering lamps, fragrant flowers… I see you in everything, my dear flowerhorn. Where did your flowerhorn soul vanish? Do you still exist somewhere, glowing like a sphere of light? Can you see me from wherever you are?

Right now, I feel like a lousy writer; my inability to describe how the flowerhorn oscillated between life and death for fifteen days fills me with shame. I, who could describe anything with extravagance of language, am forsaken by the words I now need. It pains me that I cannot find the words to eulogize and immortalize my flowerhorn.

I recall a scene in Fellini's *La Strada*. In the movie, Gelsomina and Rosa are sisters. The latter is sold to Zampanò, a street performer. She dies during travel. Zampanò returns to the girl's house with a sum of money and a request to be allowed to take Gelsomina in her sister's place. Gelsomina was to Zampanò what a monkey is to a monkey-trainer. He is chauvinistic and physically abusive towards her. At one point, she tells Il Matto, the fool, "I am useless and I'm sick of this life!"

To this, Il Matto replies, "If Zampanò keeps you with him instead of chasing you away, what does it mean? Doesn't he keep you around because he profits from you? If not, why would he continue to keep you? So tell me now, why do you think you are useless? If it had been me, though, I wouldn't have kept you for a minute. It is my belief that he loves you."

"Zampanò loves me?"

"Yes, poor man! He is like a dog and dogs can show their love only by barking. I too could have been like him, but unfortunately, I happened to read a book or two. There is nothing that is useless in this world. Look, even this pebble under my feet has some use, it means something."

"Which pebble?"

"This one, and not just this. Everything in this world has a meaning. I don't know what purpose this pebble has, but it does have one. If it has no use, then everything in this world is useless starting from the stars above us."

The novel ends here, my friends. You are probably disappointed; perhaps you think it lacks a proper ending. Tell me, other than death, is there any interesting end to life? I plan to write about my experiences in the Himalayas on another occasion. Now all that is left is this mountain and myself.

Silence.

A vast silence surrounds me.

EPILOGUE

When I finished the novel, I waited for a year instead of immediately handing it over to the publisher. I don't know why. It's probably because I felt that this epilogue had to be written.

It's been a year since I've returned from the Himalayas. Certain incidents witnessed by me after my return deserve mention here.

First, let me talk about Anjali. There used to be a huge gooseberry tree in front of her house that has since been cut down as the owner of the house needed space for a garage. Anjali could not digest this. The tree was the first thing she saw, the first thing that waved at her, every time she opened her bedroom window. Birds had built their nests there, so she used to wake to birdsong every morning. Where would those poor birds go now? The house owner destroyed those helpless creatures' homes to meet his own selfish ends. Here are some of the messages Anjali sent me on the subject:

> At first I thought they were cutting only some of the branches. When I heard they were going to fell the tree, my heart sank like a lead balloon.

> I opened the window to see a branch from the tree hanging from the balcony wall.

I don't know if you can understand how I feel about this.

As I looked at that branch, I felt like the tree was being cruelly and painfully dismembered.

I closed my window as I couldn't bear to see the skeleton that lay before me.

When I saw all those chopped branches, I felt such a stab of sorrow. The pain was indescribable.

I used to talk to that tree every day, Udhaya, and to the birds and the squirrels that lived in it. I would gaze at it every morning.

Now, I have a fresh problem. When I'm alone, I hear the window opening on its own. Maybe it was just my imagination…?

I heard the sound again. Maybe it was the wind…

I hear the sound of spirits weeping about me as I write to you now. I am *not* imagining it. Their cries are piercing my ears like sirens.

It's terrible, Udhaya. I curse myself for having such a fragile mind.

The tree bore plenty of fruits.

I used to draw the curtain back a bit before going to sleep so that I could see the tree. I'm not going to sleep in that room anymore.

The branch hanging from the balcony wall seems to be telling me something. It seems like it's looking at me in wretched misery.

Those spirits are still hovering around me.

Have I gone mad?

Or is this mere illusion?

Or perhaps I am just making a scene, as Suresh likes to say.

But no! my feelings are real! The sobbing of these spirits is real! These spirits have been with me even before, but I have not told a soul other than you.

Do you know how deeply this has wounded me? When I was driving, I felt like ramming into a bus and getting myself killed. I'm worried now. What if… what if I actually *do* it? This is why I'm thinking of seeing a psychiatrist. I am not in my right senses when I go out these days.

When nobody is around, the silence of this house is deafening.

I sense the spirits moving when I turn on the TV.

I leave the fans and the lights on when I leave the house because I don't want to return to a house in darkness.

When I am home alone, I feel their presence. They're trying to tell me something.

I don't like this. I'm afraid.

Perhaps I am imagining all this…

But the spirit must be good. It doesn't try to harm me. That's a good sign, right?

Maybe there is more than one spirit.

Please tell me I'm imagining all of this!

My head feels heavy – like there's a block of iron in it.

I don't understand anything. I feel so confused.

What is happening to me? Is it real or is it some kind of illusion?

I am not going to sleep until sleep comes for me.

The day after I received all these messages, I met Anjali at her house.

Laughing, I asked her, "Did a spirit try to get to know you better today?"

"Don't say that, Udhaya! They can hear you…"

It wasn't cold, but I shivered in fear.

One day, a fledgling crow fell out of its nest. Blackie bounded towards it. The fledgling was saved, but the next minute, a murder of crows descended on us, circling our heads, cawing raucously. Their cacophony would have been enough to wake the dead. Terrified, dog and man ran into the house. On that day I had been to Nochikuppam to buy fish. Just then all of a sudden, a ferocious crow dropped a huge chunk of saliva on my head and flew away! (Not fabricated for the sake of the story, it happened thus.)

For the next three days, an army of crows attacked Perundevi, Blackie and me whenever we crossed our threshold. Knocks from their beaks were like raps on the head from a bouncer with knuckle dusters. Perundevi had to cover her head with the pallu of her saree and hold an umbrella when she had to draw the *kolam*.

Blackie soon started having conversations with the fish. The fish responded to him just like they did Perundevi. Blackie would bark fondly at them and they would acknowledge his presence with aquatic tricks. The dog was particularly close with the flowerhorn that remained.

One day, that flowerhorn, like its deceased counterpart, began to float upside down. Maybe it had grown old too. It wasn't dead. It was still breathing. Blackie would bark at it angrily, so as to say, "Get up and play with me! What's all this upside-down business supposed to mean?" The fish, having understood Blackie's meaning, wiggled for a few second and then went limp.

Blackie continued to bark, but the fish did not respond. Blackie gave up after some time. He mournfully barked his goodbye and walked away.

* * *

One day as I was wandering through the mountains I saw a single blue *himkamal* as big as a saucer, growing from between two rocks and half-buried in snow. I started looking at it and my mind entered into a dialogue with this beautiful snow lotus. I said, "Why are you here all alone? Your beauty is meant to be adored. You should give yourself to someone before your petals fall and return to the dust."

As the breeze blew its stem, it shook and then bent toward me, saying, "Do you think I am lonely being all alone?" All alone means all in one. I enjoy these heights, the purity, the shelter of the blue umbrella above."

Living With the Himalayan Masters

Swami Rama

Glossary

Ekadashi	the eleventh day after new moon or full moon day
Bogar	A siddhar who lived circa 550 BC, also believed to have brought yoga to China. His books including 'Bogar 7000' are available even now. He was an expert in alchemy.
anney	elder brother
arivaal	sickle
military hotel	Till early 2000s, non vegetarian restaurants were called military hotel
Pancha bhoota	earth, water, fire, air and sky
Vaikunta ekadashi	According to Padma Purana, Lord Vishnu took the form of a female ('Ekadasi) to kill demon Muran. This occurs during December – January.
Thoothuvalai	Solanum Trilobatum, a herb
Tamasha	a fuss
Jala Samadhi	death by drowning
akka	elder sister
Mandapam	pillared outdoor hall

Karthikai	eighth month in Tamil calendar
Satsang	spiritual gathering
Enthiran	Robot, a Rajinikanth starrer released in 2010
Poramboke land	denotified land
benami	transaction made in the name of another person, not in the name of the one who has financed it
patta	a title deed to a property
nungu	palm tree fruit
Zamindar	landlord
TASMAC	Government owned liquor outlet
Masala movie	cheap action movies with comedy, romance and melodrama
behenchod	a cursory word; sister fucker
nilavembu kashayam	decoction of Andrographis paniculata
samadhi	meditative absorption and trance
veshti	men's garment worn in southern part of India
paramapadham	game of snakes and ladders
devadasi	a girl dedicated to the service of god by the pottukattu ceremony. The wealthy keep these women as concubine but their wards cannot go on to become heirs. They excel in fine arts like music and dance.
pallaankuzhi	traditional Tamil game played by women
paandi	Tamil hopscotch game
gandoori	Urs
ejamaan	master

arivaalmanai	vegetable cutter
karuvelam tree	Prosopis juliflora, a shrub
vettiyan	one who burns corpses, digs graves
upanyasam	spiritual discourse
rajasam	passion
thamasam	inertia
Ramalinga Adigal	a famous Tamil saint also known as Vallalar
Aadi and Thai	Tamil months
sthala vruksham	a tree that is indigenous to every temple
janavasam	the place where the bridegroom and his people were accommodated and the groom is taken through the streets on the eve of marriage
babus	clerks
"Idhar hi Lohri banayenge!"	We will celebrate Lohri here itself
Lohri	a popular Punjabi winter festival celebrated with bonfire; it marks the end of winter
gilli-danda	village street game in which a smaller stick (gilli) is hit with a larger stick (danda)
adda	a place where people gather for conversation
chutiya	arsehole, moron
panchakarma	a herbal therapy, a fivefold detoxification treatment involving massage
Qira'at	recitation of Al-Quran
Maalik	master
Chamchagiri	sycophancy
nimboo paani	lemonade

agraharam	a street adjoining a temple resided by Brahmins
chachi	aunt
bhabhi	elder brother's wife
bewakoof	stupid
kooththan	dancer, here it means Lord Shiva
sothupindam	(derogatory) one who eats but does no job
jallikattu	sport that involves bull taming; played during Pongal in southern parts of Tamil Nadu
kamarkattu	village confectionery
akkada	there
ikkada	here
thambi	younger brother
kumkum	vermilion
kaili	men's wear; it's also called lungi/sarong
sura puttu	a dish made out of shark
sattvik	righteous
raati	cow dung cake used as firewood

Acknowledgements

There was a Tamil writer called Gopi Krishnan (1945 – 2003). He lived his life like the characters out of Haruki Murakami's 'Norwegian Wood'. Not surprisingly, the characters he created in his own works too resembled Gopi. During his final years – none realised they were his final years since he looked like a forty year old then – he asked me for a help. It was perhaps the year 2000 when he approached me and said, "If I had Rs. 500 a month I can survive." That was sufficient for his daily tea and cigarettes. He used to smoke a brand of cigarette I had not heard of – it was the length of my forefinger. At the time he called in this favour, I was on the breadline myself. So he came up with an idea to raise money: give one story to a magazine every month in return for five hundred rupees. A magazine, that time, gave me 80 rupees for a story of mine. And the literary magazines were in no position to pay at all. When the editors were selling off their household effects to keep the 'literature' alive, how could they afford to pay authors?

I went with Gopi's stories from one magazine to another.

All the editors said, "We don't know this Gopi Krishnan. Give us one of your stories instead." When I had finally managed to sell one of the stories - getting three times the amount Gopi was bargaining for - he was no more.

My situation would have been more or less similar but for my friends who came to my rescue. One of them took care of my house rent, one paid my telephone bill, one covered my air travel expenses within India, another paid for my clothes while the fifth catered for my breakfast. Another friend had a special assignment: every time I sent her a Whatsapp message she would ensure an excellent meal arrive at my doorstep within an hour's time. Till four years' back, when I still enjoyed a drink, a friend used to send me a bottle of *Rémy* Martin every week. (I requested him to credit that amount to my account now that I had stopped drinking, and that friend vanished without a trace.) Some friends used to occasionally supply Chinese Wenjun, Japanese Sake, French Pastis, Bailey's, Absinthe and similar exotic beverages. When I stopped drinking these friends too disappeared. Is it such a big sin to turn teetotal?

My thanks are due to a long list of people who saved me from Gopi Krishnan's fate. I have often wondered how to repay them for their love and kindness, but I have nothing to offer in return save for my writing. So all I can do is continue writing for their sakes.

Nalli Kuppuswamy, Ramesh – Venkatesh – Ambarish (these three belong to the Dinamalar establishment), Jega, Karl Marx, Ramasubramanian, Nirmal, Melmaruvathur

Ramesh, Selvakumar, Bhuvaneswari, Kumaresan, Arathu, N. Sathyamurthy – and many more. I am nothing without them.

Further, Suparna Sharma (Asian Age), Tarun Tejpal, Geetan, Mark Rappolt and David Terrien of ArtReview Asia, Sharmista Mohanty, Prabhu Kalidas, Muthukumar, Arunachalam, Kabilan, Shalin Maria Lawrence, Srivilliputhur Raghavan, Guru, Ve. Irayanbu, Priya Kalyanaraman, Nandita Aggarwal.

I also thank Irwin Allan Sealy who wrote a wonderful foreword to this novel. Not to forget, Avantika, my wife, for encouraging me every time I felt depressed, saying you are 'this' and you are 'that' (strangely, she really believes that I'm a 'this' and 'that') - I remember them all with gratitude at this juncture.

photo credit: prabhu kalidas

Charu Nivedita is a postmodern Tamil writer born in 1953. He was born and raised in a slum until the age of 18, worked in the government services and survived as a wanderer. Since his writings are transgressive in nature, he is branded as a pornographic writer. For a longtime he was writing clandestinely under the pseudonym 'Muniyandi'.

He was selected as one among 'Top Ten Indians of the Decade 2001-2010' by the Economic Times. He is inspired by Marquis de Sade, Georges Bataille and Andal. His columns appear in ArtReview Asia, The Asian Age and several other magazines.

He lives a reclusive life in Chennai, with his wife, two dogs and a cat.